Praise for Ryan Steck

Set in Montana's breathtaking Big Sky Country and packed with intense, hard-hitting action, *Out for Blood* reaffirms Ryan Steck's prowess in the thriller genre, demonstrating once again why his character, former Marine Raider Matthew Redd, is a force to be reckoned with. If you're looking for action, this one's coming in hot!

JACK CARR, former Navy SEAL sniper and #1 *New York Times* bestselling author of the James Reece Terminal List series

Matthew Redd, introduced in Ryan Steck's debut novel *Fields of Fire*, is back and ready for trouble. Redd, a former Marine Raider turned Montana rancher, takes on a gang of outlaw bikers where the buffalo roam. The Wild West has never been wilder. Intense, brutal, and faster on the draw than a gunslinger; *Lethal Range* delivers a fresh take on your grandpa's Western.

NELSON DEMILLE, #1 *New York Times* bestselling author of *The Maze*

Intense, riveting, and ultimately wild escapist fun, *Lethal Range* is a powerful modern Western. It's *Sons of Anarchy* crashing into *Yellowstone*. Steck is a talented cinematic writer and has created a character in Matthew Redd that is both larger than life and remarkably relatable. Buy this book!

DON WINSLOW, #1 bestselling author of *The Force* and *The Border*

A white-knuckle ride from start to finish, *Lethal Range* takes off with one of the most intense scenes I've ever read, then builds to a thunderous crescendo. It's one of this summer's hottest thrillers. Like the best kind of roller coaster, the tension rises to an incredible climax.

T. J. NEWMAN, two-time *New York Times* bestselling author of *Falling* and *Drowning: The Rescue of Flight 1421*

Ryan Steck's latest *Lethal Range* is a high-stakes thriller that starts at a run and races faster with every flip of the page. The mix of spy tradecraft, gutsy action, and nonstop mayhem is what I love in a book. Pair that up with the return of Matthew Redd, a hero as ballsy as Jack Ryan and as street-smart as Jack Reacher, what's not to love? I can't wait to see what trouble Redd must tackle next!

JAMES ROLLINS, #1 *New York Times* bestselling author of *Kingdom of Bones*

Matthew Redd is a hero many readers will find comfortingly familiar while refreshingly different, and Steck wields him with precision in *Lethal Range*—a spectacular follow-up to his stellar debut. If you're a skeptic who thinks Ryan Steck can only write *about* thrillers, you're missing out on one of the hottest new authors in the genre. You'll be far from disappointed in this installment and eager for more.

JACK STEWART, author of *Unknown Rider*

[*Lethal Range*] contains all the danger, treachery, and intrigue that a thriller reader could hope for. It's a gritty tale, with tangled threads, full of action and drama. More than enough angst and adventure to keep you reading long into the night.

STEVE BERRY, *New York Times* bestselling author of *The Last Kingdom*

Steck and Redd are back! Crisply written and beautifully researched, *Lethal Range* rips the reader from Majorca to Big Sky Country. Packed with twists and cliff-hangers, this classic thriller from world-class thriller expert The Real Book Spy roars like a beast.

GREGG HURWITZ, *New York Times* bestselling author of *The Last Orphan*

Full of fists and fury, Ryan Steck's *Lethal Range* is a masterfully plotted battle of good versus evil. With unforgettable characters, lightning pace, and a story frighteningly similar to today's headlines, this book entertains and educates. If you like C. J. Box or Vince Flynn, you will *love* this book!

LARRY LOFTIS, *New York Times* bestselling author of *The Watchmaker's Daughter*

OUT FOR BLOOD

RYAN STECK
OUT FOR BLOOD

A **MATTHEW REDD** THRILLER

Tyndale House Publishers
Carol Stream, Illinois

Visit Tyndale online at tyndale.com.

Visit Ryan Steck online at therealbookspy.com.

Tyndale and Tyndale's quill logo are registered trademarks of Tyndale House Ministries.

Out for Blood

Cover designed by Dean H. Renninger

Edited by Sarah Mason Rische

Published in association with The John Talbot Agency, Inc., a member of The Talbot Fortune Agency, LLC, 180 E. Prospect Ave. #188, Mamaroneck, NY 10543.

For information about special discounts for bulk purchases, please contact Tyndale House Publishers at csresponse@tyndale.com, or call 1-855-277-9400.

Library of Congress Cataloging-in-Publication Data

A catalog record for this book is available from the Library of Congress.

ISBN 978-1-4964-8597-7 (HC)
ISBN 978-1-4964-8598-4 (SC)
ISBN 978-1-4964-8594-6 (Kindle)
ISBN 978-1-4964-8595-3 (ePub)
ISBN 978-1-4964-8596-0 (Apple)

Printed in the United States of America

30	29	28	27	26	25	24
7	6	5	4	3	2	1

For my mother, Rhonda Steck,
who I love beyond words. You have no idea
just how proud I am to be your son, Mom.
Thank you . . . for everything.

"A true warrior is not one who conquers others, but one who conquers their own fears."

TU LAM, retired Green Beret and founder of Ronin Tactics

Prologue

Winters in Montana can be deadly, but it wasn't the cold that was killing Matthew Redd.

Only eighteen hours earlier, one of the worst storms the state had ever seen had begun sweeping across Big Sky Country. Forecasts predicted two feet of snow, subzero temperatures, and winds in excess of fifty miles per hour. When he first heard about the forthcoming blizzard, Redd had been worried about practical things, like making sure they had enough gas for the generator, plenty of bottled water in case the pump went out or a pipe burst, and enough food and baby formula in case they were stuck at the ranch for a few days.

Now he was on his back, lying in eighteen inches of fresh powder, bleeding profusely, and only minutes away from certain death.

With the little energy he had left, Redd tipped his head up and turned it slightly to the side. The snow around him was stained a dark shade of crimson. The blood had cooled enough that the falling flakes had ceased melting away upon contact. Evidently, the spreading pool was no longer being refreshed from the source. For a moment, he thought maybe the bleeding had slowed, perhaps due to the frigid temperatures slowing the beating of his heart.

That, he thought, *or I'm almost out of blood.*

His eyes grew heavy, and Redd fought to keep them open.

He was no longer cold. That wave had already come and passed. Now Redd was numb. Numb to the bone-chilling temperatures. Numb to the wetness of the snow melting under him. Numb to the pain of the knife wounds that had spilled his blood.

Snow was still falling at a rate of several inches per hour. Laying his head back down, Redd looked to the sky. All around him, snowflakes fell from the heavens—brilliant ice crystals, no two the same. It was beautiful, he thought. Peaceful, even.

He could feel the life draining out of him, and in his final moments, his thoughts turned to his wife and son.

Emily . . . Junior . . .

They were safe, and that's all that mattered. But Redd found himself wishing he could hold them one last time. Tell them he loved them.

Moments after he got the phone call that kicked off the chain of events leading to him clinging to life on the mountain, he'd promised Emily that he'd come back to her.

I'm sorry, Em. I'm so sorry . . .

Through the howling wind, Redd heard voices. But he knew the men after him weren't coming to rescue him. Quite the opposite.

They were there to finish the job.

Too injured to move from the spot he'd collapsed into, Redd accepted his fate. And he had no regrets. From a hard childhood in Michigan, to the death of his mother, to then growing up on the ranch in Montana with his adopted father, Jim Bob Thompson, before joining the Marines, Redd, against the odds, had made something of himself. There had been heartache along the way—losing his whole team during an ambush, losing Jim Bob, and almost losing his ranch. But Redd had had a full life, far more than he'd ever expected. It wasn't easy, and ranching was hard work, but he had a wife he adored who loved him back and a son who was his whole world.

The voices grew louder.

This is going to be hard on Junior, he thought.

"Over here!" someone shouted. "We've got him now!"

Please, Redd prayed, *keep my family safe.*

He tried to look at the man coming to finish the job, but dark circles filled his vision. Almost like a smoky haze, the circumference of clarity getting smaller by the second. He sensed the man's presence now more than he saw him. He was close.

"Found him!" the voice called to someone else. "He might already be dead."

"Make sure of it," said another voice. This one deeper than the first.

Redd blinked heavily, fighting to open his eyes one last time. He could see the outline of both men now, one holding a gun that was pointed at his head.

This is it, he told himself.

Redd was determined to look his killer in the eyes, but he couldn't find them. Then he realized the man with the gun had turned away and was facing the opposite direction, focused on another target.

On what?

Redd couldn't see anything.

The haze grew thicker. His eyelids were heavier than ever. He squinted, trying to focus. The gunman was now aiming at something else. Redd looked past him.

There!

He caught sight of something but couldn't tell what it was. Redd squinted again but couldn't make out the figure. It looked like a black blob moving through the snow. It was coming toward him. No, toward the man with the gun. And it was moving fast.

Realizing what was about to happen, Redd felt a thin smile form across his face.

A moment later, everything went dark.

ONE

As he closed the rear cargo door of the Chevy Tahoe, Matthew Redd caught a glimpse of his reflection in the window and barely recognized himself.

It wasn't anything physical. Save for a scattering of snowflakes in his dark hair and beard, giving him a salt-and-pepper look that aged him beyond his twenty-eight years, his appearance mostly matched his mental image of himself. No, the difference was something else, something much harder to pin down. Something under the skin.

Then his gaze dropped to the foil-wrapped baking dish he held in both hands, and he realized what it was.

I'm not the man I used to be.

This was not exactly news to Redd. In the last two years, his sense of who he was and what he wanted out of life had undergone a tectonic shift. He was no longer *just* Matthew Redd, former Marine Raider. Not anymore. He was Matthew Redd, husband of Emily, father of Matthew Jr., owner and operator of Thompson Ranch. That was how he thought of himself now, and it didn't bother him one bit.

Honestly, he didn't miss his former life.

"Hey, cowboy, are you going to bring that ham in here sometime today?" Emily said playfully.

Redd looked away from his reflection and grinned back at the vision of beauty presently leaning out the door of the twenty-two-foot travel trailer that was, for the time being at least, home sweet home.

"Coming now."

"What you thinking about over there, Matty Redd?"

Emily could always read him. And in a lot of ways, she knew him better than he knew himself. When nobody else could get through to him—Redd had a notorious stubborn streak that hadn't cooled much as he approached his thirties—Emily could.

"Uh," said Redd, embarrassed he'd been caught looking at himself, "nothing."

"Just get it in here before it gets cold." As if to emphasize the point, she swiped a hand in front of her face, sweeping away the snowflakes that were drifting lazily down from the silver-gray sky.

It had been threatening to snow for the better part of a week, but that was nothing special in Big Sky Country.

Still, according to the Weather Channel, a snowstorm this deep into winter was said to be "record-breaking" in terms of volume and intensity. A note from the governor, courtesy of the statewide messaging system, advised everyone to stay put, as traveling would be "near impossible." Power outages were likely too. But they were ready for it, or as ready as one could be. Redd had made all the necessary preparations. Now it was a waiting game, with only a brief window before most of the state would grind to a halt.

Thankfully, the full fury of the storm wasn't supposed to hit until later that evening, but the snowfall seemed to have picked up just since they'd gotten back from Emily's parents' house. And it was already sticking.

Getting used to winter again had been a challenge. Redd remembered growing up with Montana winters, which sometimes started in October and could last until May, but when he'd gone off to join the Marines at eighteen, he'd lost the tempo of the seasons. He had been stationed in perpetually sunny Southern California, and even though deployments and training cycles sometimes took him to places where the temperatures dropped precipitously in winter, he had only ever looked at the weather as a challenge to be overcome in the moment. Here, with a ranch to run and cattle to tend, it was just a fact of life.

He hurried over to the trailer door, balancing the baking dish in one hand while he worked the doorknob. As the door swung open, a dark shape—specifically a dark shape that was 130 pounds of purebred juvenile rottweiler—erupted from the trailer like a torpedo blasting out of a launch tube and shot past him, barely avoiding a collision.

"Whoa there, buddy," he shouted over his shoulder. "Slow it down. This is a residential zone."

The dog, who was now zipping back and forth across the open ground, seemed not to have heard.

Forgot one, he thought. *Matthew Redd, Rubble's human.*

Rubble was the most recent member of the family, acquired after the untimely death of his former owner, Redd's attorney and friend, Duke Blanton. Blanton had been savagely murdered by members of an outlaw biker gang. The same gang had menaced Redd and his family, and ultimately burned down the ranch house where Redd had not only grown up but begun his new life with Emily, which was why they were now living in an old travel trailer.

As tragic as it was, losing the house marked the final transition between the old Matthew Redd and the new one. Prior to that, he'd been living a divided life—keeping one foot in the world of special operations by working as an FBI contractor, leading a paramilitary "fly team" on a worldwide search for an international terrorist, while still trying to have that "normal" life with Emily and Junior.

The fire itself hadn't been a wake-up call or anything like that. It had simply coincided with the successful completion of his mission for the FBI, freeing him up to focus on the things that he now realized mattered the most to him.

Building a new house was of course the first step on that path. Redd had already begun the process of clearing the site, and with the first part of the insurance settlement in hand, he hoped to be in their new home before the end of summer. Until then, they would just have to put up with living in close quarters.

He stepped inside and placed the dish on the tiny counter between the tiny sink and the even smaller two-burner stove. Emily was setting the table, crowding the place settings around an assortment of foil-covered pots and pans that contained various side dishes to accompany the ten-pound spiral-sliced ham Redd had just brought in.

Emily had spent the better part of the day preparing the meal, which they would soon be sharing with their friends Mikey and Elizabeth Derhammer. Rather than attempt such an undertaking in the trailer's woefully inadequate kitchen space, she had done the work at her parents' house, in a more suitable kitchen. Redd still wasn't clear on why they couldn't just take the prepared meal over to the Derhammers' home, where there was an actual dining room, and he'd said as much when Emily proposed the idea of having Mikey and Liz out to the ranch for dinner.

"Because, Matty, having them over for dinner at their house wouldn't make much sense, would it?"

"It makes more sense than trying to cram four adults and two babies into this shoebox," Redd had replied.

Emily shook her head. "It's our turn to host dinner. Liz and Mikey have had us over more times than I can count."

That was certainly true. Since the fire . . . since they had lost almost every personal possession, they had eaten more meals at the Derhammers' place or with Emily's parents, Elijah and Dora Lawrence, than they had at home. So Redd could understand why Emily might feel compelled to repay their kindness. For his part, he treasured their friendship with the Derhammers. He just couldn't quite wrap his head around the symbolic significance of hosting the meal inside their little temporary abode.

Outside the trailer, Rubble's insistent barking signaled that something had changed. It could have been anything from a racoon trying to sneak up on the garbage can to one of the cattle wandering too close to the fence, but Redd was pretty sure he knew what it was. He tugged aside the curtain over the little window in the door and looked out to see Mikey Derhammer's Billet Silver Dodge Ram 3500 dually rolling up the drive. It was, according to Mikey, "more tank than truck." Redd didn't disagree.

As boys, Redd and Mikey had been the best of friends. Now they were more like brothers, and Redd considered him family. Liz too.

Working the ranch with his adoptive father, J. B. Thompson, hadn't left a lot of time for extracurricular activities. As a result, Redd had cultivated few childhood friends. Nevertheless, two people had managed to break through his self-imposed social shield—Emily Lawrence, his first and only love, and Mikey.

When J. B. had been badly injured in a fall, Redd had secretly blamed himself. Maybe if he hadn't been wasting time with his friends, J. B. wouldn't have gotten hurt in the first place. To atone for this perceived failing, he'd dropped out of high school and out of his friends' lives and managed the ranch single-handedly until J. B.'s recovery was complete.

J. B. hadn't been able to stop him from quitting school, but he had insisted that Redd get his GED, a necessary step if Redd was going to realize his lifelong dream of enlisting in the Marines. When Redd had told him that he was done with that dream and that he was going to stay and work the ranch, J. B.—a former Marine himself—had put his foot down.

"I can't make you take the oath," he'd told Redd. "But don't you use me as an excuse."

J. B.'s particular brand of tough love and encouragement was exactly the kick in the pants Redd had needed. The only problem was that in leaving Montana he'd permanently closed the door on his relationships with Emily and Mikey. Or at least it had seemed that way at the time.

Nearly two years prior, when J. B.'s death had brought him back to Stillwater County and the ranch just outside the little town of Wellington, he'd been both surprised and humbled to discover that those relationships had not died, but merely gone fallow. It had taken a little effort to rekindle his romance with Emily, a fiercely independent and successful nurse practitioner working at the county health clinic, but with Mikey, it was like not a single day had passed.

Matthew Redd, friend of Mikey.

"They're here," Redd called out.

"Rubble beat you to it," retorted Emily. "Don't shout. You'll wake Matty."

He looked at her sidelong. "You think Matty won't wake up the second Luke walks in the door?"

Lucas, Mikey and Liz's son, was about two years older than Matthew Jr., and the two boys were frequent playmates. Like fathers, like sons.

Emily sighed. "I suppose you're right." She gave the table a final inspection. "Well, I guess this is as good as we're going to get it."

Redd opened the door, careful to keep Rubble out, and went to greet their guests. Mikey, who had already stepped out from behind the wheel, took Redd's proffered hand but then pulled him into a fierce bro hug. Though he definitely wasn't a hugger, Redd, who was a good six inches taller than Mikey, couldn't resist a smile as he stared out over the top of his friend's head.

"All right," he murmured, gently pushing Mikey away. "Go help your wife bring the kid in out of the cold."

Liz picked Luke up out of his safety seat and laid him down alongside Matthew Jr. The adults used the brief respite to enjoy the appetizer course Emily had prepared, along with the chardonnay Liz had brought.

"So, tell me all about your plans for this place," said Mikey after emptying both glass and plate.

Redd laughed. "You should ask Em. I'm letting her take point on the design."

"Matty would have been happy with a one-room log cabin," interjected Emily.

"And what would be wrong with that?" he said playfully. He was only half joking.

"Come on, Matt," said Mikey. "It's the twenty-first century. You've at least got to have a man cave."

"I'll let him have his man cave," replied Emily. "But I put my foot down when he wanted to put in a panic room."

Redd's easy smile wilted a little. Although Emily was making light of it, Redd was not at all pleased with his wife's resistance to the idea.

During his time as a Marine Raider and then subsequently working with the FBI, he'd made more than his share of enemies—enemies every bit as dangerous as the outlaw bikers who had destroyed their home and murdered Duke Blanton. As much as Redd wanted to believe that he had left all that behind, some of those enemies were still out there, just waiting for a chance to settle the score. If . . . *when* the day of reckoning came, Redd would do whatever it took to protect his family. And the best way to do that was to make sure they had a safe place to go when the bad guys rolled up without warning.

Emily, who chose to believe in the fundamental goodness of humanity, had dismissed his precautionary thinking as paranoia. Contrary to what she was telling Mikey and Liz, the matter was far from resolved.

"It's not a *panic* room," Redd insisted. "It's a *safe* room. Think of it as a refuge. Like a big fancy storm shelter."

Emily rolled her eyes. "More like a bomb shelter."

Mikey scratched his chin. "I don't know, Em. I think I'm with Matt on this one."

"What a surprise," Liz remarked dryly. "You two taking the same side. Who'd have predicted that?"

"It's just common sense," Mikey went on. "It's like the Boy Scout motto—be prepared."

Redd flashed a triumphant grin at Emily and offered an open-hand *see what I mean* gesture toward Mikey.

"Like either of you were ever Boy Scouts."

"I wanted to be one," countered Mikey and then in a small voice added, "Mom wouldn't let me join. She didn't get along with the den mother. Said she was a drunk—well, you know. A word she probably shouldn't have said in front of kids."

"Den mother?" said Liz. "Isn't that just for Cub Scouts?"

"Same thing," Mikey said defensively.

"I'm sure it's not," said his wife, laughing.

"Well, after Mom put the kibosh on it, I kind of lost interest." He waved his hand as if to preempt further discussion. "All I'm saying is, it doesn't hurt to plan ahead."

"I don't disagree," said Emily. "I just think there are better uses for our limited resources. We're not exactly made of money."

Mikey inclined his head to cede the point, then turned to Redd. "Well, she did say you could have a man cave, bro. Now we'll have a sweet spot to watch football. Take the win."

Redd opened his mouth to reply, but before he could say another word, his phone rang. His brows creased in consternation as he took the device from his pocket and looked at the screen. "It's Gavin," he muttered, frowning.

Emily gave him a distressed look. "Be nice, Matty. He's trying."

Redd shook his head. "I'm sure it's a work thing." He stared at the display a moment longer, debating whether or not to let it go to voicemail. "I should probably take this," he said, tapping the screen to accept the call.

In an instant, everything changed.

TWO

As the Boeing 737 banked right and lined up for final approach to runway 17R/35L, west of the main terminal of Will Rogers World Airport, the right foot of the man sitting in the fourteenth row, left side aisle seat, began unconsciously tapping out an anxious rhythm. Gavin Kline, executive assistant director of the FBI's Intelligence Directorate, was not a nervous flyer, and even though he recalled hearing somewhere that the most dangerous part of any flight was when the aircraft either took off or touched down, he was not worried about the possibility of an impending crash. Rather, he was concerned with what would happen after the jet stopped moving.

The plane was one of a fleet of four aircraft—three 737s and one Saab 2000 turboprop—operated exclusively by the Justice Prisoner and Alien Transportation System—JPATS. Informally known, even among insiders, as "Con Air," JPATS had one mission: the transport of federal prisoners between regional detention facilities. On a typical flight, the plane might have as many as 126 prisoners, secured with up to three sets of handcuffs and ankle chains—for violent offenders, hand restraint mitts and face masks were also used—all of them overseen by a team of up to twelve specially trained US marshals.

There was nothing typical about this flight, however.

With just eighteen souls aboard, including the two-person cockpit crew, the 737—flight designation DOJ125—was flying well below its max capacity, but in fact, the purpose of the flight was the transport of a single VIP passenger.

Gavin Kline was not that man.

Like the eight FBI special agents and six US marshals also traveling aboard the aircraft, Kline was only there to facilitate the safe transfer of a man who had, not so long ago, been one of the wealthiest men on earth: Anton Gage.

Gage was, no doubt, accustomed to having an aircraft mostly to himself. The only difference this time was that he had very little control over his destination.

That, and the handcuffs.

Gage had amassed his billions from groundbreaking biotechnology innovations, particularly in the specialized field of genetic engineering. Subsequently, he had invested not only his money and influence but also his unique genius in support of a criminal conspiracy aimed at radically depopulating the earth in pursuit of a twisted vision of sustainability.

Previously, Gage's mad plan to poison America's heartland with a genetically modified crop disease had been narrowly averted by a tactical team operating under Kline's aegis. Gage had been taken into custody and almost right away had done what most dirtbags in his position did: he'd begun cooperating. Selling out his coconspirators in hopes of receiving leniency and—this was especially the case for Gage—securing protection from the powerful men he was about to betray.

Until his arrest, Gage had been a member of a secret cabal of uberwealthy individuals, known informally as "the Twelve," who collectively possessed most of the planet's wealth and therefore wielded outsized influence over both the global economy and the political landscape. They were, not to put too fine a point on it, above the law, which made prosecution for their heinous crimes something of a problem. Gage himself had only been brought to heel after his collusion with a notorious bioweapons engineer had come to light, which in turn had caused the Twelve to withdraw their cloak of protection. Now, to save his own skin, Gage was going to return the favor.

During the weeks since his arrest, he had named names, identifying the principal members of the Twelve as well as promising to expose several elected officials who were actively collaborating with them.

Most of the names on the list came as no surprise; in fact, Kline would have been astonished had he learned they were *not* part of the Twelve. The few that were not already on his radar were unfamiliar to him only because they were not American citizens, like the Mexican telecom billionaire who presently ranked seventh on the list of world's wealthiest. Most of the Twelve were among the twenty richest people alive, and those few that were not were, in all likelihood, hiding their true net worth to avoid public scrutiny. Their combined wealth—not to mention the influence that came with it—was going to make prosecuting them a Herculean task. It would take more than Anton Gage's uncorroborated testimony to even convince the Department of Justice to begin the investigation, never mind bring the case before a judge.

Nevertheless, knowing the identities of the Twelve was a place to start, and that made Anton Gage a very important person in the truest sense of the word. Yes, he was a prisoner, or more precisely, a federal detainee, but he was also a witness and as such had a great big bull's-eye on his chest. The Twelve had already demonstrated on more than one occasion that they possessed the ability to arrange "accidents" and "suicides" for people who, having run afoul of the law, were willing to testify against them. Kline's former boss at the FBI, Rachel Culp, was just the latest such victim.

Which was why Gage had spent the weeks since his arrest sequestered in an off-the-books safe house in Denver, Colorado, watched over by a small team of agents handpicked by Kline, instead of in federal lockup. But despite very real security concerns, Kline couldn't keep Gage on ice indefinitely. In order to move forward with any kind of plea deal, Gage would have to submit to the judicial process, and that meant not only stepping out into the open but also accepting the outcome of the proceedings. Given the serious nature of the crimes Anton Gage stood accused of—never mind the pervasive influence of the Twelve—there was a very real possibility that the judge hearing the case might reject the plea agreement Kline had worked so hard to secure and put Gage in the federal prison system to await trial. If that happened, all bets would be off.

So Kline was justifiably anxious. Anxious about Gage's safety, and anxious about prosecuting the case against the Twelve. In his career, he'd taken on mobsters, international terrorists, and psychotic *narcotraficantes*, but the Twelve were something altogether different. Gage's testimony alone wouldn't be enough to bring them down, but without it . . . without it, they were untouchable.

Thank goodness Matt didn't just put a bullet in the back of his head.

The thought brought a fleeting smile to Kline's lips.

Matty . . .

Matthew Redd despised the affectionate nickname, but that was how Kline had always thought of him, even if he wasn't allowed to call him that. A former USMC Raider now "advising"—a euphemism if there ever was one—the FBI fly team dedicated to bringing Gage and the rest of the Twelve to justice, Redd had been responsible not only for bringing Gage in but also for twice thwarting his diabolical plans when no one else could even get close to the man. Yet Redd was more than just a highly skilled security contractor. He was Gavin Kline's biological son and as such a source of both pride and regret. Pride in all that Redd had accomplished. Regret for the fact that he—Kline—had been absent for almost all of it.

Kline had not even been aware of Matthew Redd's existence for the first decade of his son's life. He had only learned about his child, the product of a short-lived fling, when Matthew's drug-addicted mother had died of an overdose in a Michigan trailer park. Kline, wholly career focused, had recoiled at the thought of raising a child and had instead handed the boy off to Jim Bob Thompson, a Montana rancher and a former Marine he had served with. Jim Bob had been what Kline never could have, a father to young Matthew, instilling in him the values and work ethic that forged Matthew Redd into the man he now was—warrior, husband, father.

Entrusting Matthew to Jim Bob had been the right decision at the time, the best choice for everyone involved, but there was no denying that it had poisoned the well of Kline's relationship with his son. Still, Kline remained hopeful that the rift could be . . . if not healed, exactly, then at least bridged.

The sudden roar of the jet engines supplying braking thrust to slow the aircraft brought Kline fully back into the moment. He set aside both his big-picture concerns and his family problems, and instead focused his attention on the immediate task of moving Gage off the plane and into the Federal Transport Center facility.

Located on the western edge of the airport, less than half a mile from the runway on which the plane was now setting down, the FTC had its own dedicated terminal, so there would be no risk of exposure during transfer. Transporting Gage from the FTC to the William J. Holloway, Jr. federal courthouse in downtown Oklahoma City for his formal arraignment would be a different story, but that was a problem for later in the day. The immediate concern was making sure that Gage remained safe and sequestered during his stay at the FTC. While Kline had taken every precaution, conducted background checks on every marshal and corrections officer who might have reason to interact with or simply occupy the same room as Anton Gage during his temporary incarceration, it was simply not possible to cover every contingency. That was why the fly team had come along for the ride.

A noise like a thunderclap jolted Kline out of his musings.

That was an explosion, was his first thought.

At almost the same moment, the cabin lights flickered out. Even with daylight streaming in through the unshuttered porthole windows, the plane's interior was plunged into deep gloom. The deck underfoot began to vibrate—not the normal rumble of wheels on tarmac, but something more intense. A violent, side-to-side shaking as if the pilot was rapidly working the rudder back and forth. Throughout the cabin, heads began turning, looking for the source of the disturbance.

As loud as the initial noise had been, it had definitely come from somewhere outside the aircraft. The aluminum skin of the fuselage had absorbed or deflected some of the explosive energy, making it difficult to determine where it had originated. In the moment of relative quiet that followed, Kline heard someone—one of the marshals, he thought—sitting on the opposite side of the cabin remark, in an almost offhand manner, "I think we just blew an engine."

Kline strained against his seat belt, trying to get a look across the aisle.

Even as some part of his brain attempted to wrap itself around this relatively innocuous explanation for what had just happened, another part—the part that had been forged in the fire of combat—knew better.

Explanations didn't matter.

This was an attack.

THREE

A mile away, perched atop a decaying pole barn in an all-but-forgotten maintenance yard, Chad Beaudette peered through the objective lens of a Schmidt & Bender PM II High Power 5-45×56 scope and surveyed the results of his handiwork.

The 25×59-millimeter HEDP—high-explosive, dual-purpose—round, which he had only a moment ago fired from his XM109 Anti-Materiel Payload Rifle, had streaked across the flat landscape and unerringly found its target. Although the charge in the twenty-five-millimeter round—more a miniature grenade than a bullet—was small, it packed more than enough punch to utterly destroy the jet engine's inner workings. The 737 was still moving, still rolling down the runway, but the trail of black smoke billowing out from the engine nacelle slung under its right wing signaled that the plane was in trouble.

Still, Beaudette couldn't help feeling just a bit disappointed. He'd been expecting something a little more . . . dynamic. The damage to the plane was significant, and well within the parameters for mission success, but part of him had hoped the destruction of the engine would trigger a secondary explosion, one big enough to rip the wing right off or maybe blow the entire plane in two.

Yeah, that would have been pretty cool, he thought.

Beaudette liked blowing things up. It was one of the reasons—not the only one though—why his Navy SEAL teammates had anointed him with the call sign "Bamm Bamm."

He wasn't a SEAL anymore, and his new outfit didn't go in for colorful call signs, but his enthusiasm for causing fiery destruction remained undiminished, which was no doubt why the boss had assigned him this detail.

The boss appreciated Beaudette's talents in a way the Navy never had. Entrusting Beaudette with the AMPR—a modified version of the high-powered Barrett M82 .50-caliber sniper rifle, one of twelve prototypes produced by Barrett Firearms Manufacturing for the United States military but never fielded—was proof of that, as was assigning him the critical task of disabling or, if possible, destroying the 737.

But there would be no big bang today. The HEDP round had done its job and nothing more. The jet engine's internal fire suppression system had quickly extinguished the flames before they could ignite the fuel storage tanks in the wing. And while losing an engine upon landing would pose a challenge to the flight crew, it was by no means an insurmountable one. It was a possibility that every pilot trained for. Even now, Beaudette could see the plane wobbling down the runway as the pilots fought to correct the imbalance.

They would, of course, succeed, provided nothing else went wrong. It was Beaudette's job to ensure that something did.

With his eye still pressed to the scope, he swiveled the gun on its bipod a few degrees until the reticle was centered on his secondary target and continued tracking the plane's movement down the runway. As he did, he keyed his lip mic.

"Dagger Six, this is Arrow One," he said, speaking in a low whisper even though there was nobody around to hear him. "I'm taking the second shot, over."

The boss's reply came back right away, without brevity codes or commo protocols. Just two words. "Do it."

A smile touched Beaudette's lips as he put the crosshairs on the cockpit windscreen, shifted it a few ticks forward to compensate for the time it would take the twenty-five-millimeter explosive round to cross the intervening distance, and then squeezed the trigger.

FOUR

Chad Beaudette was not the only person observing the wounded 737 make its way down the landing strip. Half a mile to the west of the runway, looking out through the window of the ground access portal on the south side of the octagonal terminal building of the FTC, FBI Special Agent Stephanie Treadway watched with growing concern as a finger of black smoke began trailing out behind the aircraft.

"That doesn't look good," she murmured.

"No, it doesn't."

If Treadway had been looking for reassurance, this comment from her traveling companion, Aaron Decker, had exactly the opposite effect. Decker wasn't normally one to volunteer his opinion. To say that he kept his own counsel was a monumental understatement, so the fact that he answered with anything more than an indifferent shrug did not augur well.

Admittedly, Aaron Decker was a puzzle that Treadway had made little progress in solving. She had a gift for quickly building rapport with people, especially men who found her good looks and winning smile irresistible. It was a talent that had served her well in her career with the Bureau, and especially in her current role as Gavin Kline's protégé. But during her short acquaintance with Aaron Decker, she had yet to figure out what made him tick. All she really knew about the man was that he had previously worked with Kline in some unspecified, unofficial, and legally questionable capacity and that he had subsequently faked his death, gone off-grid, and built a new identity for himself.

Kline had called Decker a ghost, and that seemed appropriate on many levels. In addition to being legally dead, Decker had a knack for vanishing into the background. He did not occupy space so much as *haunt* it. And if her suspicions about him were anywhere close to true, Decker was a genuinely scary individual.

Treadway's gut told her that Decker was a wet-work specialist—an assassin. Possibly military or CIA, maybe with official sanction, but definitely off the books. She could think of no other explanation for Kline wanting to bring him back to life, as it were. Her best guess was that Kline planned to turn Decker loose on the Twelve if the judicial system failed to bring them to justice.

She wasn't going to come right out and ask either man if any of that was true. Frankly, she didn't want to know, though some part of her recognized that an extrajudicial solution to the problem of the Twelve might be the only recourse.

Regardless, Decker was a professional, that much was obvious, and not someone given to hysteria or flights of fancy, so for him to admit that there might be something wrong with the plane carrying Anton Gage, along with Kline and the fly team, was reason enough for concern.

If he thinks there's a problem, then it's probably a lot worse than I thought.

Then, Decker upped the ante. "Something's wrong. We need to get out there."

This time, he spoke loud enough to be overheard by the other man accompanying them, Deputy Marshal Craig Doherty. Doherty was the primary liaison between Kline's team, JPATS, and the onsite personnel at the FTC.

"The marshals aboard that plane have a protocol for emergency situations," said Doherty. "If they need backup, they'll call it in."

Treadway did not fail to note Doherty's use of the word *emergency*. If she needed confirmation that something was wrong with the plane carrying her boss, Anton Gage, and several of her FBI comrades, the marshal had just provided it.

"Regardless," Doherty went on, "we're staying put. There are people trained to deal with these situations. Let them do their job."

Treadway knew he was right. Whatever was wrong with the Con Air jet . . . whatever was happening or going to happen . . . it was so far beyond their ability to help or remedy that they might as well be watching it on a television broadcast.

Decker didn't reply. Not even a shrug. He just continued to watch the plane rolling down the runway. Aside from the long, trailing plume of black smoke, the aircraft appeared to be intact and under control, and for a fleeting second, Treadway dared to believe that the crisis would be resolved without any outside interventions. But then she saw a bright flash from the nose of the aircraft, followed immediately by a second puff of smoke, and knew that things had just gotten much worse.

What happened next was almost surreal.

The 737 began to spin. Like a ballet dancer performing a pirouette, the entire aircraft rotated to the left. Despite the rotation, inertia was still the dominant force, so the plane began corkscrewing down the runway, shrouded by tire smoke and dust. The tail swung around, then the opposite side of the plane presented, showing the undamaged engine, still blasting out braking thrust—the cause of the uncontrolled spin. Then the nose of the jet flashed into view, revealing the gaping hole where the front windscreen had been.

Treadway only caught a glimpse of the damage before the spin removed it from her sight, but it was enough for her to make a logical connection. The flash she had witnessed just before the plane went out of control had been an explosion, blasting the cockpit of the 737 and everyone in it to oblivion.

Jet engines blew up sometimes. There might be a plausible explanation for that. But there was nothing inherently explosive in a jet's cockpit, which could only mean that an explosive device had somehow been placed inside the plane. Intentionally.

Beside her, Aaron Decker reached the same conclusion. "They're under attack."

Marshal Doherty started to say something, but before he could get even a syllable out, Decker was moving. He slammed through the heavy glass door like it wasn't even there and took off across the tarmac at a full sprint.

Doherty recovered his wits just enough to shout, "Wait!" but Decker was already long gone. The marshal threw a worried glance in Treadway's direction. "What's he think he'll be able to do out there?"

It was a fair question. Right now what the people on the plane needed most was the assistance of first responders—firefighters with protective gear and heavy-duty rescue equipment, paramedics with the training and materials to begin treating the injured. If there was an extant threat, someone actively assaulting the aircraft, Decker, who was, as far as she knew, unarmed, would be of little help.

And yet, Treadway couldn't help but admire the man's decisiveness. She faced Doherty and shrugged. "I guess whatever he can."

And then, surprising no one more than herself, she was running too.

FIVE

Upon recognizing the nature of the crisis, Kline's first impulse had been to move, to seek cover so he could assess the threat. His hands immediately went to the buckle of his seat belt, fingers fumbling to find the release mechanism. It was something he'd done countless times on ordinary flights, and yet now, in the midst of a real crisis, his muscle memory deserted him.

As if divining his intent, one of the marshals shouted, "Keep your belts on! Stay in your seats!"

The marshal was absolutely correct, of course. Even though the wheels had touched down, the plane was still moving faster than a car on an open highway. When they'd been preparing to take off in Denver, the senior marshal had given them the Con Air version of a preflight safety briefing, and while it was not substantively different than the one flight attendants regularly gave to commercial airline passengers, there had been a few distinctive instructions relating to both the safety and security of the prisoner. In a nutshell, the marshal's advice had been, *"If something happens, follow our lead."*

Easy to say when there was no threat.

But Kline knew that the marshals had trained for emergencies like this, and so, fighting a primal urge, he let go of the safety belt and instead gripped the armrests of his seat. It was a decision that probably saved his life, for at that instant, another loud bang rippled through the cabin, and suddenly the aircraft went into a flat spin. The g-force of the rotation hurled him sideways, bending his upper torso over the armrest of his seat. From the corner of his eye, he glimpsed a body—he couldn't make out a face, but the man wore the tactical-gear uniform of the fly team—flying through the air to slam into a bulkhead with a sickening crunch.

Kline barely registered what had happened. His head was reeling from the violent acceleration. His extremities felt like they had been filled with fresh concrete. A smell like burnt wiring assaulted his nostrils as whorls of smoke began filling the gloomy cabin. A sudden jolt shook the still-spinning airframe as the shrieking tires left the tarmac and veered onto the grassy margin. The abrupt change in the surface quickly stole away the plane's remaining momentum, but not before the aircraft described two more full rotations, throwing up a great brown cloud of dust that completely engulfed the 737, shrouding it in near total darkness. The only source of illumination in the cabin now was from the strip lights on the floor.

With another violent lurch, the plane finally came to a full stop. The rebound whipped Kline back and forth in his seat, and even though the plane was no longer moving, it was a few seconds before the world stopped spinning. Outside the aircraft, the remaining jet engine continued screaming ineffectually, but over the din, Kline could hear the marshals shouting orders.

He again fumbled for the buckle of the seat belt. His fingers felt numb, disconnected. He knew he'd probably sustained whiplash.

Or worse.

It's just the adrenaline, he thought and hoped it was true because the alternative was too terrible to contemplate.

Finally, he felt the clasp open and the belt fell away. He reached out for the seat back ahead of him and tentatively pulled himself erect.

Through the gloom, he could just make out a group of figures moving down the aisle toward the rear of the aircraft. A face materialized in front of him, one of the marshals, one raised hand jabbing urgently in the direction the others were moving. Kline returned a nod and heaved himself into the aisle ahead of the other man, joining the exodus.

He hadn't gone ten steps when it occurred to him to check on the status of the fly team. He recalled that at least one of them had been tossed around the cabin during the spin. Had that agent simply gotten up and walked away? In the chaos, it was impossible to tell. He couldn't see much past the man ahead of him, couldn't even tell where they were all going.

He turned around, fully intending to head back and search for any stragglers, but instead found the marshal buddy-carrying a dazed Special Agent Bryan Tanaka.

"Is that everyone?" Kline meant to shout the question, but when he drew in a breath in preparation, the smoke that filled his lungs triggered a coughing fit, and he could barely choke out the words.

"Cabin's clear," replied the marshal. "Can't get to the flight deck. Too much smoke."

Kline didn't question the assessment. The thickening smoke was proof enough that, even though the plane had stopped moving, the danger was far from past. He reached out to help Tanaka, but the marshal waved him off. "I got this. Just go. Go."

Kline reluctantly obeyed, hurrying down the aisle to catch up with the rest of the group. The smoke stung his eyes and was so thick that he didn't see the exit until he was within a few feet of it.

Another marshal waited there, urging him forward. "Arms like this," he said, demonstrating the correct position by holding both arms out in front of him, palms down. "Jump and slide. Go! Go! Go!"

Barely comprehending, Kline followed the first part of the direction, extending his arms, but then stepped over the edge of the opening as if exiting at the terminal. It was only when his foot failed to make contact with a solid surface that he realized his mistake. He plunged headlong, cursing as he fell, and landed face-first on the evacuation slide that had deployed from the side of the aircraft. He tumbled the rest of the way down, rolling off the slide and onto the ground where another marshal was waiting to pull him clear.

Still engulfed in the dust cloud, it took Kline a few seconds to locate the rest of the plane's complement. With the exception of the two marshals still aboard and the injured Bryan Tanaka, the passengers had all moved about a hundred yards away from the plane, with the fly team deploying in a defensive perimeter around a cluster of marshals huddled around a still-shackled Anton Gage.

Kline knew from experience that the detonation of an explosive device was often just the opening move in an ambush, but if there were hostile forces lying in wait, they had yet to make their move. It was of course possible, probable even, that the unknown enemy behind the attack had been counting on the plane's total destruction and that there would be no follow-on attack, but Kline wasn't going to breathe easy until their prisoner was safely inside the FTC. He drew his service weapon, a Glock 19M, and moved in a low crouch to join the agents on the perimeter.

A familiar voice reached out over the shrill din of the jet's still-turning engine. "Boss! Over here."

Kline scanned the area until he spotted a man waving to get his attention. It was Rob Davis, the fly team's weapons specialist and acting team leader in Matthew Redd's absence. Under normal circumstances, Davis would have simply made contact over the team radio net, but they'd been forbidden from using their commo equipment during the flight. In his haste to exit the plane, Kline had not even thought about retrieving his kit bag.

He ran over and dropped down beside the other man. "Sitrep?" he asked.

Davis just shook his head. "Not a clue. Can't see a thing, but nobody's shot at us yet. I don't know if this is an attack or just bad luck. What I do know is that we need to get off the X. We're way too exposed out here."

"I hear you, but we're not running this show. Stay sharp. I'll be right back."

Kline scrambled over to the knot of marshals surrounding Gage and conveyed Davis's assessment of the situation.

One of the marshals, however, shook his head. "The FTC is half a mile away. That's too much open ground to cover on foot. We stay put until secure transport arrives."

"You called for transport?" As far as Kline knew, the marshals were also without radios.

"It's SOP. First sign of trouble with a transport and our emergency response team activates. They'll deploy as soon as the fire crew gives the all clear."

Kline's forehead creased in a frown. "How long will that take?"

"Not long." He nodded in the direction of the main airport complex. Kline followed his gaze and, through the brown haze of settling dust, saw flashing red and blue lights in the distance. "The firefighters will be here in about thirty seconds. They just have to make sure it's safe for our transport van to approach."

Kline did some quick mental math. Thirty seconds for the fire trucks to arrive. A couple more minutes for them to assess the situation, and then maybe two or three more for the transport team to make it out to the crash site.

Five minutes, give or take.

That was too long.

On the other hand, it was doubtful that they could reach the FTC in five minutes on foot, and so far, they hadn't taken any fire. Maybe staying put was the best option.

Kline clapped the marshal on the shoulder. "I'll let my team know."

He hurried back to update Davis. As he did, a pair of bright yellow vehicles materialized beneath the flashing lights. One of them appeared to be an ordinary fire truck, but the second, larger vehicle looked to Kline like a repurposed USMC Logistic Vehicle System Replacement transport. A true monster truck, with a 600-horsepower diesel engine, eight-wheel drive, and a sixteen-ton carrying capacity, the LVSR platform could be adapted to serve a variety of roles—cargo hauler, tanker, wrecker—so it stood to reason that it might be used in the civilian world as a fire truck.

The mere sight of something that evoked memories of his military service buoyed Kline's spirits. Things had been pretty hairy for a minute or two, but now it appeared that the crisis had passed.

He dropped down beside Davis. "Help is on the way." With the sirens of the fire trucks joining the engine noise, he had to shout to be heard. "Stand by."

"Stand by?" Davis's face registered his dismay at this suggestion. "We're not moving?"

While Kline considered how best to answer, the fire trucks closed the remaining distance. When their big tires left the tarmac and rolled onto open ground, they raised more dust, further reducing visibility. The yellow trucks seemed to vanish again. Only the flashing lights penetrated the cloud.

Suddenly, Davis jolted as if he'd just been electrocuted. An oath of surprise, or perhaps pain, erupted from his throat. Kline stared at him, uncomprehending, but only for the fraction of a second it took for his conscious mind to register the tiny eruptions of dirt from the ground in front of them and the harsh, mosquito-like whine of bullets creasing the air overhead.

Someone was shooting at them.

This was what he had feared from the start. Disabling the plane had only been the opening act. The attackers had waited for the firefighters to show up before initiating the direct assault. It was a classic terror strategy, designed to maximize casualties among first responders.

"Contact," he shouted, bringing his Glock up, searching in vain for the source of the incoming fire. There had been no audible reports, no muzzle flashes that might have helped him pinpoint the shooter. Suppressed weapons, and a lot of them judging by the volume of incoming fire.

But where are they?

Beside him Rob Davis opened fire with his own weapon—a Heckler & Koch MP5—and then the air was filled with the thunder of unsuppressed weapons as the rest of the fly team and the marshals began responding to the attack the only way they knew how. Whorls in the miasma of dust and gun smoke showed the trajectory of rounds zipping past all around, yet Kline still couldn't determine where the enemy fire was coming from.

He became aware of Davis's voice, shouting in his ear. "Fall back to the plane! Protect Gage!"

The plane? Kline wondered. *Why not the fire trucks?*

Even as he thought it, he knew the answer, realizing what Davis and the others had already intuited.

The attack was coming *from* the fire trucks.

The realization galvanized Kline. From the prone, he twisted around until he was facing back toward the plane, then sprang to his feet and took off running. Through the haze he saw three marshals huddled around Gage, shielding him with their bodies, attempting to reach the relative safety of the stricken jet. They were all that remained of the transport detail—the rest lay sprawled on the ground, wounded or dead. Mindful of avoiding a similar fate, Kline took only a few steps before throwing himself flat once more, rolling to the side, bounding up again. He repeated this action several times, just as he had been taught in boot camp a lifetime ago, zigzagging randomly in an attempt to dodge any incoming fire.

It worked.

But only for a second.

SIX

Kline was just ten yards from the jet's dual-wheeled front landing gear—where the marshals, now numbering only two, had taken refuge along with their prisoner—when something punched into his lower back and sent him sprawling forward.

He wasn't dead, wasn't even wounded thanks to his Level IIIA body armor, but in the moment, death seemed preferable. Although it didn't penetrate the Kevlar mesh, the incoming round had impacted directly above his right kidney with the force of a donkey kick. The pain was instantaneous and blinding. For several seconds all he could do was writhe in senseless agony while the battle raged around him.

As conscious thought returned, Kline was dimly aware of the slackening volume of unsuppressed fire. What had only moments before been a thunderstorm of overlapping reports now was reduced to a pathetic *pop . . . pop-pop . . . pop* with long intervals of relative silence in between.

Even through a fog of pain, the significance of this was not lost on him. *They wiped us out.*

Through barely slitted eyes, he looked sidelong to where the fire trucks sat, their red and blue emergency lights flashing through the dust and gloom like a fiery harbinger of the apocalypse. Then figures began emerging from the storm— three men . . . no, four . . . six . . . seven, spreading out and walking in a picket line across the now quiescent battlefield. From Kline's low perspective, they looked freakishly tall.

Demonic.

One of them paused, looked down to regard a shapeless mass at his feet, then pointed at it with one seemingly misshapen hand . . . No, it was something in his hand . . . A gun. A machine pistol similar to those carried by the fly team, but with an extended barrel.

The weapon twitched in the man's hand. There was no report, at least not one that Kline could hear over the din of the sirens and the roar of the still-turning jet engine, but he knew, with certainty, that one of the wounded fly team agents—one of his friends—had just been executed.

A wave of desperation and anger washed over Kline. Having won the battle, the attackers were killing the wounded, moving methodically across the scene, leaving no one alive to bear witness to their horrendous crime. And they were heading right toward him.

He flexed his fingers, only now realizing that he'd lost his pistol. It had almost certainly fallen somewhere nearby, but looking for it would only draw attention his way. Even if by some miracle he found it, he would be just one man against seven. His lightweight body armor might or might not save him a second time, but a burst from a machine pistol would incapacitate him even if the rounds didn't penetrate, giving the attackers time to close in and dispatch him with a head shot.

No, trying to fight back now was suicide. His only hope was to use his shrinking window of opportunity to reach cover. And after that?

One impossible thing at a time, he told himself.

Moving slowly, he shifted his attention, calculating the distance to the jet's forward landing gear. Ten yards. Eight or nine long steps, if he could bound up and move faster than his enemies could track him.

It was a big *if,* but it was all he had.

He tensed, preparing to spring up and run, but before he could, one of the marshals edged out from behind the landing gear, brandishing his service weapon, and began blasting away at the approaching shooters. Simultaneously, two more figures broke from cover on the opposite side of the wheels, running at a full sprint toward the rear landing gear assembly. One of the running men was Anton Gage, but in the instant that Kline recognized him, the former billionaire was slapped down by a burst of enemy fire. Gage twisted, stumbled, went sprawling. The marshal accompanying him skidded to a stop, firing his weapon at the attackers as he reached his free hand out to the fallen prisoner.

Then a round caught him in the forehead, and he went down under a halo of crimson.

Sighting Anton Gage seemed to fill the hostiles with new purpose. They concentrated their fire on the remaining marshal, driving him back down behind the wheel, and then began moving forward as one, their weapons at the high ready. They swept past Kline without giving him a second glance, dividing their forces as they approached the landing gear. Three of them moved in on the lone surviving marshal, while the others closed in on the billionaire.

Gage was still alive, writhing on the ground, gasping for breath, but as the men approached, he managed to raise a hand to them, as if asking for help.

Or mercy.

From the first sign of trouble, Kline had wondered if the bold attack was intended to liberate Gage from custody or simply to liquidate him. That question was answered when one of the men from the assault team stepped past the others to stand over Gage. Ignoring the outstretched hand, he fired a shot directly into Gage's face.

If any man deserved to die for his crimes, it was Anton Gage, but his demise brought Kline no satisfaction. In that moment, all he felt was utter defeat. With Gage dead, the likelihood of the Twelve ever being brought to justice had just gone to zero. All the effort and sacrifice to bring him in alive had been for nothing.

Kline's executioner then did something unexpected. Allowing his weapon to hang by its sling, he reached into a pouch on his plate carrier, took out a phone, and held it above Gage's face.

He's taking a picture, thought Kline. *Proof of the kill.*

The man studied the phone's display for a moment, then began manipulating the screen, no doubt forwarding the photograph to the person or persons who had ordered the hit.

Kline saw the window of opportunity slide open before him. With their attention fixed on Gage's execution, the assault element had momentarily lost their situational awareness, giving him a chance to do something more than just wait for a bullet.

He lifted up, raising his head just a few degrees, and scanned his immediate surroundings until he spotted his Glock, just out of reach to his left. A sequence of moves unspooled in his mind's eye.

Twist around and grab the gun . . . Snap off a reflex shot . . . Roll . . . Shoot again . . . Bound up and dash for cover.

He knew better than to think that he could take them all out, but maybe, just maybe, he could get a little payback.

A line from an old Bon Jovi song came unbidden into his thoughts. *"Goin' down in a blaze of glory . . ."*

Well, I never thought I'd live long enough to die of old age, he thought. A moment later, he made his move.

SEVEN

Cormac Kilmeade, known to his men as Dagger Six, took a moment—but only a moment—to savor the completion of the primary mission objective. It had been a monumental undertaking, boldly conceived and executed—the kind of operation that set his soul on fire, made him feel truly alive.

Dangerous?

Absolutely.

Guaranteed to succeed?

Where was the fun in that?

Not that he had left anything to chance. Every detail of the operation had been meticulously planned, with contingencies upon contingencies. But that was exactly why the execution phase was such a rush. Setting the dominos up and then watching them fall.

Oh, he still loved running and gunning. Blowing things up. Moving under fire. The adrenaline rush that could be found in combat was just too addictive to ever give up. It was why he preferred to lead from the front rather than watching operations from a remote command center. But at the end of the day, the mission was what mattered most.

He glanced down at the image on the screen of his burner phone, the face of the man he had just killed. The terrified expression on Anton Gage's face had softened a little in the moments since his essential spark had been extinguished, the muscles relaxing so that his expression looked a little like a melting wax mask, but there was no mistaking that it was him.

Despite assurances from the Praetorian that Gage would be on the JPATS transport plane, Kilmeade's greatest concern had been that the feds would send a decoy in Gage's place. It's what he would have done. But no, this was definitely Gage. The facial recognition app on his phone had just confirmed it, even with the slight deformity caused by the nine-millimeter round from Kilmeade's CZ Skorpion machine pistol, which had entered Gage's forehead just above the bridge of his nose.

Kilmeade tapped a small icon in the corner of the screen to forward the image, tapped it again to select the number of the burner phone the Praetorian was currently using, and then one last time to send the image.

The picture was replaced by a confirmation message, and then a couple seconds later, the phone vibrated with an incoming text.

A thumbs-up emoji.

Then the phone vibrated again.

Proceed to phase 2

Kilmeade swiped back to his contact list and quicky tapped out a stream of messages to a different recipient.

Phase 1 a win

Go for phase 2

The messages whooshed off into cyberspace.

A moment later, the phone vibrated again, signaling the arrival of a reply to his message, but before he could read what appeared on the screen, the noise of a gunshot tore his attention away.

He whirled around, the phone falling, forgotten as his hands sought the Skorpion, which dangled on its sling at his hip. Even as he caught hold of the weapon, he was moving, ducking low, twisting around to search for a target.

Twenty yards away, maybe less, a lone figure wearing a lightweight armored vest over street clothes and wielding an FBI standard-issue Glock was running toward the jet's front landing gear. Kilmeade fired off a reflex shot. It missed. He adjusted his aim and tried to lead the target, but before he could, the man threw himself flat, sliding behind the wheel like a runner stealing second base.

As the man momentarily vanished from sight, Kilmeade saw that Dagger Three was down, felled by the FBI agent's single shot, which had, either through luck or uncanny skill, slipped through the gap between Three's helmet and vest and ripped into his throat.

He snarled a curse, angry more at himself for his haste and arrogance in declaring victory while the battlefield remained unsecured than at the lone federal officer who had managed to stay alive a little longer than all the others.

To either side of him, the remaining members of Dagger Team were fanning out, attempting to flank the FBI man without becoming his next victim. The agent was no more of a threat than any of the men they had already killed, but for some reason they were having trouble doing what needed to be done. Dagger Three's untimely demise had left them rattled. Like Kilmeade, they all wore Level III+ armor and helmets equipped with ballistic face shields that were more than a match for anything but a high-powered rifle round, but that did not make them invincible. Dagger Three had just demonstrated that.

"Just shoot him," Kilmeade roared, charging toward the FBI agent's position.

But then a second unexpected thing happened.

From the corner of his eye, Kilmeade saw a flash of movement from the direction of the jet's forward landing gear. He knew that none of the plane's defenders had made it that far, knew also that it could not be anyone from Dagger Team, and yet someone was there.

A sick feeling, like a premonition of doom, clenched Kilmeade's gut. Somehow he knew that the tide had turned against his team, snatching defeat from the jaws of victory.

He spun around, looking for the target he knew he would find, and saw a lone figure, a man, blond-brown hair, slender but well-proportioned, wearing jeans and black T-shirt. He carried no weapon but something about him radiated danger.

Where did you come from? thought Kilmeade.

Unencumbered by heavy combat gear, the man moved unnaturally fast, arrowing toward the man nearest to him—Dagger Four, whose attention was completely focused on the forward landing gear where the FBI agent was hiding.

Before Kilmeade could shout to get Four's attention, the running man was there. He wrapped an arm around Dagger Four's neck and heaved him off his feet. Both men went down, but as they fell, the unknown attacker twisted Four's head so violently that Kilmeade would not have been surprised to see it torn completely off. Even though he couldn't possibly have heard it, Kilmeade *felt* Four's vertebrae cracking.

Kilmeade brought his weapon around but had no shot. The newcomer was almost entirely hidden behind Dagger Four's bulk. Then, impossibly, Four's right arm began to move . . . except it wasn't Four's arm at all, but that of the man who had killed him, rising with the Skorpion in his grip.

The machine pistol bucked, and Kilmeade felt a series of hammer blows against his chest. Staggered back by the impact, with the wind knocked out of him, he could only watch, helpless, as his team was caught in a crossfire between the newcomer and the FBI agent. The team's armor, like Kilmeade's, stopped the bullets but couldn't turn aside the far more insidious missile of fear that had penetrated their hearts.

Kilmeade felt it too. Fickle luck had turned against them. If they didn't leave now, they might not leave at all.

Gasping as his breath returned, he keyed his mic. "Break contact," he wheezed. "Exfil now!"

EIGHT

When he saw the running man take down one of the attackers, Kline's first improbable thought was, *Matt?*

But of course, it wasn't him, couldn't be. Matthew Redd was a thousand miles away. Besides, this man was smaller. More compact. But he moved like Redd—fast, indomitable, brutal.

"Aaron," Kline whispered, finally making the connection and mentally kicking himself for the confusion. It had been too long since he'd seen Aaron Decker in action. He'd forgotten just how purposeful the man could be. Decker was like an avenging angel, sweeping across the battlefield to deliver the touch of death upon his enemies.

It took Kline another moment to realize that Decker's timely arrival had just turned the tide of battle, giving him a chance to do more than just go out with guns blazing. In that moment, Decker succeeded in wresting control of his first victim's weapon, using it to engage and suppress the remaining enemy. Wasting no time, Kline edged out from behind cover and joined the fight.

The attackers' armor limited the lethality of his response. He'd gotten lucky with that first shot. But the crossfire had put the surviving hostiles on the defensive. One of them—the same man who had executed Gage—shouted something, then stabbed his machine pistol in Decker's direction and squeezed the trigger, emptying the magazine in a long and essentially futile burst. The rounds slammed ineffectually into the body armor of the dead man Decker was using as a shield. But the action achieved its true purpose, suppressing Decker long enough for the shooter and his remaining comrades to break away from the fight. In unison, they took off in the direction of the fire trucks. Kline fired after them until his pistol was empty, but none fell, and in a matter of seconds, they had all vanished once more into the haze of still-settling dust.

"Gavin! Are you hit?"

Kline whirled around to find Decker right beside him.

He still moves like a ghost.

Kline shook his head. "I'm good."

Except he wasn't. He was anything but good. Gage was dead, and his team had been wiped out.

A body lay just a few paces to his left, sprawled out on the grass. It was the marshal who had tried to cover Gage's ill-fated retreat. Kline knelt beside him, intending to check for a pulse, but stopped when he saw that the right side of the man's head was missing.

He lurched away from the dead man, then raised his eyes to meet Decker's stare. "Check the others," he rasped. "There might be survivors."

Decker nodded mutely and pivoted away, following the trail of bodies back to where the assault had begun. It was only then that Kline realized one of the fire trucks—the big one that looked like an LVSR—was still there, its lights still flashing a false message of imminent rescue.

"Boss?"

The shout, barely audible over the still-screaming jet engine, tore his attention away from the fire truck. He turned to find Special Agent Treadway emerging from the haze, approaching from the same direction Decker had come.

"Steph! Get over here. Help us look for survivors."

The request brought her up short. He could see her mouthing, *"Survivors?"*

Her eyes went wide as she beheld the carnage the attackers had left in their wake, but she recovered her wits and hurried over to join in the search. She began beside the unmoving form of Anton Gage.

"Whoa!" She looked over at Kline. "Gage is dead?"

"Forget about him," snapped Kline. "Our people are out here. Hurting. Dying."

She nodded, but then stooped over and picked something up. "Look at this."

Kline recognized it immediately. It was the phone that Gage's executioner had used to confirm the kill. Momentarily forgetting about the search for survivors, Kline ran over to Treadway, taking the phone from her.

It was a cheap Nokia, the kind sold with prepaid cellular plans—a burner—and Kline doubted it would contain anything that might help nail down the identities of the men who had led the attack or, more critically, the person or persons who had ordered it, but the mere fact that it had been left behind felt like a small ray of hope.

Even better, the phone was still unlocked, displaying a text message exchange. Two outgoing messages:

Phase 1 a win

Go for phase 2

Followed by one incoming reply:

We're already wheels up and on our way. ETA 30 minutes. Let the hunt begin!

"Who do you think these guys were?" said Treadway, looking over his shoulder. "Mercs hired by the Twelve to shut Gage up permanently?"

Kline thought about the audacity of the attack and shook his head. "They were a lot more than just hired guns. To pull this off . . . it would have taken some pretty serious resources."

"What do you think phase two is?"

Kline had been wondering that too. "The next target."

Well, that much was obvious.

"Whoever it is, he's got half an hour before his world turns upside down."

Let the hunt begin.

For some reason, that part of the message was especially troubling to Kline.

Phase two. The hunt.

Gage was dead, along with almost everyone who might have known what he planned to reveal in his testimony.

Who was left to silence?

What had started as a mere tingle of apprehension flared into a full-blown wildfire of anxiety as Kline considered the question. Deep in his gut, he knew the answer.

We're already wheels up and on our way.

He took out his own government-issued mobile phone and dialed a number.

The call was picked up on the first ring. Kline had the phone pressed to his ear, both hands cupped around it in an attempt to block some of the background noise, but he still had trouble hearing the voice at the other end. "Intelligence Directorate, Special Agent Mejia speaking."

"Rajun, it's Kline. I need you to look something up for me."

Tony Mejia, who went by "Rajun," though Kline wasn't sure where the nickname came from, was a wizard at anything that involved a keyboard. Bearing a striking resemblance to the actor who played Ned in *Spider-Man: Homecoming*, Mejia jokingly referred to himself as "the man in the chair."

"Boss? Where are you? I can barely hear you."

Kline raised his voice to a shout. "I need you to get the flight plans of all private aircraft currently in the air."

"All? There must be hundreds of them. Maybe even thousands. Can you narrow it down a little for me?"

"No, sorry." Then a thought occurred to him. "CONUS flights only. Arrival time will be about thirty minutes from now, give or take."

Mejia grumbled in his ear, but after a few seconds announced, "Well, I've got it down to about two hundred."

Two hundred?

Kline groaned, then said the thing he had been dreading, following his gut. And his worst fear. "Okay, try this. Are there any flights going to Montana?"

"Uh, okay, let me just . . . Stand by . . . Yeah, I've got one. A Gulfstream G500, operated by Livingston Charters. Fourteen pax. Left Chicago about three hours ago. Destination, Three Forks Airport."

"Three Forks?"

"It's a general aviation field about thirty miles northwest of Bozeman."

The sick feeling in Kline's gut intensified.

Mejia was still talking. "Looks like there's a weather system moving in. Heavy snow in the forecast. ATC asked them to divert to Bozeman Yellowstone International Airport, but the operator insisted on Three Forks. Even hired someone to come out and plow the field."

Kline knew that no sane pilot would choose to land a plane at a regional airport in the middle of a winter storm unless he had something to hide. "Tell me about the carrier. And the client."

There was a brief pause, and then Mejia came back. "Livingston Charters is, if you'll forgive the technical language, pretty sketchy. The airline equivalent of a no-tell motel, if you know what I mean. The client listed on the manifest is Dogpatch Inc., but I'm not finding anything about them except a PO box in Wilmington, Delaware."

"A shell company," breathed Kline, thinking aloud. "I'll bet money that the names on the manifest are bogus."

"Want me to chase this rabbit?"

Kline shook his head, knowing it would be a futile pursuit. Unless he was very much mistaken, the people capable of executing the assault on Gage's transport—in broad daylight and on the grounds of a major American airport—would have gone to great pains to cover their tracks. Besides, right now launching an investigation was pretty low on Kline's list of priorities.

"I'll get back to you," he said, ending the call and immediately dialing another number.

Treadway, who had been standing beside him during the call, spoke up. "Montana? You think they're going after—"

He held up a hand to silence her as the call was picked up at the other end.

NINE

MONTANA

A noise like a tornado tore from the phone's little speaker, assaulting Redd's eardrum. He pulled the device away a few inches before speaking.

"Gavin? What's that noise?" The ongoing roar from the phone had prompted him to raise his voice, which earned him a reproving look from Emily.

For a few seconds, all he heard was the persistent rushing sound; then a hoarse and breathless voice said, "Matt? Where are you?"

"I'm home, Gavin. Where else would I be?"

"I need you to listen to me. I don't have time to explain all the details. I'll tell you later . . . if I can . . . Right now you just need to . . ." He was speaking so fast Redd had a hard time understanding him. Kline paused a beat as if to catch his breath, then said, "They're coming for you."

That got Redd's attention. His gaze flashed about the room, taking in the expectant and increasingly worried-looking faces around him.

He covered the phone with his hand, trying to project his voice without raising his volume. "Bottom-line me, Gavin."

"We got hit. Hard. They got Gage."

"Got him?" Redd asked, though he had a good idea exactly what Kline meant.

"He's dead, Matt. It was a bloodbath. We found . . ." There was a disturbance on the other end of the line, somebody yelling. Redd couldn't make out what was being said at first, but then Kline stopped talking for a moment, and he heard another voice shouting. *"Why did they leave the other fire truck?"*

Then Kline came back. "There's another hit team . . . Could be a dozen shooters . . . They're about to touch down in Montana. You're the only other target that makes sense. They have to be coming for you."

Redd's blood went cold. A thousand questions bloomed in his mind, but only one really mattered. "How much time do I have?"

"They're coming into Three Forks. The weather might slow them down—"

Redd knew Three Forks. It was a little town south of Wellington. "How long, Gavin?" he growled, cutting Kline off.

There was a pause, and Redd heard more shouting about the fire truck—not just the other voice, but Kline and someone else, a female. "Forget the fire truck," Kline shouted, then said, "We're coming, Matt. Just as soon as we can . . ." He seemed to choke up for a moment. "You just have to hunker down somewhere safe. Stay alive until we get—"

"Gavin!" Redd yelled. "How long?"

Across the table, Liz jumped, startled by the intensity of his voice. On the bed, Junior whimpered and began squalling.

"Matty," said Emily. "What is it? What's wrong?"

Redd waved away the question, then rose from the table, opened the door, and stepped outside. Doing so did nothing to reduce the background noise at Kline's end of the call, but being outside, surrounded by the gently falling snow, helped Redd focus.

"Best guess?" Kline said after a moment. "You've got an hour till they get there. Maybe less. Matt, these guys aren't fooling around. You have to find somewhere to hole up."

Redd swore. He didn't need to ask who was behind the threat, or why.

When he'd taken Anton Gage into custody, he'd spent some quality personal time with the man. Gage, in a bid for self-preservation, had sung like a canary, which put Redd on a very short list of people who knew the identities of the Twelve, as well as the names of several noteworthy and influential individuals who were deep in their collective pocket.

He had known there would eventually be some fallout from taking down Gage, and part of him had expected them to launch a full-blown offensive. Maybe not *this* big though, and not before Gage had his day in court.

But now, apparently, Anton Gage was dead.

That changes everything.

The Twelve, it seemed, were taking a scorched-earth approach to snipping off any loose ends.

"I'll be there as fast as humanly possible," Kline continued, "but you're going to have to look out for yourself until—"

"Gavin." The female voice at the other end cut in, loud enough that the woman had to have been shouting in Kline's face. "They left the fire truck behind."

"So?"

"They left it behind, Gavin. Think about it. We need to get out of here. *Now!*"

Then the voices were swallowed up in a tumult of incoherent noise, a mixture of static, random thumps, and what sounded like labored breathing, all played over the ongoing loud rushing sound.

"Gavin?" Redd shouted, but no one on the other end of the call seemed to hear. "Gavin, talk to me. What's going—?"

Suddenly, a noise like a shotgun blast tore from the phone and right into Redd's ear. He jerked it away, but the damage was already done. With his ear ringing, Redd stared at the phone for a moment, dumbfounded, then cautiously raised it to his other ear.

"Gavin?"

He heard only silence. The display showed that the call was still connected, but no sound issued from the device. Judging by the fact that he was temporarily deaf in his right ear, Redd wondered if the speaker in the phone had blown out. Or maybe the microphone on Kline's phone.

What was that?

The trailer door opened and Emily stepped out. "Matty, is everything okay?"

He just stared at her. His mind was racing, churning over what Kline had said, and what he hadn't.

"Another hit team . . . a dozen shooters . . ."

"An hour . . . maybe less."

"Coming for you."

Emily didn't wait for him to answer. "Liz just got a breaking news notification on her phone. A plane just crashed in Oklahoma City. Is that why Gavin called you?"

The question snapped Redd back to the moment. Leave it to Emily to put two and two together.

Oklahoma City was the location of the Federal Transfer Center, where federal prisoners were held while awaiting trial—federal prisoners like Anton Gage. Kline had told Redd that Gage would eventually end up there, though the details of the move had been a closely guarded secret, even from Redd.

The timing of the plane crash could not be a coincidence.

"We got hit . . . It was a bloodbath . . ."

He shoved his now useless phone back into his pocket. "Show me."

Inside the trailer, Liz had turned her phone over to Mikey while she was busy trying to soothe the children, both of whom had awakened.

"This is pretty crazy," said Mikey, holding up the phone for Redd's inspection.

Redd focused on the screen, which, according to the little graphic in the corner, was displaying a live stream from Oklahoma City. The feed was grainy, probably shot from a distance with a phone camera zoomed in, but it clearly showed the broken and burning remains of a large jet aircraft.

"The thing just blew up a second ago," Mikey went on. "You just missed it."

Redd met his gaze. "What do you mean?"

"When the report came in, it said the plane had crashed on landing. Someone started live streaming it from the main terminal, and the network picked it up. The plane looked like it was on fire, but then just a few seconds ago, there was a big explosion. They'll probably replay it in a minute."

Redd shook his head. He didn't need to see the replay.

He had *heard* it happen.

His mind raced as he sorted and assembled the data. The picture was incomplete, a puzzle with too many missing pieces, but Kline's warning kept repeating in his head.

"Coming for you . . ."

Okay, what are my options? Stand and fight, or run and hide?

Kline had explicitly advised the latter. *"Find somewhere to hole up,"* he'd said. He had also promised, *"We're coming . . . Just as soon as we can."*

Only now Redd didn't think Kline was going to be able to keep that promise.

I'm on my own.

He shook his head. *Focus. Deal with the problem.*

Kline had said there were at least a dozen shooters inbound, and if the attack in Oklahoma City was any indication, the hit team would be packing some serious firepower. Redd had guns too. What he didn't have was an unlimited supply of ammunition for those weapons. More to the point, he didn't have a defensible position. Neither the trailer nor the barn would afford any kind of protection.

A panic room would sure come in handy right about now, he thought darkly, though he knew better than to say it out loud in front of his wife.

Staying and fighting wasn't an option. As much as he disliked the idea of running, he had no inclination to deprive his wife and child of their husband and father out of a sense of misbegotten honor.

Run and hide then. But where?

If the hit team had the resources to attack a federal prison transport plane, the movements of which were a closely guarded secret, and on the grounds of a major airport no less, then they certainly had the ability to track him down. Throwing his phone away and driving his work truck—an old F-250 Super Duty that definitely wasn't GPS enabled—would slow them down a little . . . maybe . . . but eventually, they would find him. It wasn't inconceivable that they might have an advance team keeping the ranch under surveillance.

Even if he managed to make a clean getaway from the ranch, where could he go? Not to his friends or to Emily's family—that would just put them in danger too.

That didn't even address the real problem with either alternative—he wasn't alone. He could not do anything to put Emily and little Matty at risk.

"Matty!" Emily's voice snapped him back into the moment. "Talk to me. What's going on?"

He looked back at her, glanced over at Mikey, then took in Liz holding little Lucas and gently rocking him back and forth, and made his decision.

He had to put as much distance between him and them as possible. And fast.

TEN

"I don't have time to explain everything right now," Redd began, "so you all need to listen carefully and do exactly as I say. We need to move quick."

He paused a beat, then got to the point. "What happened in Oklahoma City wasn't a plane crash. It was an attack on a federal prison transport, and it's connected to what happened here a couple of months back."

He did not need to explain that point further. Emily knew the whole story, and Mikey knew some of it—knew that Redd sometimes worked for the FBI and that the business with the outlaw biker gang had been part of something even bigger. Mikey, a voracious reader of mystery and thriller novels, especially ones from Brad Thor and Jack Carr, was smart enough to fill in the blanks.

"Gavin just told me that there's another hit team heading here. They're coming for me."

Despite his earlier admonition, Emily immediately broke in. "Wait. Coming *here*?" She moved her index finger around the trailer. "Then we need to go. Now!"

"Agreed." Redd turned to Mikey. "I need you to take Em and Junior with you. Don't go home though. And don't go to Elijah's place. I don't think they'll come after you, but if they do, those will be the first places they look."

"Hold on just a minute," said Emily. "I'm not leaving you."

"You *have* to," Redd declared with as much finality as he could manage.

"They are coming for me, Em. Just *me*. I can handle them, but not if I'm trying to keep you and Junior safe at the same time."

Mikey and Liz said nothing, but judging by the looks on their faces, they were having trouble processing what he was saying. Emily, on the other hand, stared back at him with the intensity of a laser beam. "We're a team, Matty. Whatever this is, we're going to get through it together."

He shook his head. "Not this time. These guys are pros. They'll make those bikers look like a . . ." He glanced at Mikey and offered a rueful grin. "Like a pack of Cub Scouts." He returned his focus to Emily. "The only way I'm going to be able to survive this is if I can get them in the open and isolate them. I know the land, I can use that to my advantage, but first I need to know that you're safe."

"And how exactly are you going to 'handle them'?"

"I'm going to ride up into the hills. Get them to follow me."

"Ride? In case you hadn't noticed, there's a blizzard coming."

He nodded. "It will level the playing field. I know my way around up there. They don't."

Emily shook her head. "This is crazy, Matthew."

Redd did not fail to notice her use of his full first name. She only called him Matthew when she was upset with him.

Then she went on. "Can't Gavin send some FBI agents out here?"

"There's no time. The bad guys will be here in less than an hour." He decided not to tell her that he was pretty sure Gavin Kline was already dead.

"Then call Sheriff Blackwood."

He shook his head again. "These guys would rip right through his deputies. No, this is the only way, Em. You have to trust me on this. And you have to go. *Now.*"

He saw the hesitancy in her eyes, her jaw muscles tight with resistance, but then she nodded slowly. "All right. If it's the only way to keep our son safe."

"It is. Now go."

Mikey finally overcame his silent shock. "You mean right now? This is really happening?"

Redd reached for the door. "Leave your phones here. That way, they won't be able to track you."

Liz continued to stare at him in disbelief. So did Mikey.

Emily, however, took out her phone, set it on the table, then looked to her closest friend. "It's going to be all right, Liz," she said. "Let's just do as Matty says."

The admonition broke Mikey and Liz free from the grip of inertia. Mikey surrendered both his phone and Liz's. The latter was still showing the live stream from Oklahoma City.

Emily nodded toward the door. "Let's get the kids loaded up. Mikey, can you get Junior's car seat out of the Tahoe?"

Mikey seized the idea like it was a lifeline. He gave a vigorous nod, then bolted out the door into the snow. Liz, still moving a little like someone in a daze, followed with Lucas in her arms.

When they were gone, Emily turned to Redd. "I guess you should get going," she said. Her face and voice were completely neutral, betraying none of the emotions he knew she had to be feeling.

"Yeah."

He wanted to say more, knew he ought to. He should tell her how much he loved her and Junior. He should assure her that everything would be okay, even though he knew he could not guarantee it.

But he couldn't bring himself to say it.

Deep down, he knew there was a chance that whatever he said now might be the last words he would ever say to her. And admitting that, if only to himself, would be like admitting the possibility of defeat. That was something he could not afford to do.

So he simply turned and reached for the door.

"Matty."

He stopped but did not turn back to her. *Please don't say it . . .*

"Yeah, Em?"

"You'd better come back to me." A tear rolled down her cheek. "If you get killed out there, so help me, I will bring you back and kill you myself."

Redd felt the corners of his mouth twitch up into a smile. He nodded.

Love you too, Em, he thought but didn't say it aloud.

Then he opened the door and headed back out into the storm.

ELEVEN

OKLAHOMA CITY

Cormac Kilmeade realized his mistake almost right away, but by then it was too late to do anything about it. Aboard the smaller fire engine, with Dagger Two at the wheel, racing back toward the airport fire station, he could not have gone back if he'd wanted to.

He knew exactly what had happened, how it had gone wrong. One of the FBI agents had been playing possum, caught them all flat-footed, and Kilmeade, in his haste to return fire, had dropped his phone. Then when that other guy had shown up and killed Dagger Four . . . well, the only thing on his mind had been bugging out.

In the grand scheme of things, it wasn't a huge problem. The phone was a burner, untraceable, as were the phones he'd called or texted from it—one of them belonging to the Praetorian and the other in the hands of his brother, Colin. There was nothing in his call history nor in the messages themselves that could lead to any of them.

He glanced back at the towering column of black smoke rising above the runway. He could just make out the remains of the firefighting vehicle, a dark smudge amidst the flames and smoke, and behind it, the skeleton of the 737.

Odds were good that the phone would never be recovered. The spot where Kilmeade had dropped the phone was now a smoking crater, thanks to the improvised explosive device he'd detonated after the exfil. A hundred pounds of ANFO, mixed with diesel and aluminum powder, secreted aboard the Oshkosh Striker aircraft firefighting vehicle they'd ridden out to the crash site, was a very effective method for sanitizing the scene.

Not to mention providing a nice diversion for their exfil.

Even so, he would have to contact the Praetorian and let him know that his current burner was compromised. That was not a call he was looking forward to, not because he was particularly worried about raising the man's ire—this was, after all, the reason they used burner phones—but because it would mean admitting to a mistake.

Mistakes were a sign of weakness.

If it had been one of his men, he would have torn the man's head off. Unfortunately, there was no one to blame but himself.

Pick up and drive on, he told himself.

He knew he ought to be more upset at the loss of two of his men, but he felt no sense of grief at their deaths. They had died a warrior's death; what more could any man ask for?

He had not been close to either man—fraternization was discouraged in the outfit for this very reason. The emotions that accompanied losing a friend could cloud a soldier's judgment. Sorrow and rage, the thirst for revenge—these were distractions that could prove fatal in battle. It was why he and Colin led different teams.

If anything, he was more troubled by the logistical challenge. They were, of necessity, a lean outfit, but in an operation like this, casualties were to be expected, and with phase one complete, there would be time to recruit and train replacements.

He put aside these concerns as the airport fire station came into view. Although the mission objective had been satisfied, there remained one final hurdle. Getting Dagger and Arrow Teams into the airport had been an easy thing. Getting them out, especially after the mayhem they had just caused, would be a little trickier, but unlike the assault on the prisoner transport plane, it would be accomplished with finesse and deception rather than brute force.

He noted with amusement the black SUVs with flashing emergency lights parked near the corners of the station house, anchoring the cordon ostensibly designed both to keep people from getting in and to keep those inside from getting out. The first objective was about to be tested—several more emergency vehicles were racing toward the building. Evidently someone in airport security had figured out that there was something fishy about the fire engine leaving the scene mere moments before the big Striker blew itself and the 737 to kingdom come.

"All right," he announced as the engine coasted into the open garage bay. "Showtime."

The remaining members of Dagger Team did not need any reminders about what to do next. Once Dagger Two brought the engine to a full stop, they all debarked quickly and began removing the magazines from their Czech-manufactured machine pistols. As they did, two figures attired in tactical gear identical to what Dagger Team wore—save for a few distinctive embellishments—approached from the rear of the garage, carrying several M4 carbines in their arms, which they began distributing to the operators of Dagger Team.

"You put on a hell of a show out there," said one of the newcomers—Rick Ross, otherwise known as Arrow Seven. As he passed a carbine to Kilmeade, he asked, "Who did you lose?"

"Johnson and Lake," answered Kilmeade, draping the weapon's sling over one shoulder. "One of the feebs got a lucky shot off. Took Johnson in the throat. And then this other guy showed up out of nowhere and took out Lake."

Ross offered a rueful shrug. "It happens."

"That it does," Kilmeade replied, in a tone that invited no further discussion. He reached into a cargo pocket and brought out a rolled-up parcel, which he handed to Ross. "All right, set me up. We're tight on time."

Ross unfurled the package, which contained two large Velcro-backed patches exactly like those worn by Ross and the other member of Arrow Team. In large white block letters, the patches proclaimed: *POLICE*. Below, in slightly smaller text, were the words *Homeland Security Investigations*.

When all the members of Dagger Team had similar patches affixed to the front and back of their plate carriers, Kilmeade and the others followed Ross to a small office where another member of Arrow Team waited, standing guard over four people seated on the floor, their faces hidden under blackout hoods, wrists and ankles secured with flex-cuffs.

Kilmeade nodded toward the prisoners. "Get 'em up."

In a matter of seconds, all four were on their feet, hands and feet loosed from restraints, hoods removed to reveal four men with scraggly hair and beards, blinking furiously as their eyes, accustomed to darkness after many hours under the hoods, were slow to adjust. As they did, looks of bewilderment quickly gave way to fear. Only one of them showed anything remotely resembling defiance.

"What kind of Gestapo crap is this?" he snarled.

I'll show you Gestapo crap, you good-for-nothing hippie, thought Kilmeade. He turned to Dagger Seven. "Do it."

The team needed no further prompts. Acting in unison, they approached the prisoners, thrusting their emptied and cleared Skorpion machine pistols into the hands of the unsuspecting quartet, and then just as quickly moved away.

The previously outspoken hippie looked down at the weapon in his hands with disgust. "What are you doing?"

Another of the group, perhaps sensing what was about to happen, threw down the gun and raised his hands. "Please. Don't do this."

Behind his face shield, Kilmeade's lips twitched into a sardonic smile. Facing the prisoners and affecting a flat, disinterested tone, he said, "Drop your weapons or we'll shoot."

Almost as soon as the last word was out, the room was filled with the thunderous reports of several carbines firing simultaneously. Torn apart by the fusillade, the hippies didn't even have a chance to scream.

Before the pall of gun smoke could begin to dissipate, the shooters approached the slain prisoners, inserting the partial magazines they had earlier removed back into the Skorpions, charging the machine pistols so that they were ready to fire.

Satisfied that the tableau they had created would support the eventual narrative he would promote, Kilmeade keyed his radio mic. "This is Dagger Six. Target building is secure. All tangos are down. I'm coming out, over."

Leaving the rest of the team to finish staging the scene, he moved through the building and ventured outside to where the rest of Arrow Team was holding back the airport police response team. The tension between the opposing groups was palpable, even from a distance. Arrow Six appeared to be engaged in a heated exchange with a policeman wearing riot gear over his gray uniform shirt.

Kilmeade hurried over and entered the fray, displaying his credentials and addressing the officer, who wore a single silver bar on his collar.

"HSI counter-terrorism division," Kilmeade said, using his best authoritative *don't mess with me* tone. "I'm the special agent in charge of this operation, so you can direct all your questions to me."

"Questions?" the police lieutenant spluttered, evidently unable to articulate his thoughts.

Kilmeade continued to hold his badge case up, just in case the policeman was entertaining any doubts about the authenticity of the credentials. Evidently, he was not. Had the officer looked more closely, he would have noticed that they had been issued to someone named Zachary Carter.

"Well then, I'll just read you in," Kilmeade went on, flipping the case closed. "We're HSI special operations division. I doubt you've heard of us, and we want to keep it that way. Long story short, we've been tracking a group of left-wing radicals operating out of Portland. We got a tip that they were going to try to assassinate a senior FBI director who was on that plane." He jerked a thumb in the direction of the still-rising smoke column in the distance.

"Unfortunately," continued Kilmeade, "we didn't know how or when the hit was going to go down, and by the time we figured it out . . ." He shook his head and allowed a solemn beat to pass. "From what we can tell, they overran the fire station, murdered all the firefighters inside in cold blood, and then used the station to launch the assault on the plane, posing as first responders. It looks like they turned one of those fire trucks into an IED to finish the job.

"If there's a silver lining, it's that we were waiting for them when they came back. That's why we couldn't let you and your men inside. But now that the situation is under control, I'm prepared to hand it off to you."

The police officer just gaped at him.

"I know it's a lot to take in all at once," Kilmeade went on. "The bottom line is that the situation is now under control. Yes, you've got a mess to clean up, but the immediate threat has been neutralized. It's your show now." He turned to Arrow Six. "Let's pack up. We need to get back to HQ for the debrief, ASAP."

Arrow Six keyed his mic and in a low voice said, "All Dagger and Arrow elements, implement the exit plan, over."

In his earpiece, Kilmeade heard the individual team members—including Arrow One, the sniper who had taken out the plane with his anti-materiel rifle—acknowledge the order.

This seemed to jolt the lieutenant out of his confusion. "Wait, you're leaving?"

"I told you. It's your show now."

"But . . ."

Kilmeade raised a hand. "Someone from the division will be in touch. They're probably already talking to your chief. My guess, they'll backstop things to make it look like your department and mine were cooperating all along."

Behind him, the shooters from Dagger and Arrow were filing out of the firehouse, making their way to the other SUV on the perimeter.

Kilmeade clapped the lieutenant on the shoulder. "Don't sweat it, LT. Just get in there and do your job. Heck, they'll probably give you all the credit."

Without another word to the police officer, Kilmeade and Arrow Six climbed into the nearest team vehicle.

Kilmeade waited until they were rolling to let out a relieved sigh.

From the driver's seat, Arrow Six shook his head. "Can't believe he actually bought that load of horse crap you were shoveling."

"Of course he did." Kilmeade grinned. "We're all on the same team." He paused a beat. "Hey, let me use your phone."

Arrow Six gave him a sidelong glance but did not question the request as he handed over his burner.

Kilmeade punched in a number and waited to see if the man at the other end would pick up.

"Yes?" There was a note of curiosity in the question. No doubt the Praetorian was wondering why he was getting a call from someone other than Kilmeade.

"It's me. I had a problem with my phone."

"A problem?"

Just rip the Band-Aid off, thought Kilmeade. "I dropped it. Out there."

He paused, bracing himself for an explosion of anger. Beside him, Arrow Six shot him a sidelong glance, but the Praetorian said nothing, so Kilmeade went on. "I don't think it will be recovered, but just in case, you should probably get rid of the phone you're using."

"Yes, that would probably be advisable," agreed the Praetorian with pronounced disinterest. "Listen, I'm glad you called. I've got another task for you. You did a great job out there today, but we've still got work to do."

"If you mean phase two, Colin is—"

"No, this is something else. Call it phase three, if you like."

Kilmeade was hesitant to argue with the Praetorian but felt he owed the man an honest assessment of their operational status. "We sustained some losses today. We need time to reset."

"This won't require a team. It's a one-man job, and I want you to handle it personally. Discreetly."

Kilmeade understood that the Praetorian was not *asking* him if he wanted to do the job. "All right. What's the job?"

"You put out the biggest fire today, but there are some hot spots that need to be permanently extinguished. Eleven of them, to be precise."

TWELVE

MONTANA

Redd made the trek up the snow-covered driveway to the barn on autopilot. His thoughts were a stew of worry and doubt. He kept telling himself that he had made the right call, the only possible call. The best way to protect his loved ones from what was coming was to keep them as far away from him as possible.

But what if I'm wrong? he wondered.

What if they decide to go after Em and Junior first? Try to use them against me?

Though it remained a possibility he couldn't dismiss, he thought it unlikely. If the men comprising the hit team were, like him, former military operators, they would move directly against the primary target, confident in their abilities and numerical superiority. They would come in hard and fast, laser-focused on their mission objective—him.

The unassailable logic of his decision did little to quell his anxiety.

If he was wrong, Redd knew he could never forgive himself.

After even a few minutes out in the cold, the barn's interior was almost uncomfortably warm thanks to the combined body heat of the dozen or so head of cattle that had elected to weather the storm under cover rather than out in the open. Upon seeing them, Redd's first thought was that he would need to go out to check on the rest of his stock—it was just one of the routine tasks he undertook on an almost daily basis.

Then he remembered that ranch duties were no longer his top priority.

He pushed through the herd and moved over to Remington's stall. Remington was a dappled-gray quarter horse that had been on the ranch almost as long as Redd himself. J. B. had owned several horses during the years Redd had spent growing up on the ranch, but loyal and dependable Remington had always been Redd's favorite. Together they had ridden every inch of the property on a regular basis, so often that they both could find their way around in the dark and blindfolded. They also ventured out past the fence line, into the mountain wilderness beyond.

Remington was more than just a horse to Redd; he was a friend. A friend that Redd had mostly forgotten about when he'd gone off to join the Marines. During his long absence, J. B. had been forced to sell off all his livestock, but thankfully he'd held on to Remington. When Redd had come home to discover that J. B. was dead and the ranch all but defunct and underwater financially, he'd taken no small measure of comfort that Remington was still there, still his. Saving the ranch, running it almost single-handedly had been a challenge for Redd, but without Remington, it would have been impossible.

Now well into his twenties, Remington was old for a working horse and closing in on the age where Redd knew he would have to put the old boy out to pasture. In Redd's mind, that meant exactly what it sounded like, even though the harsh reality of ranch life was that you didn't hang on to an animal that served no practical purpose.

Fortunately, Remington hadn't shown any signs of wanting to slow down.

When Redd opened the stall door, Remington dutifully strolled out as if he already knew what Redd expected of him.

"Sorry to do this to you, old buddy," said Redd, ruffling the gray's mane. "But we're gonna have to ride hard and fast for a little while. Can you do that for me?"

Remington nickered and shook his head as if to say, *Let's get on with it.*

Working with a quickness born of long practice, Redd saddled the horse and then began gathering the equipment and provisions he would need for an extended ride into the back country. With the supplies lashed to the saddle, he went over to the corner of the barn where he'd dragged his Old Glory gun safe after salvaging it from the ashes of the old ranch house.

Although the fire had blackened and oxidized the safe's exterior, the thick steel walls had preserved its contents from the flames. Unfortunately, in the moments before the fire, Redd had removed most of his small arsenal of firearms in order to defend the cabin against an attacking force of outlaw bikers, and not all of the guns had fared as well as the safe. His shotgun and hunting rifle—a lever-action Henry .45-70—had been badly scorched and were presently on the workbench of Paul Van Dunk, a prolific gunsmith Redd had enlisted to determine whether they were safe to use.

Redd had met Van Dunk, a former competitor with nearly two decades of shooting experience, back when he was with the Marine Raiders. They were introduced at the time through one of Redd's teammates. Van Dunk was one of the gunsmiths at Agency Arms LLC, and he and Redd had hit it off from the start. Since then, Van Dunk—known for his thick dark beard and mohawk—had gone on to found PACE Performance Consulting. Though he was no longer a full-time gunsmith, there was nobody Redd trusted more to check out his rifle and shotgun. If they could be saved, Van Dunk would have them working and looking good as new in no time.

Thankfully, Redd still had his Ruger Vaquero .44 Magnum—the first firearm he'd ever shot—and an FBI-issued H&K MP5SD6, which wasn't really practical for the kind of situations he typically encountered on the ranch but would definitely come in handy facing a small army of dedicated killers. He also had a Remington Model 700 hunting rifle, which belonged to Mikey Derhammer. Mikey, who only used the gun during hunting season, had made an indefinite loan of it to Redd.

Redd took all three, along with all the ammunition he had for each. He also took a fixed-blade hunting knife and an eight-pound Fiskars splitting maul. He'd added the latter to his combat load-out back in his days as a Marine Raider, intending to use it as a breaching tool, and had held on to it, finding it to be a lot more useful than he'd ever imagined.

It wasn't much of an arsenal, but it was all he had. He would make do with it because he had no other choice.

Once the weapons were either secured to his person or lashed to Remington's saddle, he donned a heavy Carhartt duck jacket and a pair of cowhide gloves—both lined with sherpa fleece—and then led the horse through the barn door, closing it behind him to keep the cattle inside from straying out into the driveway.

Outside, the snowfall seemed to have grown heavier, with fat flakes forming an almost impenetrable curtain around him, limiting visibility to only a few yards. Leading Remington by the bridle, Redd crossed the drive, heading back toward the trailer, navigating more by memory than sight.

When he saw that Mikey's truck was gone, he felt as if a weight had been lifted off his shoulders. He had expected more resistance to his evacuation order, and not just from Emily. Although Mikey was not like Redd—not a fighter by nature—when his loved ones were threatened, he did not back down. Redd valued that kind of loyalty, but he valued the lives of his family and friends even more. The kind of men who were willing to blow up an airplane at a busy airport just to kill one man would not draw the line at murdering innocents if they got in the way of their target.

At the door to the trailer, an unexpected surge of emotion swelled Redd's throat. Even though it was only a temporary dwelling, because it was a place where Redd and his family had lived in happiness, he had come to think of it as home. Now with everyone gone, the interior was cold and unwelcoming.

The thought that he might never come here again popped unbidden into his head. He dismissed it with a muttered curse.

The dinner Emily had prepared sat forlornly on the table. Redd didn't know if it had been intentionally left behind for him or merely forgotten in the haste to depart, but he wasn't about to let it go to waste. Working quickly, he transferred garlic mashed potatoes, baked macaroni and cheese, a plate full of dinner rolls, and several pounds of ham carved off the bone into gallon-sized Ziploc bags, which he then stuffed into a day pack. If he was to survive the coming ordeal, he would need calories as much as ammunition. He left the green salad behind, not because he disliked leafy vegetables but rather because he knew it wouldn't travel well.

To the pack, he also added three pairs of heavy wool-blend socks and a set of silk long underwear. As he riffled through cupboards and drawers looking for sundry items that might come in handy, he realized that he was just procrastinating. A quick check of his G-Shock watch told him that he'd already spent nearly twenty minutes of the hour—*maybe less*—remaining to him before the hit team came knocking.

It was time to go.

When he stepped back out into the weather, he first sensed then saw a dark shape on the ground alongside Remington. It was Rubble, sitting on his haunches with his head cocked to the side, looking up at Redd.

Redd felt a pang of guilt. In his haste to get Emily and Junior to safety and make his own preparations, he had forgotten someone. "Sorry, boy. Did you get left behind?"

Rubble woofed an affirmative.

"Well, I can't let you in right now because there won't be anyone to let you out. You'll have to stay in the barn, okay?"

Rubble, who knew a question when he heard one, let out another short bark, and when Redd took hold of Remington's bridle and led the horse back toward the barn, Rubble followed. However, when Redd opened the barn door, Rubble refused to go in. Instead, he just gazed up at Redd with an expectant look. In the short time that he had been with them, Rubble had accompanied Redd on his rides and clearly thought this was just another ordinary day at the ranch.

Redd shook his head. "I can't take you with me this time, boy. You've gotta stay here." He pointed to the open door and then, with a more commanding tone, said, "Inside. Now."

Rubble shook to clear away the snow that had settled onto his coat, then eased back onto his haunches.

"Come on, boy. Just get in there. I don't have time for this."

The dog remained unmoved by his appeals.

"You're not going to let me leave you here, are you?"

Rubble continued to stare up at him.

Redd sighed. "All right. You win."

As soon as the barn door was closed, Rubble was up, his nub wagging in anticipation of another ride with his master. After mounting Remington, Redd looked down, fixing the dog with a hard stare. "I better not hear you complain about how cold it is."

THIRTEEN

A hundred and fifty odd miles away, from the comfort of a Gulfstream G500 cruising at thirty thousand feet above the open prairie of central Montana, Colin Kilmeade followed Matthew Redd's departure with a growing sense of unease.

Displayed on the plane's large flat-screen monitor, the feed from the General Atomics MQ-9 Predator B unmanned aerial vehicle that had been flying circles above Redd's ranch property for several hours now clearly showed their target on horseback, riding east through an increasingly dense fall of snow.

The weather was getting worse, much worse than he'd anticipated when they'd put together the operation plan.

When Cormac had put him in charge of phase two of the operation, he'd thought he'd gotten the easier job.

Sneaking into an international airport and launching a daylight assault on a federal prison transport plane on the runway?

Only Cormac Kilmeade could pull off something like that.

Fly to the middle of nowhere and whack some ex-Marine-turned-cowboy?

"I'll let you handle that piece of cake," Cormac had told him.

Piece of cake. Yeah, right. He shook his head. *Thanks for nothing, big brother.*

His assault team had brought along their cold weather kit, so plunging temperatures wouldn't be an issue, but the snowstorm would hamper their movement.

It was already slowing them down. At last report, the runway at the backwater airport where they were supposed to land was still waiting on the arrival of a snowplow. If it didn't show before they arrived, they would either have to circle the area until it did or divert to Bozeman, where it would be considerably more difficult to unload their equipment and weapons discreetly.

And then there was the challenge of movement to the objective. It was a forty-mile drive to Redd's ranch—forty miles through falling snow. The vehicles waiting for them were supposed to be four-wheel drive with snow tires, but road conditions would nonetheless slow them down considerably.

At least the snow wasn't a problem for the UAV. With its suite of surveillance equipment, which included thermal imaging and synthetic aperture radar, it could "see" right through the weather to provide a startlingly accurate image of what was happening on the ground. The resolution wasn't good enough to give them positive ID, but the phone tracking software confirmed that the man on the horse was their target. So even if the blizzard wrecked their timetable, they would always know exactly where to find Matthew Redd.

The weather wasn't what was really nagging at him.

"What's he doing?"

"Looks like he's going for a ride," supplied Bull Dooley, Colin's second-in-command. In a military unit, Dooley—operational call sign Saber Seven—would have been the equivalent of a platoon sergeant, but their organization didn't employ ranks or titles.

"I can see that, Bull. But why? What's he up to?"

"He's supposed to be some kind of cowboy, ain't he? Cowboys ride horses."

"Not in the middle of a blizzard."

Bull just spread his hands in a helpless gesture.

Colin shook his head. "I don't like it. Why didn't he leave with the others?"

They had been watching the feed since leaving Chicago, had seen the arrival of the target and his family, and then a little bit later, a big pickup arrived with another family. Not long thereafter, everyone except the target had climbed into the pickup and left, while Redd—or at least someone carrying Redd's phone—had gone to the barn and fetched a horse.

"Could he have been tipped off?" wondered Colin.

"If he saw what happened in Oklahoma on the news, he might have figured it out on his own."

Colin allowed himself a humorless chuckle. Cormac would not have left anything to chance on his end, but had he even considered the possibility that his actions might spook the target before phase two could be executed?

It was just like his big brother to do something outrageous without considering the potential for blowback.

Cormac Kilmeade wasn't really Colin's big brother. They were identical twins with roughly the same physique. Cormac was the firstborn but only by a few minutes, and unlike many elder twins, he never brought it up in casual conversation. But of the two, Cormac had the outsized personality—the confidence and audacity that buoyed him to the top of whatever endeavor he set his sights on, whether it be their high school varsity football team or leadership of a DEVGRU squadron. Wherever his ambition took him, he always made sure that there was a place for his brother.

Little did he suspect that instead of feeling like he was at Cormac's side, Colin felt more like he was standing in his big brother's shadow.

"If so, then he might be making a run for it," said Colin.

"Probably thinks he can hide out in the wilderness. Like he's Jeremiah Johnson."

"Who?"

"You don't know Jeremiah Johnson?" Bull snorted. "Kids today have no respect for the classics."

Colin waved a dismissive hand. "I don't care who he thinks he is. He can't hide from us."

He stared at the screen. Although Redd and his horse were clearly visible as an amorphous black shape in the center of the screen, the swirling snow made it look like static noise. "Still," he went on, "maybe we should see about getting some snowmobiles."

FOURTEEN

When they reached the highway, Mikey tilted the mirror to give him a view of the rear cab, where Emily sat with both kids in their car seats. "Decision time," he announced. "Where should we go? I was thinking somewhere public. Maybe the mall."

"You want to drive all the way to Bozeman in this?" said Liz, gesturing to the steady fall of snow just beyond the windshield.

"Good point."

"Go into town," said Emily. "To the courthouse. We need to let Sheriff Blackwood know what's going on."

Mikey turned to look over his shoulder at her. "Matt said—"

"I know what he said, Mikey. He's wrong. The sheriff needs to know."

"Emily, I think Matt knows what he's talking about."

She shook her head. "No. He's just doing what he always does whenever there's a problem. Shutting us out. Insisting on doing it all by himself. He thinks he's doing it to protect us, but . . ." She sighed. "We're supposed to be there for each other. You know how much I love that man, but it's the one thing about him that just annoys me to no end."

"Just the one thing?" Mikey asked, unable to suppress a grin.

Emily rolled her eyes to avoid laughing out loud. "Okay, one of the things."

Mikey laughed but then quickly sobered. "Well, you're not wrong. I don't think Matt ever learned how to ask for help." He paused a beat. "You really think Blackwood can do something to help him out?"

It was a valid question. She had come to believe that Stuart Blackwood was, fundamentally, a good man, but as the senior law enforcement official in a rural Montana county, there was a lot of daylight between what he might want to do and what he was actually capable of doing.

"I don't know," she admitted. "But if there's even a chance that he can, then we have to tell him what's going on." She shook her head. "I don't know what else to do, but I have to do something."

"I hear you." Mikey turned to face forward and pulled the Ram out onto the highway, steering left toward Wellington. The pavement was covered in snow that was still too fresh to be packed down into a drivable surface. Emily could feel the truck's tires slipping. Mikey geared down and shifted into low-range four-wheel drive, which eliminated that problem, but at a cost. In low range, top speed was about twenty miles an hour.

"Well, this could take a while," said Mikey. "I was hoping they'd have the plows out already."

"I'd rather you take it slow," said Liz, sounding just a little apprehensive. "Especially with the kids in the truck."

Mikey nodded, leaning forward in his seat as if by so doing, he might extend the limited visibility. Liz turned on the radio, running through all the stations in broadcast range in hopes of getting an updated weather report, but after a minute of fruitless searching, Mikey asked her to turn it off so that he could concentrate on the drive. After that, they drove in silence for several miles—the only sound the otherworldly hum of tires moving through snow.

Driving into falling snow was always a surreal experience. The individual snowflakes seemed to materialize out of the indistinct white fog, immediately curving toward the windshield like little guided missiles, only to be swept away by the wipers. The effect was hypnotic, made all the more so by the persistent quiet.

Alone with her thoughts, Emily could not help but worry about her husband.

FIFTEEN

If the mountain had a name, Redd had never learned it. J. B. had only ever called it "the hill," as in, "I'm heading up the hill and look for strays." At less than six thousand feet above sea level—only about a fifteen-hundred-foot elevation change from the ranch—it was a minor peak in a minor and, as far as Redd knew, unnamed range. In a state with dozens of mountain ranges and hundreds of significant peaks, this pine-topped summit certainly seemed more like a hill than a mountain, especially since it was possible to drive almost all the way up.

Or at least, it had been.

Redd had not made that drive in almost two years—there hadn't been a compelling reason to—and the last time he'd ridden partway up, looking for strays, he'd discovered that the old rutted two-track was slowly being reclaimed by nature. Now with the heavy accumulation of snow, it was almost impossible to tell where the road had been.

It was slow going, partly because visibility was next to zero, and partly because he knew the fresh snow might conceal any number of tripping hazards that could seriously injure Remington. A broken leg wasn't always a death sentence for a horse, but under these conditions, it would be. And possibly for Redd as well.

But it was the reduced visibility that posed the greatest challenge. And the greatest risk. Redd had heard stories of how people caught in blizzards could get lost and ultimately die trying to get from their house to a barn. Now he was experiencing it firsthand.

The contour of the terrain and the narrow corridor between the trees helped him stay on what he thought was the old road. Whenever he spied pine boughs through the veil of falling snow, he would course correct in what he thought was the right direction. All he really knew for certain was that he was climbing.

Oddly, the cold didn't bother him. Between his warm attire and Remington's body heat, he felt only the mildest chill on the exposed skin of his face. Nevertheless, he knew only too well how quickly that could change, especially after the sun went down.

Enveloped in a white haze, he not only lost track of time but also his sense of urgency. His thoughts drifted with the snow, and he had to struggle to remember why he was riding and what was at stake.

Another hit team . . . A dozen shooters . . .

Coming for you.

He pushed up the sleeve of his jacket, checked his G-Shock, and was astonished to see that he had been riding for almost an hour.

An hour . . . Maybe less.

Had the hit team reached the ranch? Were they already on his trail, closing in?

He had to believe the snow would hamper their pursuit, just as it was slowing his escape, and yet he knew it would be a deadly mistake to underestimate their capabilities. He fervently hoped they would underestimate his.

Another uneventful hour passed. The grade grew steeper, and from time to time he thought he remembered certain sections of the ascent. Even draped in snow, some of the trees still looked familiar, especially as he neared the cabin.

Like something from a fairy tale, it seemed to materialize out of the snow. A dark squarish shape surrounded by white, the old hunting lodge was exactly as Redd had left it but nothing like he remembered.

Perched on the mountain's flank, near a pass that led down into National Forest land, the rugged little log building had served many generations of Thompson family sportsmen as a base camp from which to hunt all manner of wild game in the wilderness beyond. Redd and J. B. had used it thus many times, but Redd's fondest memories were of sneaking away to it with Emily during the years of their high school romance.

His last visit to the cabin had been memorable for all the wrong reasons.

Nearly two years ago he had retreated to the cabin accompanied by a wounded Gavin Kline and Hannah Gage, Anton's psychotic daughter. To save Kline's life, he had reached out to the only person he knew with the requisite medical training—his estranged former sweetheart, Emily Lawrence. Emily had hurried to the cabin and begun treating Kline's injuries, only to be caught up in the siege when a team of killers sent by Anton Gage arrived.

Redd had done the only thing he knew how to do—he had gone on the offensive. In the ensuing firefight, one of the shooters had lobbed a grenade into the cabin where Kline and Emily huddled, and for a moment or two, Redd had feared the worst. Fortunately, Emily had been foresighted enough to seek refuge in the cabin's root cellar, under the floor. Both doctor and patient had survived the blast more or less unhurt.

Redd had not been up to the cabin since that night. He had every intention of fixing it up, repairing the blast damage and making it habitable again, but had not been able to make time for it. Between spending time with Emily and Junior, running the ranch, and working with Kline's FBI fly team to hunt down Anton Gage, he'd just been too busy to think about it.

He regretted that now. The cabin would have been a nice refuge from the storm, if only for a little while. But now it was little more than a husk, shot full of holes. The grenade had shredded the beds, shattered the old wooden chairs, and knocked the wood-burning stove off its hearth.

Worse, as he discovered after stomping a path to the entrance, not only had the door been blown off its hinges, but several large gaps had been opened in the roof, allowing snow to drift in. Now the interior of the cabin did not look altogether different than the exterior.

Yet, even if it had been completely restored, the cabin wouldn't have been much good to him. Not with at least a dozen killers coming after him. That was a lesson he'd learned the hard way almost two years ago. The cabin was no place to hide and no place to mount a defense against an overwhelming enemy.

But even if it couldn't give him brief respite from the winter weather, Redd knew of a couple ways it might still prove useful.

SIXTEEN

Although the roads had not yet been plowed, the drive became easier as Mikey's pickup neared town. Limited visibility was still a problem, but there had been enough vehicles coming and going from Wellington to pack the snow down into a surface the Ram's big tires could hold on to. Emily wasn't at all surprised to see that the parking lot at Spady's Bar and Grill was three-quarters full.

It took a lot more than a blizzard to keep Montanans at home, especially at happy hour.

Nevertheless, as they made the turn onto Broadway and headed through town toward the courthouse, they saw that most of the local businesses were closed. Although the main thoroughfare was covered in packed snow, the sidewalks and most of the parking spots along the street were buried under waist-high drifts.

The old brick courthouse, on the other hand, was a hive of activity, with county vehicles and sheriff's department patrol cars coming and going from the gated county lot. Emergency flashers threw out a dazzling light show of red, blue, and orange, glittering magically in the falling snow. But the street parking situation was much the same as downtown. Mikey circled the block twice in a futile search for a place to park.

"Just stop here," Emily said, as Mikey drove past the entrance to the sheriff's department offices for the second time.

"In the middle of the road?" asked a disbelieving Mikey.

"Yes." Exasperation bled through into her reply. "If you want to keep driving around in circles, knock yourself out, but I need to get in there."

Grumbling, Mikey eased the brake down and flipped on the hazard lights. Even before the pickup came to a full stop, Emily threw open her door and stepped out onto the packed snow. After more than an hour in the warm environment of the truck, the cold went right to her bones. Hugging her arms around her upper body, she made her way toward the sheriff's entrance to the courthouse building, keeping her weight slightly forward so that her feet wouldn't slip out from under her.

She had to bulldoze her way through the drift covering the sidewalk, but once she was through it, the going was easier. Nevertheless, when she finally stepped through the glass doors and into the lobby, her legs from the knees down were caked in clinging snow. She stomped her feet several times but only managed to shake some of it off. Frustrated, she pushed through into the office and approached the front desk where the sheriff's receptionist, Maggie Albright, guarded entry into the kingdom as fiercely as any mythical dragon. A plump woman with hair dyed bright scarlet, Maggie regarded Emily through her designer knock-off glasses, then raised a finger, signaling her to wait just a moment.

"No, honey, you're not listening," said Maggie, her eyes rolling up toward the ceiling. "Sheriff Blackwood can't just hook a plow blade up to a patrol car. It doesn't work that way."

Emily stared back at her, confused until she saw that Maggie was wearing a low-profile headset. She wasn't speaking to Emily, but rather to someone on the other end of a phone call. While Maggie fielded what was evidently a complaint from a concerned citizen, Emily looked past her to the television set on the wall, which was tuned to a twenty-four-hour news station. The volume was turned down, but the graphic crawl at the bottom of the screen, not to mention the familiar image of a large aircraft burning on the runway, was easy enough to follow without supplemental audio.

The blizzard might have been big news locally, but the plane crash in Oklahoma City was the top national story.

"No, honey," Maggie went on. "We've got a call out to Dale, but he's already out on a job . . . Well, that's his business, isn't it? We'll all just have to wait until he's done . . . No, the sheriff can't arrest him for that, but I'll be sure to let him know you called . . . No, I . . . No . . . Okay, bye-bye, now."

Maggie stabbed a finger down on her phone console, blew out a sigh of irritation, then brought her attention back to Emily. "Dr. Redd, what can I do for you?"

Emily had long ago stopped trying to explain to the good folks of Stillwater County that she wasn't a doctor but a nurse practitioner. She supposed as far as they were concerned, it was a meaningless distinction.

"I need to speak to the sheriff. It's urgent."

"Oh, honey, everyone urgently needs to speak to the sheriff. Maybe you hadn't noticed, but we're having some weather—"

Before she even knew what she was doing, Emily brought her hands down on the desk. She did not slam her fists down, but the loud smack of her open palms landing on the desktop had the same effect. Maggie let out a yelp, recoiling as if the slap had been directed at her.

Emily did not know Maggie all that well, didn't know if condescension was her default setting or merely the result of cumulative frustration at having to field an unusually high volume of complaints. Emily suspected the latter and ordinarily would have cut the woman some slack.

But not today.

"Maggie! Sheriff Blackwood. *Now*."

The other woman gaped at her for a moment. Then she reached out one trembling hand and tapped her console. "Sheriff, Dr. Redd is here to see you," she said in a small voice. A moment passed, and then Maggie said, "He'll be out in a moment."

Emily took a deep breath, realizing only then that her heart was racing. She made a mental note to apologize to Maggie . . . but later. After the crisis passed.

The moment might have stretched out into an uncomfortably long silence if not for the ringing of the telephone, which drew Maggie back to her duties. Just from listening to one side of the conversation, Emily surmised that the caller wanted to know why the county roads had not been plowed. Maggie's answer, and the weary tone in which she delivered it, suggested that this was not the first time someone had inquired about the issue. Evidently, the county did not own snowplow trucks but contracted out the service to someone named Dale who was otherwise engaged with a job somewhere else. More calls came in before she could give a satisfactory answer to the first caller, and Maggie soon began a complex juggling act of placing calls on hold and parceling out information. Emily, whose patience had already been stretched thin with the knowledge that her husband was in mortal danger without any backup, had to fight the urge to grab the phone handset and shout at the callers, telling them to just deal with it. Her rising ire quickly cooled when Sheriff Blackwood finally appeared in the doorway behind Maggie.

Wet snow clung to the shoulders of his heavy coat and the brim of his Stetson, but it was his frown that immediately commanded Emily's attention.

Stuart Blackwood was a tall, rangy man with steel-gray hair and a drooping mustache that made him look much older than his fifty-two years. Emily knew he had spent many of those years battling the demons of post-traumatic stress disorder—resulting from the horrors he'd been party to on the Saddam Line during Desert Storm—and alcoholism—his way of trying to self-medicate the former. After decades spent working as a policeman in Chicago, with his marriage in ruins and his career and pension at risk because of drinking and the taint of suspected corruption, Blackwood had been at rock bottom. Then he had been approached by a group of Wellington businessmen—real Chamber of Commerce types—who had enticed him into running for sheriff of Stillwater County. They had not counted his personal and professional flaws as a liability, but rather as an advantage. They saw him as a useful tool, someone who would selectively enforce law and order to advance their goals of transforming the county into a high-priced wilderness playground and resort town for the rich and famous.

Then something interesting had happened. Nearly two years earlier, Blackwood had taken a bullet in a shoot-out with a team of hired guns sent to kill Matthew Redd. Instead of relapsing into depression and drinking, Blackwood had emerged from the incident with a new lease on life, resolved to perform his sworn duties with the utmost professionalism. He'd even hired Matty as a weapons and tactics trainer for his deputies. Redd and Emily counted him as a friend, which was why she found his frown just a little concerning.

"Mrs. Redd," he rumbled. "Why don't you step into my office?"

His manner was also alarming. Why had he assumed that she would want to speak in private?

Does he already know? Did Matty call him?

And he never called her "Mrs. Redd."

She followed him through the door and into his private office, a utilitarian and unwelcoming little space. There was a flat-screen television mounted to the wall, and like the one in the lobby, it was tuned to the news channel and displaying the same footage of the plane crash. Blackwood closed the door behind her and then moved to the other side of his desk but did not sit down. Instead, he leaned over his desktop, hands flat, arms outstretched and supporting his bulk so that he could look her in the eye. "Can I ask what this is about?"

So he doesn't know. But something's still off here. She took a breath. "Matty got a call from his father . . . his biological father, Gavin Kline . . . the FBI director."

Blackwood knew who Kline was, and knew of his relationship to Redd, but Emily hoped that mentioning Kline's affiliation would impress upon the sheriff the seriousness of what she was about to tell him.

"Gavin warned him that there's a team of killers on their way here. Coming after him." She flicked her gaze toward the television. "It has something to do with the plane that went down in Oklahoma City."

Blackwood's frown deepened. He seemed to sag a little and then leaned away from the desk, collapsing into his chair.

"Did you hear what I just said?" pressed Emily. "A team of killers. Coming here. Coming after Matty."

He stared back at her, his expression twisting as if experiencing pain. "How certain are you of that?"

"How certain—?" Emily heard her voice rising with a flash of anger. She took a breath to regain her composure. "Pretty certain. Matthew is heading up into the mountains, trying to draw them off. But he's all alone out there. And these men are professionals. They're coming here. For all I know, they might already be here and looking for him. He needs help, even if he's too stubborn to admit it."

Blackwood let out a weary sigh. "Emily, I'm not quite sure how to . . ." Another sigh. "Is there a chance that you and Matthew . . . or maybe Kline . . . are reading this all wrong?"

Emily was taken aback. "Reading it wrong?"

"A couple hours ago, I got a call from Martin Shores . . . He's the SAC for Homeland Security Investigations up in Helena. He was calling to let me know that HSI agents would be operating in the area. It's customary for federal agencies to inform local LEOs when they're working in their jurisdiction. Professional courtesy. But this was something else. Martin told me why they were here, what they were doing. And he warned me to stay out of it. He said that any interference might be construed as criminal obstruction."

Emily shook her head. "I'm not following, Sheriff. What does Homeland Security have to do with this? Are you telling me they already know about the hit team?"

Blackwood pursed his lips together for a moment, as if summoning the courage to face Emily's wrath. "I don't know anything about a hit team. All I know is what Martin told me—that agents from Homeland Security Investigations were on their way to Wellington to take Matthew in for questioning, and that I wasn't to interfere."

"Take him in?" Emily's voice rose another octave. "They're coming to arrest Matty? That's ludicrous. Why?"

"They didn't say. But Martin didn't say they were arresting him. They just want to ask him some questions."

"About what?" Even as she asked, Emily felt a creep of dread run up her spine. Was it something to do with those bikers?

When the outlaw biker gang had begun their campaign of harassment, Blackwood had been unable to use the power of his office to protect Emily and Junior, so Redd had done what he always did—he'd confronted the problem head-on, declaring all-out war against the bikers, killing several of them. The killings were justifiable as self-defense—at least, those that had occurred on the ranch property when they had set the house ablaze. When he'd gone out to confront them in their hideout, he'd strayed into legally uncertain territory, but nobody in local or state law enforcement saw a problem with what he had done. And by the end of it, Kline had shown up, sanctioning Redd's actions as part of the FBI's ongoing criminal investigation of the bikers, immunizing him from criminal or civil consequences.

Had someone in Washington changed their mind about that? Was that what Kline had really been trying to tell her husband? Had Matty misunderstood the warning?

But a glance at the plane burning on the runway in Oklahoma City reminded her that, whatever else was going on, the threat was real.

She faced Kline again. "You didn't think that was something we needed to know about?"

Blackwood shook his head. "My hands were tied. If I called to warn Matthew that they were coming, they'd have me up on federal charges."

"That's crap and you know it. Matty's your friend. And if they wanted to ask him questions, all they needed to do was call us up and ask. Matty wouldn't run from them."

Blackwood spread his hands. "I'm sorry, Emily. They didn't give me a choice."

"Is there a way to contact them? The Homeland agents? Let them know about the hit team?"

Blackwood considered this for a moment. "I can call Shores and pass it along . . . but are you sure this wasn't some kind of miscommunication?"

Emily didn't think it was, but the timing was suspicious. For the Homeland Security agents to show up at almost exactly the same time as the hit team was just too coincidental to be a coincidence.

There was an easy way to find out though. "Can I use your phone?"

"Emily, you can't contact Matthew about this."

"I'm not going to," she snapped, feeling her ire rise again. "I don't think he even has his phone with him. I want to call Gavin. Maybe he can clear this up."

Blackwood frowned, as if trying to think of a pretext to deny the request, but then relented, pushing the phone console toward her. She picked up the handset and punched in Kline's number, grateful that Matty had pressed her to memorize important phone numbers as a matter of personal security.

The outgoing call tone rang twice, and then a generic voicemail introduction began playing. Emily thought about hanging up and trying again, but if Kline was screening his calls, he might not pick up on an unfamiliar number. Instead, she waited for the tone and then left her message.

"It's me." For reasons she couldn't quite explain, she decided not to use names or supply any details. "I need to talk to you as soon as possible. Call me back at this number."

With any luck, he would check the voicemail as soon as the notification popped up and then return the call promptly. With a little more luck, he would tell her that, yes, it was all a misunderstanding, and no, there wasn't a hit team inbound, and it would all be cleared up with a phone call, and then they could get back to their lives.

But as she ended the call, from the corner of her eye, she saw the bottom screen crawl on the television displaying a new message in bold letters:

SOURCES SAY OKLAHOMA CITY PLANE CRASH "AN ACT OF TERRORISM"

And below that:

FBI assistant director killed in explosion

A gasp escaped her lips. She staggered backward as if struck physically by this revelation. Blackwood was on his feet in an instant, circling around the desk to steady her.

She barely felt his hands guiding her into one of the visitors' chairs.

FBI assistant director killed . . .

Gavin.

There were probably dozens of assistant directors in the Bureau, but somehow she knew he was the one who had died.

Did you know, Matty? Was that why you didn't want to ask him for help?

Emily was not as close to Gavin Kline—her father-in-law and the grandfather of her son, whether or not Matthew wanted to admit it—as she would have liked to be, but she had always hoped that one day he would truly be part of their family.

Now it seemed that day would never come.

Yet that was not the real reason why the news had left her feeling so despondent, so hopeless.

If Kline was dead, then it was unlikely that any help was coming.

Matty was on his own.

"No," she whispered, shaking her head, refusing to give in to despair. "No, he's not."

You're not alone, Matty.

She was on her feet before she knew it, out the door and heading for the exit. Blackwood's voice chased after her. "Emily! Where are you going?"

Emily didn't answer. She couldn't answer because she didn't really know where she was going or what she was going to do when she got there. She only knew that her husband needed her, and somehow she was going to be there for him.

SEVENTEEN

OKLAHOMA CITY

Despite the rumors sweeping across the internet, Gavin Kline wasn't dead, though for a while after he regained consciousness, he might have argued that death was preferable to the way he felt.

He remembered Treadway and Decker shouting about the fire truck left behind by the hostile assault team, remembered finally grasping the reason for Decker's concern. Remembered running. After that . . .

After that, his next memory was of a pair of blurry shapes hovering above him and a voice, muffled as if someone was shouting through a pillow, asking, "Boss, can you hear me?"

He tried to reply, aware that what had come out of his mouth was an incoherent mumble, and then attempted to sit up.

Big mistake.

Pain seized control of his body, transforming him into a blob of jelly. There was a taste of blood in his mouth and a smell like exploded fireworks and dust in his nostrils. His ears still rang, and although his visual acuity seemed to be returning, he realized that what he had first taken to be two shapes looking down at him was actually just one—one disheveled Stephanie Treadway, bifurcated into two unaligned images because his eyes were no longer working together to produce binocular vision.

Concussion, he thought, and then, *I hope that's the worst of it.*

It didn't feel like the worst of it. The expression *"I feel like I just got run over by a freight train"* did not seem at all hyperbolic. If anything, it was an understatement.

A bomb. A bomb on the fire truck. If Aaron hadn't warned us . . .

If Aaron Decker hadn't recognized the threat, he wouldn't be feeling the way he felt right now.

"Uhhhnn," he managed to say.

"Don't try to move," said Treadway. "Help is coming."

Her voice seemed more distinct than before, which he took to be a sign that his cognitive abilities were returning.

"H-h-h-how m-m-m . . . ?" He gave up trying to phrase the question. Even the mere act of trying to talk set his synapses on fire.

"There was a bomb on the fire truck," she said, answering a question he hadn't asked. "A big one."

"T-t-t-team . . . ?"

"It's bad," she said. Only now did he hear the emotion in her voice. "Aaron is okay. He's helping to recover the . . ." She choked up. "It's bad, boss."

Somehow that felt even worse than the pain. The team . . . his team . . . He knew for certain that some of them had been killed in the initial firefight. He vividly recalled the attackers moving through the battlefield executing the wounded. The appearance of Anton Gage—the primary target—had caused the assault team to break off, so it was possible that some of the fallen had survived until . . .

Until the truck bomb detonated and blew everything in a fifty-meter radius to kingdom come.

All dead, he thought. *I should have seen this coming. It's my fault.*

It wasn't, of course, but in the moment he couldn't bring himself to believe otherwise. Survivor's guilt was a terrible demon to face.

Almost two years earlier, in a desperate bid to save Matthew Redd . . . to save his own son . . . Kline had contrived a way to keep Redd on ice, separating him from his Marine Raiders team in the hours before they were to deploy on a compromised mission. The team had been wiped out and Redd had blamed himself for not having been there with them. When Redd had subsequently learned of Kline's meddling, it had been like throwing a frag grenade into the already fragile dynamic of their relationship. At the time Kline had thought he understood why Redd felt so angry about having been kept out of the mission, even though his presence would not have changed the outcome one iota . . . except that he, too, would have been among the dead. Now he realized that he really hadn't understood what Redd was going through at all.

He drifted in and out of consciousness for a while. After an interval that might have been only minutes, he was roused by a paramedic who asked him a few questions, assessing him for symptoms of concussion, which he did not doubt that he had sustained. When he was gently transferred to a litter, a surge of pain brought him fully awake and then overwhelmed him, letting him fall back into oblivion.

Later—how much later, he could not say—he was roused again by a bright light shining into his right eye. He flinched reflexively, realizing only then that someone was holding his eyelid up. The lid was released, allowing him to blink, but then the procedure was repeated on the left eye.

"Pupils are responsive," murmured a male voice.

Kline was pleased to discover that his hearing seemed to have mostly returned, and after blinking his eyes a few times, he found that his vision was also normal again. He saw that he was no longer outside on the ground, but in a bed—a hospital bed. Even better, the debilitating pain he had experienced before was now merely a dull throb. Aside from that and a weird metallic taste in his mouth, he actually felt pretty good. His body felt almost like he was floating.

"Director Kline, can you hear me?"

Kline rolled his eyes in their sockets until they settled on the face of a bearded man wearing blue scrubs. "Mmm-hmm. Loud and clear," he mumbled.

"You got your bell rung pretty good," the man, presumably a doctor, went on. "You've got some cracked ribs, and I want to monitor you for TBI, but I think you're pretty lucky, all things considered."

Lucky. The word was quite pleasing to his ear.

I am lucky, he thought. *By all rights, that bomb should have killed me.*

With that thought, the euphoria he had been feeling vanished with the abruptness of a light switch being thrown. He tried to say something, but between his brain and his mouth, the words got jumbled into an incoherent mess. One word, however, emerged from the tangle. A name. "Treadway."

"I'm here, boss."

He rolled his head to the side and saw her, standing a few steps away on the opposite side of the bed.

Treadway looked to the doctor. "Can I talk to him? Privately, I mean?"

"We're weaning him off the pain meds, so he may be a little disoriented for a while. But sure. I'll give you the room."

Treadway waited until they were alone to approach the bedside. "Well, the good news is, you're going to live."

Kline didn't think that was such good news.

"Fleetwood, Tanaka, and Baylor are alive," continued Treadway. "For now, at least. Docs say they're in critical condition. I'm not really sure what that means, but . . ." She trailed off.

Kline knew what it meant—three of his agents were barely clinging to life. He could also do the math.

Three alive meant five dead.

Five husbands and fathers who wouldn't be going home to their families.

After a pause, Treadway spoke again. "An HSI critical response team moved on the firehouse that the terrorists were using as a staging area."

"Terrorists?" Kline mumbled. Even in his fuzzy-headed state, he knew that sounded wrong.

"Yeah. Preliminary reports are saying that this was the work of radical anti-government extremists. From what I'm hearing, you were the primary target, not Gage."

Kline couldn't believe his ears. If Treadway had told him that the assault force had ridden away on unicorns, he would have had an easier time accepting it. "No." He tried to sit up. "No, that's not right."

"Take it easy, boss. You're still pretty banged up."

Unable to convince his muscles to comply with his intentions, Kline sagged back into his bed. His mind felt sharper, however.

"Those weren't terrorists." He spoke slowly, letting the words fully form before trying to utter them. He wanted to say more, to explain that the gear and tactics employed by the assault team were far too sophisticated to be in the repertoire of a homegrown terror network, but that was more than he could manage. "And they weren't after me. If Homeland thinks so, they're wrong."

Treadway spread her hands. "All I know is what I've heard. Which isn't much."

Kline's thoughts were racing ahead of his ability to express them. It was plainly obvious to him that the evidence implicating homegrown terrorists had been planted in an effort to divert attention away from the real culprits. He was a little surprised at the gullibility of the Homeland Security investigators.

"Smoke screen," he managed to say. "Let me talk to the SAC."

"I'll try to get someone over here, but they aren't exactly being forthcoming. They're claiming jurisdiction on the investigation because it happened at an airport. I don't get the impression that they're interested in sharing."

Kline shook his head . . . or tried to. Grimacing through a throb of pain, he said, "Federal agents died. A federal witness . . . That makes it our jurisdiction."

"Maybe you'll have better luck convincing them of that than I did."

I will, thought Kline. *Just as soon as I can string more than a few words together.*

He began strategizing, rehearsing what arguments he would use, what assets were at his disposal, and what favors he could call in, to make sure the threads of evidence that must, he felt sure, lead back to the Twelve would not get tangled up in the red tape of bureaucratic ineptitude. Yet deep down he knew that it was already too late. There would be no evidence. The Twelve would not have left anything to chance. They had served up a plausible explanation for the heinous attack, along with a perfect patsy, and that would likely be the end of the matter, no matter how loudly Kline protested.

"Where's Decker?"

"He's around here somewhere. Want me to get him?"

"No. Just tell him I said . . ." Kline trailed off, realizing that with his next words, he would be stepping off a cliff.

Up to this point, it had been a purely theoretical exercise. If the Twelve could not be brought to justice through the legal system . . . if they were indeed above the law . . . then didn't he have a moral imperative to go outside the law in order to bring them down?

It was the kind of work that Aaron Decker had specialized in, once upon a time. If anyone could wipe them off the board—

No, say what you mean. Kill them. Exterminate them.

—it was Aaron Decker. It wasn't just that he was an expert tracker and—when circumstances demanded it—a stone-cold killer. What made Decker special was that he left no footprints whatsoever. His targets died without anyone ever suspecting that they had been marked for death. If Kline went after the Twelve, it would merely appear that the world's wealthiest men had all simultaneously experienced a run of fatally bad luck. No one would ever know that their deaths had been ordered by Gavin Kline.

He had told himself that it was just a contingency, and somehow that had made it easier to contemplate ordering the murder of eleven human beings.

It wasn't theoretical anymore. The Twelve had just demonstrated their contempt for the rule of law by killing Gage and nearly wiping out the entire fly team.

And yet, if he set Decker loose, wasn't he showing the same contempt for the rule of law?

If that's what it takes, Kline thought, *I'll carry that burden.*

He took a breath. "Tell him . . . green light. He'll understand."

Treadway bit her lip, and Kline realized that she understood too. But then she nodded. "I'll tell him."

Kline let out his breath with a sigh. Now that the order was given, he actually felt better, as if making the decision had cut through the fog of moral uncertainty. The Twelve deserved to die. There was no ambiguity concerning that judgment. They were responsible for many deaths and had plotted to kill countless millions more. They had sent men to kill his agents, to kill him, and were, even now, hunting Matthew . . .

Matthew!

How could I have forgotten about Matthew?

The killers were on their way. Maybe they were already there. He'd warned Redd, but had the warning come in time?

"Steph, wait!"

Treadway paused at the door and looked back.

"Montana. You have to go to Montana. You have to help Matt."

If it's not already too late. But he couldn't bear to say it.

Kline could see the questions in her eyes, but to her credit, she left them unsaid. She knew what he wanted her to do, knew that he was asking her to do the impossible. And she knew that, somehow, she would do it.

She gave a grim nod. "On it, boss."

EIGHTEEN

MONTANA

"We've got him," said Colin Kilmeade, stabbing one white-gloved finger down on the screen of a tablet computer on which an overhead satellite photograph was displayed.

The image was from eight months ago and showed the property identified as Thompson Ranch and the surrounding area as it would have looked without the blanket of heavy snowfall. Roads and trails, which were now impossible to distinguish in the real world, were revealed, as well as structures that were now hidden from aerial view under several inches of accumulation. Curiously, the photo map showed a large house that no longer seemed to exist, while omitting the small travel trailer where Colin now sat with Bull Dooley, planning the next phase of the operation.

From continuously monitoring both the drone feed and the tracker on Redd's phone, Colin had surmised that they would not find Redd or anyone else inside the ranch buildings, but the fourteen men of Saber and Javelin Teams had nevertheless made a rapid, dynamic insertion, charging in on their rented snowmobiles—seven Ski-Doo Expedition Sport 600s, all equipped with a rear seat—as if they were storming a heavily fortified enemy base. As expected, they found the trailer completely abandoned and nothing but cows in the barn, which accounted for the unusually strong heat signature that appeared as a large black square on the thermal display from the drone.

With the full fury of the snowstorm now upon them, the drone's capabilities were greatly reduced, which had led the UAV's operator to recommend recalling it to base. Colin had decided to keep it on station a little while longer, just in case.

The signal from Redd's phone, however, continued to come through loud and clear and presently showed him stationary at a seemingly random position several miles to the east. When the phone finder app was superimposed onto the satellite image, the reason for Redd's lack of movement became apparent. The little red dot indicating Redd's location—the exact spot where Colin was pointing—marked a small square structure, situated in a clearing just off an old Jeep road that wended up and over a mountain pass.

"What's he doing up there?" wondered Dooley.

"Who knows," replied Colin. "Like you said, cowboy stuff. Maybe he's camping or something."

Dooley gave an ambiguous grunt of acknowledgment.

"The important thing," Colin continued, "is that he's probably settling in. We can move in and be on him before he realizes what's going on."

"Those snow machines aren't exactly stealth equipped," said Dooley, folding his arms across his chest. "He'll hear us coming from a mile away."

"More like a few hundred yards. Maybe not even then. The snow will act as a natural sound dampener."

"You're kidding."

Colin shook his head. "I read it in a science magazine. Fresh snow absorbs sound waves, just like foam insulation."

Dooley continued to regard him with a skeptical eye. "Even a few hundred yards will take away the element of surprise. He could be armed."

"It's a chance we'll have to take. Unless you want to spend all night humping up to that cabin in the snow." He clapped the other man on the shoulder. "Come on, Bull. On the snowmobiles, we can be up there in fifteen . . . twenty minutes, tops." He made a gun with his fingers and wiggled his thumb. "Bang, bang. Mission accomplished. Twenty more minutes to get back to the highway. We're on our way back to the plane inside of an hour."

✖ ✖ ✖

Colin's schedule proved to be overly optimistic. While the Ski-Doos were capable of reaching speeds well in excess of eighty miles per hour, the conditions, not to mention the relative inexperience of the riders and the fact that each machine was bearing two full-grown adults, each carrying an additional sixty pounds of gear, gave him an expected rate of progress closer to thirty miles per hour. Once they started climbing up into the mountains, that pace was halved. Colin had plotted their route into a GPS device, using waypoints derived from the satellite map of the old road, so they didn't have to worry about wandering off the trail, getting lost, or worse, running into a tree. Nevertheless, the blizzard reduced visibility almost to nothing, meaning the riders could not see one another until they were practically right on top of each other, forcing them to motor along at a pace barely faster than a walk. To Colin, it felt like they were crawling, though had they actually been moving on foot, they would have been lucky to manage more than one mile in an hour.

His assertion regarding the sound-dampening qualities of snow, however, proved remarkably accurate. The snowfield seemed to absorb the sound like a sponge. Even from astride a snowmobile, the quiet was almost unnatural. And as the plot on the map brought them ever closer to the old log cabin, with no movement whatsoever of the dot marking the location of Matthew Redd's phone, Colin's optimism returned. Either Redd didn't hear them coming or he disregarded the muffled engine noise as inconsequential.

When they were just five hundred yards from the coordinates of the cabin, Colin called a halt and brought everyone together in a huddle for one final brief before execution. His original plan—a variation on their standard operating procedure of having Saber Team move to contact, with the expert marksmen of Javelin providing fire support from a distance—would not work because of the reduced visibility, so instead, they would all advance toward the target on foot. Javelin would establish a perimeter on three sides, and then Saber would move in and clear the cabin. In the unlikely event Redd managed to survive their dynamic entry and slip out the back door—if there even was one—he would find himself caught in Javelin's overlapping fields of fire.

"Any questions?" asked Colin when all the assignments were given. There were none. "Then let's do this."

They moved out in a close Ranger file—close because attired as they were in winter overwhite camouflage shells, they had to maintain constant visual contact with the next man in line to avoid getting lost—until the cabin finally appeared before them. Colin gave the hand signal to halt and then passed back the signal that would send Javelin on ahead to establish their overwatch positions. Even though the nearest positions were just twenty yards away, Colin quickly lost sight of the men. Their SOP called for using only hand and arm signals this close to the objective, but without being able to see his men, that method of communication wouldn't be effective, so Colin broke protocol.

Speaking in a whisper, he sent a message out over their comm network. "Javelin elements, be advised. Visual signals aren't going to work. When you get in position, break squelch with your roster number. Over."

After a few more minutes, he heard the faint static scratch of someone keying their mic three times. Javelin Three was set. Not long thereafter, Javelin Two checked in, with the rest following suit. It was a tedious, time-consuming process, and by the time Javelin Team was finally in position, Colin was so amped up that he felt like just rushing the cabin by himself.

He keyed his mic again. "Javelin, stand by. Saber is moving to target. Will break squelch once when we are set, and once more before we execute. Break radio silence only in the event of unexpected contact. Saber Six, out."

There was a long trough-like depression in the snow, the path Redd had trod up to the cabin entrance, now already mostly covered over. The log building was smaller than Colin thought it would be, and the snow piled up against the exterior walls made it look even more compact. As he got closer, he could smell the distinctive aroma of woodsmoke and then, through the curtain of snowflakes, saw a curl of smoke rising from the cabin's roof.

He imagined Redd sitting inside, huddled close to a woodstove, his boots off, feet held close to the fire, unaware, vulnerable.

This is going to be so easy.

He motioned for the rest of the team to stack up to the left of the doorway, which required them to leave the path and wade into the accumulated snow. Judging by the exterior dimensions, there wouldn't be room inside for the entire assault team to go in, so he went down the line, tapping each man on the shoulder and giving them their final instructions. Only three would go in; the others would remain outside as a reserve element, just in case the unthinkable happened. When the team was set, Colin keyed his mic, signaling Javelin Team that they were set, then returned to the front of the stack and started his mental countdown. Then after breaking squelch a final time, he gave the signal to go kinetic.

There was no knob or lever on the door, just a simple wooden handle and a sliding bolt above it, presently in the open position. At *go*, Saber One, the team's designated breacher, gave the door a gentle push to see if it would open and when it did not yield, proceeded to fire a twelve-gauge TKO breaching round from his Remington 870 shotgun into the latch.

After the prolonged quiet of their approach, the report was thunderous. The compressed zinc slug not only obliterated the exterior latch along with a plate-sized chunk of the door but hit with such force that the entire door toppled backward as if blown off its hinges. Colin imagined Redd panicking as the loud boom filled the tiny enclosure.

As soon as the door was down, Colin bolted forward, sweeping through the open doorway, his primary weapon—a Colt M4—at the high ready, looking for a target . . . and was immediately engulfed in a haze of white smoke.

As unexpected as this was, Colin did not miss a beat. The team routinely rehearsed dynamic entries under every imaginable condition—including entering smoke-filled rooms—and so, while part of his brain was trying to reason out why Redd's cabin was a literal smoke box, his muscle memory kept him moving. He hooked to the left, clearing the doorway for the next man in the stack, all the while looking for someone to shoot. But if Redd was in the cabin, Colin couldn't see him. He couldn't see anything. His eyes were stinging, and he was struggling to hold back a coughing fit after breathing in the choking miasma.

From off to his right, he heard a strangled voice call out, "Clear. There's no one here."

Then someone else added, "I'm outta here."

Colin was loathe to leave the cabin without knowing for certain that Redd wasn't there, but he knew that until they could clear the air a little, a visual inspection would be impossible. "Move out," he gasped, turning and groping along the wall until he found the exit.

Although none of them had realized it from inside the cabin, the simple act of opening the door had begun the process of exchanging hot smoke for cool outside air, and in a matter of a few seconds, the interior of the cabin was revealed in the beam of the tactical flashlight mounted to the Picatinny rail of Colin's M4. Not surprisingly, there was nobody inside. On the far wall, smoke billowed from the broken chimney stem of a potbellied stove, swirling around inside the cabin on its way to the hole in the ceiling where the chimney had once been attached. The floor of the cabin was hidden under a layer of snow, but in the center of the room, sitting atop a small nest of rags, was a mobile phone.

Matthew Redd's mobile phone.

Beside him, Bull Dooley muttered a curse. "He knew we were coming. Knew we were tracking his phone."

Colin shook his head. "How? No, never mind how. *Why?* Why go to the trouble of setting this up? He could have just left the phone back at the trailer. Or turned it off and pulled the battery."

"He wanted us to come here," said Dooley. "Used the phone as bait."

Colin felt a jolt of adrenaline hit his bloodstream. He keyed his mic. "Everyone, stay alert. The cowboy knows we're here."

"I doubt he's hanging around to see if we fell for it," Dooley went on. "He can't see through this snow any better than we can. This was just a diversion. He's probably miles away by now."

"Even so, we've already made the mistake of underestimating him." Colin took out his tablet and layered in the feed from the Predator drone. As before, it showed an indistinct image of the surrounding landscape, with a few scattered heat blooms—animals, no doubt—appearing and then just as quickly disappearing from view. One of them might well be Redd, but which?

He ran the time index back to the moment when both the signal from Redd's phone and a fairly substantial heat signature reached the cabin—nearly ninety minutes before their arrival. Colin then ran the feed forward at four times normal speed. For a long while nothing moved, but gradually, the heat return from the structure began to increase—no doubt the interior warming as Redd built the fire that had turned the cabin into a smokehouse. Finally, after an hour in real time, a small black blob seemed to detach from the cabin, moving into the woods.

"That's him," Colin said, tagging the signature. He slowed the playback to 2X normal and followed the tagged item as it moved away, heading into the surrounding woods.

"Do you smell that?" asked Dooley.

Colin, engrossed in the video feed, shook his head.

"Something's burning." Before Colin could point out the obvious, Dooley amended, "I meant plastic or something. Not woodsmoke."

Even as the other man said it, Colin caught a whiff of the same odor—not the pleasant aroma of a campfire, but the acrid smell of chemical substances burning.

"What the—?" Colin started to say, but Dooley's shout cut him off.

"The snowmobiles!"

Saber Team's second-in-command took off running as fast as conditions would allow, kicking through the snow and following their tracks back to where they had left the vehicles. Colin followed close behind, with a sinking feeling in his gut. He already knew what they would find when they reached the snowmobiles.

The burning plastic smell increased as Colin drew closer, and then, despite the dense screen of falling snow, he saw harsh orange firelight directly ahead.

Four of the snowmobiles were ablaze—searing pillars of fire reaching heavenward. The heat was so intense that it melted the snow out of the air in every direction and had already turned the accumulation underfoot to wet slush. Three of the machines remained untouched, though a second glance revealed that the five-gallon jerricans of fuel each one had carried were now missing.

Dooley shouted impotent curses and tried heaving armfuls of snow at the conflagration but couldn't get close enough to smother the flames. Colin just stared at the burning vehicles, unable to even begin articulating his anger and frustration.

Redd, he thought. Then realization dawned. *He's here.*

Colin began searching the snow around them, trying to catch a glimpse of their target. He had assumed that after the deception with the phone at the cabin, Redd would have tried to put as much distance between himself and his pursuers as possible. It was what any sane person would have done. But Redd had gone on the offensive, risked everything by remaining in the area, waiting for the teams to come to him, waiting for them to give him an opening.

More members of the team were arriving, and one of them—Saber Four—had the presence of mind to grab a fire extinguisher from one of the undamaged snowmobiles. Braving the heat, he moved in close to one of the burning vehicles and discharged the canister, spraying its contents into the flames. Unfortunately the extinguisher, which was designed to put out small electrical or gas fires before they could get out of control, contained a relatively small amount of dry chemical powder and ran empty without having much effect.

"Forget it," snarled Colin. "They're toast."

Dooley spat another oath, then shouted, "Sweep the area! He can't have gotten far."

Colin was quick to countermand the order. "Belay that. That's what he wants us to do—split up so he can start picking us off one by one." He shook his head. "Maintain three-sixty security." He held up his tablet. "We'll let the UAV lead us to him. I'm not going to make the mistake of underestimating him again."

NINETEEN

A hundred yards away, from the concealment of a hastily dug snow cave just beyond the tree line, Matthew Redd peered through the scope affixed to Mikey Derhammer's Remington Model 700. The falling flakes made it difficult to distinguish much of anything in the surrounding landscape, never mind a flesh-and-blood target, but the four burning snowmobiles shone through like warning beacons.

Redd knew that by lingering in the area he was playing a dangerous game with the hunters. He couldn't afford to get into a firefight with them, not yet, but if he could pick off a couple of them, bloody their collective nose as it were, without giving himself away, the survivors might think twice about taking him on. More importantly the odds would improve in his favor, if only slightly. But if they were actively searching for him now, they were staying beyond his limited visual range, and if he stayed where he was, they would eventually find him.

It was time to get moving again.

He got to his feet slowly, so as not to give away his location, and headed away from the fires. The tracks he had left earlier had not yet filled in, and he followed them back into the woods, where Remington and Rubble waited. Powdery snow clung to his clothes, providing a degree of camouflage, but distance would hide his presence much more effectively.

Once in the saddle, he coaxed Remington into motion. Rubble ran ahead of them. Redd stayed in the trees, giving the cabin a wide berth as he circled back toward the old road and kept an ear cocked for the sound of snowmobile engines.

He debated now whether he should have taken the time to destroy all seven of the snowmobiles. His decision to leave three of them intact had been a strategic one. Had he sabotaged all of the vehicles, the hit team would have just two options—attempt to track him on foot or wait for replacement snowmobiles to arrive. He had given them a third option. With three functioning snowmobiles, six men could continue after him, while the others either trailed along on foot or waited for a resupply. Doing so would divide their forces—they would certainly realize that—but with a six-to-one advantage, it might be a chance they would be willing to take. Redd certainly preferred six-to-one over taking on the entire assault force at once, but he needed to stay ahead of them. If they anticipated his next move, headed over the pass to cut him off instead of sign-cutting and tracking him the old-fashioned way, then any benefit gained by dividing the enemy forces would be lost.

Everything depended on reaching the pass ahead of them.

He pushed Remington as hard as he dared, riding upslope and staying close to the pine boughs where the accumulation was relatively shallow. For his part, Remington negotiated the ascent with sure-footed ease, and soon the familiar contour of the road came into view. Even though he could not see it, he knew the summit of the pass was only a few hundred yards above his present position.

Almost there, he thought.

He reined Remington to a stop and listened for a moment. Hearing nothing, he nudged the horse out into the open and rode for the top of the pass. Not thirty seconds later, however, Rubble stopped dead in his tracks, cocked his head to the side, and let out an alarmed *woof.*

Redd halted Remington again and cupped a hand to his ear, turning slowly in the saddle until he heard it too—the strident whine of a small engine, getting louder with each passing second.

He immediately coaxed Remington into motion again, this time with an audible command that urged the horse to a full gallop. Without the slightest hesitation, Remington bounded forward, kicking up clouds of powder as he raced up the slope. For a moment, the noise of his hooves alternately compressing and scattering the snow drowned out the engine noise, but the latter grew steadily louder until it was all he could hear. Redd risked a glance back but couldn't see anything through the whiteout cloud left in Remington's wake. If the ever-increasing engine noise was any indication, the snowmobile was nearly upon them.

Then almost miraculously, Remington crested the summit of the pass. On a clear day, Redd would have had an unrestricted view of the valley below and the maze of ravines and draws that wended through the range. Today, however, there was merely an impression of emptiness above and a long descent below.

Redd hauled on the reins, bringing Remington to a skidding halt, turning him hard to the right. The horse gave a whinny of protest at this unexpected direction, as if to say, *I know what I'm doing, boss,* but grudgingly complied, cantering to a full stop. Rubble, who had raced along beside the horse, spun around in a full circle to face back the way they'd come, barking an animated challenge to the approaching riders.

Redd vaulted out of the saddle, hunting rifle in hand, and threw himself down into the snow just as the dark outline of the lead snowmobile loomed out of the haze right in front of him. He brought the rifle to his shoulder and snapped off a reflex shot in the general direction of where he thought the driver would be. The Model 700 bucked in his hands, the report echoing weirdly, but it was the sudden bloom of red in the midst of the stark white tableau that revealed the effectiveness of the shot.

In the next moment, the snowmobile became fully visible as it crested the pass, almost close enough that Redd could have reached out and touched it, had he been so inclined. Harder to see were the two figures sitting astride it. Their all-white attire made them virtually invisible, but the vivid crimson bloom on the chest of the man in the front seat was unmistakable.

With the rifle still braced against his shoulder, Redd worked the bolt, twisting his upper torso to follow the snowmobile as it continued past. As soon as the second round was seated, he pulled the trigger again.

This time, there was no immediate visual indication that the shot had found its target. The snowmobile, however, veered off its original course, swung to the left, and plunged into the trees along the roadside. A moment later, a resounding crunch signaled the abrupt end of its journey.

Redd had no time to savor this victory as a second snowmobile reached the summit. He twisted back around, worked the bolt, sighted, and fired in one smooth motion. He couldn't tell if the shot struck home but at almost the same instant that he fired, the driver jerked the handlebars hard to the left.

Too hard.

The sharp, sudden turn flipped the machine over into a sideways roll, and it tumbled crazily down the slope, flinging up huge clouds of snow that hid its final fate from his view.

Redd quickly snapped his attention back to the summit where the third snowmobile was materializing out of the snow haze. He worked the bolt and this time took an extra half second to sight in, aiming the weapon right at the snow machine's bubble-like windshield, before squeezing the trigger.

As soon as the rifle bucked against his shoulder, he worked the lever again, ejecting the spent brass and advancing the last round from the internal magazine, all the while maintaining a fix on the snowmobile as it roared past. But before he could fire again, he saw the rear-seat rider twist around, pointing a familiar if indistinct object in his direction. The white wrap tape on the upper receiver and heat shield could not hide the basic shape of an AR-type assault weapon.

Redd immediately rolled to the side, half burying himself in snow, even as bright yellow flame erupted from the rifle's muzzle, unleashing a burst that tore into the spot where he had been lying only a moment before.

Redd came out of the roll ready to fire again, but the snowmobile had vanished in the fog of snow thrown out by its treads. More reports cracked out from the haze. The gunman had to be firing blind, spraying and praying, but the rounds were sizzling into the snow a lot closer to Redd than he would have liked.

In the midst of the mayhem, Remington stood his ground, evidently unruffled by the noise. A working horse who had accompanied both Redd and J. B. on trail rides and hunting expeditions, he'd long since become inured to the sound of gunfire and, perhaps not understanding that the loud bang often preceded a painful or even fatal injury, did not spook. When a round creased the air beside him, kicking up a puff of powder a dozen feet away, he merely swished his tail as if trying to shoo away a horsefly.

Redd felt enough fear for both of them. If a stray round took Remington down, it would likely spell the end for him as well.

Rubble, on the other hand, had been whipped up into a frenzy. As the snowmobile passed, he bolted after it, disappearing into the haze.

"Rubble, no!" Redd shouted, but if the dog heard the command, he was beyond caring. With his superior olfactory and auditory senses, the rottie did not need to see the snowmobile to pursue it. Redd had no idea what the dog would do if he actually caught up to the machine.

Unable to do anything to protect his animals, Redd could only hold his ground and wait for the snowmobile to come back for another pass at him. A few seconds later, it did.

The changing pitch and intensity of engine noise not only signaled the imminent attack but revealed the driver's intent a fraction of a second before the machine materialized in front of him, aimed right at Redd. The driver was going to try to run him down.

Redd snap-fired his rifle's last round, then rolled to the side, out of the way.

As if anticipating his evasion, the rider swung wide in the other direction even as Redd loosed his shot. The reason for this maneuver became evident a moment later when the snow machine slowed to a full stop, not ten yards from where Redd lay, and the rear-seat rider took aim with his carbine.

In an instant, stretched out like taffy, Redd considered his short list of options. He could try rolling again, making himself a moving target. That might work for a second or two, but no more. He could fling the empty rifle at the shooter, maybe spoil his aim, but again, that would buy him only a momentary reprieve. Or he could forget about trying to avoid getting shot and instead spend his last remaining moments fighting back. The rifle was useless, but his fully loaded Ruger was in its holster on his hip.

I'd rather go out shooting, decided Redd, dropping the rifle and reaching for the Ruger. He didn't dare to hope that the shooter would miss, not at such close range, but thought maybe he could break leather before the bullet snuffed out his candle forever.

Then before the man could pull the trigger, Rubble exploded out of the whiteout and hit the shooter like a wrecking ball. The rottie's powerful jaws clamped down on the man's right forearm, knocking the carbine out of his hand, even as the dog's mass and momentum swept both riders off the snowmobile.

Redd was up a moment later and, with the Ruger in hand, charged toward the melee. The driver was already recovering, reaching for the carbine slung across his back. Redd quickly pumped a shot from the Ruger into the man's ski goggles, shattering the lenses along with everything behind them, then brought the muzzle of the smoking hand cannon to bear on the second rider, who was thrashing in the snow, trying to tear loose from Rubble's jaws, even as the dog shook him like a rag doll.

With man and dog so closely entangled, Redd hesitated to pull the trigger, but when he saw the black-powder-coated blade of an oversized fixed-blade fighting knife appear in the man's left hand, he decided he couldn't wait any longer. When the man raised the knife, preparing to plunge it into Rubble's body, Redd took aim at the upraised hand and pulled the trigger. The Ruger thundered, and a .44 Magnum round blasted both the knife and the hand that held it into oblivion.

The resulting shriek of pain gave even Rubble pause. He let go of the man, retreating to Redd's side and giving the latter the opening he needed to fire one more shot to take the man out of the fight permanently.

As the last echoes of the report were absorbed by the snow, an eerie silence fell up the mountain. The snowmobiles, all equipped with safety tethers, had shut off automatically once their riders lost their seats, and now the only sound was Rubble panting to catch his breath.

Redd reached down and patted the dog's head. "Who's a good boy?" he whispered. "Who's a good boy?"

Rubble answered the question with an enthusiastic *woof.*

Redd stared out into the snowy nothingness, searching for the other assaulters. In the near whiteout conditions, he couldn't locate them. He figured two or three of them might still be alive, bruised and battered, but not out of the fight. Eventually, they would regroup and come after him, and when they did, he wouldn't hear them coming.

It was time to get moving again.

TWENTY

Sheltered in the warm kitchen of the Water of Life Community Church, with a mug of hot cocoa in hand and surrounded by people she loved, Emily could almost forget about the winter storm raging outside. What she could not so easily put aside was the thought of her husband being out in the storm, fighting for his life.

Alone.

After her failed effort to enlist the help of Sheriff Blackwood, Emily had been at a loss for what to do next. Matthew had advised against reaching out to her parents, and she understood why. If the men hunting him chose to come after her, perhaps as a way of gaining leverage against him, the first place they would look for her would be her parents' home.

Matthew had, no doubt, intended that she, along with the Derhammers, should take refuge in a place where they had no obvious connections. Somewhere his enemies would never think to look. The problem with that strategy was that Emily had no intention of crawling under a rock and staying put while clinging to the hope that everything would turn out all right in the end. It wasn't in her nature to simply stand by and do nothing. Wishful thinking was not an effective treatment against any medical condition that she knew of.

Emily understood why Matty wanted her and Junior safely out of the way, but what *he* didn't understand was that she wasn't going to let him face this trial alone.

She knew better than to think that she could saddle up and grab a gun, charge out into the wilderness, and take on the men hunting Matty like some kind of avenging angel. She wasn't Rambo. She didn't have the same skills and training as her husband. More importantly, she possessed the wisdom to know that even attempting such a course would do neither of them any good. She had originally thought the best way to help him was to make sure that he got some backup, but unfortunately, the people she had been counting on to provide that help—Sheriff Blackwood and Gavin Kline—weren't available. After leaving Blackwood's office, she had returned to Mikey's truck, laying out the problem and expressing her resolve to find some other way to help Matty.

"The church?" Mikey had asked when she had given him their next destination. "Matt said—"

"I know what he said, Mikey." It was becoming a familiar refrain. She made an effort to temper her frustration. Mikey was, after all, trying to look out for her . . . for them all. "He said not to go to my parents' place. The church is neutral ground."

"Do the bad guys know that? If they google *Reverend Elijah Lawrence*, they're gonna realize that the church is the second place they should look for you."

"We're not going to stay there. Not for very long. But I need a phone."

Mikey seemed to accept this and made the short drive to the church, which was situated in a corner lot in the residential neighborhood three blocks north of the courthouse. The Ram's big tires easily negotiated streets that had not seen any vehicle traffic since the storm began.

Reverend Elijah Lawrence's open-door policy in his church was almost literal. The doors were never locked, and anyone was welcome inside anytime, regardless of whether they were part of his congregation or not. The food in the pantry was freely available to anyone who needed it, and to the best of Emily's knowledge, nobody had ever abused this privilege. On the one or two occasions when teenaged hooligans had crept in and vandalized the interior, the community had acted quickly to repair the damage while emphatically shaming the perpetrators.

Emily had half expected to find her father or some other church volunteer waiting inside to help organize a relief effort for those in the community who might have lost power or been otherwise caught unprepared, but the church, like the parking lot, was empty. Once inside, Liz began heating water to prepare cups of Swiss Miss, while Emily called her father and asked him to join them.

Elijah Lawrence was nobody's idea of what a rural pastor ought to look like. At eighty-one—he'd been over fifty when Mrs. Lawrence, several years his junior, had given birth to Emily—he should by all rights have long-since retired, slowing down to enjoy his twilight years. Instead, he not only served the congregation but still put in a few hours every day at the auto body repair shop he'd built up from nothing as a young man. Whippet-lean and tough as a two-dollar steak, he looked more like an aged former bantamweight boxer turned trainer than someone who had devoted his life to shepherding God's flock. Yet despite his craggy exterior, when he spoke from the pulpit he rarely ventured into fire-and-brimstone territory. The message he shared emphasized love and neighborliness, not judgment. Emily thought he had probably only ever entertained unchristian thoughts toward one person—the young man who had wooed his only daughter and then broken her heart. Fortunately for them all, Matthew Redd had returned like the prodigal son and made everything right. He'd also given Elijah a grandson.

Once he arrived, Lawrence listened without interrupting as Emily explained the situation, beginning with the call Matthew had received and ending with Blackwood's revelation that he had been warned off giving any assistance to Redd by Homeland Security agents. Then she sketched out her plan to help her husband.

When she was done, Lawrence steepled his fingers under his chin in a thoughtful pose. "I have to ask . . . Is it possible that Matthew has misread the situation? That these men he believes are hunting him are actually law enforcement?"

"No." She shook her head. "I mean, there might be real Homeland Security agents looking for him, but they aren't who blew up Gavin's plane. I think the kill team Matty talked about is real."

"Trust me, sir," said Mikey. "If Matt says there are dudes after him, it's real. I've seen it firsthand." Mikey had a close relationship with Elijah. In fact, he'd worked for him for so long, Elijah had all but appointed Mikey to run his auto repair shop. Emily knew her father trusted Mikey and his judgment.

Lawrence nodded slowly. "Then mightn't it be possible that the Homeland agents are trying to protect Matthew from these other men?"

Emily frowned then shrugged. "I don't know. I guess. But Matty doesn't know about them. He thinks he's facing these killers alone."

"And so you want to ride out and tell him." Lawrence's tone became stern, more a father than a pastor. "I don't need to tell you how foolhardy that is."

"Then give me an alternative," she fired back.

"Have you looked outside, Emily? It's not fit for man or beast out there. And how on earth are you even going to find him?"

"I know how he thinks, Dad. He's not just going to wander around. He'll use the hunting camps for shelter."

"We're in the middle of a blizzard," countered Lawrence, exasperation creeping into his tone. "Those camps are miles away. In some of the roughest country there is."

"I can find them. I just need a good horse."

Lawrence shook his head. "I can't let you go out there, Emily. You have a child to think of."

Emily's reply was just as passionate, but respectful. "I *am* thinking of him. I want Junior to grow up with his father still here to protect him." Before he could protest, she raised a hand. "I'm doing this, Dad. I didn't call you here to talk me out of it. Please, I need your help."

"I'm eighty-one, Em. I've got no business riding a horse in the best of conditions."

"I'm not asking you to. I need you to help *me* get a horse. You must know someone who has one I can borrow."

Lawrence's deep frown indicated that, much to his chagrin, he did.

"I'll need to borrow one of your hunting rifles too," she went on. "But what I really need most is for you and Mom to find a safe place for little Matty." She thrust her chin in Mikey's direction. "And them. Matthew seemed to think that Mikey and Liz might be in danger as well. In fact, you should probably make yourselves scarce too. These people might come after you, thinking they can get to us through you."

"Emily, are you hearing yourself? You want to ride out into this blizzard. Alone. On a borrowed horse with a gun . . . to what? Help Matthew fight off an army of killers? He knows how to survive out there. He's been trained for it. You haven't. It's an unnecessary risk, and if he were here, he'd tell you the same thing."

"Well, he's *not* here," she fired back. "And if he was, I would tell him that he doesn't have to keep taking on the whole world by himself. I'm going, Dad." She paused a beat, then went on. "Matthew doesn't know about these Homeland Security agents. He needs to be told, and this is the only way to reach him."

Lawrence turned to Mikey. "Maybe you can talk some sense into her?"

Mikey, who had been staring down at his empty mug throughout the conversation, took a deep breath before raising his eyes to look at Lawrence. "She's right. Matt needs help, and there's nobody else who can do this."

Emily felt a rush of gratitude at the unexpected support, but before she could verbalize it, Mikey added, "I'll go with her, sir."

"Mikey," Liz gasped. "You can't go out there. Are you kidding me right now?"

He turned to her. "I have to, Liz. He's my best friend. He's like a brother to me, and you know if it were me out there, Matt wouldn't let anything stop him. He'd ride out and find me and help however he could. That's what I'm going to do."

She opened her mouth to protest, but then something in her eyes changed. She glanced at Emily, then looked back at Mikey and nodded slowly. "No, you're right. Of course, you have to go." She let out a nervous chuckle, looking to Emily once more and then to Lawrence. "This is what we do, isn't it? Look out for each other? Help each other in times of need? That's what family does. I can help with little Matty; don't you worry about him." She turned to Mikey. "But you better be careful out there. I want our son to have his daddy too."

Mikey nodded. "Always."

Lawrence's grizzled face twisted in consternation. "There's help, and then there's plumb foolishness, and I can assure you, this is the latter."

"With respect, Reverend Lawrence," said Mikey, "it's not. I may not be a Marine like Matt, but I can handle myself in the back country. So can Emily."

"This isn't just an overnight pack trip. You'll be riding into a blizzard. And there's a good chance you might run into men with guns."

Mikey started to say, "We'll be careful," but Emily spoke over him.

"That's why we *have* to do this. Matthew is all alone out there."

Lawrence threw up his hands and pivoted away from the table. For a moment, Emily thought he was going to storm out of the church without another word, but after taking just two steps, the old man stopped in his tracks. Without turning back, he put his hands on his hips. "Chuck Boardman has a couple of geldings that I trust for something like this. I'll give him a call. Explain to him that you're doing the Lord's work."

He turned and gave Liz a long, appraising glance. "I've always believed that a supportive wife is a gift from God. I pray you don't ever have cause to regret this."

"Me too," Liz said, her voice almost a whisper.

Lawrence put his hands on his hips. "Well, why don't you load the kids up in my truck. There's bound to be someone in the congregation with some extra room."

Emily came around the table and approached her father. Undeterred by his disapproving body language, she threw her arms around him. "Thanks, Dad. I love you."

After a long moment, he returned the embrace. "I love you too." He swallowed down a lump of emotion, then added, "I'll be prayin' for you, sweetheart."

TWENTY-ONE

OKLAHOMA CITY

It was dark by the time a young FBI special agent, sent out from the OKC field office, delivered Gavin Kline to the airport, but thanks to the deployment of a small army of portable light towers on and around the west runway, he had no difficulty finding his way back to the scene of the attack. Getting through the jurisdictional roadblocks proved somewhat more challenging.

He knew something was up when he tried to cross the outermost perimeter, which consisted of wooden crowd-control barricades manned by OKCPD officers. Upon presenting his credentials to the officer manning the entry checkpoint, he had been told in no uncertain terms that, since he was not on the list of people authorized to be on the scene, he could not go in.

"Sergeant . . ." He searched the man's uniform for a name badge but didn't see one. "I'm the FBI director of intelligence. That means I'm the one who decides who gets on that list of yours."

The police sergeant appeared unimpressed. "Then I guess you won't have any trouble adding your name."

Kline scowled at the man. He still hurt all over. In fact, he was hurting even more than he had when he'd left the hospital AMA—*against medical advice*—a little over an hour earlier, and the pain was interfering with his ability to remain diplomatic. "Who's in charge of the investigation? I want to talk to him."

"That would be SAC Bergen."

"SAC of what?" Kline demanded, even though he had a pretty good idea.

"Homeland Security Investigations. They're handling this." The sergeant's eyes flicked toward Kline's badge case. "Not the Bureau."

Kline fought the urge to fling verbal acid at the officer. "Is SAC Bergen out there?" He pointed to the field.

"I believe so."

"Can you contact him and let him know that I'm here? I think he'll want to speak with me, inasmuch as I was out there—" he pointed again—"when all this went down."

The sergeant narrowed his eyes for a moment, then took out his phone. He turned away as he made the call, so Kline couldn't hear either side of the conversation, which seemed to go on for several minutes. Finally, the policeman put the phone away and faced Kline. "He's sending someone out."

Kline thought that would be the end of the matter, but he was soon disabused of that notion when an HSI special agent—not Special Agent in Charge Bergen, but one of his lackeys—came out to the barricade to "take your statement."

Kline thought the man must be joking and told him as much.

The other man regarded him coolly. "I was under the impression that you wanted to cooperate with our investigation, Director Kline."

"That's exactly why I'm here. Take me to SAC Bergen so I can set him straight. I hear you're pursuing a theory that this is the work of left-wing extremists."

"It's not a theory," retorted the Homeland Security agent. "It's a fact. We have them dead to rights. Well, dead, anyway. Our special operations team took them out."

Kline shook his head. "No. That's all wrong. The guys that hit us weren't a bunch of crunchy granola anarchists. They were pros."

The agent regarded him for a moment, then took out a notebook and a pen. "Describe these 'pros'?"

"Oh, for the love of . . . Just let me talk to your boss."

Things continued in this vein for several more minutes before an exasperated Kline threatened to call the Secretary of Homeland Security. It was mostly a bluff. As an executive assistant director of the FBI, Kline was only three steps removed from the attorney general—a cabinet position on the same level as the secretary of the Department of Homeland Security. While the DHS secretary might not have taken Kline's call, the AG would have and would have certainly made some noise about the lack of interdepartmental cooperation. But whether or not Kline could use that political leverage to move the mountain of red tape blocking his access to the investigation was less certain.

Evidently it was a bluff the junior HSI agent did not feel comfortable calling because he agreed to pass Kline's request along to the special agent in charge running the investigation.

"No," Kline said. "You're going to take me to him."

Having already ceded the victory, the young agent caved and led Kline out to the runway where the shattered remains of the JPATS plane and the airport firefighting truck marked the place where he had almost died.

The scorched field was crawling with agents in blue windbreakers with bold yellow letters declaring *Police HSI*. Kline knew that Homeland Security Investigations—the investigative branch of Immigration and Customs Enforcement, or ICE—was primarily tasked with investigating things like human trafficking rings and international smuggling, and to a lesser extent, preventing terrorism. As Kline understood it, they had claimed primary jurisdiction because the incident had occurred at an international airport. While they certainly possessed the capability to investigate the attack on the Con Air flight, it was not their specialty. They lacked the resources and experience to pursue the kind of in-depth investigation that would eventually lead back to the real culprit. Interagency rivalries notwithstanding, Kline couldn't fathom why DHS wasn't begging the FBI for help.

He found the special agent in charge in the ad hoc command center, which consisted of several folding tables set up under a collapsible canopy positioned on the edge of the tarmac near the crash site. SAC Bergen, a fit man who looked to be in his midforties, greeted Kline with a firm handshake. "Director Kline. We thought you were dead."

"I'm not," Kline replied. "But a lot of good men are."

Bergen acknowledged this with a somber nod. "At least we got the dirtbags responsible."

"That's why I wanted to speak with you. Do I understand correctly that you are treating this as an act of domestic terrorism, carried out by political extremists?"

The Homeland agent regarded him with a suspicious look. "That's right. One of our SOD teams has been tracking them for a couple weeks. We knew they had something planned but didn't know that you were the target until today. The team interdicted them at the airport firehouse. They were too late to stop the attack, but they took the terrorists out. All of them that didn't get blown up in the explosion."

"You're saying you had intel that an attack was imminent? Maybe that was something you should have shared with us?"

Bergen's eyes narrowed, as if the question had been a personal attack. "With all due respect, Director, you of all people should know how this works. On any given day we're tracking dozens . . . hundreds of bad actors who might be planning something. That doesn't mean we always have actionable intelligence."

"They've got you chasing your tail," said Kline. "You have no idea what's really going on here."

"I think we've actually got a pretty good handle on it. We recovered a ton of physical evidence from the scene. Weapons. A laptop with their manifesto and a target list. It all tracks. Now we're just trying to figure out how these guys managed to infiltrate the airport."

Kline shook his head. "You think this action was targeted against me. I promise you, it wasn't. The real target was the prisoner we were transporting. He was a key witness in the investigation of an international conspiracy. His testimony would have brought them down, so they had to silence him. They have the resources to make it happen. It's not the first time they've taken out a witness in federal custody. Everything you've found pointing the finger at left-wing nutjobs is a smoke screen designed to distract you from the real bad guys."

"You think the terrorists were recruited by this conspiracy?"

"There aren't any terrorists," snapped Kline, his patience about to boil over. "I saw the men that executed this attack. They were trained professionals. They wore military-grade body armor. They killed—" he choked up and had to take a breath to compose himself—"killed more than a dozen federal agents."

"That doesn't sound like the guys we took down."

"No, it doesn't. Because the guys you took down were set up to take the fall by the men who really did this."

Bergen shrugged. "Frankly, that's not the story the evidence is telling."

"Then the evidence is lying." Kline's voice had risen almost to a shout, drawing the stares of several HSI agents working nearby. With an effort, he brought his ire down a notch. "I'll need to talk to someone from this special operations team."

Bergen folded his arms over his chest. "They've been quarantined. That's standard procedure after any operation, especially one where there are fatalities on the scene."

"Don't stonewall me, Bergen. I'm not a reporter. This attack targeted DOJ personnel, so you can bet that we're going to be conducting our own investigation. You are going to need to produce those men for questioning."

Bergen considered his response for a long moment. "I'll have to push your request up the chain."

Kline mirrored the other man's pose. "Do that. I'll wait."

Bergen stared daggers at him, but then seemed to have a change of heart. "Okay, Director. In the interest of interagency harmony . . ." He took out his phone, placing a call to a number from his contact list, then held up a finger, indicating that Kline should wait. A moment later, he said, "Dave, I need a location on those SOD guys . . . the ones involved in the airport incident."

There was a long pause as the party on the other end of the line gave an answer that was evidently not to Bergen's liking. His eyebrows came together in a perplexed frown.

"No," he said after a moment. "They were supposed to check in after they got settled."

There was another pause. Kline didn't need to hear Dave's side of the conversation to know that something was very wrong.

"Just give me the number for the lead agent. Carter, I think it was . . . You're kidding. Who the . . . You know what, never mind. Put me through to somebody in the Special Operations Division."

Without lowering the phone, Bergen looked over at Kline. "Just a little bureaucratic mix-up."

"You aren't going to find them," Kline replied gravely.

"Of course I will. Their division office will know how to contact them."

"The division office is going to tell you that they've never heard of those men." Kline sighed. "But I think I can help with part of your investigation. You said you were trying to figure out how the terrorists were able to infiltrate the airport. Well, I'll tell you how they did it. They flashed a badge. Just like yours."

TWENTY-TWO

MONTANA

The snow stopped falling not long after dusk, the clouds overhead parting to reveal an almost magical transformation of the wilderness landscape. The snow-covered slopes seemed to almost glow a deep blue in the moonlight. Overhead the sky was full of stars. A fringe of clouds rising in the northwest, however, suggested the break in the weather was only temporary, and Redd knew he would need to make the most of the brief reprieve if he was to reach his next destination—an old hunting camp he'd used in the past—before the snow started to fall again. If he didn't get there before the snow returned . . .

He didn't want to think about what would happen if he didn't.

With the fall of night, the temperature had dropped several degrees, and Redd was definitely feeling the cold. The adrenaline that had fueled him through the battle with the kill team had long since drained away, and now the chill was settling into his bones, making him feel sluggish. Remington appeared to be handling the conditions well enough, but Redd knew that eventually, the cold would get to the old quarter horse as well. But while Redd had the stars overhead and an unrestricted view of the mountains, he was able to orient himself, navigating cross country to the mountain where the hunting camp was situated.

For a long while after the battle with the hit team, Redd had kept an ear out for the sound of pursuit. He knew he'd permanently taken out two, maybe even three of them and believed some of the others had probably sustained serious injuries, so even if one or all three of the snowmobiles were still functioning, it would be a while before the survivors could link up with the rest of their group and resume their pursuit.

But resume it they would. He did not doubt that for a second. Yet as he put more distance between himself and them, he rode a little easier. While the snow fell and the winds blew, his trail would be almost impossible for them to find and follow.

Now that the snow had stopped, that trail would be a lot easier for them to pick up, but Redd figured he'd gone five or six miles since the encounter. They would have to search a lot of ground and expend a lot of time before eventually crossing his trail. Once they did, they would close in quickly, and he would need to be ready.

The camp was little more than a clearing on a relatively flat section of a forested ridgeline, where many generations of hunters had pitched their tents and dressed their kills. Because the site was upslope, there was no danger of it being swept away in an avalanche or mudslide, but what made the site especially desirable to the hunters—and to Redd—was the horse shelter at the edge of the clearing.

The shelter wasn't exactly a structure. It was illegal to erect any kind of permanent man-made object, even a bench or fire ring, on National Forest land, but that hadn't stopped someone—perhaps one of J. B.'s ancestors—from stacking up a few windfalls into a sort of horseshoe-shaped frame, topped with a lattice of branches. Anyone occupying the campsite could hang tarps or even fresh pine cuttings on the frame to form temporary walls and a roof, providing shelter for horses during inclement weather. The existence of the shelter wasn't a closely guarded secret, but as long as nobody made any permanent improvements to it, the rangers were content to ignore its presence.

When the snow had started falling, the open weave of the lattice had allowed most of the flakes to sift through, but as snow accumulated on the branches, the gaps shrank away to nothing, resulting in a nearly foot-thick snow dome over the shelter.

Redd scooped out the snow that had fallen through and piled it up along the open front of the structure, creating an additional wall of snow that would act as insulation to help hold in the heat. Once he brought Remington and Rubble inside, he closed up the opening, leaving just a small hole for ventilation.

Working by the light of a headlamp, he removed Remington's saddle and saddle blanket, and while the horse munched on alfalfa pellets from his feed bag, Redd began the necessary chore of rubbing him down, removing sweat that would otherwise freeze in his coat and spreading around the naturally occurring oils that would help Remington endure the frigid conditions. The rubdown was almost as therapeutic for Redd as it was for Remington. After hours of freezing in the saddle, the physical activity helped restore circulation to his nearly numb extremities. By the time he was finished, the interior of the shelter felt noticeably warmer.

He draped a horse blanket over Remington, then spread the saddle blanket out on the frozen ground and attended to his firearms, wiping them down to the best of his ability before reloading and doing functions checks on each. Only when his horse and his equipment were in order did he attend to his own needs.

All of the food he had brought was now cold, some of it completely frozen. He considered trying to make a small fire to warm both it and himself, but ultimately decided against it, not because of a fear that it might melt the walls of the shelter—Redd knew snow actually reflected back radiant heat rather than absorbing it—but because a fire, even a small one, would be visible from a distance, giving away his position. Instead, he ate his meal cold, setting aside the frozen items for later.

As he gnawed on a slice of nearly frozen ham, he was overcome with intense feelings of misery and anger. This meal . . . this cold, dreary repast . . . was the product of hours of work on the part of his wife and had been meant to be shared with their close friends. Instead, he was eating it alone, in a frozen wilderness, and all because a bunch of rich men had decided that he needed to die. The thoughts robbed him of his appetite, but he kept eating, knowing that without fuel, his body would not be able to carry him through the ordeal ahead.

Beside him, Rubble, unaffected by self-pity, gobbled down his portion of ham and then gazed up hopefully at Redd. In spite of everything, the rottie's big puppy dog eyes brought a smile to Redd's face, and he rewarded Rubble with another piece of ham.

Once they had consumed all the food that wasn't frozen solid, Redd shut off his headlamp, and then he and Rubble huddled together under a blanket and tried to sleep.

✖   ✖   ✖

A tentative *woof* from Rubble brought Redd immediately awake. He had not really slept, but rather hovered on the edge of consciousness, resting his body but keeping his mind in a semialert state, knowing that his survival might depend on a quick reaction. But aside from opening his eyes, he remained perfectly motionless, holding his breath and listening for any sound that might explain Rubble's reaction.

There might have been a perfectly nonthreatening explanation. The rottweiler was still a puppy, not a trained guard dog. He didn't have a lot of experience in the backcountry and didn't know how to differentiate night sounds. For all Redd knew, the dog might have been responding to the sound of a squirrel up in a tree or the screech of an owl. He might even have been dreaming. Whatever the reason, aside from that single bark, Rubble did not seem to be agitated, but Redd couldn't afford to take any chances.

After a full minute of listening, hearing nothing, he let out his breath and got to his feet. His muscles were stiff, his joints aching, but his mind felt clear, and after a couple quick stretches to limber up, he crept up to the ventilation hole and began carefully removing snow to enlarge the opening.

The first thing he noticed was that it had started snowing again. Not the heavy, wind-driven snow of the day before, but a gentle fall of big, fat flakes. The moon was gone from the sky and cloud cover blocked out the stars, leaving the world considerably darker than it had been during his long ride to the shelter. A check of his G-Shock showed that it was a little past 4 a.m. Sunrise was still a couple hours away, and there was not even a hint of predawn twilight in the distance. Nevertheless, he could still distinguish a few dark shapes against the white snowfield—trees that had shed some of their burden of snow, rock features that protruded here and there—and when he peered through the scope on the Model 700, he could see a lot more of them. The magnification revealed a series of shadowy depressions—the trail left by Remington's hooves, only partially filled in by fresh snow. Using the tracks as a reference point, he began sweeping the rifle back and forth in slow arcs, scanning the approach to the shelter. Satisfied that there was no activity within direct visual range of the hunting camp, he ventured out of the shelter in search of a better vantage point. Following his master's lead, Rubble bounded out after Redd and then ran off in search of a tree to water.

Redd also began looking for a tree, but for different reasons. If the enemy was closing in on him, he needed to find cover and concealment—a defensive position from which to engage and return fire. He moved to the tree line bordering the campsite on the north and then began packing down the snow at the base of a pine bough, creating a stable shooting platform. Once in position, he glassed the slope again, sweeping the rifle back and forth in long, slow arcs, looking for anything unusual. Even so, he almost missed them.

It was the motion that caught his eye. He steadied the rifle, moving the scope back slowly to the spot where he thought he had detected movement, and kept watching until he saw it again: a small dark speck that might have been merely a pine sapling or the top of a protruding rock . . . except for the fact that it was steadily advancing up the slope.

Once it was fixed in his view, Redd began to see more detail, the outline of a larger shape around the darker speck that didn't quite match the crystalline blue-white of the snowfield. A shape that might be a man in winter overwhites wearing some piece of gear that wasn't wrapped in camouflage tape.

Then, at the edge of the circle of magnification, he spied another dark speck in motion, another white man-shape. Redd felt his blood go cold.

The enemy had found him.

TWENTY-THREE

"Saber Six, this is Javelin Two, I have a visual on the target. Repeat, I have visual at my two o'clock, three-five-zero meters. He just ducked behind a tree."

Colin Kilmeade stopped in his tracks and looked upslope, scanning the area Javelin Two had just described. In the brown-and-gold display of his Enhanced Night Vision Goggle-Binocular—ENVG-B—he had no difficulty finding the tree line Javelin Two was describing but saw no sign of Matthew Redd. Against the cool, dark snowfield, Redd's body heat should have shone like a halo, but all Colin could see was the fainter gold tracery of pine boughs, shrouded in snow. Evidently, the cover their target had chosen was completely masking his infrared signature.

The latest evolution of night vision technology was a radical improvement over the old green monochrome haze revealed in the night-optical devices—NODs— he used during his first few years with DEVGRU—but they were still a far cry from Superman-style X-ray vision. Colin took comfort in knowing that he could see a hell of a lot more than Matthew Redd could.

"This is Saber Six. I don't see him."

There was a brief pause, then Javelin Two's voice came back. "Yeah, I lost him too, but I know where he is. I can put a round through the tree if you want. Might not kill him, but it'll definitely flush him out."

On any other day, against any other target, Colin would have not hesitated to give the green light. On a search-and-destroy mission, the only thing that mattered was eliminating the target by the quickest, surest method, and often the best way to accomplish that was with a 180 grain Win-Mag round, delivered from one of Javelin Team's MK13 Mod 5 .300 caliber sniper rifles at a nice standoff distance—no fuss, but considerable muss.

Not this day. Not this target.

His shoulder still ached, and under his overwhites and plate carrier, he knew his chest was one great big bruise, but he had been a lot luckier than Bull Dooley. Dooley had been driving the lead snowmobile and had driven right into a bullet. The round had caught him in the neck, just above the collar of his ballistic armor vest. It hadn't been an instantly fatal wound; Dooley had stayed alive long enough to crash his snowmobile into a tree, breaking the arm of his rear seat rider, Saber Two, before bleeding out.

Colin had been lucky in that the bullet with his name on it had struck just a little bit lower and had been stopped by his SAPI plate. The force of the impact had hurt like a son of a gun—he imagined it was a little like getting kicked in the chest by a donkey—but it was nothing compared to what had happened when he lost control and rolled his machine down the slope, dislocating his left shoulder in the process. It was an injury he'd suffered before, and with a little manipulation—a little painful manipulation—he got the bone back into its socket. He wasn't going to let a little thing like that take him out of the fight—not today. It was personal. Redd had made it personal. And Colin was going to personally end Matthew Redd's life. He wanted to see the fear in Redd's eyes, wanted to watch the life drain out of him.

"Negative, Two," he said after a moment. "Hold your position with Jav One and maintain visual contact. If you see him again, call out. Everyone else, fan out and continue movement to target. We'll hold at one hundred meters and reassess."

Besides Colin, Saber Three was the only remaining member of Saber Team still on the field. Saber One, Colin's rear seat rider, had gotten pretty banged up in the rollover. He was mission capable, but Colin had opted to send him and Saber Two back on their one stillfunctional snowmobile so the latter could get medical treatment. Saber Three and Javelin Team had linked up with Colin to continue the hunt on foot.

Nine men to take down one. Colin should have felt good about those odds, but Redd had already reduced their force by a third.

With the feed from the Predator drone to guide them, tracking Redd's movements posed no real problem, but catching up to him involved a long march through nearly knee-deep snow. The night vision gear and snowshoes they had prudently included in their load-out made the going a little easier, but it was still an all-night slog. Colin was tired and hurting, and the only thing that would make him feel better was pulling the trigger on Matthew Redd.

Javelin Two's voice broke over the net. "I see him. He's in the prone. Looks like he's got his eye to glass. I have the shot."

Colin searched the tree line again and this time spotted Redd, a dark shape outlined in a golden corona in the display of his next-gen night vision device. The tech was so good, Colin could easily distinguish the protruding barrel of Redd's rifle and the scope through which Redd was looking.

He was about to tell Javelin Two to hold, but then an uneasy feeling came over him. *What's he doing? Looking for us? Surely he can't see anything.*

If Redd *was* scoping the hill, it could only mean that he knew they were coming. The question was, *how?*

Suddenly, a bright flower blossomed at the end of Redd's rifle.

Colin swore under his breath as he dropped flat into the snow a fraction of a second before something tore through air uncomfortably close to his head. After another second the report rolled past, oddly muted by the fresh snowfall.

Forget this, thought Colin Kilmeade and then keyed his mic. "All Javelin elements, light him up."

TWENTY-FOUR

Redd held his shooting pose as he worked the bolt, keeping his sight picture while looking for some indication that the round had found its target. He saw movement in the scope, probably his target kissing the ground, but in the darkness, it was impossible to discern anything more than that.

A miss, he decided. *But by how much?*

He felt sure of his aim. The problem was that when he had accepted the loan of the rifle from Mikey, he had not taken the time to properly zero the weapon, adjusting the scope to his unique sight picture. He regretted that now. With a spotter giving him immediate feedback, he could have made Kentucky windage adjustments—mentally correcting for the difference between his eye and Mikey's—but without knowing where the round had gone, high or low, left or right, every shot was a literal shot in the dark.

He debated firing again but decided against it, knowing that the muzzle flash would almost certainly have given his position away. *Shoot and move* was a core tenet of sniper combat. Instead, he pulled back behind the tree and crawled away, moving deeper into the woods. It was the right call. No sooner had he moved than the air around him exploded in a spray of splinters and snow as automatic rifle fire tore into the trees above his head.

The incoming fire was all high, owing to the angle of the slope, but he ducked low and kept moving, seeking another covered position from which to engage again. He stayed close to the tree line, skirting the edge of the hunting camp before dropping down to wait for another target of opportunity. After the initial burst, the rate of fire slackened but did not let up completely. The wild fusillade was replaced by a more coordinated attack, the shots coming one or two at a time from different locations. It was, he realized, suppressive fire, meant to keep him pinned down while a second group moved in to flank him—a standard infantry tactic, but knowing that didn't make him feel any more confident.

He recalled another night, not so long ago and not so far from where he now crouched in the darkness, when he had faced a similar situation—a squad of highly trained, highly motivated killers, possessed of the same skill set as he, with superior weapons, stalking him, trying to outmaneuver and ultimately neutralize him.

He had survived that night, beaten them at their own game, but there had only been six of them that time. He wasn't exactly sure how many he was facing now, but it felt like a lot more than six.

The recollection triggered another thought.

NODs.

The enemy that he had faced nearly two years ago at the old cabin had used night vision devices. What were the odds that this hostile force was also outfitted with them?

Pretty likely, he thought, with a growing feeling of dread.

During his time in the Corps, Redd had used NODs extensively, both in training and in combat, so he knew well the advantages and limitations of night vision devices. And right now the advantages heavily outweighed the limitations, skewing the odds even further against him.

If he was going to survive this, he would have to throw out the old playbook and do something to change those odds.

TWENTY-FIVE

Javelin Four—real name Dan Bailey—was the first to top the ridgeline, coming up about a hundred meters to the south of the spot where Javelin Two had reported contact. Despite being tired and cranky after hours of hard trekking in snowshoes, the adrenaline surge of contact with the target, not to mention the fact that the finish line was finally in sight, supplied him with a burst of energy. Nevertheless, he did not make the mistake of charging ahead like he was invincible. Not after what Matthew Redd had done to Saber Team.

With his M4 at the high ready, he scanned the trees, looking for any hint of Redd's location, and began advancing, one slow step at a time. The snowshoes were a pain to walk in, requiring him to raise his feet just a little higher with each step and to employ a wider, exaggerated gait so as not to trip himself up, but if there was a moment in the operation when he definitely did not want to trip, it was now.

One thing he didn't need to worry about was giving his position away with the noise of his steps. The odd squeak-crunch of compressing snow was completely drowned out by the din of suppressive fire.

When he reached the tree line, he saw a long series of craters in the snow, weaving through the boughs. Footsteps, he decided. Matthew Redd's footsteps.

This is going to be easy, he thought, then chided himself for being too cocky, thinking again about what had happened to Saber Team.

But the tracks clearly showed Redd's path of retreat. The snow was at least a foot deep, maybe even eighteen inches. There was no easy way to cover one's tracks in deep snow, and no way at all to avoid leaving prints in the first place.

He keyed his mic and spoke in a low voice. "All Javelin elements, this is Jav Four. Lift fire, lift fire. I have identified a trail and am closing with the target."

Saber Six came over the net. "Roger, Four. All elements, lift fire. Flankers, move up to support Javelin Four."

There was no discernible change in the volume of suppressive fire, but Bailey knew that the shooters would have raised their aim point, sending their rounds into the treetops to avoid hitting him. Even so, it was always a bit unnerving to move with bullets creasing the air directly above his head.

The trail of footprints meandered along the edge of the clearing for about twenty yards before hooking around the root system of a recently toppled tree. If Redd was going to set an ambush, that would be the spot for it.

Trusting his camouflage and his armor to tilt the balance in his favor, Bailey swung to the left, giving the corner a wide berth but keeping his finger on the trigger and the muzzle of his carbine trained on the spot where the tracks disappeared. He knew that, at any moment, he would spot Redd, crouched over his rifle, straining to see in the darkness, ready to fire at the first sign of movement, but even so, when he glimpsed the dark shape outlined in golden light and the protruding barrel of a long gun, a jolt of panic went through him and he hastily pulled back before Redd could get off a shot.

Bailey held his breath a moment, staring at the blind corner, expecting Redd to edge around it and take the shot, but nothing happened. Maybe Redd hadn't seen him. After all, it was dark, and Bailey's overwhites would blend in with the background.

Do it, an inner voice urged. *He can't see you. Take him out.*

Bailey took one second more to let his courage build, then smoothly moved around the corner, bringing Redd's form once more into view. He tapped the trigger of his PEQ-15, which instantly put a pinpoint of laser energy onto his target, and then squeezed the M4's trigger twice, firing a controlled pair center mass into the target.

Even as the shots were loosed, his brain began sounding a warning. There was something wrong with this whole setup. The shape behind the gun, the shape that he had assumed could only be Matthew Redd . . . wasn't.

No, it wasn't Redd. Wasn't even a man.

Before he could make sense of it, however, something hit him hard from behind, and everything went black as his goggles were torn away from his face.

He pivoted away, turning to meet the threat as he backpedaled, giving himself enough standoff distance so that he could aim and shoot . . .

Except none of that happened. Somewhere between his brain and his body, the message got lost. The connection had been severed.

Gripped by primal terror, he tried to cry out, to call for help, to warn his teammates, but something hard was pressing against his mouth, holding in his screams and blocking his ability to breathe.

Trapped in darkness, trapped inside his own mind, Dan Bailey spent the last moments of his life wondering how Matthew Redd had gotten the drop on him.

TWENTY-SIX

Redd was pretty sure that the man was dead, neck broken from the savage hit he had delivered to the back of the shooter's helmeted skull, but he kept one gloved hand clamped over the man's mouth for a full minute, just in case.

It was a long, cold minute.

For the first time since riding out, he was experiencing the winter storm without the protection of his warm, sherpa-lined Carhartt jacket, and the wind, which was starting to pick up again, cut right through his flannel shirt. But as he let go of the dead man's mouth and, by feel alone, located the night vision goggles attached to the corpse's helmet, he knew the sacrifice of his jacket had been a small price to pay.

His crazy plan had worked.

Using the coat draped over a mound of snow with the sleeves extended like arms to "hold" the Model 700, he had created a decoy to lure in one of the shooters while he lay buried in the snow and hidden from view nearby. Shivering under what promised to be his death shroud if the plan went sideways, Redd had looked out through a hole barely larger than his fist and mentally rehearsed what he would do when they came for him.

He had decided on a weaponless takedown if there was only one hostile. Not only would it be quick and relatively silent, but it also represented his best chance to capture a set of NODs. If there had been a pair of shooters, he would have had to use the Ruger—the only weapon he possessed that might be able to defeat their body armor. Had there been more than two . . . Well, he was just glad there hadn't.

Rather than trying to figure out how to unclip the night vision device from the man's ballistic helmet, Redd simply unbuckled the chin strap and took helmet and all, settling it onto his own head. When he got the binocular eye cups into position, he was stunned by the image they revealed.

"Oh, I like these," he murmured, realizing only as the words came out that his teeth were chattering. In his excitement, he'd momentarily forgotten the cold.

The view from the NODs was like something from a video game. The resolution was much better than anything he had ever used during his time in the military, but more than that, the imagery appeared to be computer enhanced, presenting a much more sharply defined picture of the world around him. The corpse on the snow at his feet was outlined in a tracery of golden light, as was the hasty decoy he'd set up. The device was a quantum leap forward in night vision technology. The significance of this was not lost on Matthew Redd.

The men who had come to kill him were equipped with gear that, to the best of his knowledge, wasn't even in wide use with the military. These weren't just run-of-the-mill private military contractors. They were connected.

He stared down at the body, debating whether to appropriate the man's camouflage shell and weapon, but decided against it. He had already spent too much time on the X, and if the shooter's buddies didn't already know what had happened to him, they would surely come looking soon.

Instead, he wrestled the body around the roots of the windfall, positioning him about where he'd staged the decoy, and then, as an added measure, draped the Carhartt jacket over the dead man's shoulders. Then he started looking for a better hiding spot.

He settled in behind a thick tree trunk about forty yards away, with a good line of sight to his decoy. Crouched down so as not to silhouette himself, he watched and waited as incoming fire continued to shatter the forest canopy.

He did not have to wait long. Two more figures appeared in the display of his NODs, outlined in yellow tracery. He figured they were at least a hundred yards out—too far, he thought, to have spotted his decoy, but obviously following the tracks he had left earlier. They moved tactically, one holding position behind a tree trunk, covering the other's advance, and then switching roles, leapfrogging forward.

Redd let them get closer. He needed them closer. A lot closer.

He saw the exact moment when one of them spotted the decoy. They reacted exactly as he had hoped they would, hastily shrinking behind the nearest cover before edging out for a second look. That was when he struck.

He'd set aside the hunting rifle in favor of his FBI-issued MP5SD6. The submachine gun wasn't as accurate at that range as the rifle, nor did it possess the stopping power of either of his other weapon choices, but it did possess one attribute that would give him an advantage against multiple targets: an integrated suppressor that would reduce both the sound of the report and the muzzle flash, making it much harder for the assaulters to fix his position.

As soon as one of the men revealed himself, Redd put the H&K's sights directly onto his NODs and squeezed the trigger. The sub-gun, set to three-round burst, had virtually no recoil or rise, and with the suppressor, the noise of the bolt cycling sounded louder to Redd than the report. A spray of bright droplets appeared in the air around the target's head—hot blood, glowing almost white in the display of Redd's NODs.

He shifted the sub-gun to the spot where the other man was just emerging into view, to all appearances unaware of what had just happened to his comrade. Redd cut him down with another three-round burst.

But as the man dropped, Redd glimpsed a bright flash in the far distance and saw a brilliant shaft of coherent light stab through the darkness, seemingly aimed right at him. He barely had time to throw himself down behind the tree before a storm of bullets tore into the trunk right above him. Even so, he felt a hard slap on his left biceps and knew that one of the rounds had grazed him.

He cursed himself for making a rookie mistake. He'd been so focused on the two close targets that he'd lost situational awareness, failing to even consider that there might be other enemy shooters closing in on him. It was, thankfully, a mistake he would survive to learn from, but first, he had to get moving again.

A quick look showed a ragged tear in the sleeve of his flannel shirt, the fabric already damp with a bright stain of spreading blood. He tore the hole open wider, revealing a bloody furrow that, thankfully, hadn't been plowed too deep. He worked the arm back and forth, flexing his fingers, and was relieved that it still seemed to be fully functioning. There wasn't even any pain, though he suspected that would soon change.

There wasn't time to bandage the wound, so he did the next best thing, shoving a handful of snow into the sleeve to hopefully slow the bleeding. Then as soon as the incoming fusillade stopped, he rolled away from the trunk, sprang to his feet, and bolted deeper into the woods.

Several more reports chased after him, tree trunks exploding into splinters all around, but none found their mark. When he'd gone about fifty yards, he threw himself behind another trunk where he rolled into a prone shooting position and waited for the enemy to come to him.

Abruptly, all shooting stopped, both in the woods and below. Evidently the hunters had determined that suppressive fire wasn't doing them any good and had decided to change up their tactics.

An almost eerie silence descended on the woods. Redd focused on his breathing, trying to quiet the runaway jackhammer of his heartbeat. He'd scratched three more of the would-be killers, but how many were left? Kline had told him to expect at least a dozen, and that number more or less squared with the number of snowmobiles they'd brought into the mountains. With at least five confirmed dead, he might still be facing somewhere between seven and nine more. Maybe ten.

Redd groaned. He'd barely made a dent in the odds.

But then he shook his head, remembering a bit of sage advice someone . . . probably J. B. . . . had told him years before—something about eating an elephant one bite at a time. He didn't need to kill all the men after him at once; he just needed to kill one or two, and then one or two more, until there were none left.

That was how he was going to beat them.

He counted to ten, then risked a peek out from behind cover. He was only exposed for a fraction of a second, but it was long enough to make out a pair of shooters, just twenty yards away. It was also long enough for them to see him.

A storm of gunfire stripped the bark from the tree above him, but this time he did not break and run. Instead, he rolled to the left, away from the tree, and came up again, this time with the extended stock of the H&K snugged into his shoulder and the business end of the weapon aimed at the spot where he thought one of the shooters was standing. His estimation was off by a mere degree or two, easily corrected, and he squeezed the trigger.

As he dropped down again, Redd glimpsed the man pitching backward, his carbine spraying one last burst straight up into the forest canopy. Even as the other man shifted his aim, Redd was rolling again, two rotations, and then he popped back up and loosed three more rounds directly into the shooter's face.

Then all was quiet again.

Scratch two more, thought Redd. *One bite at a time.*

TWENTY-SEVEN

Colin Kilmeade was on the verge of panic. "Javelin Six, report."

No reply. He glanced at his tablet, checking the latest imagery from the drone. Ordinarily, the UAV's infrared camera was capable of "seeing" through forest canopy, but the addition of snow on the branches added a layer of insulation that made penetration difficult. Difficult, but not impossible. The feed presently showed six infrared signatures large enough to be human beings, scattered throughout the woods. None were moving. Five of them were the flanking element he'd sent ahead. The sixth had to be Matthew Redd. But which one?

"Six? Are you there? Dom? Answer me, buddy."

But Dominic Russo—Javelin Six to his team subordinates—did not answer.

"Jav Five?"

Still nothing.

"Saber Three, do you copy? Somebody talk to me!"

Beside him, Javelin Seven shook his head in disbelief. "They're dead. They're all dead."

"Shut up," snarled Colin. "We don't know that."

Yet despite the knee-jerk denial, Colin *did* know.

Matthew Redd had scragged the flanking element—five men, with the best training and superior equipment, had been done in by a cowboy.

A freaking cowboy. How is this possible? He knew the answer of course. Redd wasn't just a cowboy. He was a former Marine Raider. But even so, one man should not have been able to take down an entire fire team—all of them former tier one operators.

He pounded his fist against his thigh in an impotent display of rage. *I'm going to take his scalp if it's the last thing I do.*

Colin shoved the tablet into a pocket. It wasn't going to be much help in pinpointing Redd's exact location, not until the bodies of his fallen teammates cooled, and maybe not even then. He turned to Javelin Seven. "All right, he knows our playbook, so we're gonna do something he can't possibly expect. Take your shooters up the hill and establish fire positions to the south. Five hundred meters should do it. Then start putting rounds into the trees. But take your cans off first. I want him to hear the shots."

He expected pushback at the command to have the men remove the suppressors from their weapons, but Javelin Seven's objection came from a different quarter. "You want snipers to lay down suppressive fire?"

Colin understood the other man's reticence. Javelin One and Three—the team's snipers—were carrying MK13 Mod 5 bolt-action long rifles with five-round magazines. Using them to lay down suppressive fire would be like using an artist's brush to paint a house—technically possible, but tedious and a gross misuse of a tool designed for precision.

"I don't need suppressive fire. If you have a clean shot, take it, but mostly I just want him looking ahead and to his flanks while I come in from the north and take him from behind."

Seven's look of skepticism only deepened. "You'll be walking into our fire."

"I'll take that chance. And let's stay off comms. He might have captured a radio set, in which case he'll know what's coming. I'll fire three shots one second apart to signal a kill."

"What will you do if you need help?"

"I won't," Colin replied confidently. He nodded up the slope. "Do it."

Javelin Seven cocked his head to the side in a gesture that said, *It's your funeral,* but then pivoted and relayed the orders to his two snipers. Colin didn't linger, but turned and began hiking along the flank of the mountain, moving parallel to the ridge where Matthew Redd was hiding.

When he'd gone a good five hundred yards, he turned into the slope and began climbing. With his snowshoes, he was able to stomp it down into a temporary stairway that held his weight better than the loose scree underneath. Even so, it was a time-consuming process, and he hadn't made it halfway when he heard the report of a rifle. One of the Javelin snipers was in position and firing his weapon into the forest as directed. More shots followed, and while Colin couldn't say with any certainty, he thought there were more than just two rifles being fired, and some of the shots sounded like they were coming from somewhere a lot closer to his current position. Was that Redd, shooting back at the snipers?

Colin quickened his pace, sacrificing stealth for speed, scrambling up the slope without bothering to create stable footholds. As long as Redd was busy trading shots with the Javelin marksmen, Colin could get into position and come up from behind him, but he had to do it quickly, before Redd figured out what was really going on.

Once under cover of the trees, Colin paused, looking and listening, trying to fix Redd's position. After a few seconds, something cracked through the air overhead, rustling branches, followed a fraction of a second later by the boom of a report. That, he knew, was one of the Javelin sniper rifles, its bullet traveling faster than the sound of the shot. A few moments later, there was another report, louder and closer.

That's him, Colin thought.

He put the distance to within a hundred yards, though with the dense tree cover, it might have been less.

Colin took out his tablet and checked the drone feed again. He easily found himself in the display, as well as several of the other IR signatures. Some of these were dimmer than the others—these were almost certainly the bodies of his teammates, already starting to cool now that their spark of life had been extinguished. The one about eighty yards to the southeast of his position, right on the edge of a clearing, was burning a lot brighter. That had to be Redd. Farther along the ridge, to the south, three distinct man-shapes were in the open—Javelin Seven and the two snipers.

Using the tablet like a map, Colin moved east, until he was due north of Redd's position, then began closing the distance. He moved from tree to tree, using the boughs as cover just in case Redd somehow detected his approach, but his caution proved unnecessary. Redd's attention was, to all appearances, fixed on the snipers who were still trading shots with him. Watching the feed, he realized that Redd's position wasn't static. After each shot, the bright blob marking his position would move, sometimes disappearing from view, only to reappear twenty or thirty yards away.

He's smart, thought Colin. *He knows better than to shoot twice from the same spot. But he doesn't know that I can see him no matter where he goes.*

There was another report, very loud and very close, and then a second later, something zipped through the trees over his head, followed a moment later by a single distant report. Colin waited, expecting to hear another, but there was only a long, ominous silence.

Had Redd killed one of the Javelin snipers?

Colin clenched his fists in impotent rage, vowing again to make Matthew Redd's death memorable.

Then he glimpsed something moving through the trees, a mere twenty yards away. Slowly, Colin leaned back, keeping a pine bough between himself and the figure, who moved in a fast walk, staying low, head clearly on a swivel.

It was Redd—had to be.

From his oblique angle, Colin could see that Redd was wearing a tactical helmet identical to his own, taken, no doubt, from one of the fallen members of Javelin Team, and no doubt still equipped with a set of ENVG-Bs. That at least partially explained how Redd had so effectively turned the tables on the men hunting him.

After moving another ten yards, Redd flopped down on the snow, his body positioned perpendicular to the tree line, facing the clearing, and unwittingly showing Colin his back.

Colin did not hesitate. He would not get a better chance than this to finish Redd once and for all, but he also knew he would only have a few seconds to act before Redd was up and moving again. He brought his M4 up, aiming it at a point that was just about between Redd's shoulder blades, and then activated the PEQ-15.

It was the first mistake he'd made. In his haste to end Redd's rampage, he'd forgotten that Redd's captured NODs meant he could see the laser too. It shouldn't have mattered, not with the beam pointed at Redd's back, but the device must have leaked a few errant protons or cast enough ambient infrared light to throw a shadow on the snow. Whatever it was, Redd saw it and reacted immediately, rolling aside before Colin could pull the trigger.

Even so, Colin still had the drop on him. Redd, evidently realizing that he was beaten, didn't even try to bring his weapon—a long rifle—up in his own defense. He just lay there on his back, like a lamb on the altar, waiting for the sacrificial knife.

Colin should have pulled the trigger right then. He was close enough that a couple bursts from the M4 would have nearly cut Redd in half. But something about Redd's helplessness, after nearly annihilating Colin's entire team, stayed his hand.

He wanted to savor this victory, and he wanted Redd to die knowing that he was beaten.

"You lose, cowboy," Colin Kilmeade snarled.

It was his second mistake.

TWENTY-EIGHT

In the instant that the gunman opened his mouth to speak, Redd moved.

With his left hand, he swatted a handful of snow in the other man's direction and in the same motion rolled to the right, making himself a moving target. The gunman reacted as if the spray of snowflakes were droplets of acid, flinching away, the bright shaft of his laser sweeping up and away from Redd, who then did what he hoped was something completely unexpected.

Instead of scrambling for cover behind the nearest tree, Redd launched himself at the gunman. He stayed low, like a football lineman coming off the scrimmage, all too aware of the carbine in the man's hands. The muzzle of the weapon shifted this way and that as his foe overcame his initial reflex reaction and began desperately trying to reacquire Redd as a target, but by coming in low, Redd managed to stay just one step ahead of the shooter, who couldn't depress his aimpoint fast enough to track him.

Before the man could realize that he needed to back away, Redd was inside the reach of the weapon. He immediately seized hold of the M4's barrel with his left hand, thrusting it up and away, even as he rammed his right shoulder into the man's solar plexus. The man's breath was driven from his lungs with a satisfying *oomph*, and then both of them went sprawling into the snow.

Maintaining his hold on the carbine, Redd quickly scrambled up and straddled the gunman's chest, taking the mount position, and then with both hands, thrust the weapon sideways, across its owner's body, ramming it up crosswise over the man's throat. Only then did the man overcome his surprise to begin offering desperate resistance.

Predictably, he tried to push the carbine away, gripping the heat shield and upper receiver with both hands, but Redd just locked his elbows out and bore down harder.

As if finally realizing how much danger he was in, Redd's opponent began to thrash beneath him. Anticipating his moves like a champion bull rider, Redd shifted his body to absorb each jerk without easing the pressure one bit. Frantic, the man's twisting became increasingly violent, quickly reaching a frenzied climax until, evidently spent, his hands slipped away from the gun across his throat, falling aside as anoxia sapped him of the energy and will to keep fighting.

Redd, who thought the man had succumbed a little too quickly, continued pressing the carbine against the man's throat just in case the apparent surrender was a ruse. Still, he was a fraction of a second too slow when the man's right arm pistoned up from waist level to thrust up into Redd's exposed chest.

A line of fire seared across Redd's ribs. Letting out an enraged howl, he thrust himself away from his not-quite-vanquished enemy. The repositioning had less to do with the pain he felt and more to do with the fact that the man was already attempting a backslash with the black-powder-coated five-inch blade of a combat knife.

As he scrambled backward, slipping on the snow and falling flat on his back, Redd saw bright drops of his own hot blood flying away, turning black as they splashed down on the frozen landscape. Redd quickly got his feet back under him, only to see his foe, now also back on his feet, carving the air between them, slashing back and forth in a flurry of cuts designed more to intimidate than to wound.

Redd could feel his shirt already growing damp and sticky as blood wept from the slash wound. The cut didn't feel very deep but burned like a stripe of hellfire. He was pretty sure the blade had only sliced across his ribs without penetrating any deeper—a flesh wound, just like the bullet that grazed him, but it was a bleeder, and that was going to be a problem if he didn't take the time to do something about it.

Redd needed to end the fight, and fast.

Ignoring the pain, he made a grab for the Ruger holstered on his hip, but the moment he did, his opponent dropped into a fighter's stance, raising his empty left hand up, ready to block any incoming attack and dropping his knife hand down to waist level. Then, striking quick as lightning in spite of the cumbersome snowshoes strapped to his feet, the man darted forward, stabbing the knife toward Redd's chest.

Knowing he would never break leather in time, Redd forgot about going for the gun and instead pivoted away from the knife thrust, sweeping up with his left forearm to knock the man's knife hand away, simultaneously punching out with his right fist, aiming for the man's NODs. His rising arm block failed to make contact, however, and his punch merely glanced off the side of the man's ballistic helmet.

Another line of fire seared across his left arm, the knife blade flinging away more bright droplets of his blood.

Redd stumbled back again, unable to believe how quickly the man had moved . . . was moving again, pressing another stab-and-slash attack.

The knife speared out, a striking prairie rattler, dripping Redd's own blood instead of venom, but no less deadly. Redd managed to throw himself out of the way, narrowly missing the blade as it carved a serpentine pattern in the space he had occupied only a second earlier. Then the man was attacking again, darting in so quickly that Redd had no time to think and barely enough to react.

Blood, glowing like ichor, continued to flow from Redd's veins, spraying out in bright drops, mingling with the falling snowflakes that swirled around the two combatants. Redd ducked and managed to dodge another attack, and then another. On the third swipe, he was a fraction of a second too slow. The tip of the knife caught his chest, penetrating his flannel shirt right above the left pocket, gouging deep into his pectoral muscle before raking sideways, carving out another fiery furrow as the man drew the blade back for yet another attack. The knife lashed out at Redd again and again, and each time Redd barely managed to twist away.

The cuts, relatively minor though they were, were taking a cumulative toll. He was losing blood, and that, combined with the cold, was sapping his energy reserves. He was slowing down, losing his edge, right when he needed it the most. His foe, on the other hand, seemed to be getting faster and stronger with each attack. Redd knew that if the fight went on much longer, he would be done for.

Futile though he knew it was, Redd made another grab for the Ruger. His opponent did not hesitate to attack, just as Redd knew he would. This time, as the blade arrowed toward him, Redd did not try to dodge. Instead, he stood his ground, turning his torso slightly so that the blade sliced across his chest rather than penetrating, and as the man's momentum carried him forward, Redd wrapped his left arm around the man's right, bringing his right arm around to hug the man close to him. Then Redd thrust his head forward, smashing the top of his recently acquired ballistic helmet into the other man's face or, more precisely, into his night vision goggles.

Although the foam lining system of the helmet was specifically designed to absorb high-energy impact events, Redd felt the crash reverberate all the way to his spine. It was worth it though, because the headbutt achieved its desired purpose, ramming the other man's NODs into his face with such force that the night vision device sheared away from its swivel mount and fell away to reveal a bloodied face and dazed but frantic unseeing eyes.

Redd let go of the man, shoving him away, mindful of the blood-slick blade he still gripped in his right hand. The man resumed his fighting pose, slashing the air in front of him to discourage another attack, but Redd could see the fear in his eyes as they darted back and forth, searching the darkness for any sign of his enemy.

The man stabbed out blindly with the blade, drew back, and stabbed again, but his random attacks came nowhere near Redd, who was retreating step by slow step, removing himself from the man's reach.

"Come on!" snarled the man. "You think you can take me, cowboy?"

Redd knew that if he replied to the taunt, the man might be able to home in on the sound of his voice, so he waited until the Ruger was in hand to answer.

"Yup," Redd said as he brought the Ruger up and sighted his target. He squeezed the trigger once, sending a round into the bridge of the man's nose, ending the fight once and for all.

But even as the echoes of the shot died away, Redd suddenly felt light-headed. *I'm bleeding out,* he thought.

Worse, he had no idea what he might be able to do to save himself.

Redd struggled to return the Ruger to its holster. After a few failed attempts, the big gun slipped from his grasp and fell into the snow. When he bent down to pick it up, a wave of vertigo crashed over him. He flailed his arms, trying in vain to regain his balance, and then pitched backward, sprawling on his back in the snow.

Darkness crowded his vision. The NODs, no longer serving any useful purpose, felt oppressive and unnatural against his face. He shoved them aside, then unbuckled the helmet's chin strap and flung it away. Fat snowflakes alighted on his face like tiny frozen butterflies.

With the little remaining energy he had left, he tipped his head up and turned it slightly to the side. He could see the snow around him, stained a dark shade of crimson. He thought maybe the bleeding from his wounds was slowing because of the frigid temperatures.

That, he thought, *or I'm almost out of blood.*

He was no longer cold. That wave had already come and passed. Now he was only numb. Numb to the bone-chilling temperatures. Numb to the wetness of the snow melting under him. Numb to the pain of the wounds from which his blood still oozed.

All around him, snowflakes fell from the heavens—brilliant ice crystals, no two the same. It was beautiful, he thought. Peaceful, even.

He could feel the life draining out of him, knew that this was the end, yet all he could think about was his family.

Emily . . . Junior . . .

They were safe, and that was all that mattered. He had won. One bite at a time, he'd eaten the elephant, killed the men who had come to kill him. But Redd felt no sense of victory. Only disappointment that he would never hold his wife or child again, never get another chance to tell them he loved them.

I'm sorry, Em. I'm so sorry . . .

Then he heard voices and remembered the snipers he had engaged across the clearing. His declaration of victory had been premature.

This is going to be hard on Junior.

"Over here!" someone shouted. "We've got him now!"

Please, Redd prayed, *keep my family safe.*

A darkness that had nothing to do with the night swelled about him as he searched for the killers stalking toward him. One of them was close. He could hear the crunch of snow compacting under snowshoes.

"Found him!" The voice was close; the man might have been standing over him. A moment later he added, "He might already be dead."

"Make sure of it!" came another voice, not quite as near but still too close.

Redd fought to open his eyes one last time. He could see the outline of both men now, one holding a gun that was pointed at his head.

This is it, he told himself.

Redd was determined to look his killer in the eyes, but the man with the gun had turned away, looking at . . .

At what?

The haze grew thicker. Redd squinted through leaden eyelids, looked past the gunman and saw . . .

There!

A black shape was moving through the snow. It was coming toward him. No, toward the gunman, moving fast.

Redd felt a thin smile form across his face.

Who's a good boy?

Then there was only darkness.

TWENTY-NINE

SOUTHAMPTON, NEW YORK

Aaron Decker expected to find a closed security gate and maybe even a security guard at the entrance to the palatial estate that was the primary residence of the world's third-richest man. What he had not expected was a police presence.

When he saw the jumble of patrol vehicles and unmarked cars lining the drive, most inside the gate but a few outside, one of them parked diagonally across the paved single lane to act as a secondary barrier, Decker's first thought was, *They're here for me.*

It was a rare moment of apprehension, but the possibility that the police were there to intercept him was something he could not discount. The close brush with death in Oklahoma City had rattled him more than he cared to admit. Despite every precaution taken by Kline and at least three federal agencies, the killers had gotten inside the secure area, attacking with overwhelming force and firepower. The only plausible explanation was that the assaulting force had some kind of inside connection, and if that were true, it meant that his mission, despite being a closely held secret between him and Kline, might already be compromised.

But his instincts, which had saved his life more times than he could remember, told him that this was something else, so he stuck to his original plan, turning the rented Ford Transit van into the driveway and continuing toward the blockade as if he had every right in the world to be there.

Gavin Kline often likened Decker to a ghost, citing his uncanny ability to carry out missions—specifically targeted assassinations—without being detected, and often without anyone even realizing that the deaths were any more suspicious than they appeared. However, there was nothing supernatural about how Decker operated. His prodigious success rate was due solely to meticulous intelligence gathering, planning, and attention to detail during the execution phase. He did not move against a target until he knew everything there was to know about the person.

Back in the days of the Global War on Terror, when he had worked with Gavin Kline to hunt down and eliminate known terrorist financiers and facilitators working in Europe, North Africa, and the Middle East—men who could not otherwise be brought to justice—the task had been a challenge. The targets had been borderline paranoid about maintaining secrecy, as any good operator ought to be.

Building target packages for the men Anton Gage had exposed as members of the Twelve, on the other hand, was ridiculously simple. Their lives were a matter of public record. He had easily learned everything there was to know about each of them, right down to where they were at any given moment, and had developed appropriate contingencies for carrying out the execution phase for each of the eleven names on the list.

As he rode the brake to a halt about twenty yards from the patrol car, a uniformed officer got out and approached. Although she walked with a casual air, Decker did not fail to notice that one hand rested on the butt of her holstered service weapon.

He lowered the window and greeted her with a smile. "Amazon delivery," he chirped. "Just need a signature."

She cast a suspicious glance past him, her gaze falling briefly on the small corrugated cardboard box resting on the passenger seat, and then on the stack of boxes of varying size and shape arrayed behind him in the cargo area, before coming back to meet his eyes.

"Can't do that," she said matter-of-factly. "I need you to clear the driveway."

He debated whether to protest or beg the officer to make an exception for him but decided to simply go with it. "I'll just mark it as 'no response.' Can you give me a rough idea when—" he made a show of checking the address label on the box—"ah, Robert Bridger or his designated representative will be available to receive the package?"

The officer stifled a chuckle. "Yeah, I don't think that's going to happen."

"Why's that?" asked Decker, taking a chance that the officer might be willing to share more information.

"Watch the news tonight. You'll figure it out." She thrust her chin back toward the main road. "Move along, please."

Decker shrugged, then put the van in reverse and backed away.

The officer's cryptic hints, combined with the substantial police presence, pointed to an obvious conclusion: Robert Bridger, computer magnate and philanthropist, one of the world's wealthiest individuals, and the man Anton Gage had identified as "One," the leader of the Twelve, was dead under suspicious circumstances.

Decker wondered when it had happened. Probably sometime during the night, while he had been in the air, riding a red-eye from DFW. Will Rogers International had been so backed up following the attack on the JPATS transport that he'd elected to make the three-hour drive to Dallas in order to get a flight out.

If he had just waited a day, he could have saved himself the trip.

He should have counted himself lucky. After all, his sole purpose in flying to New York and making the two-hour drive out onto Long Island had been to end Bridger's life, not to mention his murderous ambitions, and the fact that someone had already taken care of it meant that he could move on to the next name on the list. But Aaron Decker didn't believe in coincidences.

Bridger's death could only mean one of two things: either the billionaire had killed himself, perhaps fearful of what would happen when his complicity in the genocidal plots of the Twelve was made public, or someone else had killed him. The latter seemed more likely, especially since the Twelve's assassins had already plugged the leak Anton Gage had created, but the question of motive remained unanswered.

Decker, however, had a theory.

Bridger, for all his wealth, had always struck Decker as possessing a rather weak character. He was—or rather had been—pale and soft in appearance, nurturing a public image that looked like someone sent over from central casting to play the part of a computer nerd. A little over a year out from an acrimonious divorce after more than twenty years of marriage, exposed as—surprise—an adulterer, he seemed like someone who would be quick to make a deal to save his own skin, and that was reason enough for one of the other members of the Twelve to want to preemptively silence him.

If this theory was correct, the Twelve might be on the verge of destroying themselves without any assistance from him. And while a civil war within the group might seem like a net-positive development, in the near term, it would put the remaining ten men on a defensive footing, which would make Decker's mission that much more difficult to accomplish. Moreover, the ultimate result of an internal purge would likely be the elevation of the most ruthless member to a position of unassailable power. In fact, the timing of Bridger's death, coming as it did on the heels of Gage's assassination, suggested that both events were directed by the same strong hand.

As he rolled down the narrow, tree-lined suburban streets of Southampton, eventually finding his way back onto State Route 27, heading back toward the city, Decker mentally reviewed his target list, reprioritizing based on the likelihood of each member to be the presumptive alpha, and settled on the man Anton Gage had designated "Eight"—one Holton Fish.

Fish, much like Gage himself, had built his fortune on a foundation of celebrity rather than market savvy. His management style was ruthless and exploitative. His public persona was a caricature of masculinity that inexplicably had earned him a cultish following on social media platforms, particularly those favored by adolescent males. Despite leaving a string of failed businesses and bankruptcies in his wake, he had somehow acquired a reputation for being a brilliant innovator, and in an age when perception was reality, his net worth continued to grow despite ongoing problems with his brand.

His association with the Twelve had always been problematic as he had never shown any indications of being an ideologue. According to Gage, Fish had joined the cabal more out of a desire for prestige than to save the world. To Decker's way of thinking, Fish was the man most likely to want to seize control of the Twelve by any means necessary, and that moved him to the top of the list.

Fish owned four homes, two of them outside the United States, but the latest intel put him at his beach house in Malibu, California. Decker could be back at JFK Airport before noon. Seven hours in the air to Los Angeles, but with the time difference, it would only be late afternoon when he arrived, leaving him plenty of daylight to reconnoiter the target.

If Fish was behind both the internal purge and the attack in Oklahoma City, he would probably be on a defensive footing, which would pose a challenge to Decker, but not an insurmountable one.

Not for a ghost.

THIRTY

MONTANA

Stephanie Treadway had seen snow before, lots of times in fact, but as she picked up the keys for her rental car—a Ford Edge, which the agent at the Hertz desk at Bozeman Yellowstone International assured her handled great in the snow— it occurred to her that she had somehow managed to avoid ever driving in it. Fortunately, the main roads had all been plowed and graveled, and the SUV, equipped with standard all-wheel drive, antilock brakes, and all-weather tires, performed as promised.

She drove cautiously, staying a good ten to fifteen miles per hour under the posted speed limit, which seemed like the smart thing to do. It also gave her plenty of time to take in the picturesque beauty that surrounded her, even if she wasn't really in the right mindset to appreciate it.

She was still haunted by the events of the previous day. The attack on the Con Air flight and the loss of several fellow FBI agents—many of them close friends—not to mention her proximity to the IED blast had taken both an emotional and a physical toll. The detonation had knocked her off her feet, but she'd come away with only some bruises and sore muscles. Better off than Kline, and a lot better than the rest of his team.

By all rights, after a trauma like that, she should have taken a couple days' leave at a minimum, but there hadn't been a chance to slow down even a little. On Kline's orders, she had driven up to Wichita to avoid the air traffic snarl in Oklahoma City and then flown up to Bozeman, by way of Denver, catching the last flight of the day.

She had arrived at Bozeman Yellowstone International at half past nine in the evening—not too late, she had thought, to make the forty-five-minute drive up to Wellington—only to discover that the western half of the state was experiencing the worst snowstorm in recent memory and that travel under such conditions was not advisable. As urgent as her mission was, she reasoned that she wouldn't be much help to Matthew Redd if she drove her car off the side of the road and got buried in a snow drift, so she booked a room at the Comfort Suites near the airport to pass the night, hoping to get an early start the next morning if conditions permitted.

Yet as tired as she was, sleep had eluded her. Her mind kept replaying the final moments before the blast. Decker frantically trying to explain the danger to Kline . . . Kline finally figuring it out . . . Their mad dash to get out of the blast zone. And then, the desperate search to find survivors amid the carnage. The worst part, though, was the gap—the minutes before, during, and after the explosion that were simply gone, permanently erased, shaken from her memory like the image on an Etch A Sketch.

It was not the first time something like that had happened to her.

Six years earlier, working for a different alphabet-soup government agency, she'd experienced a similar close call during a visit to a forward operating base in Helmand Province, Afghanistan. A bomb, hidden aboard a truck driven by a turncoat Afghan National Army soldier, had detonated inside the compound, killing half a dozen Afghan recruits, two US Special Forces operators, a CIA chief-of-station, an Afghan interpreter, and the senior Taliban leader who had been taken into custody less than twenty-four hours earlier.

Treadway had no memory of that explosion either. All she knew was that one moment, she had been standing a few feet away from her boss, interrogating the detainee, and the next, she was in the med tent, dazed, bruised, but miraculously alive. During the months of physical and psychological rehabilitation that had followed, that period of lost time had been what troubled her the most. At times she seriously wondered if she had fallen through the looking glass—been transported into a parallel reality where the people she had known and worked with simply didn't exist.

Although she'd eventually been cleared to return to active service, the memory—or rather the absence of the memory—had continued to gnaw at her soul. Fearful that she'd lost her nerve, a potentially fatal condition for an intelligence officer, she'd backed away from a couple highly coveted field postings and before long had found herself deskbound. She had been on the verge of quitting altogether when a chance encounter with Gavin Kline—who had been the FBI point of contact in the Joint Terrorism Task Force to which she had been relegated—had convinced her to come down from the ledge. After a single conversation with her, Kline had declared that what she really needed was a win, something to bolster her confidence, and he made it his personal mission to make sure she got one. And eventually, they did. Together, they wrapped up a nascent ISIS terrorist cell operating in upstate New York. Not long thereafter, he'd convinced her to submit her application to the Bureau.

At first she had assumed that Kline saw her as the child he had never had, but when she learned that Kline actually had a son—Matthew Redd—she had grasped his true motive. By mentoring her, Kline was trying to atone for being absent from Redd's life. For her part, Treadway *did* think of Kline as a father figure, even though she was close to both her father and her stepfather.

And now he was the one who had almost been erased from existence.

A bottle of pinot grigio was her customary prescription for banishing the darkness, but she knew she would need a clear head in the morning, so she endured the sleepless hours, rising well before dawn and downing several cups of hotel room coffee before venturing out into the cold.

The weather was something she had not anticipated when making her travel arrangements. She did not have any cold weather clothes in her go bag, just her blue FBI windbreaker, which was better than nothing but not nearly enough to keep her warm with the temperatures well below freezing. She had arrived in Bozeman too late to go shopping and was leaving well before any of the shops opened. The SUV's heater was working just fine, as were the heated seats, so she was warm enough during the drive but didn't like her chances of finding adequate winter clothing in Wellington.

She arrived at the Stillwater County courthouse a little past 7 a.m. and was relieved to see that the building was already open, the concrete walk leading up to the sheriff's department entrance shoveled and deiced. This was not her first visit to the sheriff's office, but it had been a couple years. A smile touched her lips when she saw the gold lettering on the door indicating that Stuart Blackwood was still Wellington's top cop. Treadway and Blackwood had history.

During her last visit to Wellington, while driving together on a mountain road north of town, a member of a different hit team hunting Matthew Redd had shot up Blackwood's patrol vehicle. Blackwood had caught a bullet, but when the killers had moved in to finish the job, Treadway had gotten the drop on them, saving his life. Little things like that had a way of creating a lasting bond between two people, especially in law enforcement.

When she presented herself to the receptionist, flashing her credentials, the tired-looking woman eyed her suspiciously, showing not a hint of recognition, but mere moments after announcing her over the intercom, Sheriff Blackwood rushed from his office, his gravelly voice booming out her name. "Special Agent Treadway! To what do I owe the pleasure?"

She thought he sounded genuinely happy to see her, but before she could answer, his face suddenly morphed into a look of suspicion. "This wouldn't by any chance be concerning Matthew Redd, now would it?"

The question was not as prescient as it might have seemed. Blackwood was aware of Redd's connection to the FBI, so there was a better than even chance that if an FBI special agent came to town, it probably involved Redd. But Treadway sensed something else behind Blackwood's remark.

"What makes you ask that?" she said, probing.

Blackwood nodded. "I figured as much. I take it Emily filled you in on what's been going on?"

"Emily?"

Blackwood frowned. "Mrs. Redd. I assumed that she called you."

Treadway shook her head. "I haven't spoken to her or Matt. I'm here at the direction of EAD Kline. But you're right in thinking this concerns Redd. We've become aware of a threat to him. A threat that's coming here, to your county."

Blackwood crossed his arms over his chest. "That's what Emily said, and I'll tell you what I told her." He sighed. "I have explicit orders to steer clear of Matthew Redd."

Treadway was momentarily dumbstruck. Finally, she managed to ask, "Orders from who?"

"SAC Shores from the Helena field office of Homeland Security Investigations. They've sent a team of agents to bring Redd in for questioning. I'm afraid that's all they told me. That, and that I should stay out of their way."

Homeland Security again, thought Treadway.

Kline had briefed her the previous night concerning his working theory that the attack in Oklahoma City had been carried out by men posing as a special operations team from the Department of Homeland Security. He was still in Oklahoma, trying to pick up the trail of the impostors.

"Someone lied to you, Sheriff. DHS has nothing to do with this."

Blackwood shook his head. "I know Martin Shores. He's legit."

"Okay. Then someone lied to *him*. The people behind this are the same ones who carried out an attack in Oklahoma City, and they did it by posing as HSI agents. It sounds like they're going to try doing the same thing here."

Blackwood narrowed his eyes at her. "You can confirm that?"

"I can." She wasn't exactly sure how just yet but thought her certitude would suffice to convince the sheriff.

Blackwood's frown deepened and he breathed a curse. "So what you're telling me is that a gang of killers is hunting Matthew Redd in my county right now?"

"That's about the size of it."

Blackwood took out his phone and, after a moment of scrolling, put it to his ear. He listened for nearly a minute, evidently without making contact, then lowered the phone and tried again with the same results. "They aren't picking up. Not Matt or Emily." Concern spread across his face. "I hope we're not too late."

Treadway hoped so too but didn't say it. "Matt would know to ditch his phone. He doesn't like anyone tracking him, let alone a hit team. I'm sure he told his wife to get rid of hers too."

Blackwood pursed his lips together in thought. "Emily said that Matthew was going to head up into the mountains. Why would he do that?"

"Fieldcraft." It made perfect sense. Treadway knew that out in the wilderness, Redd would hold the advantage because he knew the land. The men pursuing him wouldn't. He was severely outnumbered, but taking the fight into the wild, especially in the current elements, was an equalizer.

Smart. If he doesn't freeze to death.

"Fieldcraft," repeated Blackwood. "Meaning?"

"Meaning it won't be easy for a bunch of out-of-towners to track him down up there. Not impossible, but it should buy him some time."

Blackwood blinked at the ceiling. After several seconds, he turned to Treadway. "Are we sure they're not just trying to bring him in for some sort of questioning? Maybe there's some kind of misunderstanding here or somethin'."

Treadway held his gaze. "Sheriff, these men blew up a federal prison transport and killed over a dozen federal agents. We need to get out there and find Matt before they do."

"In *this*?" Blackwood waved an arm toward the window, where powerful wind gusts blew flurries of snow in a circulation motion. "Even if I wanted to . . . and I *do* want to help Matthew . . . my hands are tied until the storm passes. Nobody has the resources to launch a manhunt right now."

"These men have resources you can't imagine, and they're going to throw everything they've got into hunting Redd down. And if they do find him, it won't be to drag him in for questioning."

"Whelp." Blackwood sagged as if she'd just let the air out of him. He shook his head. "Then heaven help him. Because until this storm passes by, I don't think anyone else can."

THIRTY-ONE

Cormac Kilmeade usually enjoyed watching people die. It wasn't that he derived sadistic pleasure from seeing someone breathe their last—he wasn't a psychopath. What he felt was a sense of satisfaction. In his profession, the dying and dead he had occasion to observe were invariably targets whom he had just dispatched, missions he had accomplished.

Today, however, he just wasn't feeling it.

Sitting in a Midtown Starbucks, with a Caffè Americano in one hand and an iPad in the other, Kilmeade watched, via live video from a microdrone hovering high overhead, the scene unfolding two blocks away. A pair of EMTs were working furiously to revive the man who had, only a few minutes earlier, keeled over mere steps from the entrance to the office building that housed his uber-successful capital management firm. Their efforts would prove futile. The man was already gone. The fatal dose of suxamethonium chloride—a powerful paralytic agent—which Kilmeade had surreptitiously injected in the man's buttocks during a brush pass as the man got out of his limousine, had already effectively killed him.

Another operation had gone like clockwork, another name had been crossed off the Praetorian's list, and yet Kilmeade felt only deep anxiety. His sense of dread had nothing to do with the current assignment. Rather it was his brother's mission in Montana that was the source of his inner turmoil.

Twelve hours earlier, Colin had called in to report that he'd hit a snag. The target had somehow been forewarned and was proving harder to run to ground than expected. Cormac got the impression that his brother was downplaying the seriousness of the situation, probably out of a sense of embarrassment that things hadn't gone according to plan, but he had not pressed for a more thorough situation report, preferring to let his brother deal with the problem in his own way.

Early that morning, however, not long after crossing off another name on the list out on Long Island, Cormac had suddenly been overcome with a deep sense of foreboding, a completely irrational belief that something had gone terribly wrong in Montana.

He knew better, of course. Colin had superior numbers and firepower, not to mention a suite of tracking tools at his disposal, so there was no earthly way that Matthew Redd would escape with his life. Yet the feeling did not go away.

And now Colin was overdue for a scheduled check-in.

Cormac knew he should try to establish contact with his brother. That was standard operating procedure. More than that, he desperately wanted to call, just to make sure that everything was okay. But doing so would be tantamount to a vote of no confidence in Colin's leadership abilities.

Colin Kilmeade suffered from a completely irrational inferiority complex, constantly comparing himself to his brother and always coming up just a little short in his own estimation. Any effort on Cormac's part to dispel this notion always backfired, making the ever-so-slightly younger twin feel even more diminished. Cormac had long ago determined that it was better to let Colin find his own way to shine or, in this instance, solve whatever problems had arisen with the mission.

But SOP was SOP. Colin would just have to get over it.

Kilmeade tapped a button on the screen of the iPad, ending the feed from the drone and recalling it automatically to base, which in this instance was the rooftop of the same building that housed the Starbucks. Then he took out his new burner phone, but before he could begin entering Colin's number, the device began vibrating in his hand.

The number displayed on the ID was not Colin's, but it was from one of the phones issued to Saber Team. Kilmeade's first reaction was relief, but that quickly gave way to another bout of apprehension.

Why wasn't Colin making the call?

He accepted the call and said, "Go for Dagger Six."

"Saber Two here. I'm . . . uh . . . calling because . . . uh—"

"Spit it out," growled Kilmeade. "Why are you calling me? And why hasn't your Six called in?"

The latter was all that Kilmeade really cared about.

"Sir, that's actually why I'm calling you. I've lost contact with him."

A flush of adrenaline dumped into Kilmeade's veins.

"It's probably just the mountains," Saber Two went on. "Cell coverage is pretty sketchy up where they're operating."

Kilmeade seized on this idea like a lifeline. Of course, cellular coverage would be sparse in Montana. The state was mostly wilderness, and besides, what did a bunch of dumb cowboys need with 5G connectivity?

But what was Colin doing in the mountains? Kilmeade unconsciously shook his head. "Start from the beginning. What's been going on? Why is your team split up?"

After a brief hesitation, Saber Two launched into an account of the team's pursuit of Matthew Redd, albeit consciously avoiding any language that might flag the conversation for further review by the authorities and careful not to use any names. Redd was simply "the objective." Things got complicated when Saber Two tried to explain how Redd had managed to single-handedly almost wipe out Saber Team.

The revelation left Kilmeade shaken.

He's just one man. How could this have happened?

How did Colin let this happen?

"Six sent me back with Saber One for medical treatment. I haven't heard from him since. He anticipated making contact with the objective sometime during the night, but I haven't heard from him, and . . . well, to be honest, I'm a little . . . concerned."

So am I, thought Kilmeade, but to the man on the other end of the line, he said, "It's probably like you said. He can't get a signal out. I'm sure he'll make contact as soon as he can."

Not quite able to bring himself to believe this platitude, Kilmeade added, "I'm going to send Arrow Team out there, just in case you all need some additional backup. If Six does make contact, have him call me immediately. I'll call again when Arrow is ready to link up with you."

"Appreciate that, sir," replied Saber Two, sounding immensely relieved. "I'm sure everything's A-okay out there, but . . . like you said, just in case."

"Just in case," echoed Kilmeade as he ended the call.

Colin's got this, he told himself. *He'll call just as soon as he can get a signal through.*

But as he left the café, heading upstairs to retrieve the drone, intent on continuing on to the next name on the Praetorian's list, his sense of foreboding only deepened.

What's going on out there in Montana?

THIRTY-TWO

MONTANA

The skies cleared shortly before dawn, and the sunrise over the mountains was spectacular. The snow-capped peaks glistened against the expanse of azure sky that had earned Montana its nickname. Riding through the snow, following the contours of the valley that wended through the range, Emily Redd chose to interpret the break in the weather as a hopeful sign.

Her original plan—to ride through the night to Matthew's aid—had been frustrated by the storm. The road out of Wellington was impassable for anything but a four-wheel drive, which meant that while Mikey could have driven his truck out to the Boardman spread, and even as far as the fire roads that they intended to follow into the national forest, he could not have done so with a loaded horse trailer in tow. So instead of taking immediate action, she'd spent a long, sleepless night worrying about her husband, all alone in the wilderness.

Nevertheless, the change in the weather allowed her and Mikey to get an early start. Towing a trailer with three of Chuck Boardman's best trail horses, along with all the food, water, and survival gear they could scrounge, they'd headed out before sunrise. The highway and most of the county's main roads had been plowed and sanded, which allowed them to get a lot closer to the mountains than they would have been able to had they set out the previous night. On balance, the delay had not really cost them anything and had probably spared them a great deal of effort and discomfort, but it was hard for Emily to see it that way.

Especially when she hadn't heard from her husband.

The drive passed by in silence, neither of them willing to fill the resulting void with conversation or speculation about Redd's fate. Even though both of them were confident in Redd's ability to endure any hardship, unsupported expressions of hope and optimism would have rung hollow. Instead, by unspoken mutual accord, they elected not to put their hopes or fears into words.

At the turnoff to the fire road, Mikey pulled to the roadside. As soon as he shut the engine off, the cab instantly turned into a refrigerator. The chill seemed to radiate from the window glass. Emily pulled her coat tighter and donned her gloves before opening the door and dropping down into snow that was almost knee-deep. Working together and yet hardly saying a word, they off-loaded the horses, saddling two of them and loading the third with panniers full of food, water, blankets, and anything else they thought Matthew might need. Then, without any further discussion, they started out, riding single file with Mikey in front up the snowbound fire road just as the sun appeared over the tops of the mountains.

Hours passed in relative silence. The only sounds were the crunching of hooves compacting snow and the soft swish as it was brushed out of the way. The snow covering the road was mostly pristine, though as the day wore on, they encountered animal tracks crisscrossing the snowfield. At the top of every hour, Mikey plotted their location on a topographic map of the area, using back azimuth readings to triangulate their exact position. Based on those readings, they were making good time, but their destination—the nearest of several hunting camps where Emily thought Redd might have chosen to take refuge—remained maddeningly distant. While they remained in the valley, the going was relatively easy, but to reach the first of the camps, they would have to climb, and that would slow their pace to a crawl.

Not long after the two o'clock map check, a loud *whump* echoed down the valley. All three of the horses started at the sound, overcome by sudden panic. Emily quickly reined her mount in, but Mikey's efforts to do the same with his were complicated by the fact that he was also tethered to the pack horse. Absent a rider to soothe him, the animal wheeled around and bolted back down the way they'd come, pulling Mikey's horse—and its rider—along with it. Mikey quickly pulled back on the reins, trying to halt his horse, but with the pack animal still trying to drag them both along, Mikey's horse was caught in a tug of war. Reacting to what it perceived to be the more immediate problem, it shook its head, trying to get some slack in the reins, and then reared, trying to shake its rider off. Mikey shifted his weight forward, hugging the animal's neck in a desperate bid to keep from being unhorsed. He managed to stay in the saddle but lost his grip on the reins, and with them, what little control he had possessed. The horse bucked once more, then shot forward, chasing after the pack horse.

Seeing Mikey's distress, Emily brought her mount around and coaxed it to a full gallop, racing after the runaways. Because it was untethered and carrying less of a total load, her horse closed the distance quickly. She came abreast of Mikey, glanced over to see him groping for the reins, which shook and slithered about as the horse moved, and then continued ahead, going after the pack horse. The tether that connected the two animals was short—only a little more than a single horse length—and she drew even with the frightened creature just a few seconds later. As she did, she turned her own horse into the other animal, leaning over as the gap between them narrowed and throwing one arm around the pack horse's neck, pulling back with steady pressure, all the while murmuring to it in a soothing voice.

"Shhh. Calm down now. It's okay."

Whether because of her touch, her voice, or merely her presence, after a few more strides, the horse slowed. As she relaxed her hold on it, easing back into her own saddle, the pack beast shook its head, nickering, and then came to a full stop. Mikey, now once more in control of his own mount, rode up along the opposite side and reined to a halt.

For a long moment, everyone—horses and humans—strove to catch their breath. Finally, Mikey managed to speak. "That sucked." He looked to Emily. "Thanks."

"Don't mention it," replied Emily, her voice a little shaky with leftover adrenaline.

"What was that noise?"

Emily had an idea of the answer but glanced around, searching the slopes for confirmation. Sure enough, off to the southeast, something that looked like a large white cloud—in an otherwise cloudless sky—seemed to be creeping up the flanks of a not-too-distant mountain.

"Avalanche," she finally said aloud. "These are the perfect conditions for one. A couple feet of fresh snow sitting on top of old snowpack and ice. When the sun warms it up enough to start melting, it doesn't take much to start things moving."

Mikey, suddenly looking ill at ease, followed her gaze, then glanced up at the slopes looming directly above them. "Perfect conditions, huh?" He swallowed, then straightened his back, putting on a show of courage. "Well, I guess we'll just have to keep our voices down from here on out."

Emily managed a smile. "Loud noises aren't really an avalanche trigger. That's a myth."

Mikey raised an eyebrow. "No?"

She shook her head. "When the snowpack is ready to let go, it just does. Short of that, it takes something big—like an artillery shell—to get things moving. That's what the Forest Service uses for avalanche management. A shout or even a gunshot won't do it."

Mikey considered this for a moment, then looked at her. "How did you get to be such an expert on avalanches?"

"I had to attend an emergency medicine seminar. Avalanches are a leading cause of death and injury in the Mountain West, so it's something we need to be ready for. The presenter took us through the whole process, from how they happen to what kind of damage they can do."

Mikey nodded slowly. "I guess I'm lucky to have you along. That way, if we get caught in one, you'll know how to save us."

Emily's own smile slipped. "Self-rescue from an avalanche is almost impossible. You're literally buried alive. You can't move. Your arms and legs are pinned, and depending on whether you've got any head space, you run out of air pretty quick. It's not the cold that kills but asphyxia. If you aren't rescued by someone in about fifteen minutes, the chances of survival go down to about twenty percent. Beyond forty-five minutes . . ." She let her voice trail off, realizing that she had probably said too much. "We should be okay if we avoid riding below the steeper grades. The danger zone is on slopes between thirty and forty-five degrees. Steeper than that and the snow doesn't really get a chance to pile up. Less . . . say, twenty-five degrees, you can still have a slide, but it won't get enough momentum to cause a real problem."

"Not that I don't love the doom-and-gloom approach here," he said sarcastically, "but did your seminar talk about what to do if you get caught in one? Aside from just bending over and kissing your own butt goodbye?"

She nodded. "First, don't try to outrun it. You can't. Your best chance is to try to move laterally, parallel to the slide, and try to reach the outer edge where it has less mass and moves slower. But if you do get caught, you're supposed to move your arms and legs like you're trying to swim to the top. If you're about to get completely buried, put your arms over your head—" she crooked her elbows, bracketing her face with her arms—"to create an air pocket."

"Like I'll be able to remember any of that if it happens."

She conceded the point with a rueful smile. "If we're careful . . . and lucky . . . we won't have to find out."

Her tone and manner projected confidence, but deep down she couldn't escape a feeling of dread, not for herself and Mikey, but for Matthew, who was facing the same natural dangers as they while also being hunted by a team of professional killers. For all she knew, the avalanche they had just witnessed might have swept him away, with nobody to rescue him.

"Do you think Matt knows what to do in an avalanche?"

"Yeah," Emily said, more confidently than she felt.

"I'm not sure they teach that kind of thing in the Marines, you know."

Emily shook her head. "Matty might have been a Marine, but deep down, that man's a cowboy. He grew up out here. He'll know what to do."

"I grew up here too, ya know. That's the first time I've ever seen an avalanche."

"Yeah, but Matty spent his time outdoors. You were too busy sitting inside, playing *Call of Duty*, when we were kids."

Mikey rolled his eyes. "Like Matt wasn't flying through chores on the ranch to play with me. We were a duo! You wives just wouldn't understand."

Emily laughed. All of them—her, Matty, Mikey, and Liz—had grown up together. She was thankful they were all still together now. They'd come a long way. Mikey, who was in many ways like a brother to her, had been there for her since she could remember. From oil changes to helping her fix stuff around her house when she lived alone before Redd had come back to Montana, he'd always been a loyal, dependable friend. To Redd, yes. But also to her.

Emily tucked a strand of hair behind her ear. "Thanks for being here, Mikey."

He shrugged. "Don't mention it."

✖   ✖   ✖

About an hour after observing the avalanche, Emily and Mikey began ascending toward the ridgeline where the first hunting camp was situated. The route was long and tedious, meandering back and forth across the slope in a series of switchbacks that appeared on the map as a distinct trail but were harder to pinpoint under more than a foot of snow. As they moved back and forth across the mountain, they did so under the looming threat of another avalanche. Twice during the climb, they heard the distinctive *whump* that signaled the beginning of a slide, but always in the distance. The snowpack above them held together, and the horses did not react as before.

It was late afternoon by the time they crested the ridge. After hours in the saddle, both riders were happy to dismount and stretch out muscles that had

grown stiff with inactivity and exposure to the cold, but Emily had an even more pressing reason for climbing down off her horse.

Covered in snow, the old shelter looked more like a terrain feature than a structure. There was no evidence of any activity around it—no footprints in the snow—but there was a small hole in the drift piled up like a wall that might have been intentionally put there, perhaps to provide ventilation to the interior. Approaching it, Emily felt her hopes begin to rise for the first time since Matthew's departure.

He's here, she thought, unable to temper her relief with caution. *He's safe.*

And as she high-stepped through the snow, almost running to the shelter, she heard the distinctive sound of a whinnying horse issue from the little opening.

"Remington!" she called out, her spirits surging. "Matty! It's me. Mikey's with me."

She reached the front of the shelter and immediately began scooping away the drift, enlarging the hole. Warm air, infused with the distinctive smell of horse urine and manure, wafted out of the opening. Although the interior remained shrouded in gloom, Emily caught a glint of light reflected in a single dark eye.

"Remmy! Is that you, buddy?" The hole was now big enough to confirm the identification. There was no question that the animal standing in the middle of the shelter, a horse blanket draped over his flanks, was Matthew's old quarter horse. When he saw her, he shook his head and gave a snort of recognition.

But Remington appeared to be alone in the shelter.

Emily's relief at finding tangible proof of her husband's presence evaporated, replaced by an even deeper sense of dread.

"Matty, are you in there?" She pushed through the opening, scattering loose snow onto the uncovered grass floor. Remington's saddle rested in one corner, and a shapeless backpack lay on the ground beside it, but Matthew Redd was nowhere to be found.

She stumbled back out of the little structure, suddenly frantic. "Mikey, he's not here. He's not here. Where is he?"

Mikey, who was tending to the horses, began looking around. "I'm sure he's here somewhere. He's probably scouting the area on foot or something."

"Then where are his tracks? Nobody's been through here in hours. Not since the snow stopped."

"He's got to be around here somewhere, Emily." Mikey sounded more desperate than confident. "He wouldn't just leave Remington behind."

She ran past him, searching the area for tracks as she closed the distance to the wood line. "Matty!" she called out. "Matty, where are you?"

There was no answer.

THIRTY-THREE

Matthew Redd drifted in and out of consciousness, drawn up by the sound of voices and the sensation of movement only to settle back once more into the dark embrace of oblivion. He could never quite make out what the voices were saying. He recognized the individual words, but their meanings slid away like droplets of water dancing on a hot skillet whenever he tried to make sense of them. He was certain about one thing. One of the voices was definitely Emily's.

But no, that couldn't be right. Emily was far away. Safe from the death and violence that had found him. Safe with Junior and Mikey and Liz and Lucas.

A dream then, he decided.

He recalled an old short story . . . What was the name? Something about a bridge . . . A man being hanged on a bridge . . . The hangman's rope breaks and he falls into the river. He then makes his way home to his wife, and just as he's about to embrace her, the rope snaps taut and breaks his neck. His escape had been a dream, a delusion experienced in the instant of his death.

A dream as I die, he thought and then fell once more into darkness.

Later, but how much later he could not say, the voice—Emily's but not Emily's—brought him back again, and this time he saw her face floating above him, her luxurious hair hanging down, brushing against his skin. He tried to speak her name but heard only an indistinct rumble of unformed words.

It wasn't Emily. Couldn't possibly be her, because she could not possibly be here with him. Either he was dying on the side of a mountain, bleeding out, freezing to death, alone except for his delusions, or he was already dead, floating into the great beyond.

Yet the apparition hovering gently above seemed real enough. Did that mean he was already dead?

Redd believed in heaven, though he wasn't sure he deserved to be there. But if this was heaven, then it couldn't be Emily here with him, because she was alive and safe and far away.

If not Emily, then who?

It occurred to him that perhaps it was his mother.

He had not thought about her in a long time, and when he did, his emotions were always conflicted. He missed her dearly, that was true. But there was also a side of him that was angry with her. Not for being an addict, but for not fighting harder to overcome those demons. She had missed out on so much life. And not just her own or even Redd's, but Junior's too.

Linda Redd had become pregnant with him after a one-night stand with a young Marine named Gavin Kline. It had been only one of many bad choices she had made and would continue making. Whether because of pride or shame, she had hidden the knowledge of his birth from young Matthew's father and had instead turned to a series of successively worse boyfriends, many of whom had beaten both her and Matthew. Because they fed her drug habit and sometimes gave her a roof to sleep under, she had defended them, telling her son that the beatings the two of them received were their own fault. When he was eleven years old, he had come home from school to find her dead of an overdose, the needle still in her arm.

Jesus forgives us, but first we have to ask. And Mom wasn't about asking for anything . . .

He immediately felt guilty for thinking it. For all her flaws, she was his mother. His flesh and blood. She had given him the gift of life, and for all that it hadn't always been easy, he cherished it because it had brought Emily and little Matty to him. Sure, Linda Redd had made some bad decisions, but who was he to judge? Without J. B.'s patient guidance, he might very well have gone down the same road.

Maybe that's why he was seeing her now, so that he could tell her the things he'd never gotten a chance to say to her when she had been alive, the things he needed to tell her if he was ever going to be able to forgive her in his heart. If God could forgive a person their sins, surely Matthew Redd could do so too.

Okay, then, he thought, *just say it.*

"I love you, Mom."

The face above him broke into a smile, and the sound of gentle laughter rained down upon his upturned visage. "Mom? Well, I don't know whether to be flattered or insulted."

Redd jolted in surprise at the voice. It wasn't his mother, wasn't Emily, wasn't anyone familiar. In that instant, Redd knew that he had been wrong about everything.

This wasn't heaven, and he wasn't dead. He could feel his body, the beating of his heart, the sensation of a semisolid surface under him, and the weight of a blanket pressing down from above.

He was alive. And there was a stranger standing over him.

His vision sharpened, the face coming into focus. Blonde hair. Not the same as Emily's. The shape of her face was different too. She was also considerably younger than Emily, possibly just a teenager. Redd felt sure that he had never seen her before in his life, but he knew with undeniable certainty that she was real—flesh and blood, not an angel, not a delusion.

A memory of his battle with the hit team flashed through his mind, and suddenly, he felt very vulnerable.

He looked past her, his eyes darting around the . . . not a room, but a tent. A medium-sized olive drab canvas tent—Army surplus by the look of it. An electric lantern hung from the center pole, and there were several plastic totes lined up against one wall, but the small enclosure was otherwise empty.

The young woman put a restraining hand on his arm. "Hey, take it easy. You'll tear your stitches if you start thrashing around."

Stitches?

He recalled getting cut, not just once but several times. As if awakened by the memory, the wounds began to throb with fresh pain.

He brought his gaze back to the woman as if seeing her for the first time. He decided he was not wrong about her age. Her plain face was smooth and unlined, with just a trace of baby fat in her cheeks. The rest of her was mostly hidden under a bulky, fur-lined, dark-blue parka.

"Who are you?" he demanded. "Where am I?"

Her expression became tentative, and she withdrew her hand quickly, as if the mere act of touching him had been a mistake. "You're safe," she said, and then retreated a step.

Redd now saw that beneath her parka she wore a long sack dress that reached down almost to her ankles. The garment looked like something from a *Little*

House on the Prairie rerun, which made the parka and the heavy snow boots on her feet seem even more incongruous.

"I'll let Papa know that you're awake," she continued. "He'll explain everything."

Sensing that she was about to leave and desperate for more answers, Redd tried to sit up. "Wait!"

As if in response to his outcry, he heard an inquisitive whimper and then saw an enormous black-and-tan head rise into view beside him.

"Rubble!" Despite his confusion, Redd felt immediately relieved to see the rottie.

The woman, who had been on the verge of opening the flap to leave, stopped and looked back. "Is that his name? Rubble? That's one loyal dog you've got there, mister. He was sitting with you, barking and howling until his poor little throat was raw. That's how we found you, ya know. We weren't sure he was going to let us help, but then he must have figured we were okay. He hasn't left your side since we got back."

The utterance sent questions swirling through Redd's mind. *Who is "us"? And where is "back"?*

But the girl had said all she was going to say. She turned away again, opened the flap, allowing a wave of cold air to rush in, and then was gone.

Redd sagged back, the mere act of trying to rise leaving him spent. A moment later he felt something pressing against his thigh and looked down to find Rubble nuzzling him. He smiled despite himself and reached down to scratch the dog's ears. "Who's a good boy? I owe you one, buddy."

Rubble gave a soft but contented sigh, as if to say, *No problem.*

"What do you make of this?" continued Redd, gesturing toward the tent flap. "You really think these people . . . whoever they are . . . are okay? Or did we just jump out of the frying pan and into the fire?"

If Rubble shared his master's apprehension, he gave no indication. He just licked Redd's hand and then sat back on his haunches, regarding his master with an adoring look.

Redd took a moment to make a more thorough survey of his surroundings. He lay in an old-style canvas military cot, consistent with the tent, but the blanket covering him was a patchwork quilt. Under it, he had been stripped down to his underwear, the waistband of which was crusted with blood. Thick bandages covered the wounds on his arms and chest. The dressings looked professional— whoever had attended to his injuries had evidently received medical training.

One bandage, covering the inside of his left elbow, was conspicuous for both its low profile—nothing more than a small gauze pad held in place by several turns of self-adhesive wrap—and by the fact that he couldn't remember having been cut there. The bandage looked more like what might be used after a blood draw.

A check of his G-Shock revealed that it was a little past 4:30 p.m., meaning that he'd been out for a good twelve hours. Evidently a lot had happened to him during that time.

Mindful of not putting stress on the wounds, he rolled onto his side and pushed up into a sitting position to get a better look at the tent. The floor was nothing but a waterproof tarp, and when his bare feet touched it, he immediately felt the chill of frozen ground underneath, a stark contrast to the air in the tent, which felt, if not exactly warm, then at least tolerable. The reason for this, he discovered, was a portable catalytic heater, positioned at the foot of the cot, fighting a close proximity battle against the chill.

He pulled the quilt around his shoulders and was about to stand up when the tent flap opened. Expecting it to be the young woman, Redd pulled the blanket together in front of him in a probably pointless attempt at modesty, but to his surprise the person who stepped through was an older man.

Tall and broad, with a bushy gray beard that reached down almost to his barrel chest, and dressed in buckskins with a fur hat, the newcomer looked like an old-fashioned mountain man. He regarded Redd from the tent's entrance for a moment, then gave a nod of acknowledgment and stepped through. "Bekah said you were awake," he said, as if unsure how to begin the conversation. His voice was a deep baritone that seemed to rumble out of his chest.

Redd made a mental note of the young woman's name. "I am," he replied and then gestured to his bandages. "Thanks to you, I guess."

The man made a grunting noise that might have been a laugh. "You've got that right. If we hadn't come across you when we did, you'd probably be stone-cold dead right now."

"Well, I'm grateful." Redd studied him for a moment, trying to decide if the man's aloof demeanor signaled a threat of some kind. "I'm Matthew Redd," he said, hoping the offering of his name would prompt reciprocal action. "I own the ranch just west of here."

"That so?" The man folded his arms across his chest. "And just what sort of trouble are you in, Redd?"

It was a natural enough question to ask of someone found nearly dead on the side of a mountain and surrounded by corpses.

Okay, thought Redd. *Skip the small talk and cut right to the chase.*

He took a breath, trying to decide how much to say. He didn't know this man, didn't know whether he was someone who could be trusted or who might, for the right price, hand him over to the next wave of killers.

Still, the girl had seemed friendly enough.

"Some folks got it in their head to come gunning for me," he said. "I fought back."

The man made the grunting sound again. "You fought back." His voice had a sarcastic edge, but Redd thought he detected a trace of admiration. "You didn't answer my question. What sort of trouble? Why were they after you?"

"Have you been following the news? You know about Oklahoma City?"

Under his bushy steel eyebrows, the man's eyes narrowed. "That was almost thirty years ago. What's that got to do with anything?"

Thirty years? The answer confused Redd, but only for a moment. *He's talking about the Timothy McVeigh bombing of the Murrah Federal Building.* "No, not that. The terrorist attack at the airport yesterday."

The man shook his head. "Don't know anything about that." His eyes narrowed again. "You have something to do with it? Is that why they were after you?"

"What? No. I . . ." Redd trailed off, the import of the man's question finally sinking in. *He thinks I'm the bad guy. Why? And if he believes that, why hasn't he already contacted the authorities? Why save my life?*

"The men I fought with were the ones who were behind it," said Redd, choosing his words carefully. "There was a prisoner on that plane that they wanted dead. Why they wanted him dead is a long story. The short version is that he was going to implicate some powerful people in a conspiracy, and they wanted to shut him up permanently. And since I know what he knew, they came after me as well."

As he spoke, Redd noticed a change in the man's expression, suspicion giving way to something like satisfaction. When Redd finished, the man shook his head. "I knew it. Had to be something like that. Those jackbooted thugs will do anything to hold on to their power."

"You've got that right," agreed Redd, mildly surprised at the insight.

The man regarded him again, this time with an appraising stare, and Redd got the sense that he had just passed some kind of test. "You killed all of them? Just you?"

Redd nodded toward Rubble. "I had a little help."

That elicited another grunt. "Yeah, I figured it wasn't you that tore out the throats of the last two. But we found close to a dozen of 'em scattered across the mountain. And you took 'em all out. That's pretty impressive, Mr. Redd. You have some sort of training."

It wasn't a question.

"I was a Marine," Redd offered, as if that was explanation enough.

"Yeah? Well, I expect some of them had similar training to yours." He reached into the folds of his buckskin jacket and took out something that looked like a wallet, which he proceeded to toss over to Redd. "Took these off 'em."

As it flew through air toward him, Redd glimpsed a flash of gold, and when he caught the object, he immediately felt its weight in his hands. He flipped it over to reveal a gold badge, shaped like a shield with an eagle on top. Raised letters set in dark-blue enamel read *Homeland Security Investigations*. Below that was the seal of the Department of Homeland Security, with the letters *U* and *S* to either side, and below it, on a blue enamel ribbon, were the words *Special Agent*.

Homeland Security?

Redd had never seen a DHS badge before and had no basis for disproving its authenticity, but he figured that if the kill team had decided to pose as federal agents, they wouldn't have skimped on their props. The more important question was why they were pretending to be federal agents in the first place. He was about to tell his host that the badge had to be a fake, but then had a thought.

The old guy believes it's real, which means he thinks I just killed a bunch of federal agents. And yet he doesn't seem the least bit bothered by it.

With that realization, the pieces of the puzzle began falling into place. The camp, the man's buckskins, and his evident contempt for federal authorities . . . even his odd reference to the 1995 Oklahoma City bombing . . . Everything pointed to one inescapable conclusion.

Redd's saviors had fled civilization to live in the wilderness.

He wasn't sure what to call them. Survivalists? Doomsday preppers? Sovereign citizens? Modern-day mountain men?

Probably fugitives from justice too.

Redd had heard stories of wanted men escaping into the wilderness, avoiding justice and living mostly off the land. Some were violent criminals, like serial bomber Eric Rudolph, the domestic terrorist who had targeted the 1996 Olympics in Atlanta and had eluded capture for years by hiding out in the forests of North Carolina. Others were guilty of less spectacular crimes like tax evasion but saw their resistance to the federal government and their rejection of mainstream society as an expression of a heroic ideal.

Even if they weren't on the run because of some criminal act, the man and . . . Bekah? His daughter, presumably, though he looked old enough to be her grandfather . . . They were breaking the law simply by living on National Forest land, presumably poaching game, and might well view Redd's mere presence as a threat, especially if they thought that federal law enforcement agents were out looking for him.

He would have to tread carefully.

He set the badge on the cot beside him. "How did you find me?"

"Are you kidding? It sounded like World War Three up there. Once the shooting stopped, we came out to have a look-see. Heard your dog, which led us to you and a whole lot of dead feds. For a while there, it looked like you might be on your way to joinin' 'em." He paused a beat, then added, "We debated just letting nature take its course, but . . ."

He trailed off as if unsure how to finish the thought.

"Well, I'm glad you didn't," Redd put in quickly.

The man nodded. "It was pretty clear to us that they were after you, and . . . well?" He shrugged. "I've always had a soft spot for the underdog. Especially when he's being targeted by agents of the fascist shadow government."

The comment further confirmed Redd's suspicions about his still unnamed savior, but it was his earlier admission that he had almost left Redd to die that was the most troubling. *He's still not sure saving me was the right decision. He's afraid that I'll bring my trouble to his doorstep.*

It wasn't an unfounded concern.

"I can't thank you enough for saving my life," said Redd, "but last night was just the first round. They've probably got reinforcements on the way already, and the longer I stay here, the more danger you and . . . your family will be in. I'd feel terrible if you got caught up in my trouble. So, if I can just get my clothes, I'll be on my way."

The man laughed again, this time more of a guffaw than a grunt. He shook his head. "You've got steel, Redd. No doubt about it. But you're in no shape to leave."

"I'll be fine."

"I beg to differ. You lost a lot of blood before we found you. If it hadn't been so cold, you would have bled out completely. Took two units and a liter of saline solution just to get your volume up to where we could measure your blood pressure. Probably could have stood to have a couple more, but two pints was all Justin could spare."

Justin, thought Redd. *That makes at least three of them.*

It took a moment longer for the real significance of the man's words to sink in. He looked down at the wrap around his elbow and suddenly felt as if there were spiders crawling under his skin.

Wait . . .

"You gave me a blood transfusion?"

Reading his unease, the man raised his hands. "Don't worry. We know what we're doing. Justin is type O negative. Universal donor. This isn't the first time we've had to tap him."

Redd found this assertion less than comforting. While a blood-type mismatch would probably have been fatal, of greater concern was the possibility that he had been exposed to a blood-borne pathogen—HIV or hepatitis. HIV was a ticking time bomb—a disease that could be treated, but never cured, and one which might not even show up on a test for months. It was a risk that could not be completely mitigated even under the best of circumstances.

And now a stranger . . . some crazy man living in the woods . . . had just pumped his blood into Redd's veins.

He tried to tell himself that it didn't matter, that he was alive, and if the man wasn't exaggerating the seriousness of his injuries, that the transfusion was the reason why, but the irrational part of his brain was slow to accept this.

He took a breath, swallowed, then met the man's eyes. "Tell Justin I'm grateful."

The man regarded Redd for a long moment, then seemed to reach a decision. "I'll let you tell him yourself. It's just about suppertime. I'll have your clothes brought over, and then you can come meet the rest of the family."

The invitation seemed to go beyond mere hospitality. It was as if saving Redd's life was one thing, but breaking bread with him required a degree of trust that the man still felt uncertain about.

Shouting down his paranoia regarding the blood transfusion, Redd replied, "That sounds wonderful . . . I don't think I got your name."

Redd knew that his host had intentionally withheld that information and was curious to see just how far the man's willingness to trust him would extend.

The man appeared to consider the request for a moment. Then, fixing Redd with a stare that felt like a challenge, he answered, "The name's Strong. Josiah Strong."

Because he wasn't expecting to hear a familiar name, Redd failed to hide his surprise.

Strong's eyes narrowed. "I take it you've heard of me."

Redd nodded slowly. He had recognized the name instantly, just as he would have David Koresh or Ted Kaczynski.

Infamous to most, inspirational to an unhinged few, Josiah Strong had been the founder and leader of an extreme antigovernment group known as the Montana Strongmen, which had existed in the 1990s at the peak of the militia movement. In 1996, a three-month-long standoff with federal agents at the Strongmen compound in northeastern Montana had ended in an apocalyptic raid, in which several of Strong's followers were killed, along with three ATF agents. Strong's body had not been among those recovered in the aftermath, and it was widely believed that he had escaped to Canada or possibly even died from injuries sustained during the bloody firefight. The enduring mystery of Strong's whereabouts had only added to his legend.

Mystery solved, thought Redd. *He was living in my backyard all along.*

Strong continued to scrutinize Redd. "I sense in you a kindred spirit, Mr. Redd. I hope that my trust is well placed."

For all its seeming benevolence, there was a subtle threat underlying the words. Redd knew that, even though Strong had saved his life, his fate still hung in the balance.

He managed a smile and a nod. "You said something about supper? I'm famished."

Strong laughed. "Let's get you dressed first."

After he was gone, Redd glanced down at Rubble. "Josiah Strong," he muttered. "Can you believe that, boy?"

Rubble answered with a plaintive whine.

Redd sighed and shook his head. "Out of the frying pan."

THIRTY-FOUR

The news of Robert Bridger's death broke while Decker was somewhere above flyover country. According to a preliminary report from the Southampton Police Department, the death was the result of foul play—a murder-suicide carried out by Bridger's ex-wife. That was the extent of the detail in the report, but Decker felt certain that the evidence supporting that conclusion would be abundant and incontrovertible.

And wrong.

Both Bridger *and* his ex-wife were victims of homicide.

Decker's suspicions on that score were reinforced a couple hours later when, shortly before his plane set down at LAX, another high-profile death made the news. Werner Heissman, CEO of what was arguably the world's most successful capital management firm, had joined Bridger in the great beyond, dropping dead on a Manhattan sidewalk. There was nothing outwardly suspicious about Heissman's death—he was eighty-eight years old, after all—but when two of the world's wealthiest individuals died within the space of twenty-four hours, people noticed. A certain snarky TV news pundit had remarked that it was a bad day to be rich in America, while in the darker corners of the internet, conspiracy theorists began spinning their webs.

The latter, Decker knew, would have a field day as the rest of the men on that list started dropping like flies. Somebody was doing Decker's job for him, preemptively clearing the board of players, and he was determined to find out who it was.

He felt a grudging professional admiration for the Heissman hit. Making a death appear to be the result of natural causes wasn't easy, not when the target was a high-profile individual. Medical examiners always went the extra mile with celebrity deaths, knowing that their conclusions would be scrutinized in the media.

Bridger's death, on the other hand, or rather the killing of the ex-wife in order to make the death appear to be a crime of passion, was something Decker found contemptible. That was the work of a sociopath.

Decker did not enjoy ending the life of another human being, but he did take satisfaction in the knowledge that by taking one life, he might save many others, or at the very least, find justice for those already lost. Killing someone with only a tangential relationship to the target? That was unacceptable.

Traditional military doctrine held that it was sometimes necessary to destroy a building, or even an entire village, just to take out one high-value target. Simply put, sometimes bad men needed to die. They were like tumors that, if left untreated, would metastasize, spreading evil and destruction throughout society. But if the "treatment" involved unnecessary death, often of innocent bystanders, how was the cure any better than the disease?

Finding a better answer to that question, a better alternative to even the limited collateral impact of drone strikes, had played no small part in Decker's decision to accept recruitment into Kline's off-the-books program in the first place, and it was why he had agreed to come out of retirement in order to end the threat of the Twelve. Decker saw himself as a scalpel, a precision tool for excising the cancerous cells while leaving the surrounding tissue virtually untouched.

Did his dead visit him in dreams? Sometimes. But it was the people who died because he had not acted quickly enough that truly haunted him. And if he didn't get out ahead of this apparent civil war for leadership of the Twelve, more innocents might get swept up in the war of assassins.

Decker still liked Holton Fish as the mastermind of the coup, but whether the man was in fact the guilty party or just another target for the real killer, he was sure to be on heightened alert, which posed a problem.

Decker's original plan had been to use the delivery driver routine to begin surveilling the target, just as he had planned to do in Southampton. It was the most effective way Decker had found to conduct close reconnaissance in a developed nation like the United States, better than utility repairmen or gas company line inspectors responding to "reports of a leak in your area." Not only had freelance delivery drivers become ubiquitous, unlikely to draw any attention, but everybody, even billionaires, loved getting deliveries. Even if the targets didn't take receipt of the packages personally, entrusting that task to a personal assistant, once the contents were judged to be harmless, they would eventually find their way to the right person, little suspecting that the object—be it a prototype mobile phone or a piece of designer jewelry—contained miniaturized surveillance equipment that would allow Decker to pinpoint the target's location and identify whatever local security measures might be in place along the way. But if Fish had adopted a defensive posture, he would be wary of anything unexpected.

Decker had developed his contingency plan during the short drive to a nearby self-storage facility where he kept a variety of untraceable weapons, tools, costumes, and props—anything he might need to carry out an operation. He maintained similar storage units in several major cities around the globe, all paid in advance for at least another eighteen years, out of the same black budget that had financed his earlier operations, because even though he had retired from that life, Aaron Decker, like Mikey Derhammer, believed in the Boy Scout motto.

He spent just half an hour in the storage unit, making a few refinements to a forged document, and then, after changing into attire more in keeping with his new legend, locked up and got on the road to Malibu.

Los Angeles traffic being what it was, it took him about an hour and a half to make the twenty-eight-mile drive to the foot of the Santa Monica Mountains where Holton Fish was currently taking up residence in a six-bedroom, six-bath, 6,500-square-foot palace in Palm Canyon, overlooking Malibu Lagoon. Decker pulled to the side of the road near the house's driveway and used a burner phone, which he had spoofed to a Washington DC area code and prefix, to call Fish's personal cell phone.

He didn't actually think the billionaire would pick up and so was mentally composing the voicemail message he would leave when, to his surprise, the call connected.

"Who is this?"

Decker recognized Fish's voice from the many interviews and livestreams he'd watched while compiling target packages for the Twelve. In his television appearances, he came across as both lackadaisical and arrogant. Now, however, he sounded anxious.

Decker launched into his rehearsed cover story. "Mr. Fish, this is Assistant Director Gavin Kline of the Federal Bureau of Investigation. I'm parked just outside. It's urgent that I speak with you privately. It concerns a possible threat to your life."

"Threat?" replied Fish. Then, hesitantly, he asked, "How did you get this number?"

"I'm an assistant director of the FBI, Mr. Fish. It wasn't that hard. Now, with your permission, I'm going to come up your driveway and present my credentials at your front door."

He expected Fish to do what most powerful men did when confronted by a law enforcement official and redirect him to a lawyer, but Fish surprised him a second time. "Yeah, okay. Come on up."

Decker wondered at the motive behind the man's apparently cooperative behavior. If Fish was orchestrating the assassinations of the Twelve's leadership, then he might well have reasoned that refusing to speak with an FBI agent would appear suspicious. On the other hand, it was entirely possible that Fish's monstrous ego was in the driver's seat and that he saw talking to the FBI as a challenge, a battle of wits—a battle that might ultimately turn into a life-and-death struggle. So Decker was on his guard, head on a swivel, as he made his way up to the front porch of Fish's palatial home.

The door was closed, but after a moment, Fish's disembodied voice issued from an intercom speaker beneath the doorbell. "Hold your badge up to the camera."

Decker displayed his forged credentials, modified to bear Kline's name, and replica shield, and after the briefest of pauses, the door swung open. Wary of an ambush, but not wanting to show it, Decker stepped through quickly, clearing the doorway and conducting a rapid visual sweep of the spacious room beyond.

The front room was enormous—easily eight hundred square feet with a vaulted ceiling and one entire wall made of glass, giving an unrestricted view of the Pacific Ocean. Minimalist furnishings—just a sectional arranged in an incomplete square around a coffee table in the center of the room—made it seem even bigger. Yet aside from Fish, who was still holding the door, the room was empty. There was no entourage of bodyguards, personal assistants, or hangers-on loitering about, waiting to address the billionaire's every whim. Fish appeared to be alone in the house.

He looked nothing like the smug, confident bon vivant who had made regular appearances on late-night talk shows and YouTube videos. Haggard and drawn, his chin bristling with stubble, eyes puffy and bloodshot, Fish looked as if he hadn't slept in days.

He did not invite Decker farther inside but merely stood where he was, staring at Decker. After a long moment, he began working his jaw as if struggling to form words. "You here to kill me?"

The question stunned Decker.

Does he already know?

"What makes you ask that?"

"I thought maybe you were . . ." Fish trailed off, then squared his shoulders. "You mentioned some kind of threat?"

Decker narrowed his eyes at Fish. "That's right. But something tells me that doesn't surprise you."

Fish waved a dismissive hand. "I get death threats all the time. Have you seen my Twitter feed?"

Decker had. He also knew that the other man was dissembling. Fish was, in fact, terrified.

I've got this all wrong, thought Decker. *He's not the mastermind. But he might know who is.* "Mr. Fish, have you been following the news?"

Fish laughed without humor. "Oh yes. Believe me, I'm paying attention."

The remark was too vague, so Decker pressed. "Then you know about the deaths of Robert Bridger and Werner Heissman?"

"Don't forget Anton," supplied Fish. "Anton Gage. He was on that plane in Oklahoma City."

Interesting that you knew that, Decker didn't say aloud. "The official line is that there's no connection. That the timing of their deaths is a coincidence. But I think we both know that's not true."

Fish nodded. "Just a matter of time before . . ." He trailed off again.

"So, you are aware of this threat?"

Fish hung his head, refusing to meet Decker's gaze, but said nothing.

This wasn't going anything like Decker had expected. "Fish, if you know something . . . know who's behind this, you've got to tell me."

"Makes no difference. You can't stop them."

"Not if I don't know who they are." When Fish did not respond, Decker continued. "I need a name, Fish. Whoever it is, they're no match for the FBI."

Fish met his gaze and gave another humorless laugh. "That's what you think." He looked down again. "They're untouchable."

"Nobody is untouchable," countered Decker.

Fish regarded him for a moment. "You know much about history?"

Decker, who held advanced degrees in the subject, felt certain that he knew a good deal more than the billionaire, but affected impatience. "Can you just get to the point?"

Fish ignored the admonition. "In the Roman republic, there was a special group of men—an elite group of legionaries—who served as bodyguards to senior government officials and military officers. They were called the Praetorian Guard. Over time they grew in power and influence, eventually turning into the emperor's private army for dealing with internal problems.

"Which was all fine and good when the emperor was somebody with his head screwed on straight. Then this madman named Caligula came along. I'm sure you've heard of him. Literally a crazy person. He sent the army out on pointless missions. Turned the palace into a brothel and tried to appoint his horse to be a proconsul. So do you know what his elite bodyguards did?"

Decker did know, but he made a rolling motion with his finger. "Get on with it."

"They assassinated him. For the good of the empire. But really for their own good, because their fortune was tied to the fortunes of the empire. Over the next three hundred years, the Praetorian Guard assassinated a total of fifteen emperors. They were the real power in Rome. If an emperor didn't want to play ball . . ." He drew a finger across his throat.

"Enough with the history lesson," growled Decker. "What's your point?"

"We've got our own Praetorian Guard in this country." He laughed. "It started out innocently enough, just 'protecting the homeland from terrorists.'" He made finger quotes and affected an accent that was somewhere between Kennedy and Reagan. "Pretty quick though, it turned into the president's private little army.

"And just like in Rome, they became the real power in this country. You've probably heard the term *shadow government*. Well, they're it. Not even the president can control them. If the Praetorian doesn't think the president is good for the country, he can . . . persuade him to make some changes. He doesn't need to kill anyone, though if he wanted to, he would probably get away with it. Like I said—untouchable. He knows all the secrets. Where the bodies are buried. Literally in some cases."

"He? You're saying there's one man calling the shots? Who?"

"We thought we could beat him at his own game," Fish went on, ignoring the question. "We had dirt on *him*. Video of him partying with underage girls on a certain private island . . . I think you know the one I'm talking about. It was only an insurance policy. Just in case he needed a reminder to stay out of our way."

"We?" Decker decided to take a chance. "You mean the Twelve?"

For the first time since they'd begun talking, Fish was rendered momentarily speechless. He gaped at Decker for a moment, then in a small voice said, "You know about us?" He sagged. "Of course you do. That's why you're really here. Anton talked, didn't he?"

"It's why you killed him. To shut him up."

"We didn't kill Anton. There was no need. It would have been his word against ours anyway. We would have just painted him as some conspiracy-spinning lunatic."

"Then who killed him?"

"Haven't you been listening? It's the Praetorian. He probably thought Anton would drop his name too. Put the word out about the tape. A scandal like that would be fatal to him. Even he's not immune to that kind of publicity. So he decided to be proactive. I guess shutting Anton up wasn't good enough. He's going to make sure nobody ever has that kind of leverage again. He's knocked off Bob and Werner, and I'm sure someone will come for me soon. And there's not a thing any of us can do to stop him."

"If that were true, then he wouldn't need to kill you," Decker pointed out. "Come in. We can keep you safe."

"Like you kept Anton safe?"

"If we had known about this Praetorian, we might have been able to take appropriate measures to protect him." *Not to mention the FBI agents and marshals we lost,* Decker added silently.

The irony of the situation was not lost on him. He had come here with the intention of ultimately killing Holton Fish, and now he was making a case for preserving the man's life. But he felt sure that Kline would not want him to pass up a chance to bring in a new witness against the Twelve.

"You won't be able to stop him," said Fish, hanging his head.

"You've got a better chance with us than on your own," pressed Decker. "Now that we know what we're up against . . ."

Before he could finish the sentence, two things happened almost simultaneously.

The first was a sound—a loud *crack*—which came from the direction of the window wall off to Decker's right. Decker knew without looking that what he had just heard was the sound of a bullet striking the glass.

The second, which Decker glimpsed only from the corner of his eye, was the back of Fish's head disintegrating in a spray of red mist.

THIRTY-FIVE

Decker threw himself flat and rolled behind the sectional, removing himself from the sniper's line of sight. He cursed himself for not having moved Fish away from the glass wall, but when he'd started the visit, trying to save the man's life had been pretty low on the priority list.

Another *crack* echoed through the open room, followed immediately by an eruption of foam from a small hole in the back of the sectional, and another *crack* as the bullet finished its journey by burrowing into the wall behind him, leaving a hole about the diameter of Decker's pinky finger.

Armor-piercing rounds, he noted absently. Anything else would have deformed or fragmented on impact with the tempered glass of the windowpane. The position of the hole relative to the hole in the sectional revealed the angle of the shot—the shooter was firing up at the house, probably from somewhere down the canyon. That, however, was of less significance than the fact that the sniper was still firing, even though Fish—presumably the primary target—was already down. Evidently the shooter had orders to leave no witnesses.

The Praetorian wasn't taking any chances.

Decker hadn't heard a report, which probably meant the sniper was using a suppressor and that likely nobody in the ritzy neighborhood was even aware the attack was occurring. It also meant the sniper could bide his time, wait for Decker to make a move for the exit. How long he might be willing to wait was impossible to say; he might already have bugged out, but Decker wasn't going to take that chance. Without raising up, he took out his burner and called 911.

"This is Assistant Director Gavin Kline of the FBI," he said when the dispatcher picked up. He gave the address of Fish's home, then added, "I'm taking fire from an unknown gunman with a high-powered rifle using armor-piercing rounds. I need backup and I need an airship."

Decker doubted the local police would be able to run down the Praetorian's sniper, but the presence of a helicopter overhead would almost certainly scare the shooter off.

The dispatcher, somewhat flummoxed by the direct nature of Decker's request, connected him directly to a sergeant at the City of Malibu Police Department, and Decker was obliged to repeat his request. "I'm taking fire," he repeated, though it had in fact been at least two minutes since the last shot. "Get a helicopter in the air."

He ended the call, then immediately called Kline, who picked up on the first ring. "I see you're already taking pieces off the board," remarked Kline, eschewing a standard greeting. "Though to be honest, I expected a little more finesse."

"If you're talking about New York, that wasn't me. It seems we've got a competitor. I'll tell you all about it, but first, I need you to backstop a cover."

"Okay. What is it?"

"In about fifteen seconds, the Malibu Police are going to call the head office to verify that you are currently operating in their city."

"Me?"

"I'm you right now, and I need local backup. Someone's shooting at me."

"Shooting at you?"

"Gavin, focus. Make the call."

"Okay, okay. Hold on a sec." There was a beep and then the line went quiet. After a couple minutes, Kline came back on. "Okay, you're covered, but you'll have to hang around and give them a statement. Try not to let anyone take your picture."

"You know I'm camera shy."

"Right. Now, would you please tell me what's going on?"

"Like I told you. We've got a competitor. Somebody else is going after the Twelve, and my gut tells me it's the same somebody behind the hit on the prisoner transport." He quickly recounted what Fish had told him.

"Did he give you a name?"

"We didn't quite get that far, but he specifically mentioned 'protecting the homeland.'"

"Homeland," muttered Kline. "That can't be a coincidence."

"What do you mean?"

"The guys who hit us at the airport were posing as a Homeland Investigations special activity unit. And Stephanie says that someone in HSI is running interference for the hit team going after Matthew Redd in Montana. From what I can tell, the DHS field office thinks the request is legit. I'm heading up there myself to try to cut through the red tape, but now I'm wondering . . ."

He trailed off, so Decker prompted, "Wondering what?"

Kline didn't answer.

"Gavin, wondering what?"

Decker could hear Kline sigh across the phone connection. Finally, he said, "I think I know who the Praetorian is."

THIRTY-SIX

MONTANA

Redd's clothes were returned to him clean, but the fabric felt stiff and scratchy against his skin and smelled of woodsmoke, no doubt a result of having been dried on a line in front of an open fire. The knife slashes had been expertly mended, but the bloodstains, like his memory of the life-and-death struggle that had caused them, were not so easily erased. Still, as he pulled on the garments, moving gingerly to avoid tearing his stitches and reopening the wounds, Redd felt as if he'd been given a new lease on life.

He wasn't out of the woods just yet, not by a long shot. He was, after all, still on the mountain with an unknown number of killers after him. He hadn't made contact with Emily and was worried about her and Junior. And though his injuries were, for the moment, taken care of, there was always the possibility that, given the less than sterile environment where he was treated, he could contract a serious infection. But that was a problem for another day. For now, Redd was back in the fight. That he owed his rescue to an antigovernment fugitive—an extremist—was more than a little troubling, but what really mattered now was how to make the best use of this unexpected gift.

His status with Strong and his followers was unclear. They had saved him, at no small risk to themselves, and had chosen to bring him into their midst. But did they view him as a guest or a prisoner?

Or something else entirely?

Strong had intimated that his group's first inclination had been to simply let him die. What had tipped the balance and caused them to instead act to save him? And how would they react when Redd expressed his desire to leave their camp and return to his life?

He was certain of one thing: he would see Emily and little Matty again. No matter what curveballs the universe threw at him, no matter how many more battles there were to fight, he would be reunited with his family.

No matter what.

Redd's Carhartt jacket had been among the articles of clothing returned to him, and as he pulled it on, he noted the small holes—now stitched closed—in the front left and back panels. The damage had been caused when one of the shooters had fired at his hasty decoy, giving him the chance to turn the tables on the attacking force. The heavy coat had always been a dependable shield against the elements, but now it had saved his life in a very different way, and he was glad to have it back.

Finally armored against the elements, Redd threw back the tent flap and stepped out to meet the unknown. The first thing he saw was the young woman who had been with him when he'd awakened, evidently waiting for him to come out. "Papa asked me to bring you to dinner," she said, answering an unasked question.

Papa again, thought Redd, wondering at the age discrepancy. Now that he was conscious and standing upright, he was even more certain that she was an adolescent. Maybe eighteen, but probably younger. "Thanks," he said. "It's . . . Bekah, right?"

"Papa told you?"

It had been his intention to pump her for information, but the look of adoration in her eyes suddenly made him feel uncomfortable. He decided to forgo further questioning lest it be misinterpreted as real interest.

"He mentioned it in passing," he said and quickly looked away, surveying the surrounding area. The tent in which he had recuperated was just one of a half dozen that he could see, arranged in an apparently haphazard fashion under the forest canopy. There were no other people in evidence, but the well-trod path in the snow connecting the tents suggested the presence of several people.

"Papa said your name is Matthew," Bekah was saying. "Should I call you that or just Matt?"

Redd didn't look at her. He didn't want to do anything to encourage further attention. He almost answered her with a terse *"You should call me Mr. Redd,"* but decided that might backfire spectacularly. Instead, he muttered, "Matt's fine. Where's everybody else?"

"They're in the mess tent. C'mon, I'll show you."

At that moment, Rubble wriggled out from under the tent flap to stand alongside Redd. He gestured to the dog. "Is everyone welcome?"

"Gross, no. I mean, he's a sweetie, but no, we don't let dogs in the mess tent."

"Fair enough." Redd glanced down at Rubble and made a shooing gesture. "Stay here, boy. Go explore. I'll save you some leftovers."

Rubble gave what Redd interpreted as a woof of understanding and then charged off into the trees, following his nose.

"And don't mess with the local wildlife," Redd called after him.

As he followed Bekah through the camp, Redd kept an eye out for any landmarks that might help him figure out where he was, but the forest was too dense to offer more than an occasional glimpse of the sky. He would need a better idea of where the camp was situated before he could begin formulating an exit strategy.

Bekah brought him to a larger tent from which white smoke was pouring via a chimney vent. As they drew close, Redd detected the unmistakable smell of roasted venison, and his mouth immediately began to water. Until that moment, he hadn't even realized how hungry he was.

Inside he found Josiah Strong seated at the head of a long table—actually, a series of lightweight folding camp tables arranged in a line—in the company of six other men. Two looked to be roughly the same age as Strong, while the others were Redd's age or younger. All wore long unkempt beards, save for the youngest, who had only a pubescent sprout of hair on his chin and upper lip. Unlike Strong, the men wore commercially manufactured attire—Mossy Oak camouflage was a popular choice—though the garments showed their age.

There were also three women in the tent, not including Bekah, all of them attending to final meal preparations. Bekah immediately went to join them. The women appeared to be in their mid-to-late thirties, though it was hard to say with any certainty. None wore makeup, not even lip gloss, and the faces looked a little leathery, no doubt a result of their rugged lifestyle. Like Bekah, they wore long sack dresses. One displayed a pronounced baby bump—Redd estimated she was seven months along.

Strong rose to his feet when Redd entered, as did the rest of the seated men. Redd glanced at them quickly, noting expressions that ranged from curiosity to barely concealed hostility, then looked to Strong, who regarded him with a cautious smile.

"Mr. Redd." Strong gestured to an open seat to his immediate left. "Please join us."

Redd nodded and moved directly to the chair—a lightweight foldable sling chair, designed more for slouching in front of a campfire than pulling up to a table. Mindful of his injuries, Redd lowered himself slowly into the chair, and as he did, the rest of the group took their seats in unison.

Strong gestured to a man seated diagonally across from Redd. "You mentioned wanting to express your gratitude to Justin here for providing the transfusion."

Redd took the opportunity for a longer look at the other man. Justin had been among those who had regarded Redd with wary curiosity. He didn't look much different than any average Rocky Mountain denizen who could be found on a barstool at Spady's—thickset and powerfully built, a bit on the heavy side but with a core of muscle that owed more to hard manual labor than workouts at the gym. He appeared to be in good health, which was Redd's chief concern, but Redd knew looks could be deceiving where certain illnesses were concerned. Nevertheless, he managed a smile and nodded to the other man. "Thanks. I guess I owe you my life."

Justin's only reply was a slight tilt of the head.

"Justin may have given actual blood," Strong went on, "but all of us gave some sweat on your behalf. Carrying your litter was no easy feat, let me tell you."

And just how far did you carry me? Redd wondered.

Six men carrying a litter—and Redd's 265-pound body on it—through the snow would have been lucky to manage two miles an hour. That probably meant he was no more than ten or twelve miles from where the battle had occurred. Probably a lot less.

He was tempted to ask but decided a question like that would—correctly—be interpreted as a signal of his desire to leave at the earliest possible opportunity. Something told him that the hospitality of his host might quickly evaporate if he expressed that desire.

"Thank you all," Redd said, with as much sincerity as he could muster. "I'd be dead without you. I really do appreciate what you did."

The looks from some of the men suggested that him dying would have been their preferred outcome, but none gave voice to that opinion.

Redd decided to seek a little goodwill from his hosts. "Truly," he went on, recalling something from one of Elijah's sermons. "I was a stranger, but you took me in anyway. You had no idea who I was or what I was doing out here, but you tended to my wounds, and now you're feeding me. It's like the parable of the Good Samaritan. I assume you're familiar with the story?"

Strong gave Redd a thoughtful look. "You a believer, Mr. Redd?"

"Well, I'm trying," Redd answered honestly. A few years ago it would have been an outright lie, but since Emily had come back into his life, he'd had occasion to rethink the matter. It helped that while his father-in-law was a pastor, and Emily a strong believer herself, nobody pushed or forced anything on him. Whenever it would come up, Emily was always very encouraging but steadfast in her belief that Redd needed to choose for himself based on his own convictions, not because of what she might want for him. In time his curiosity about the Bible and its teachings had grown into much more. He was learning, often reading passages underlined by J. B. in the old family Bible he'd left and passed down to Redd. But his faith was a private matter. Not because he was ashamed of it, but more because he didn't feel qualified to speak on it just yet.

Strong gestured to the men sitting around him. "Well, everyone here is free to *believe* what they want. We serve all gods."

"Amen to that," a voice said from Redd's left.

So . . . not like the Good Samaritan, thought Redd. *Not even close.*

Strong looked away and made a *come along* gesture to one of the women. Immediately, she and the others began carrying dishes to the table. One enameled cast iron platter held what looked to Redd like a large shoulder roast, sliced into thick slabs oozing juices. Other bowls contained cooked potatoes, gravy, green beans, and bread rolls. Once the dishes were placed, the women moved to fill empty seats at the table. Bekah sat alongside another woman who bore more than a passing resemblance to her. A much older sister or . . .

It's her mother. Redd almost recoiled at the realization. *She must have been just a kid herself when she gave birth.*

Then he remembered that Bekah had called Strong "Papa."

That's his wife? But he's got to be at least thirty years older than her.

If the woman was indeed his wife, then she would have practically been a toddler when Strong had gone on the run. So how had they connected? And how old had she been when Strong had taken her into his bed?

Redd's sense of unease deepened. Disagreeing with government tax policy was one thing—the Founding Fathers had done no less. But taking a child bride? That was a bridge too far.

Not only was Josiah Strong *not* a Good Samaritan, but to Redd he was not a good man at all. He may have on camo and boots, but he was, Redd knew, a wolf in sheep's clothing. If he was right, and he had a sneaking suspicion that he was, Strong's warped religious views were likely used in a sick and twisted way to try and spin things, justifying his actions and way of life. Worst yet, if Strong truly believed he was in the right, that made him a true believer. And that made him dangerous.

At the head of the table, Strong bowed his head and murmured, "Let us pray."

A chill suddenly went up Redd's spine.

THIRTY-SEVEN

There was almost no conversation during the meal. Most of the men ate with what seemed like grim determination, as if consuming the food was a necessary but unpleasant task. The scene reminded Redd of his early days at boot camp when he and the other recruits raced to finish their meal before one of the drill instructors came along and decided they had eaten enough. As each man finished, one of the women would move quickly to remove his plate and utensils, cleaning and drying the items before returning to her own repast. The men remained at the table, evidently waiting for a cue from Strong, who seemed to be taking his time. For his part, Redd savored the simple fare. He would need the calories, not to mention the protein, both for healing his wounds and for facing what lay ahead.

The dinner menu, Redd noted, included items that could not have been foraged. The green beans, he felt certain, had come from a can, and while it was possible that Strong had a potato patch somewhere, it seemed more likely that they'd come in a ten- or twenty-pound bag from the IGA.

Despite giving the appearance of living a self-sufficient life off the grid, Strong and his people were evidently in contact with civilization, and likely receiving support from someone living in a community. Maybe Wellington but probably one of the larger cities like Bozeman or Helena. Likely, that was where Strong had recruited his current coterie.

And his women.

But where were the children? The other wives? It seemed unlikely that Redd was looking at the entirety of the group. The man presumably had some way of recruiting new members, but even so, the life he could offer them would have limited appeal, particularly—or so Redd assumed—to women, who, from what he could tell, were treated almost like chattel slaves.

After Strong's plate was cleared away, he turned his gaze on Redd. "I'd like to hear more about what happened to you out there. Just because I don't hold with the current illegitimate government, it doesn't mean that I excuse lawbreaking. I need to know that you aren't a drug pusher or something worse."

Redd had anticipated this conversation and had crafted an explanation that had the benefit of being mostly true. "Well, it's a long story. The gist of it is that somebody wanted my property. I didn't want to sell, so he started playing rough. It all kind of spiraled from there."

Redd figured Strong would be sympathetic to the idea of someone just trying to protect his private property, so he conflated the schemes of Wyatt Gage—Anton's son—with those of Anton himself. If Strong possessed outside contacts with the ability to fact-check Redd's story, they would find ample evidence of Wyatt's attempted land grab and strong-arm tactics.

"He was mixed up in some other stuff too," Redd went on. "Illegal stuff. And rubbing elbows with some powerful people who wanted to make sure he would never be able to testify against them when the feds caught him. Because I knew all about it, they decided to come after me too. It's as simple as that."

Strong regarded him thoughtfully throughout this statement and for several seconds thereafter. "Nothing's ever 'simple as that,'" he said finally, shaking his head. "I feel like you're holding out on me."

Redd spread his hands. "I don't know what to tell you. That's how it is." He paused a beat, then added, "If you've got a way to check the news, you'll see that I'm telling you the truth. The man's name was Gage. Anton Gage. He was on a federal prison transport plane that was attacked when it landed in Oklahoma City. The men responsible for that are the same ones who came after me."

"Federal agents attacked a federal prison transport?" Strong shot back.

It was, Redd had to admit, a sticking point. He decided to play to Strong's paranoia. "I'm sure they made it look like someone else was to blame. You ever heard the term *false flag operation?*"

Redd could tell by the look in Strong's eyes that he'd plucked the right string. "I'll look into it," said Strong. His tone, however, suggested that he found the explanation sufficient. "If I may ask, what do you intend to do now?"

"I guess I hadn't thought that far ahead," admitted Redd. This was also mostly true, but not for the reasons Strong probably thought.

"The government isn't likely to stop coming after you. Not when they realize just how bad you've bloodied their noses."

Redd nodded slowly. "I guess you're right about that."

"This life . . ." Strong made an expansive gesture. "Living on the run. It's not easy. Take it from someone who knows. There have been times when I thought about giving up. Surrendering. Taking my chances in court, maybe get a chance to tell my side of it all." He shrugged. "If they let me live that long, which they probably wouldn't.

"Other times," Strong continued, "I thought about just going out in a blaze of glory." He shook his head again. "But that's the coward's way. Life. Freedom. Those are the gifts God gives us. We should treasure them, not squander them."

Redd had an idea of where Strong was going with this monologue, but remained silent, letting the other man make his point.

"If I'm not mistaken about you," Strong went on, "you're someone who feels the same way. That's why you fought back. And you've got the skills to keep yourself alive as long as it takes." He paused a beat before sinking the hook. "I could use someone like you."

This comment elicited a snort from one of the other men seated at the table. Redd didn't see who it was, but Strong shot a withering stare in the direction of someone seated across from Redd. Redd glanced over and saw that the offender was one of the younger men, and that despite Strong's reproving look, he was regarding Redd with open contempt. Evidently Strong's opinion of Redd was not shared by all his followers. The fact that the men were not afraid to openly disagree with Strong suggested that his hold over them was not as absolute as Redd had first imagined.

He returned his attention to Strong. "You want me to join your group?" This too was something he'd been expecting, but he tried to sound surprised, even a little awed.

"Our *family*," Strong corrected him. "We know how to avoid the authorities. Been doing it for thirty years. On your own, how long do you think you'll last?"

Redd made a show of considering the request. He wasn't certain how Strong would respond to a refusal, or even the appearance of equivocation. He suspected that if he said no, Strong would make a show of acceptance, but then have one of his men shoot him in the dead of night. That way, when the authorities discovered his remains, they would stop combing the woods in search of him, thus reducing the likelihood of their inadvertently discovering Strong and his followers. Judging by the looks he was getting from the other men at the table, there would be no shortage of volunteers.

Still, if he didn't push back a little, it might appear suspicious. "I've got a family, Mr. Strong. A ranch to take care of. I can't just leave all that behind."

"That's exactly what you have to do," declared Strong. "That part of your life is over. I know that's a bitter pill to swallow, but that's just how it is."

"What if I brought them with me?"

"The feds will be watching your folk, waiting for you to try to make contact. They'll never give up. Better your loved ones think you dead so they can move on."

It wasn't lost on Redd that, *technically* speaking, he was FBI. He was the leader of the fly team—whatever was left of it, anyway. If Strong found that out, it would be game over.

Redd affected a look of dismay while he appeared to contemplate this possible future. "This is a lot to take in," he said.

And it ain't ever going to happen.

"Ordinarily, I wouldn't even consider bringing an outsider into our midst. You see, we're not some gang of outlaws. We're a family, bound by our faith and traditions. Some of our ways will seem a little strange to you at first, but I think in time, you'll come to see that we're walking the path the gods have set before us." Strong smiled. "I sense something in you. Like I told you, you're a kindred spirit. You're tough. Not afraid to shed the blood of the unrighteous. Finding you feels like . . . like an answer to our prayers."

I don't know who you're praying to, thought Redd, *but it's not God.*

"How so?"

Strong's earnest smile slipped a little, as if the question had tapped a reservoir of shame. "We've been wandering in the wilderness so long that I'm afraid we're losing heart. You can teach us how to fight. Weapons. Tactics. Military discipline. You could transform us into an army. An army of righteous crusaders."

Yup, thought Redd. *He's a true believer. And he's dangerous alright.*

Redd surveyed the room once more, taking in where everyone was standing in his peripheral vision. For a brief moment, he considered making a move. He'd fought numerous men at once before. Though he was a big man, Redd was quick. So quick that he figured he could flip the table, grab Strong, and use the man as a human shield before anyone else was able to draw their weapon. But then what?

No, what he needed was to stall for a bit longer.

Knowing he had to be careful in how he responded, Redd rubbed his chin slowly. He wanted to buy himself enough time to gather Rubble and make a break for it. "This is . . . a lot to consider," he finally answered. "Could I sleep on it?"

Strong did not seem the least bit put off by the request. "Of course. But I will need an answer by morning. We're breaking camp first thing. There's another wave of federal agents coming, you can bet on it, and I aim to be long gone when they find this place."

"So soon?" Redd grimaced. "But I'm sure you're right."

Strong nodded then rose to his feet and turned his attention to the rest of the group. "Turn in early. I want to be packed and ready to go before sunrise."

The group rose in unison and immediately dispersed to go about their respective duties. Redd stood as well, feeling light-headed—the lingering effects of decreased blood volume—and had to sit down quickly to avoid blacking out. If Strong noticed Redd's moment of weakness, he gave no indication, but exited the tent along with the other men, leaving Redd in the company of the women who were busy clearing the table. Redd took a few deep breaths until the wave of vertigo passed, then rose again, slowly this time. As he did, Bekah approached, holding a large bowl full of meat scraps.

"For Rubble," she said, holding the dish up.

Although she wasn't smiling, her eyes held the same look he'd noticed earlier. It wasn't adoration, but he couldn't place it. "Thanks," he mumbled.

She gazed up at him. "You look a little peaked. Come on. I'll walk you back to the med tent."

As he couldn't disagree with her diagnosis, Redd nodded and let her lead the way. Although he didn't experience another near-fainting spell, he did feel a bone-deep fatigue, as if the mere act of digesting his meal was a Herculean effort. Given what he'd just been through, he knew he should count himself lucky, but he also knew that his ordeal was far from over. He wasn't going to be able to give his body the time it needed to recover.

"So, you going to stay with us?"

Bekah's comment broke him out of his reverie. "Uh, yeah," he said. "Looks like I might not have much of a choice."

"You sure that's what you want?"

Redd had to struggle to maintain a neutral expression. Although she'd made no effort to hide her curiosity about him, he had not expected such an overt expression of interest.

She's prying for something, but what?

Rubble chose that moment to bound out of the woods, racing to join them. Bekah quickly turned her attention to the dog, scratching behind his ears as she waved the food dish in front of him and set it down. Rubble immediately buried his nose in the dish and began greedily devouring the meat scraps.

Bekah watched the dog eat, avoiding Redd's gaze. Only when the bowl was licked clean a couple minutes later did she look at Redd again. "Stay or go, whatever you decide, you'd better do it quick."

Is she warning me?

Then without waiting for a response, she retrieved the dish, turned, and walked away.

THIRTY-EIGHT

After a heated debate, it was Emily, reasoning that Matthew would not have left Remington behind unless he intended to return, who made the decision that she and Mikey would wait at the hunting camp.

If they went out looking for him, she had argued, there was a very real possibility of missing him altogether.

Where are you, Matty?

Please, God, she prayed, *just give me a sign. Help me find my husband.*

She and Mikey had taken turns assuring each other that finding Remington was in fact a hopeful sign. It was proof that Redd had been at the camp, Mikey claimed. Probably only a few hours before.

She hoped desperately that that was the case.

While Emily could not fathom his reasons for leaving the quarter horse behind and venturing out on foot, she knew he would not have gone far.

But as the afternoon shadows lengthened, with no sign of Matthew, hope began to give way to despair.

Then they heard the distant whine of snowmobile engines echoing up the valley.

Emily's heart skipped a beat. She tried to tell herself that it meant nothing. People went snowmobiling on fire roads all the time. There was no reason to think that this was anything other than some kids enjoying a little winter recreation after a major snow event.

But she couldn't bring herself to believe it.

"We should hide," she told Mikey.

He nodded. "You get the horses inside. I'll try to cover our tracks."

That he had not disagreed told her it was the right decision.

While she led the horses back into the shelter, Mikey went about trying to brush away all their telltale foot- and hoofprints with a pine branch. It wouldn't hold up to a close inspection, and there was no disguising the trail they'd left back and forth across the mountain and all the way back to the main road, but then if the snowmobiles were already following that trail, it wouldn't matter how well Mikey was able to sweep the area. They'd be found in no time.

The engine noise continued to grow louder for a while, but then just as Mikey was about to join her and the horses in the too-small enclosure, the sound abruptly ceased.

Emily held her breath for a moment, as if afraid that in the sudden silence her exhalations might be heard, but then realized what nonsense that was. The snowmobiles were still a ways off, somewhere down in the valley below. She let the breath out, then looked over at Mikey.

"What do you think?"

"Could be nothing. Then again . . ." He shrugged. "Probably safer if we don't find out."

She nodded, then looked through the large opening at the front of the shelter, wondering if there was time to cover it with snow, further camouflaging their presence.

But another thought popped into her head.

Why?

They had come out here to help Matthew, not to cower in fear at the first sign of trouble.

She turned back to Mikey. "Let's go. I want to get a closer look."

Mikey was aghast. "*What?* No. Absolutely not. What if those are the guys hunting Matt?"

"Don't you think it might help to know that before they show up to kill us too?"

"Emily, this is not what we came out here to do."

"We came out here to help Matty," she insisted, fixing him with a stare that brooked no further argument. "We can help him by getting a better idea of what he's up against." Then she softened a little. "Let's just get a quick look. C'mon, Mikey. Two minutes. Tops."

Mikey let out an audible sigh. "You're just as bad as him, you know that? He never listens to me either."

"Mikey?"

"Yeah?"

"Shut up." A smile stretched across Emily's face. "Let's go!"

She heard him give a little growl of frustration, but he offered no further objection, so she stepped through the opening and headed out across the clearing. Mikey was right on her heels. As she neared the edge, she dropped to all fours so as not to present a large silhouette to anyone in the valley below and continued forward at a crawl. As she neared the precipice, the valley was gradually revealed.

Then she saw the snowmobiles.

"There," she whispered to Mikey, pointing.

There were seven of them, all idle and, at first glance, riderless. It took her a moment or two to discern the human shapes standing in a loose knot nearby because all of the men were wearing white and were hard to distinguish against the snowy background.

Camouflage, she realized.

"I don't think those guys are just out playing in the snow," mused Mikey.

Emily glanced over at him. He was peering down at the men through a pair of binoculars.

"What do you see?" she asked.

He lowered the glasses and passed them over to her. After adjusting them to her eyes, she zoomed in on the snowmobilers and this time was able to make out details, like the white tactical chest rigs the men wore and the weapons they carried. Most were armed with what looked to her like AR15s, wrapped in white tape to break up their outline, but two of them had long rifles—really long rifles—slung across their backs. The guns were so big that they protruded skyward at least a foot above the heads of the men carrying them.

As if tuned in to what she was seeing, Mikey commented, "A couple of those guys have got Barrett sniper rifles."

This information seemed more like something Matthew would have keyed in on, but then Emily remembered that Mikey was a voracious reader of mystery and thriller novels and had probably picked up a lot of gun trivia by osmosis. For her part, all Emily needed to hear was *sniper rifles.*

The mere fact of their presence settled on her like a heavy weight. Throughout the long ordeal, some part of her had secretly hoped that Matthew was just being paranoid. That he'd misread the situation and there was no hit team coming after him. But seeing them with her own eyes utterly erased such hopes.

She continued watching the meeting in the valley below. After a few minutes of discussion, the group broke up and returned to their snowmobiles, after which the noise of small engines filled the valley. One of the snowmobiles zoomed away back down the valley while the others moved out in pairs, heading in different directions. One of the pairs seemed to be heading up the slope directly below the ridge.

"We should get back," advised Mikey, and this time Emily was in full agreement. She handed the binoculars to him, and then together they crawled away from the edge a few yards before standing up and starting their return trek to the shelter. Yet even before they made it back, the increasing volume and pitch of the engine noise told them that the two snowmobiles were indeed coming up the mountainside.

Emily's mind raced through a list of possibilities.

We could make a run for it.

Not on foot. They'd never be able to outdistance the snowmobiles. But horses could go places that snowmobiles couldn't. Unfortunately, they'd already unsaddled their horses, giving them a break after the long ride in, and Emily very much doubted they had enough time to get them ready for another outing before the men on the snowmobiles reached them.

Riding bareback was an option, but not a great one. Emily hadn't ridden without a saddle since she was a teenager and had no idea if Mikey had ever done so. It wasn't a skill that could be learned on the go.

Or . . . they could fight. They had brought along hunting rifles and a shotgun and had plenty of ammunition. With the element of surprise on their side, they had the advantage.

"Get inside," Mikey said, as if reading her thoughts. "We'll wait until they're right outside and then let them have it."

But Emily shook her head. "No. It's no good."

"Em, we're out of time. We won't get another chance. We have to do this."

"As soon as we start shooting, we'll bring the rest of them right to us."

"Then we'll fight them too," insisted Mikey. "We don't have another choice."

She shook her head again, refusing to take another step. She wasn't squeamish about the prospect of taking a life. She'd done so before to protect herself and her family, and she wouldn't hesitate to pull the trigger if the need arose. But because she was a mother, with a family to think about, the idea of going out with guns blazing didn't sit well with her.

They might get lucky the first time. Kill both riders quickly. But once the element of surprise was gone, the opposing force would have all the advantages.

Numeric superiority, better weapons, better tactical training. A heroic stand against overwhelming odds might be Matthew's style—and he seemed to have a real knack for beating the odds—but it wasn't for her.

There's got to be another way.

The engine noise continued building to a fever pitch. The riders weren't bothering with the switchback trail but were coming straight up the slope.

"Emily, we have to do this!" Mikey started for the shelter entrance.

"No. Mikey." She reached out and took his hand, gripping it as if trying to squeeze her certainty into him. "There's a better way. Trust me." Then seeing the uncertainty in his eyes, she added, "They're not looking for us. They have no idea who we are."

"They're killers. They won't even bother to ask."

"I think they will. If things start to go south, we can always go for our guns."

Mikey looked unconvinced, but the point was rendered moot when the snowmobiles seemed to leap up over the precipice, stirring up clouds of powder as they crested the ridge. The riders spotted Emily and Mikey almost right away and immediately steered toward them, closing the remaining distance in a matter of seconds. The noise was so loud that Emily felt like covering her ears. Over the din she could just make out the horses in the shelter whinnying and stamping out their irritation at the disturbance.

The snowmobiles raced toward them like heat-seeking missiles, and for a fleeting moment, Emily thought, *I've made a terrible mistake.* But then when they were just ten yards away, the riders banked and skidded to a stop, shutting off their engines and dismounting quickly. One of them brought his weapon around, holding it with the muzzle pointed down at the snow, but in such a way that it could be raised and fired point-blank in the blink of an eye. The other man, however, approached with empty hands, his long rifle—*his Barrett,* thought Emily—slung across his back.

"Howdy, folks," he said, a big plastic smile pasted on a face that was ruddy from the cold. "Mind if I ask what you're doing up here?"

Emily's heart was pounding, but she managed to match his smile. "We're just up here checking on our hunting camps after the storm," she replied, then cocked her head to the side. "Mind if *I* ask *you* the same question?"

The man uttered a short laugh, then used his teeth to pull off the glove on his right hand, after which he reached into a large slit in the side of his all-white overgarment. Emily stiffened, ready to move if the man produced a handgun, but when he brought out his hand, it held only a wallet. He flipped it open and held it up, displaying a government-issued identification card and a gold shield.

"Homeland Security. We're conducting a sensitive operation in this area."

A memory of her visit to Sheriff Blackwood the previous night flashed through Emily's mind. What had he said? *"Agents from Homeland Security Investigations are on their way to Wellington to take Matthew in for questioning."*

The badge looked real enough.

Had Blackwood been told the truth after all? Was that what was really going on? *But if they just want to question Matthew,* she wondered, *why send out snipers?*

"Homeland Security?" asked Mikey. It came out as a nervous croak, but he kept talking. "Don't you guys hunt terrorists? Never heard of any terrorists in Montana."

The man's smile did not slip. "We hunt all kinds of bad guys," he said, putting the badge case away. "Not just terrorists." He then made a show of looking past Emily and Mikey, directing his gaze to the dark entrance to the shelter. "Whatcha got in there? Mind if I take a look?"

Emily sensed the question was rhetorical. He was going to look regardless of any objection on their part. She shrugged. "It's public land. I can't stop you. But be careful. Our horses are in there. You don't want to spook them."

The man laughed again, perhaps misunderstanding the reason for her warning, and then strode past both of them. He did not go inside the shelter but instead took a small flashlight from his chest rig and shone it inside.

"Four horses," he remarked. "But just two of you."

"The others are pack horses," said Mikey. Emily thought he said it a little too quickly, though it was only half a lie and completely plausible.

As long as he doesn't notice that there are three saddles in there.

"Pack horses?" The man looked to his counterpart, who was still standing by the snowmobiles and holding his weapon at a casual low ready. "That a thing?"

Emily almost laughed aloud at the question.

This guy doesn't have a clue.

The other man nodded. "Yeah. It's a thing." He said with a pronounced Texas drawl, which presumably gave him the authority to comment on anything having to do with horses.

The man with the sniper rifle accepted this with a shrug, then turned back to Emily and Mikey. "How long you folks been up here?"

"We rode up this morning," said Emily. "Been here a couple hours."

"Yeah? You seen anyone else out here?"

"Just you guys." Emily allowed this to sink in for a moment, then asked, "Why? Should we be looking out for anyone?"

The sniper regarded her for a long moment.

Too long, she thought. *He doesn't believe us.*

In her head, she tried to calculate how many steps it would take to reach the entrance to the shelter, grab one of the rifles, and start firing. Of course, the real question was how far she would get before the other man opened fire on her.

But then the sniper shook his head. "Probably not. All the same, you folks might want to consider heading back."

Emily couldn't tell if the remark was merely a suggestion or a politely stated ultimatum. "It'll be dark soon," she countered. "Better to wait out the night. That was our plan anyways, stay the night and head home in the morning."

The sniper exchanged a look with his partner, then nodded to Emily. "Yeah, that's probably a better idea. Don't want to be traipsing around out here after dark. Never know what you might run into."

He strolled past them, returning to the snowmobiles, threw one leg over the saddle, and settled astride it. After replacing his glove, he reached for the starter button, but then hesitated, looking back to Emily and Mikey. "Listen, if you folks hear any shooting, don't pay it no mind."

Emily nodded and flashed an upraised thumb.

The sniper laughed, then pressed the starter. The two snow machines roared to life almost simultaneously and then cut across the clearing, leaving a cloud of snow in their wake. In thirty seconds, they were lost completely from sight, with only the distant whine of their engines attesting to their presence.

As she watched them go, Emily felt her spirits rise. It wasn't just that they had survived what had looked at first glance like a potentially fatal encounter. The visit by the Homeland Security agents had counterintuitively filled her with hope.

Beside her, Mikey blew out his breath in a long sigh. "Well, that was tense. But . . . you were right. That was the smart play. So are we really leaving in the morning, or was that something you said just to get rid of that guy?"

She turned to him, unable to suppress a smile. "They're still looking for him."

"Yeah. So?"

"They're looking for him because they haven't found him yet. He's still out here. He's still alive."

Mikey nodded slowly in understanding, and then he too began to smile. "Like there was ever any doubt. We're not going anywhere, are we?"

"Not without Matty."

THIRTY-NINE

Earlier that day, as he had made his way from the terminal to the baggage claim area to collect his beloved XM109—presently disassembled and nestled inside a bombproof Pelican 1750 hard case—Chad Beaudette had passed a large poster showing a panoramic cityscape emblazoned with the legend: *Welcome to HELENA, Queen City of the Rockies.*

He'd given a derisive snort, thinking, *It oughta say, Welcome to Montana, the back end of nowhere.*

The Baton Rouge native had been of that opinion long before arriving at the regional airport in Helena. In fact, he'd decided it the moment that the boss called, interrupting a well-earned day of chillaxication at Daytona Beach, and told him to get to Montana ASAP. Nothing he'd seen since arriving had changed his mind. The so-called Treasure State was big, cold, and empty.

And somewhere out in that big, cold emptiness, Javelin Team was MIA.

When the call had come in, he'd figured the missing team had probably just gone into a dead zone—it was the back end of nowhere, after all—and that they'd probably pop back up on the radar by the time Arrow Team put boots on the ground.

But that hadn't happened.

Instead, Chad—in full winter overwhites, astride a snowmobile with the

191

AMPR slung across his back—had ridden out with the rest of his team into the frozen wasteland, following Javelin's GPS track. The device had stopped transmitting sometime during the previous night, but the log-in record showed the team's final location several miles from the nearest road. At last report, Javelin, led by Saber Six—Colin Kilmeade—had been tracking their target on foot, which sounded truly hellacious to Chad, but which also meant that they hadn't gone as far as they might have if they'd been on snowmobiles. Unfortunately, when Arrow Team reached Javelin's last known location—a valley covered in a couple feet of snow—they'd found no trace of their comrades.

Just as with the communications breakdown, there might have been a perfectly reasonable explanation for this. The GPS unit might have been damaged, or the batteries might have gone dead. But whether or not that was the case, the team was missing, and nobody had any earthly clue where they had gone.

Unable to get a signal out, Arrow Six had made the decision to ride back until he could make contact with Dagger Six—Cormac Kilmeade himself—to report the initial findings and request aerial support in the form of the DHS MQ-9 Predator drone Saber and Javelin Teams had been using during their search the previous day. While he was doing that, the rest of the team was sent out in pairs to comb the area. Chad's search partner was his spotter, Jack Wagner—Arrow Two.

Since it had been nearly twelve hours since the final GPS contact, the search area comprised a circle about twelve miles across—an area of over a hundred square miles. It was a lot of territory to cover, but Chad figured that eventually someone from Javelin would hear them coming and try to initiate communication.

He still clung to that hope half an hour later when he glimpsed a spot of red in a snowdrift. He immediately shut off his snow machine, dismounted, and went to investigate.

"Whatcha got?" asked Wagner, after turning his snowmobile off.

Chad knelt down to investigate the crimson spot, which was about the size of a half-dollar coin. "Looks like blood."

Wagner came over to stand beside him. "Man, how'd you see that?"

"I got good eyes, Jack. It's why I'm the sniper." He searched the immediate area looking for more color, but instead saw something else in the drift.

"What's that?" he murmured, brushing away some of the snow. It fell away, revealing an open eye, staring sightlessly back at him.

Chad recoiled, a curse slipping past his lips. Behind him, Wagner breathed something similarly profane, adding, "That's a body."

Chad stared at the revealed face for a long moment, then begin brushing more of the snow away. The substance was a grainy crust, more ice than powder, as if it had partially melted then refrozen, which he realized was exactly what had happened. The body had been warm when laid here, and the snow covering it had begun to melt even as the body cooled.

The rest of the face gradually appeared, somewhat distorted by the terrible trauma visited upon it at the instant the candle of the man's life was extinguished. The deceased's other eye was gone, blown away by what could only have been a large-caliber bullet. That same bullet had also blasted out the back of the man's skull. Yet even with the disfigurement, there was no question as to the man's identity. He was, after all, the spitting image of his twin brother.

"That's . . ." Wagner pointed at the dead man, the gesture saying what he could not seem to put into words.

"Yeah," Chad muttered, feeling suddenly nauseous.

The dead man was Colin Kilmeade.

Chad's reaction had nothing to do with the grisly state of Colin's remains. Rather, he was overcome with both disbelief and dread. Disbelief that Colin was dead, to all appearances killed by a mere cowboy from the back end of nowhere. Dread at the prospect of having to report Colin's death to Cormac Kilmeade.

He took several deep breaths until the urge to vomit passed, then bent to the task of fully uncovering the remains. Even before the excavation was half finished, it became apparent that there were more bodies hidden in the drift, stacked up like cordwood and hastily covered over.

Javelin Team.

Elite operators one and all, and the cowboy had wiped them out.

"The boss is going to crap a brick," said Wagner as the fourth body was revealed.

"I think he knew something was wrong," Chad replied. "Why else did he send us out here? After what happened to Saber Team, it was obvious that the cowboy was a lot more dangerous than anyone thought."

"We gotta call this in."

Chad nodded dully, understanding that what his spotter really meant was, *You've gotta call this in.* He keyed his mic. "Arrow Seven, this is Arrow One, over."

When he got no reply, he tried something different. "Arrow One, calling any Arrow element, over."

Still nothing. The Motorola radios they used for intrateam communications supposedly had a range of over fifty miles, but that was dependent on a lot of variables such as terrain and atmospheric conditions. Evidently the little valley they were in was blocking his signal. If Montana was the back end of nowhere, they were firmly lodged in its butt crack.

Suddenly, a terrible thought occurred to him.

The cowboy is still out here.

He looked around quickly, seeing the landscape as if for the first time, no longer as a cold, empty wasteland, but rather through the eyes of a sniper.

We're exposed here.

He thought about unslinging the XM109 but immediately dismissed the idea. Without a target the AMPR was worse than useless, while the mere act of shifting to an alert posture might provoke an attack. Instead, he turned slowly to Wagner.

"Jack, we need to find cover. Now."

A look of confusion flitted across the other man's face, but just as quickly, understanding dawned. "Ready to move," he said, barely louder than a whisper.

"On three," replied Chad, and when he had given the three count, they hurtled into motion, circling around the drift, plowing through the snow to seek shelter in the nearby stand of trees. Chad expected to hear a report chasing after them, though he didn't think he'd catch a bullet. The odds of anyone, even a master sniper, picking them off on the move were pretty slim. But there was no shot. For several seconds thereafter, as he lay prone on the frozen ground, the only sound he could hear was the fierce beating of his heart.

Finally, Wagner spoke up. "What do you think? Is he out there?"

Chad shook his head. "No idea. But if he is, he knows that we know. He won't hang around." He rolled over to face his teammate. "Ride out until you can get a signal, then let the rest of the team know that the mission has changed."

Wagner's face screwed up a little, no doubt contemplating how much danger he would be in as he ventured out into the open, but then he gave a nod. "What are you going to do?"

Chad hefted the anti-materiel rifle. "I'm going hunting."

FORTY

The Helena field office of the Department of Homeland Security was located a literal stone's throw from the entrance to the Helena Regional Airport, in a bland, rambling one-story structure that seemed almost to vanish into the snowy landscape. Without guidance from her phone's map app, Stephanie Treadway would probably have driven right past it without even noticing.

The drive up to Helena had not been quite as harrowing as her earlier journey from Bozeman to Wellington. Traffic had been light, the roads were plowed and sanded, and the snow had stopped falling, though if weather reports were correct, there was another wave on the way. Even so, Treadway's forearms were aching from nearly two hours of relentlessly gripping the Edge's steering wheel. Her fingers felt like they were permanently curled into claws. Yet as stressful as the drive had been, she was grateful to actually be doing something.

She'd spent most of the day sitting idle at the Stillwater County courthouse, waiting for some indication of what to do next. The sheriff had finally come around, accepting her version of what was really going on and admitting that Matthew Redd was "in a heap of trouble," but without a clear idea of what to do to help him, the sheriff's hands were tied. Redd had gone off the grid, and Blackwood lacked the resources to initiate a manhunt to find him. Further complicating matters, the winter storm with all its attendant crises was keeping his department fully occupied.

"Until Matthew decides to reach out to us," Blackwood had told her, "there's not a whole lot we can do for him."

Determined to be there if and when Redd made contact, Treadway had settled in for a long wait, and there she had stayed until, late that afternoon, Gavin Kline had called with a revelation that had changed everything. Aaron Decker had put a name to the entity behind both the Oklahoma City attack and the hit order on Matthew Redd—the Praetorian.

And just like that, Treadway knew how to help Redd.

Until that moment, Treadway had believed, much as Kline himself had, that both the assassination of Anton Gage and the hunt for Matthew Redd had been carried out by men posing as Homeland Security agents, and thus there would be little purpose in reaching out to the actual Department of Homeland Security. But Kline's theory about the Praetorian's identity and a better understanding of the scope of his power and influence had opened up new possibilities, particularly where the DHS was concerned.

Steeling herself in anticipation of the frigid external environment, she exited the Edge and hastened to the building's main entrance. She presented her credentials to the security guard at the front entrance and, as she had an appointment, was directed to the office of Special Agent in Charge Martin Shores.

She had called ahead, partly as a matter of professional courtesy, but mostly to ensure that Shores would be in his office and not taking a snow day. She had not given him any details regarding the nature of her visit but merely couched it in terms of coordinating activities.

Shores, who looked like Hollywood's idea of a heroic G-man, did a double take when she entered his office and quickly got to his feet, extending a hand to greet her. Treadway got the distinct impression that, had she been a male or even objectively less attractive, he would have remained in his seat, but that little bit of sexism was just fine with her if it greased the wheels.

After the handshake, which lasted just a second or two longer than it ought to have, Shores gestured to a guest chair. "Well, Special Agent Treadway," he began, grinning as he stated her full title, as if doing so was some sort of inside joke. "What can the Department of Homeland Security do for the Bureau today?"

She took her seat and returned her most radiant smile before answering. "Actually, Martin . . ." She caught herself. "Forgive me, SAC Shores—"

"Marty's fine . . . Stephanie."

She inclined her head. "Marty. Actually, I think there's something the Bureau can do for DHS."

"Do tell."

"It's come to my attention that HSI is looking for a certain Matthew Redd."

Shores's smile plummeted. He leaned forward in his chair. "I'm afraid that's not a subject I'm at liberty to discuss, Special Agent Treadway. I'm sorry you came all the way out here for nothing."

The suddenness of the reversal was a little shocking, but Treadway had anticipated resistance and stuck to her script. "Marty, I think you have the wrong idea about this. I'm here to help. Matthew Redd is a Bureau asset. We can bring him in for you. Or at the very least give you critical intel that might help you find him."

Shores regarded her for a few seconds as if weighing the sincerity of the offer, but then he shook his head. "No, I think you've got the wrong idea. This office isn't part of the Matthew Redd investigation. That's happening at a higher level. My involvement was solely in the role of liaison with local LEOs, telling them to keep out of it. And that, by the way, is what I've been ordered to do as well."

"But surely if you were able to bring Redd in—"

"These orders came down from the office of the director," Shores said. "Matthew Redd is a live wire, and I'm going to keep my distance and then some."

She dialed her smile down a little, just enough to show that she was disappointed but not mad at Shores. "Well, that's too bad. But my information is still solid, and I'd like to get it to someone who can use it. Maybe you could put me in touch with whoever is leading the search?"

Shores shook his head again. "Can't help you with that because I don't know. You're welcome to call the director's office. Maybe somebody there will talk to you." He shrugged. "But I wouldn't count on it."

Treadway let go of the smile and instead turned her lips down in a pout. "Well, that's really a shame." She gave Shores a long, scrutinizing look. "Are you sure there isn't some way you could put me in touch with the guys on the ground? You know, help me cut through some of the red tape?" Sensing an imminent objection, she added, "Nobody would have to know it was you that helped me. But I would be grateful."

The last statement seemed to give him pause. She could see the wheels in his head turning; the unspoken question was in his eyes. *How grateful?* But then the curtain fell again. "I wish I could help you, but . . ." He shrugged. "I just don't have access to that information."

Realizing that she was up against an impenetrable wall, Treadway decided to change tactics. "Listen, I was in Oklahoma City yesterday."

Shores raised an eyebrow. "You were?"

She nodded. "Right in the thick of it. Now, I know that the search for Redd is connected to what happened there, so as you can probably guess, I've got a personal stake in this. I lost several friends yesterday. I know that an HSI special operations unit is taking the lead. I also know that those guys are never a hundred percent independent. There's got to be a trail. Intel requests, travel vouchers, hotel recommendations . . . something. A thread I can pull on to find the right person to talk to."

The fact that Shores did not refuse the request out of hand told Treadway that she was getting somewhere.

"You've got something, don't you?" she pressed.

"It's . . . ah, not exactly a smoking gun. But . . ." He sighed. "It's also not exactly a closely guarded secret."

She brought back her smile and turned it up to eleven.

"For the last couple days, one of our UAVs has been deployed to the Stillwater County area."

"UAVs? A drone?"

"A Predator MQ-9. We mostly use them along the southern border, but occasionally we request one to help with cross-border smuggling from Canada. Anyway, I don't know who requisitioned the air support, but I can access the nav logs and tell you when and where the aircraft was operating. I know it's not much . . ." He shrugged.

Shores was right. It wasn't much, but it was something. Treadway nodded. "Show me."

The SAC swiveled his chair toward his computer keyboard and, after entering a few commands, turned the monitor so that Treadway could see the display. The screen showed a topographic map with few landmarks, superimposed with brightly colored lines that looked like the errant scribbles of a toddler.

"Each of these tracks is a different mission," explained Shores. "The first flight— the yellow track—launched from Nevada yesterday morning at about 0600 hours."

Treadway focused on the yellow line, which entered the map from the south. Most of the lines overlapped above a mountainous area with few roads, but the yellow line bypassed the mountains to fly back and forth above an area near what appeared to be a major highway running north-south.

That's Redd's ranch, Treadway realized. *They had him under surveillance yesterday. Before the attack in Oklahoma City.*

"It arrived on station at around noon and patrolled for a couple hours," said Shores. "Then came up here to refuel."

"I thought those things could stay aloft for days."

"I've heard forty hours is the limit, but we don't like to test that for obvious reasons. My guess is that the guy in charge wanted to top off the tanks before going operational. See the blue track? That mission lasted over nine hours."

Treadway took note of the blue line, which meandered back and forth in an area due east of the yellow track. *That was them following Redd into the mountains,* she thought. *But did they get him?*

"Looks like they RTB'd early this morning," continued Shores.

RTB'd—returned to base. They wouldn't have done that if there was a reason to stay.

It felt like an ominous development.

"Now this is interesting." Shores used his mouse to zoom out, revealing the yellow and blue lines tracing back to their origin in southern Nevada. When he did, a third line was revealed—a red track that began at the same origin point and appeared to be following the same path through the skies. "It looks like they're bringing it back up here for another mission."

Treadway barely managed to stifle a gasp.

He's still alive. They haven't found him yet.

"When will it get here?"

Shores's head bobbed as he did some mental math. "Probably not until after dark." He stared at the screen for a moment longer, then shrugged. "That's all I've got really. Like I said, it's not much."

"Actually, it's very helpful." She held his gaze a moment. "I don't suppose you would be willing to share that GPS information. You know, interagency cooperation and whatnot."

Shores appeared to be considering the request, so she added, "Maybe when I get finished up here, I'll let you buy me a drink at the local watering hole."

A drink or two with Special Agent in Charge Martin Shores was a small price to pay for access to the navigational tracks of the DHS drone. With that information, Sheriff Blackwood just might be able to find Redd before the kill team and get him into protective custody.

Her suggestion brought his smile back in full force. "Just give me your number and I'll text it to you."

"Clever." She grinned and handed him her business card.

FORTY-ONE

Redd lay on his cot in the med tent, not quite asleep but in a deeply relaxed state like a hypnotic trance. His senses remained on full alert, his body on standby like a car idling in neutral, waiting for the signal to switch gears and go. As tired as he was, and as much as his body needed real, restorative sleep, he couldn't afford to relax his vigilance.

Outside, he could hear the sounds of Strong's men moving about, packing up their gear in preparation for an early departure the following day. He wondered at the logistics of the move. Based on what he had seen during his brief outing to the mess tent, there was a great deal more equipment in the camp than could be easily transported by such a small group, especially given the winter conditions. Did Strong have other followers in the camp that Redd had not seen? Or was he counting on support from accomplices outside his little community?

It was a passing thought, and ultimately not something he cared to expend brain power on. He was going to be long gone before Strong's people broke camp in the morning.

Redd waited to arise from the cot until 2300 hours—11 p.m. It was earlier than he would have liked. Two-thirty or three would have been optimal, but he figured that if any rogue elements in Strong's organization were going to make a move on him, they would fixate on the idea of coming at midnight.

With the electric lantern switched off, the interior of the tent was pitch black, but he made his way to the flap by memory and eased it open. Outside, the glow of starlight reflecting from the snow provided more than enough illumination for him to ascertain that Strong had left no one to stand guard at the med tent. Redd remained there, watching and waiting, just in case there was a roving sentry on patrol, but if there was, he was somewhere else. All was still in the camp.

He glanced down at Rubble, who sat expectantly beside him, and raised a finger to his lips. Although it was wishful thinking on his part to believe that Rubble would understand the signal, the dog did not answer with his customary *woof* but just stared up at him expectantly, as if to say, *Well, what are you waiting for? Get on with it.*

Redd shoved his bare hands into his pockets—his gloves had not been among the articles returned to him—and started forward slowly, circling around to the back of the tent to keep it between himself and the rest of the camp. He was all too painfully aware of the *crunch-squeak* noise of his boots compressing the snow underfoot, but as there was nothing he could do to mitigate it, he continued forward, hoping that it wasn't as loud as it seemed.

He soon left the camp behind and found himself fully enveloped by the dark woods. Here there was little light to guide his way, and he had to grope forward, keeping a hand out in front of him to avoid walking into a tree or getting raked by a low branch. The temperature was well below freezing, and he could only tolerate a few minutes of exposure before necessity forced him to switch hands.

At first he had no clear idea of direction and could only hope that he was keeping to a more or less straight line, but he soon realized that he was on a slope. He turned into it and began climbing, hoping that eventually he would reach an elevation where he could get above the trees to get a better look at both the terrain and the sky. If he could get a rough idea of where he was and determine cardinal directions from the position of the north star, he felt certain he would be able to find his way back to the old hunting camp where he'd left Remington. After that he would have to play it by ear.

His strategy soon bore fruit as the spacing of the trees opened up, allowing more starlight to penetrate the overstory. He wasn't yet able to spot any familiar constellations to guide him to the north star, but with more light, he was able to move faster and keep his hands warm.

His first hint of trouble came when he realized that Rubble was no longer beside him. He turned and spied the dog just a few paces back, motionless but fully alert, staring back down the slope. Rubble had detected something, heard a faint noise or caught a scent that had arrested his attention. That he was motionless and not raising an alarm or going on the attack suggested some uncertainty on his part about what it was, but Redd wasn't going to take any chances. If his premonition about a midnight attack was correct, then Strong's men were already aware of his departure and might have decided to come after him.

He did not have to wait long for confirmation. No more than a minute after taking cover, he spied a glow moving through the trees just below his position. A moment later the glow resolved into the beam of a flashlight illuminating the snow and revealing the tracks of both man and dog. The light obscured the identity of the person holding it, but from what Redd could tell, there was only one of them.

That will make this easier, he thought.

He watched the figure's approach, letting the person come closer while mentally rehearsing the takedown. If he was lucky, the man would be armed and Redd would be able to equip himself with his weapon, thus improving his odds in any future encounter. If he was really lucky, the man would be wearing gloves, size extra large.

As the light drew nearer, Redd looked away, shielding his eyes to protect his night vision, and instead focused on the sound of the man's footsteps. He tensed, ready to spring out as soon as the figure drew even with his hiding spot, but just then the footsteps stopped and the light moved, seeking out a dark, motionless shape farther up the hill.

Breathing a silent curse, Redd launched himself at the now unmoving figure. Yet even as he moved, he heard a familiar voice whisper, "Rubble, is that you, boy?"

Redd barely managed to stop himself before colliding with the figure, which he now understood was not a man at all, but a young woman.

It was Bekah Strong.

FORTY-TWO

Instead of wrapping an arm around her neck and putting her in a chokehold, as he'd originally planned to do when he'd thought she was someone else, Redd clamped one hand over Bekah's mouth to stifle any cries and, with the other, snatched the flashlight out of her hand, shoving it inside his coat pocket to hide the beam.

Rubble, who had begun bounding toward her the moment she spoke his name, came to a halt just a few feet away. Although unable to fathom why his master was wrestling with the nice lady who had given him dinner earlier, the violence of Redd's actions evidently clued him in to the fact that something was wrong. His hackles went up and he began emitting a low growl through bared teeth.

"Easy, boy," Redd murmured. "I've got this."

Bekah had immediately begun struggling, a reflexive action, but he maintained a firm grip, leaned close to her ear, and whispered, "I'm going to let go of you. Don't make a sound. Got it?"

Her struggles ceased as soon as he spoke, and a moment later, he felt her head bob in what he took to be a nod.

"Okay. I'm letting go." He loosened his hold, only a little at first, ready to tighten his grip again if she decided to rethink her pledge to remain quiet. Finally, he spun her around to face him. "What are you doing out here?" he hissed.

"Looking for you, obviously," she replied, managing to sound defiant despite a tremor of fear in her voice.

"*Obviously*," he retorted. "Why?"

"Because you're leaving, and I want you to take me with you."

Suddenly, it all made sense to Redd. No, it was never adoration she held for him, but rather hope. She viewed him as her ticket to getting away from Strong and his group, or "family."

I don't have time for this.

He sighed. "Did you come alone? Does anyone know you're out here?"

"Yes," she said. "Alone, I mean. And no, nobody back at the camp knows. At least, not yet."

"What do you mean *not yet*?"

"They're going to figure it out pretty quick when they realize that you're gone. They'll probably think you took me along as a hostage."

Perfect.

Redd muttered an oath under his breath. He had been expecting someone from Strong's camp to pursue him sooner or later but had not anticipated that it might be Bekah. This was a complication he didn't need.

"All right, back to my first question. Why did you come after me?"

"I told you. I want you to take me with you. And . . ."

"And *what*?"

"I was trying to save you," she said. "Kevin is planning to kill you. I overheard him talking to Devon about it. I came to warn you, but you were already gone."

"You came to warn me?"

She didn't respond.

"Look, I appreciate it, but you don't need to worry about me, Bekah. You need to head back before your father finds out that you're out here. *Go.*"

"I'm not worried about you," she said defiantly. "I'm worried about *me*. And now that I'm out here, there's no just going back."

"Go back," Redd repeated. "Tell them you tried to stop me. Bekah, seriously, you don't want to go on the run with me. I'm sure you've had a hard life, but what I'm heading into isn't easy, especially if your friends are coming to hunt me down."

Her anger flared. "They aren't my friends."

"Fine. Not friends. Call them whatever you want. But—"

"Kevin thinks he's going to marry me," she blurted. A tear crept down her cheek. "In case you hadn't noticed, there aren't exactly a lot of choices out here when it comes to finding a husband. And the other men know that Kevin wants me. They won't stand up to him. Not that any of them are much better."

Get moving, he told himself. *No time to waste.*

"You tried telling him you don't want to get married?"

She shook her head. "You don't understand. I have to get married. It's required after you turn eighteen."

"Required?" Redd had a feeling he already knew the answer to his next question, and where this conversation was going. "By who?"

"My father."

"I know your dad is the little ruler of his own traveling kingdom here, but he can't force you to get married."

"Maybe that's how it works in your world," said Bekah, her voice trailing off for a moment, "but that's not how it is in the Family."

More of the puzzle pieces clicked into place. Strong was going to use Bekah to broker power through marriage.

How could he do that to his own daughter?

"Look, Bekah, I'm sorry. I'd like to do something to help you, but right now I . . . I just can't. You need to get back to your camp."

"Matt, please. Take me with you."

The plea was so urgent, so unhesitating, that Redd realized it had probably been her intention from the moment she saw him.

I don't have time for this, he told himself. But deep down, he knew he couldn't abandon her.

"There are men hunting me, Bekah. You'd be in danger."

"I'm already in danger." She stared up at him. "Please, Matt. I can't stay here any longer. Even if I do go back, if they know I helped you in any way, or that I didn't stop you, they'll kill me."

Redd hoped that wasn't true. He hoped Strong wouldn't kill his own daughter. Then again, something told him that the alternative, whatever other form of punishment they might enact upon her, could be even worse than death.

Redd gritted his teeth in the darkness. He had already wasted too much time talking to her. He needed to get moving. "Bekah—"

"I won't go back. You can't make me. I'll just keep following you anyway, so you might as well let me come with you."

"I could just tie you to a tree," he threatened.

She put her hands on her hips. "You wouldn't."

Redd swore again. She had called his bluff. He didn't have a choice now. At least not one he could live with. Bekah needed him, and Redd knew he might be the only chance she had at getting away.

Poor kid.

He relented with a sigh. "Fine. I'll do my best to get you someplace safe."

As he said it, it occurred to him that he had no idea where that might be. His plans had mostly focused on getting away from Strong's camp. He had not given much thought to what would happen after that.

I guess I've got all night to figure it out, he thought.

"But, Bekah, I can't make any promises, okay? I can't even guarantee I'll keep myself safe. I mean, look where I ended up. These men chasing me, and I'm not talking about your father, want me dead. They're trained to kill and won't stop until they complete their mission."

"Then we better get moving!" Her triumphant smile gleamed in the starlight. Then she reached into her coat and took out a small bundle. "Here. I figured you could probably use this."

Redd took it, thinking it was a scarf or something, but as soon as he felt its heaviness, he knew what it was—his Ruger, holstered in his gun belt.

"I reloaded it," said Bekah. "It's ready to shoot."

It's a start, thought Redd, happy to see the gun returned. *But it won't be nearly enough to battle everyone.*

FORTY-THREE

With a little help from Bekah, Redd was able to get a better idea of the precise location of Strong's camp, and the distance and direction they would need to travel in order to reach the old hunting camp. If her description was correct, the site was only about six miles away, a journey Redd felt he could make in two to three hours.

It soon became apparent that this estimate was wildly off the mark. Part of this was due to conditions on the ground. The previous day's snowfall had largely settled, compressing under its own weight to form an icy crust that sometimes held their weight but was just as likely to break apart. Moving over it wasn't necessarily harder than trying to slog through fresh powder, just more tedious.

What really slowed them down, however, was the fact that Bekah was not as hardy as Redd had assumed she would be. It seemed that in Strong's organization, the menfolk went out hunting and scouting the wilderness, while the women remained behind cooking and performing other chores about the camp. While such labors were physically demanding, they did not build aerobic endurance. Despite her youth and the appearance of good health, Bekah tired quickly and required frequent rest breaks.

Redd would have found these delays frustrating if not for the fact that his own stamina was somewhat compromised. The mental tricks he had always relied on to keep him moving through grueling long-distance ruck marches when he had been a Marine could not overcome the fact that his red blood cell count was far below optimal. The exertion was, he imagined, similar to what high-altitude mountaineers experienced in the "death zone" on Mount Everest.

He tried to keep them both going, knowing that if anyone from the Family was coming after them, every second spent not moving brought them that much closer to a possible confrontation, but mere knowledge of that danger could not empower them to overcome physical realities.

At first he allowed them two minutes of rest for every fifteen minutes of travel. But those two minutes soon became five, and the interval of travel shrank to ten and then seven. Redd eventually stopped trying to force the issue and resigned himself to the fact that they might have to turn and fight at some point. When that happened, they would stand a better chance if they weren't completely exhausted.

The breaks posed another problem, however, one that Redd couldn't dismiss as easily. On the move, their exertion generated more than enough heat to keep the cold at bay, but when they stopped to rest, a chill set in quickly. When they were able to keep the rest periods brief, the cold temperatures provided an additional motivation to get moving again.

As they trudged along, clouds began scudding across the sky, blotting out the starlight. Not long thereafter, the wind picked up and fresh snow began to fall. Redd found a silver lining in these dark clouds—the wind and snow would erase their tracks, making it harder for any pursuers to track them.

Harder, but not impossible.

✖   ✖   ✖

When the attack finally came, even Rubble was caught unaware.

They were descending a pass, one Redd recognized as just a mile or so to the south of the ridge where the hunting camp was located. Given the treacherous conditions on the slope, not to mention their ever-increasing fatigue, he thought it best to negotiate the steeper portions in a series of switchbacks, which would increase the distance traveled considerably but make for easier going.

They were about a quarter of the way down when they heard the shot.

Redd couldn't fix a location for the shooter, nor did he see where the bullet went. All he knew for certain was that the shot had missed. He assumed that it had come from above, that Kevin or someone else from Strong's Family had tracked them to the summit of the pass, spotted them moving against the stark white snowfield, and fired down on them.

Redd's first impulse was to draw the Ruger and begin looking for the enemy.

His second was to find cover to avoid the next shot. But with snow reducing visibility to only a few yards, and no real idea where the gunman was, he didn't know where to aim the big handgun. Finding cover was similarly problematic. He could throw himself flat against the slope, but there was nothing to hide behind—no rocks or trees—and because the unseen enemy had the high ground, lying prone on the snow would only serve to give the shooter a bigger silhouette to aim at. That left only one tactical alternative: evasion.

A moving target was always harder to hit, but the real purpose of evasive maneuvers was offensive in nature. He could either find a better place from which to engage the enemy or shorten the intervening distance in order to get a better shot at the man. Redd figured the latter afforded him the best chance of survival. If he could zigzag back up the slope and get a visual fix on the gunman, the Ruger would take care of the problem. Unfortunately, there remained one other consideration. He wasn't alone.

Unarmed as she was, there was no good reason for Bekah to close with the enemy. Moreover, if she stayed with him, the size of their silhouette would almost double, which in turn doubled the chances that a bullet would find one of them. It made more sense for them to split up, for Bekah to continue heading down while he made his way back up.

He had only a moment in which to read Bekah in on his plan, but before he could say a word, her panic took over. She whirled away and tried to run straight downhill.

He had just enough time to shout, "Wait!" before the crust of snow broke underneath her, causing her to pitch forward. Unable to arrest her fall, she went tumbling down the slope, and in an instant, she was gone, carried along in a small avalanche of disturbed snow.

Before he could make up his mind about whether or not to go after her, another report thundered from above, then another, and this time Redd heard the bullet splitting the air close—too close—to his head. The shooter was dialing in his location. He realized then that the first shot hadn't really been aimed at them. The men from the Family wanted to bring Bekah home alive. Their intent had simply been to flush them out. And it had worked. Now that Bekah was no longer in close proximity to Redd, they weren't holding back.

Redd spun around, facing down the hill. From the corner of his eye, he spotted Rubble, barking and jumping excitedly in place, as if he knew that Redd was in trouble but wasn't sure what he could do about it.

"Go after her, boy!" Redd shouted, pointing down the slope. The dog immediately bounded away. Redd was right behind him, but unlike the dog, he did not try to run downhill. Instead, he dropped into a seated position on the snow and began sliding down the mountain on his backside.

Unexpected pain flared in his arms and chest as the sudden movement stressed wounds that had only just begun to heal. Redd felt his stitches tearing, imagined blood weeping into his bandages, but there was nothing to be done about it. That pain was transitory, replaced by the chill of snow flying up into his face and inside his clothes as he plowed his way down the mountain.

With limited visibility due to the falling snow, he quickly lost sight of any reference points, but in just a few seconds, he spied a dark shape directly in his path. It was Rubble, his coat dusted with white, standing guard over another shape, this one partially buried in a mound of snow. Driving his heels down, Redd skidded to a stop just a few feet away from the dog. He could now make out Bekah's form. A crust of ice clung to her like an exoskeleton, but she was moving, struggling to extricate herself.

Another report cracked the air overhead. "Stay down!" Redd shouted. He flipped over on his belly, drew the Ruger, and began looking for a target. Snow continued to swirl around him, obscuring the summit of the pass, but after a moment he thought he saw something moving against the white background. He sighted down the barrel and took the shot.

The big handgun bucked in his grip, momentarily eclipsing Redd's view of the target. He thumbed the hammer back, searching the area again, but saw only white. Then in the corner of his eye he saw movement off to his right and brought the Ruger around for another shot. Once more the thunderous recoil caused him to lose sight of the ephemeral target. He didn't know if he had hit anything, or if there had ever been anything there to hit in the first place, but he did know that the two shots he had fired had, in all likelihood, betrayed his location. It was time to get moving.

He slammed the Ruger into its holster, then turned to check on Bekah and tell her that they needed to keep moving, but in that instant, someone or something blindsided him, bowling him over and sending him sliding down the mountain like a runaway bobsled.

FORTY-FOUR

Half a mile away, Chad Beaudette muttered a curse as he relaxed his finger and let out the trigger of the AMPR. He'd been a heartbeat away from taking the shot. The reticle had been lined up on the target, his finger already taking up the slack, when someone came out of nowhere and bulldozed his target completely out of view.

He tried to follow the pair of entangled figures as they slid away, but shrouded as they were, not only by the flakes falling from the heavens but also the wave of loose snow engulfing the two struggling men, it was impossible to tell which was which.

One of them was Matthew Redd. He was sure of that.

Pretty sure. Sixty percent sure. And that was, as his father often joked, good enough for government work.

When he'd heard shots fired, he'd made the logical assumption that Redd was shooting at one of his teammates. After all, what were the odds that someone else was out in this frozen wasteland shooting or getting shot at? And the reports had sounded close, close enough that he'd immediately picked up from his little hide sight and begun moving in the direction from which he thought the shots had come. Sure enough, he'd spotted two people—a man and a woman—moving down the face of the mountain on the opposite side of the valley he was presently overlooking. With the magnification on his scope, he had even gotten a pretty good look at the man's face, and it did look like the picture of Matthew Redd that had been circulated to the team.

Oddly enough, Redd—or the man he thought was Redd—wasn't carrying a rifle, at least not one that he could see, which meant he hadn't been the one to fire the shots. And the man who had just plowed into Redd definitely wasn't someone from Arrow Team. Which begged the question, just what on earth was going on here? Was someone else after Matthew Redd?

Chad shook his head. He didn't have time to sort out this cowboy-meets-*Deliverance* nonsense. He didn't care who else was involved or what their particular grievances were. Matthew Redd needed to die, if for no other reason than because of what he had done to Chad's teammates, and Chad was going to make sure it happened.

A single shot from the anti-materiel rifle would do the trick. It wouldn't even require a direct hit. As the old saying went, *"Close only matters in horseshoes and hand grenades."* An HEDP round was actually better than a hand grenade because you could "throw" it from a mile away, but the operative word was *close.* Right now he had no idea where Redd was, so getting a shot close enough for the blast damage to have an effect wasn't possible. He had to get glass on target to make the shot count.

The Schmidt & Bender scope was great for magnifying a target once identified but terrible for surveying a large area. This was why snipers worked in teams with a spotter, but Wagner was watching some other corner of this godforsaken wilderness, so Chad would just have to make do as a singleton.

He tried focusing on the area directly below where he'd last seen Redd, but wherever he looked he saw only white. Returning to that original spot, however, he picked out a trio of figures—one of them the woman that he had seen with Redd, and two men that he didn't recognize. The latter were wearing, of all things, Mossy Oak camouflage, which stood out like a sore thumb against the stark white background. One of the men was gripping the woman's arm and appeared to be shouting at her, leaving Chad to wonder again what Redd was mixed up in.

It occurred to him that, if Redd had been trying to protect the woman from the men pursuing them, then he would probably try to come to her rescue, provided of course he survived his tumble down the mountain. Then again, he might not. He might just decide to cut his losses and leave the whole mess behind.

Chad felt his chances of taking out Matthew Redd slipping through his fingers. He had started with an approximate fix on Redd's location, but with each passing second, the uncertainty increased.

"Where are you?" he growled.

This was exactly why he preferred blowing stuff up. He was an excellent marksman, with an intuitive grasp of how ballistic projectiles behaved over long distances, but being good at something wasn't the same as enjoying it. There was a certain satisfaction to be had from taking a head shot at two thousand meters, but it was nothing compared to making a jet aircraft explode.

Just like that, the solution came to him.

He had been looking at the problem the wrong way, through a sniper's eyes. In Oklahoma City, he hadn't accomplished the mission by taking out the point target, but rather by destroying the area target. That was the whole purpose for carrying a weapon like the XM109 into battle.

The answer had been staring him in the face all along.

Chad Beaudette did not enjoy operating in mountain environments, especially in winter conditions. He was a SEAL, for Pete's sake, a combat swimmer, not a suck-loving Army Ranger. But that didn't mean he didn't know *how* to fight in such conditions. As part of his journey to become a SEAL, he'd attended grueling mountain warfare training schools and had, just as in everything, excelled. He knew mountains—and knew a few things about what made them so dangerous.

He brought the scope back up, finding the two men in camo and the woman they were trying to bring under control. Through the swirl of falling snowflakes, he could make out large areas of disturbed snow above and around them, great scallops where pack snow had been dislodged and broken away, revealing older ice underneath.

Perfect, he thought, elevating the rifle a few more degrees until the reticle was pointing to a spot about halfway to the summit of the pass.

"Bamm, bamm," he whispered and then pulled the trigger.

FORTY-FIVE

Emily awoke with a start. It took a moment for her to remember where she was and why she was there, and another to recognize what had brought her to consciousness. She sat up, still cocooned in her sleeping bag, and whispered, "Was that—?"

From out of the darkness, Mikey replied, "Yeah, it was."

She found him, framed in the opening to the shelter, a barely discernible silhouette against the scant light filtering down through the clouds. They had been sleeping in two-hour shifts, one of them standing watch while the other tried to rest.

Even as Mikey spoke, there was another report. The echoes of rifle fire reverberated from the mountain slopes, and Emily recalled the thinly veiled threat made by the Homeland Security agent. *"If you folks hear any shooting, don't pay it no mind."*

Yeah, like that's going to happen.

Now fully awake, she wriggled out of the sleeping bag. The chill in the air made her want to crawl back into its warm embrace, but the possibility . . . no, make that the *certainty* that her husband was, that very minute, fighting for his life energized her. She pulled on her boots and her gloves, then grabbed her rifle and went to join Mikey.

Another report echoed in the night.

"Sounds close," she whispered.

"Yeah," agreed Mikey. "What do you want to do?"

Her first impulse was to say, *Let's get in the fight*, but she knew that was reckless.

"We've got to be smart about this," she said. "Matthew doesn't know we're out here. If we try sneaking in the dark, we're liable to get shot, either by him or the guys hunting him. I say we saddle up and ride out there."

"Ride?" Mikey protested. "That will make us an even bigger target."

"Exactly. We need to be visible. Those Homeland guys won't shoot at us, no matter what they say. And Matthew will recognize us and realize that we're here to help. He'll find a way to let us know where he is."

"You willing to bet your life on that?"

Another report rang out, quickly followed by the sound of a shot with a slightly different pitch. Emily was no expert, but she felt certain that the reports were from two different weapons.

"That's him," she said, certain of it without really knowing why. "This is the best way to help him."

Mikey gave an exasperated sigh. "I should know better than to try changing your mind once it's made up."

She returned a satisfied nod. "We're going to need some light," she said, taking her headlamp from a pocket. "You might want to cover your eyes until they adjust."

"Go for it."

She clicked on a button that activated a bulb covered by a red filter. Red light, with its long wavelength, was better for preserving night vision and much harder to see at a distance. In its glow, she saw the horses standing patiently in the shelter, their eyes already open as if fully aware that they would soon be put to work.

But as Emily was about to heft her saddle onto the back of her chosen mount, another report—this one much louder and deeper—boomed in the night.

Mikey, who was just bending down to pick up his saddle, looked up in alarm. "I think that was one of the Barretts," he said in a grave voice.

Emily didn't question the assessment. She felt her heartbeat quicken with fear for Matthew. "Come on," she urged. "We've got to move."

FORTY-SIX

As soon as they started sliding, Redd's assailant seemed to lose any sense of hostility toward his intended target and instead began treating Redd like a lifeline, clutching at him in blind panic as if by so doing, he might halt their runaway plunge.

Redd, though not oblivious to the peril of an uncontrolled slide down the mountain, saw the situation differently. His attacker was the most urgent threat and so neutralizing him was the priority. Despite having no leverage, he managed to twist out of the man's frantic grasp, first locking up his limbs and immobilizing him and ultimately flipping him over into a mount position. Straddling the man's chest, Redd rode him like a sled. His dominant position afforded Redd a measure of control, and by leaning back and dragging the toes of his boots, he was able to arrest their slide. As they slowed, loose snow began piling up over them, covering the man's face completely and burying Redd to the waist.

Even before they stopped moving, Redd went in for a cross-collar choke and quick end to the fight. But as his hands closed over the man's shirtfront, the covering of snow fell away to reveal a familiar face. It was Justin, the young man who had provided the blood transfusion that had saved Redd's life.

The realization brought Redd up short. Although these men from the Family had shot at him, Redd was already hesitant to kill any of them, and not just because he had, only a few hours earlier, broken bread with them. They weren't innocent by any means, but they weren't hardened killers like the hit teams that had come after him.

And now the life of the man who had freely given some of his blood was in Redd's hands.

Justin, sensing Redd's hesitation, began thrashing and twisting like a champion bull trying to throw a rider. Redd, still in the dominant position, easily held on, but instead of going for the choke, he simply drew back his arm and delivered a hard punch to Justin's jaw. The blow snapped the young man's head sideways, spattering the snow beside him with a spray of blood. Redd recocked, ready to follow up with a second punch, but there was no need. Justin was out cold.

There was no time to savor the victory, however. Redd felt certain that Justin had not come after them by himself. But just as he was starting to rise, intent on heading back up the slope to where he'd left Bekah, a noise like the roar of a cannon boomed in the air overhead.

The sound stopped Redd in his tracks. The report was much louder than the earlier shots, suggesting a heavier-caliber round. Redd's first thought was that it sounded like a Barrett sniper rifle, which fired a .50 caliber BMG round and was used primarily by the military and police SWAT teams. He doubted that such a weapon would be in the arsenal of Josiah Strong and his followers. If someone was indeed shooting a Barrett out here, it meant Redd had bigger problems than the Family.

The hit team was back, and this time they'd literally brought the big guns.

Yet as ominous as the report was, even more disturbing was the distinctive *whump*—something felt as much as heard—that occurred almost simultaneously from somewhere high up on the mountain above him. Redd knew that sound too.

It was the sound of a small explosive charge detonating.

The significance of this was not lost on him.

There was only one reason why anyone would shoot explosive rounds at a snow-covered mountain slope. Someone was attempting to trigger an avalanche.

The dictionary definition of *avalanche*—a rapid flow of snow down a mountain slope—did not begin to express the magnitude of the danger of the phenomenon. Once an area of snow and ice broke loose from the side of a mountain and began sliding down, gathering more mass along the way—as much as a million tons—nothing could stand against it. And because the snow might move as fast as two hundred miles per hour, outrunning an avalanche was almost impossible. Anyone unlucky enough to be caught in the run-out path faced almost certain death, either crushed under the massive weight or suffocated slowly in an icy tomb. Although the number of avalanche deaths worldwide was comparatively small, the risk to those who enjoyed winter recreation—backcountry skiers, snowmobilers, and alpine mountaineers—was extremely high. Perversely, most avalanche-related fatalities were caused by their victims.

The danger had been on Redd's mind from the moment he ventured out into the mountains, especially so because the risk was highest after heavy snowfall. By avoiding slopes with moderate grades, especially in the afternoon when the sun's heat might begin melting the snow, softening and destabilizing the accumulated mass, he had minimized the risk, but it was something that could never be completely eliminated. The one thing he had not anticipated was that the men hunting him might contrive to unleash the forces of nature against him.

Any ideas he might have had about helping Bekah or dealing with the men from the Family or even fighting back against the hit team were shoved aside in the face of this new impending threat. One thought superseded all other considerations—survival.

He couldn't immediately tell if the explosion had actually triggered a slide. The Forest Service used howitzers to lob explosive shells onto slopes where avalanche risk was highest, triggering the slides in a controlled fashion to alleviate the danger, but those guns fired thirty-five-pound shells, producing a significantly greater effect. He had no idea what sort of ordnance the hit team had access to, but it definitely wasn't an artillery piece. Still, avalanches were hard to predict. Hoping that the mountain would hold together was a luxury he couldn't afford.

He looked left then right, assessing the shortest, surest distance to a place of safety. To his left, only about fifty yards away, he spied a section of rock too sheer to climb. A hundred yards to the right, several hardy pine trees clung to the slope, their dark boughs standing out in stark contrast to the white of the snowfield. As a general rule, trees were no less vulnerable to a massive avalanche than Redd himself, but based on the topography, Redd thought they might be outside the slide zone or, at the very least, on its fringe. Despite the inherent risk, Redd thought he stood a better chance there than he would clinging to the rocks in the other direction, so making a snap decision, he broke for the woods.

It was a decision he immediately had cause to question. With each step, the snow slipped away beneath his feet, causing him to stumble and fall repeatedly. Each misstep not only sent him sliding farther down the slope but also triggered mini avalanches that swept down upon him like ocean waves.

Another report boomed, followed by another explosion high above. A few seconds later, the sounds repeated again, and then once more. And then a different noise permeated the night, a persistent hiss like white noise, amplified to the volume of a jet engine, and growing louder and louder, vibrating through Redd's body like an electrical current.

Somewhere high above him, the explosive shells had broken the fragile frozen lattice clinging to the slope, setting in motion a chain reaction that would scour away thousands of tons of ice and snow and send them racing down toward the valley below, sweeping away everything and everyone on the mountain.

The avalanche had begun.

As the moving mass of snow gathered both volume and velocity, it pushed out a wall of air in a pressure wave that blasted into Redd and sent him tumbling yet again, this time engulfed in a haze of fine ice crystals borne along on the wind. What little light there had been from the stars to guide him was extinguished, plunging him into a darkness so absolute he could not tell if his eyes were even open.

He tried to get his feet under him, desperate to reach the relative shelter of the tree line, still a good fifty yards away, but the snow beneath him was already moving, carrying him along like a leaf in a river current.

Then the avalanche overtook him.

It did not slam into him so much as sweep him up, more like an ocean wave than a wall of solid matter. As the snow and ice flowed around him, he began tumbling uncontrollably, his body whipping crazily until he had no sense of his position. He felt a hard impact against his thigh and thought maybe he'd hit a protruding rock, but then more blows followed, and he knew that it wasn't rocks he was feeling but chunks of hard ice, mixed with the loose snow of the slide.

It took a few seconds for him to realize that he was no longer tumbling. In fact, he felt almost no sense of motion at all, only a lingering sensation of vertigo. In what almost passed for irony, once he was fully engulfed in the avalanche, his body position had stabilized.

He vaguely recalled being told that the way to survive an avalanche was to move one's arms and legs as if swimming. A human body was denser than snow, so a person would naturally sink, just as in water. Unfortunately, he had no idea which way was up and was afraid that he might inadvertently bury himself deeper. So instead of attempting to claw his way through the snow, he limited himself to short arm strokes and kicks, as if treading water.

It felt more like treading freshly poured concrete. Gritting his teeth, he fought against the increasingly viscous substance, forcibly pushing the snow away from his limbs even as it flowed into the gaps he created. Recalling another avalanche safety lesson, with a titanic effort, he managed to raise his arms, covering his head and creating a small air pocket in front of his face. Yet even as he managed this small victory, he felt the snow packing in around him and the tremendous weight pressing down. Simply drawing breath was a Herculean labor. It felt as if a giant hand were closing around his chest. He tried moving his arms again, attempting to create a larger void around his head, but the effort succeeded only in causing loose snow to infiltrate the existing gap, forcing him to relent and bring his arms in close to preserve what little air remained.

That was when he realized that the harsh white noise had given way to an even more terrible silence. The bone-shaking vibration had ceased. All was still. The avalanche was over, its energy expended. Yet this fact brought Redd no comfort.

He wasn't just trapped; he was buried alive.

FORTY-SEVEN

As he lay there, enveloped in darkness, unable to move, barely able to breathe, Matthew Redd recalled a short story he had once read . . . or maybe it was an old Arab proverb . . . his brain was fuzzy on that particular detail . . . Something about a man who, fearing that Death was coming for him, fled to a distant city, only to inadvertently place himself right where the Reaper had expected to find him.

As a Marine serving in combat zones, the specter of an untimely death had been a constant companion. Like many of his fellow warriors, he had coped with the stress of repeatedly putting himself in harm's way by developing a fatalistic attitude.

When it was your time to go, it was your time.

That he had survived when so many of his brothers had fallen served only to reinforce this belief. So when he had eluded certain death through the unlikeliest intervention—rescued in the middle of nowhere by a wanted fugitive who had been willing to pump literal lifeblood into his depleted veins—he had thought it a miracle.

But now, not even a day later, he was facing a worse fate, buried alive in an icy tomb.

The Grim Reaper might reschedule your appointment, but he never canceled it.

Redd found himself regretting those extra hours and the false hope that survival had brought him. He'd been ready to go, had said his goodbyes, if only in his heart. He had accepted his fate and found a peace that he had not even known he desired. To have hope dangled before him, only to be yanked away, like Lucy snatching the football away from Charlie Brown, felt especially cruel.

Maybe it is my time . . .

"No." The whisper slipped unbidden from his lips, but when he heard it, something primal awakened within him.

No. I don't accept that.

"No," he said again, aware that in so doing, he was expending his limited supply of breathable air, and then he shouted, "No!"

The defiant cry filled the tiny space around his head and set his ears ringing, but he didn't care because in that instant, he knew he was going to live.

He *had* to live. Because he had something to live for. And until God took him home, Redd would do what he was born to do.

He would keep fighting.

"Emily," he whispered. "Junior. I'll see you soon."

And with that, he drove his arms out like pistons, punching into the snow above his head.

The sudden movement triggered a minor cascade of snow falling, not down onto him but rather up, with particles of ice somehow rising into his nostrils.

I'm upside down, he realized, almost with a laugh, and then changed his plan of attack.

He tried kicking out, hoping that he might be close enough to the surface to break through, but the weight of the avalanche had him pinned. He couldn't even wiggle his feet.

But I can still move my arms.

He drove down . . . or rather up with his elbows again and again, using them like a pair of pile drivers. As more snow broke loose and fell around him, he began shifting his head from side to side, diverting the snow and compressing it under him to preserve his working space.

The exertion brought a painful reminder of his earlier injuries. Pain throbbed in his wounds, pulsing in time with his heart. He thought he felt dampness against his skin, his blood saturating the bandages and oozing out, but he ignored the sensation and kept pounding his elbows into the covering of snow. And when, after what felt like several minutes of relentless effort, he had increased his working space enough to extend his arms, he began using his hands to scrape at the snow around his upper torso. As the grip on his chest loosened, he was able to breathe freely once more, and the rush of fresh air revitalized him.

He knew that he must be burning through his limited oxygen supply, but there was no point in trying to conserve what little air he had. According to the experts, a person buried in an avalanche could only last about fifteen minutes provided they remained calm, conserved their air, and waited for rescue, but Redd knew that nobody was coming to save him. Unlike the previous day, there would be no miraculous last-second rescue. He would have to save himself or die trying.

He resisted the impulse to check his watch, rejecting the idea that he had less than fifteen minutes to live. He wasn't going to set a time limit for himself. He would stay alive as long as he had to.

Clawing at the icy walls of his tomb, scooping out hunks of snow, which he packed down underneath him, he began raising himself up as he cleared away the snow above him. Even so, his progress was incremental. He had cleared only about eighteen inches, but judging by his inverted orientation and the fact that his legs were immobilized, there was at least six feet of snow between him and survival.

If anything, this realization only made him work harder, digging and scraping with his hands, twisting his body in an attempt to loosen the grip of the snow binding his legs. As he fought, he began to feel strangely euphoric. Laughter burbled unbidden from his lips as he continued attacking the snow. Some part of him knew this reaction was not normal, but it wasn't until he felt the urge to take a break, and maybe even a little nap, that he realized he was feeling the effects of oxygen deprivation.

He knew it was a fight he could not win through brute force. The harder he worked to free himself, the faster he used up what little air remained to him, and when he reached that unalterable threshold, he would simply pass out and never wake up.

"No," he whispered again. "I'm going to live."

And so he fought on. And on . . . and on . . .

Until there was no fight left in him.

FORTY-EIGHT

Matthew Redd awoke to hot breath on his face. Then something that felt like a dry rag began swiping across his mouth and nose.

"I'm awake," he mumbled, still half-asleep. "Gimme a minute."

But the strange rubbing continued, as did the vaporous exhalations, which, he realized after a moment, exhibited a unique and familiar aroma—dog's breath. It was Rubble, licking his face.

"Okay, Rub. I'm getting up."

He raised one hand, trying to fend off what he assumed was a display of affection, and inadvertently triggered a cascade of loose snow down onto his face. The brush of cold ice grains brought him fully awake, and his memories of what had just happened returned in a rush.

Getting caught in the avalanche. Being buried alive. Running out of air.

But he hadn't died. Rubble had found him, saved him.

Rubble had survived too.

"Thank you," he whispered.

He realized that, aside from the fact that his face was now uncovered, very little else had changed. He was still mostly stuck in place, his body tilted downward at about a forty-five-degree angle. Still, the replenishment of his oxygen supply, not to mention the fact that a way to the surface was now opened, gave him a much-needed boost of energy.

And he was no longer alone.

"Come on, boy," he urged. "Keep digging."

Rubble seemed to get the message and, after letting out a sharp *woof,* drew back his head and began scratching furiously to further enlarge the hole he had created. Redd joined in, focusing his efforts on trying to loosen the avalanche's hold on his legs, and after several minutes of sustained effort, he was finally able to kick free. As soon as he did, he extricated himself from his icy tomb and then flopped down, overcome with a mixture of exhaustion and relief.

Rubble immediately dropped beside him, nuzzling into Redd's side as if they were back home in the crowded little trailer. Redd, laughing, reached down and scratched the giant rottie behind the ears. A crust of ice clung to the dog's coat, and even in the darkness Redd could see that Rubble's dark hide was liberally coated with a dusting of snow.

Redd still marveled at the dog's escape. He surmised that, just like himself, Rubble had reacted to the avalanche the only way that made sense—running as fast as he could—but unlike Redd, Rubble was better equipped for moving through the snow. He was also more than a hundred pounds lighter than Redd, so when the slide had eventually caught up to him, he hadn't been buried as deep. His instinct to survive had probably kept him doing all the right things—fighting like crazy, "swimming" through the churning snow to get back to the top—and it had paid off.

"Lucky for us both," murmured Redd.

And then he remembered something that turned his joy to ashes.

Bekah!

Muttering, "No, no, no," he scrambled to his feet and stared out across the transformed terrain.

The sky, now fully clouded over, was dark, but still provided a stark contrast to the white of the snowfield. But instead of a long, steep descent to the valley covered in a more or less uniform layer of snow, he saw a semilevel field of coarse debris spread out before him—the run-out zone of the avalanche, where the slide had lost the necessary momentum to keep pushing the growing mass of snow ahead of it. He scanned in every direction, searching futilely for a human form protruding from the flow or a scrap of dark cloth that might indicate the presence of someone below.

Nothing.

He cursed his impotence. He had failed her. She had trusted him, and he had let her die.

Redd pushed that thought from his mind.

She could have made it, he told himself. *Find her!*

"Bekah!" he tried to shout. His throat, unexpectedly raw, closed on the second syllable. He coughed and tried again. "Bekah!"

His call echoed in the valley, but there was no answer. As far as Redd could tell, Bekah was gone, swallowed up by the mountain.

Some part of him recognized that his shouts might betray the fact of his survival to the sniper who had triggered the avalanche. If the shooter was well trained—and Redd did not doubt that he was—then he was long gone, but there was a chance . . . always a chance . . . that he was wrong about that. Besides, shouting wasn't going to do Bekah any good if she was trapped under the slide.

Rubble, who had jumped up along with Redd, stood beside him, likewise staring out at the empty wasteland, no doubt wondering what his human was looking for. Redd knelt beside him.

"Rubble, go find Bekah!" When he said her name, he jabbed an emphatic finger out across the debris field. Rubble started forward, but then stopped and looked back at Redd, as if they were playing fetch and he'd just figured out that Redd hadn't really thrown the stick after all.

"Bekah!" Redd repeated, gesturing again. "Go find Bekah. The nice lady who gave you dinner."

Rubble just shook his haunches back and forth excitedly.

Frustrated at his inability to communicate his desires to the animal, Redd decided to try leading by example and charged out into the slide zone. Rubble, perhaps finally grasping Redd's purpose, gave another excited *woof* and charged ahead of him. Redd shook his head miserably. It had been too much to hope that the dog would understand what Redd needed him to do. Rubble was only a puppy, after all, and though he had displayed incredible loyalty and instincts, he was not a trained search-and-rescue dog.

Redd returned his attention to the snowfield around him, scrutinizing it again for any sign of a human presence. Finding Bekah was his first priority, but he knew that other members of Strong's Family had probably been buried in the slide too. He knew for certain that Justin, the young man who had given his blood to Redd, was out here somewhere, trapped in a frozen grave. There might be one or two others.

Even though they had come after him and tried to kill him, he couldn't just let them die.

Not like this.

For better or worse, and Redd was becoming more and more convinced that everything about them was bad news, they had saved his life.

He had to at least try and return the favor.

Up ahead he saw Rubble stop and lower his head to the ground, sniffing around. Something had aroused the dog's curiosity. But then, just as quickly, the dog was moving again, zigzagging across the debris field, following a pattern known only to him.

Still, it was a hopeful sign, and Redd made for the spot that Rubble had just inspected. He didn't see anything particularly noteworthy, but with nothing else to go on, he knelt down and began digging, pulling out double handfuls of snow and flinging them over his shoulder. When he had cleared away a couple feet of snow, he bent low to the ground and listened, straining to hear something . . . anything . . . that might indicate the presence of another living being.

Nothing.

He resumed digging, but after a few seconds, the sound of Rubble barking caught his attention again. He stood up and searched the area until he found the rottie, head down and paws working furiously at a patch of snow fifty feet away.

A faint ember of hope began to glow in Redd's chest. Abandoning his excavation, he hurried over to where Rubble was digging and, without a word, joined him. Working together, man and man's best friend dug down two feet, then three. As the hole deepened, it became necessary to shore up the sides to prevent the edges from collapsing inward. Redd focused on that, letting an increasingly enthusiastic Rubble do the bulk of the digging.

Redd soon noticed dark streaks in the white emptiness of the hole and for a moment dared to hope that Rubble was on the verge of discovering Bekah's unconscious form. Then he realized that the streaks were blood from the dog's paws and felt a pang of guilt. The incessant digging had savaged the poor animal's forefeet. And yet the rottie gave no complaint, nor did he show the slightest inclination to leave off his efforts.

As the bloody trails grew larger, Redd knew he had to intervene. The search was hopeless. Even if, by some extraordinary stroke of luck, Bekah lay beneath them, she could not possibly still be alive.

"Stop," Redd croaked. "Rubble, stop."

With just his hindquarters protruding from the hole, the rottweiler paid him no heed. Fully committed to uncovering whatever it was his nose had detected, he continued scraping away the snow with paws that were probably too numb to even feel pain.

"Rubble!" Redd said, trying to project authority into his voice but failing utterly. All but overcome with exhaustion and grief, it was all he could do to keep from breaking down in tears. "Stop, boy," he begged. "Give it up."

Seeing that Rubble would not be swayed, Redd reached down into the hole and wrapped his arms around the dog's neck, fully intending to lift his massive body out of the snow. The darkness at the bottom of the hole had grown in size, not mere streaks of blood but a large spot the size of a dinner plate. The sight of it stabbed at Redd's heart for a moment, but then he realized that what he was looking at was not blood at all but a swatch of dark fabric.

He found something, Redd realized.

Who's a good boy?

Redd heaved Rubble out of the hole but did so in order to take the dog's place. This far down, the snow and ice felt as hard as Portland cement, and Redd struggled to make any headway. It was no wonder poor Rubble's paws had been shredded. What Redd needed was a shovel, or failing that, a knife to break up the hard pack, but he had neither.

He did, however, have a gun.

He drew the Ruger from its holster and, gripping the barrel, began using the butt like a hammer, pounding away at the frozen covering. The ferocity of his assault broke the ice apart in huge chunks, which he scooped up and flung away, revealing more of the dark fabric.

It was a body; there was no question about that. Who it might be, and whether they still lived, were questions he chose not to consider.

But then the answer to the first question was revealed as his frantic digging exposed a mass of blonde hair and, just beneath it, the familiar face of Bekah Strong. He took a moment to clear the ice away from her mouth and nostrils. It was not immediately apparent whether she was breathing, and he wasn't going to take the time to check for a pulse, not while she was still held captive in the avalanche. Instead, he redoubled his efforts, hammering away at the ice to uncover her upper body and legs, until he was able at last to lift her out of the hole.

Rubble came over immediately and began licking her face, as if trying to awaken her the same way he had his master not long ago. Redd gently pushed the dog away, then knelt over her, placing his cheek just above her mouth. There was not even a trace of breath. He stripped off his gloves and tried feeling for a pulse, but his fingers were too numb, too insensitive, to feel anything at all.

Unwilling to accept that it was already too late, Redd decided to initiate CPR. He was certified, had been for years, but had never had occasion to perform the life-saving procedure in a real life-or-death situation. He racked his brain, trying to recall the steps.

Establish the airway, he told himself.

He tilted her head back and lifted her chin, opened her mouth, and inserted a finger to make sure there wasn't any snow blocking her windpipe. The rest came back to him quickly.

Give two breaths.

He bent low, pinched her nose shut with his fingertips, put his lips to hers, and blew gently into her mouth. He felt her chest rise as the air flowed into her lungs. He moved his mouth away, letting the air rush back out, then returned and supplied the second breath.

He still couldn't tell if she was breathing on her own or not, but he knew that the two breaths he had given her had definitely gone to the right place. The stale air in her lungs had been refreshed. Now it was time to make sure that the oxygenated blood was circulating through her body.

He shifted position, crossed his right hand over his left, fingers interlaced, then placed them over Bekah's sternum. From his training, he knew not to hold back—to be effective, the chest had to be compressed at least an inch and a half. Broken ribs were not uncommon.

Squaring his shoulders, he leaned over so that all his energy would be focused directly down on her heart. Before he could begin pushing, however, he heard a frantic cry.

"Matty! Stop!"

Redd froze in place, then turned his head toward the source of the shout. He could only make out the silhouette of a horse and rider, wreathed in falling snow, but even in the darkness, he instantly recognized both.

Remington.

And Emily.

FORTY-NINE

"Em? What are you doing here?"

Emily knew the question was natural enough, but she did not fail to note the layers of subtext—surprise, but also fear for her safety, anger that she had put herself at risk by coming after him, and something else . . . embarrassment, maybe?

Did he somehow think that she thought he was behaving inappropriately by trying to perform CPR on a helpless woman?

It was possible, she supposed, but far likelier that he was just so emotionally overwrought after everything that had happened that he wasn't thinking straight at all.

She reined Remington to a halt and dismounted, then hurried over to join her husband. "Don't do compressions," she said, ignoring his question. "If she's hypothermic and you start pushing cold blood to her heart, you could kill her."

She couldn't discern his face to register his reaction but noted that he immediately pulled back from the unmoving form.

Rubble rushed up to greet her, excitedly waggling his rear end, but she stopped him with a firm "Down, boy," then began checking the young woman's vitals. "How long has she been down?"

"I . . . uh, I'm not sure," Redd stammered. "I just found her. Just dug her out."

Emily checked her watch. When the avalanche had begun, fearing the worst, she had immediately activated her chronograph. That had been twenty-one minutes ago. It had taken her and Mikey that long to saddle the horses and race toward the transformed slope. She had known, as only a wife can know, that her husband had been caught in the slide, and that it would be up to her to save him, but thankfully, she had been wrong about that. Matty Redd had saved himself, just like he always did, and now he was trying to help someone else.

She thought she detected the faintest trace of a pulse in the young woman's carotid artery. "We have to get her to a hospital," she said. "ASAP."

"She's . . . alive?"

Emily knew better than to answer with anything but the truth. "I don't know. We have a saying with hypothermic patients—they're not dead until they're warm and dead. I won't lie. Even if we can bring her back, she might have taken a hit neurologically."

She thought that sounded better than saying the girl might have brain damage.

"But we can't do anything for her here," she went on. "Come on. Help me get her ready for transport."

Just then, Mikey rode up, trailing Emily's mount and the pack horse. "Matt!" he shouted, almost falling out of the saddle in his eagerness to join them. "Dude, I don't believe it. I mean, I believe it, but—"

Emily quickly cut him off. "Mikey, get me one of the sleeping bags. Quick!"

Mikey leaned to see around Emily, taking in the sight of the girl lying between her and Redd. "Whoa, what's going on? Who is she?"

Emily turned her head back toward Mikey. "She doesn't have long. Sleeping bag. *Now!*" When she saw Mikey snap to action, she turned back to her husband. "Who is she, Matty?"

"It's a long story. She saved me though. Now she needs our help. I'll tell you the rest later—but we gotta move."

Emily nodded. "Mikey!"

"One sec!" Mikey shouted.

Redd, who had not moved since her arrival, now shook his head. "Em, you shouldn't be here. It's dangerous."

"You think I don't know that?" she snapped, regretting her tone even as the words slipped out. She took a breath, trying to regain her clinical detachment. "I'm here to bring you home, Matty. I know you think you have to face this alone, but you're wrong. I never should have let you come out here by yourself. We're stronger together."

Always have been. Why won't he just see that?

"Em, you don't know what these people are capable of."

"I do. I know things you don't know. The men chasing you . . . they're federal agents. Homeland Security."

He shook his head again. "That's exactly why you can't be out here."

"You're wrong. That's why you *have* to come in. Hiding isn't the answer. Eventually, they'll find you if you're on your own. But there are good people back in town ready to stand with you."

When he did not respond immediately, Emily busied herself with gently rolling the unconscious female victim just as Mikey arrived with the sleeping bag. She hadn't been exaggerating the risk of doing chest compressions. Any sudden movement could send cold blood from the extremities to her heart. Getting the young woman out of the mountains to a care facility without causing the very thing they were trying to prevent was going to be a challenge, but under the circumstances, it was a risk she would have to take.

Emily wanted to inquire further about the woman's identity—not out of any sense of jealousy, but because she liked to have as much information about her patients as possible—but knew it wasn't the time for a conversation like that. "We need to get her up on the packhorse. But gently."

The direction shook Redd out of his torpor. He reached down, slipping his hands under the motionless form now bundled up in the sleeping bag, and effortlessly lifted her in his arms.

"Let me give you a hand," said Mikey, stepping forward, but Redd was already moving toward the horses with his burden. "Or . . . I'll just let you handle it."

As Redd moved off, Emily noticed several large dark spots on the snow where he had been standing, and a trail of smaller spots following after him. "Matty, are you bleeding?"

"It's nothing," he replied, easing the unconscious woman onto the back of the packhorse, settling her between the panniers.

"It's not *nothing* if you're bleeding," she insisted. "Show me."

"In a minute. Right now we have to find the others."

"Others?"

He gestured past her, toward the avalanche debris field. "There's more of them. Buried. We have to find them."

Emily checked her chronograph again. Twenty-nine minutes. Almost double the survivability window. While the fifteen-minute rule was by no means hard and fast—there were stories of people surviving hours, even days without serious complications—the odds fell off almost exponentially beyond that point. Every minute they spent looking for more victims—victims who were almost certainly beyond saving—reduced the chances of saving the one victim that had already been recovered.

Still, saving lives was her business, and if Matthew thought there was a chance . . . "Do you know where they are?"

"No, but Rubble can find them."

The dog gave an excited *woof* at the sound of his name. Emily glanced down and noted the bloody pawprints surrounding him. Then she glanced again at the trail of blood leading to where her husband was standing.

Dear God, what have they been through?

She shook her head. "I'm sorry, Matty, but this is a triage situation. We have to help the people who can be saved."

"Em . . ."

"And we can't stay out here," she went on. "You know that as well as I do. Those agents are still hunting you. We have to head back. *Now.* It's our best chance to get through this."

Realizing that she needed to make some kind of concession, she added, "As soon as we can get a phone signal out, we'll alert the mountain search-and-rescue team. Let them know that there are other victims out here. That's the best chance they've got."

He stood there for a minute, swaying back and forth, as if unable to process what she was telling him. She realized then just how close he was to collapsing, and so she did the thing she should have done from the very start.

She wrapped her arms around him and hugged him tightly.

FIFTY

Chad Beaudette rode a wave of euphoria through the rest of the night. He'd blown up a mountain. A mountain! He had also taken out their primary target, the cowboy dirtbag who had wiped out more than a dozen of his teammates, and that felt pretty good too.

The sense of elation carried him through the long snowmobile ride back to the staging area, where he soaked up the praise from his teammates—all of whom were equally happy to be done with this particular mission—and through the drive back to Helena. He'd been a little bummed at the fact that all the bars were closed, so there would be no celebrating their success with a round of drinks, but no matter. With the mission finally done, he could get back to Daytona and pick up his vacation where he'd left off.

He was still feeling it when, just as he was finally settling in at his hotel room to grab some shut-eye, he'd gotten a text from Dagger Six, ordering everyone to rendezvous at the airport. That irritated him, but only a little. The boss wouldn't roust them all out of bed at such an ungodly hour to congratulate them on a job well done. That wasn't his style. No, a predawn summons could only mean that he had more work for them. Which wasn't the worst thing in the world, provided Chad got a chance to blow some stuff up. He just hoped the new assignment would be somewhere a little more hospitable.

The wave finally crashed when he reached the hangar at the airport and saw the look on Cormac Kilmeade's face.

Even on a good day, Kilmeade had what Chad could only characterize as scary energy. Not psycho—just intense.

As Chad walked into the hangar, however, he got the distinct impression that this was not a good day.

Kilmeade wasn't frothing at the mouth. He wasn't raging, and he wasn't quietly fuming. In fact, he wasn't really doing much of anything—just sitting in a folding chair at a collapsible table, set up near the open entrance to a Livingston Charters Gulfstream G500, watching the screen of a tablet computer. And yet, just sitting there, doing almost nothing, he seemed almost radioactive.

Chad could tell he wasn't the only one who felt it. Everyone was giving Kilmeade lots of space.

It was understandable, he supposed. Kilmeade's brother—his twin brother—had been killed. That wasn't something you could just get over in a day or two. But still, why bring that vibe to work?

Chad gradually realized that Dagger Team—what was left of it anyway—was also present. They had probably come with Kilmeade on the plane. The two surviving members of Saber Team were there as well, despite the fact that one of them had his arm in a cast.

Including Kilmeade, the head count was fourteen shooters.

Looks like it's all hands on deck, thought Chad.

When the last member of Arrow Team arrived, Dagger Seven—Darren Richmond—approached Kilmeade and said, "All present and accounted for, boss."

Kilmeade continued to stare at his tablet, but after a few seconds, he spoke a single syllable. "Or."

The utterance was full of quiet menace.

Richmond stared back, bemused. "Boss?"

"It's supposed to be 'all present *or* accounted for,'" Kilmeade said, finally looking up. He tossed the tablet on the table and then stood, surveying the room before returning his attention to his second-in-command. "If everyone's present then of course they're accounted for. *All present or accounted for* means that you have accounted for—" he did not raise his voice, but he emphasized the words, drawing them out—"everyone who isn't present."

Chad felt a chill go down his spine. He wasn't sure what was happening, but he could tell it was bad.

Kilmeade stalked around the table and cast his gaze out at the rest of the assembled group. "Who isn't present? It seems like we're missing quite a few. Are they all accounted for?"

Richmond swallowed nervously. "Uh, everyone's here, boss. I mean, everyone that . . . uh . . . isn't . . ."

"Isn't dead?"

Richmond nodded.

"So I guess that's what you meant by *accounted for*." There was no mistaking the sardonic tone. "Maybe you should have said, 'All present or dead.' That would have been more accurate, don't you think?"

"Uh, yeah, boss."

"All present or dead," Kilmeade repeated. "There should be twenty-eight of us here. But I count only fourteen. Can anyone tell me why that is?" Kilmeade's gaze began moving to each of the men in turn. None of them answered.

Kilmeade came to Chad, who could feel the other man's stare burning into his retinas. "How about you, Arrow One? Can you tell me why fourteen of our teammates are accounted for?"

Chad's spine prickled with a sudden flare of heat.

Kilmeade's gaze lingered on him a moment longer, then moved on. "We all know that losses are just part of the job. It sucks, but it's the cost of doing business." He paused a beat and cocked his head to the side as if struck by inspiration. "You know, maybe that's why we say *accounted for*. It's just business. We lost two in Oklahoma City, and it stings. But we *got. The job. Done.*"

He smacked his fist into his hand to punctuate the statement.

Despite the fact that Kilmeade's attention had moved on, Chad was sweating. Beads of perspiration were running down his spine, soaking the waistband of his boxers.

What's he saying? he wondered. *We didn't have anything to do with what happened to Dagger and Javelin. If anything, we fixed their screwup.*

"But out here," Kilmeade continued. "Out here, we've lost twelve men. Twelve. And yet the job still isn't done."

What? Chad barely stopped himself from saying it aloud. *No. You're wrong. The job is done. I dropped a mountain on that cowboy.*

Kilmeade stalked back to the table and picked up his tablet, holding it up and showing them the screen. Chad looked, as did everyone else, but couldn't really tell what was being displayed there.

"The job still isn't done," Kilmeade said again. "Matthew Redd is still alive."

Chad shook his head, unable to hold back. "No, I saw him die. The avalanche—"

Kilmeade cut him off. "This is live footage from the UAV showing Matthew Redd, very much alive, riding out of the mountains. And he's not alone."

Now Chad's whole body felt like it was on fire. This was all on him. He had assured his teammates that Redd was finished. When Arrow Six had asked if he was sure, he'd cockily replied, *"Who walks away from an avalanche?"*

He had never been so embarrassed.

Kilmeade, however, didn't seem to be focusing on him at all. "Now, I don't know *why* he's still alive. *Why* we can't seem to get the job done. But let me tell you, that changes. Right. Now."

If it was meant to be a rousing speech, it fell flat. There were no answering cheers or fist pumps.

But shame could be a powerful motivator too.

Kilmeade wasn't done. "We are going to hunt Redd down. We're going to kill everyone who stands with him and everyone he loves. And then when he has nothing left to live for, we are going to close his account once and for all."

He then raised his hand to his mouth, put thumb and forefinger between his lips, and let out a shrill whistle that echoed in the cavernous hangar to an almost earsplitting volume, causing Chad to wince involuntarily.

Even before the noise died away, a new sound filled the air, a low rumble like distant thunder. The source of the noise was immediately apparent as men—fully a dozen of them, wearing full tactical kit and armed with an assortment of machine pistols and semiautomatic rifles, stormed from the interior of the Gulfstream, double-timing onto the hangar floor like a basketball team emerging from the locker room onto the court at the beginning of a championship game.

Chad recognized a couple of them—men he'd served with in the SEALs years ago and who had left the team in disgrace after some unforgivable lapse of judgment—and it didn't require a great leap of logic to realize who the rest of them were.

Although the Praetorian's active force was limited to four seven-man teams operating under the official aegis of a special operations division of Homeland Security Investigations, recruitment was always ongoing. There was no shortage of potential recruits, men with not only the requisite military special operations training and experience, but the right temperament to follow the Praetorian's orders without question.

Men without scruples.

Ordinarily, when a vacancy needed to be filled, a candidate would undergo a selection process similar to that used in special operations units, followed by months of intensive training and team integration exercises before ever being tapped for real world operations.

Evidently Kilmeade had decided to accelerate the process in order to replenish their diminished numbers. The hunt for Matthew Redd would be the final selection test for new recruits.

Kilmeade let his eye roam the assembly once more, then perhaps in an unconscious nod to their location, said, "Let's ride."

FIFTY-ONE

More than once, during the long ride back out of the mountains, Redd thought about wheeling Remington around and heading back into the wilderness. He could feel the sniper's eyes on him, following him, waiting for the perfect moment to take another shot. If it happened, he would probably be dead before he heard the report. That it had not happened already did not in any way lessen his almost paranoid certainty that death would strike without warning. And despite Emily's repeated insistence that she remain at his side no matter what, his fear for what might happen to her, not to mention Junior . . . and Mikey . . . and everyone else that he cared about . . . That fear ate at his soul.

If anything happens to them because of me, I couldn't live with myself.

But the expected attack never happened, and gradually, Redd almost came to believe that, after triggering the avalanche, the sniper had declared victory and left the field.

Still, it would only be another brief reprieve. Eventually someone in the Twelve would realize that Redd was still alive and send another hit team. They would never stop coming.

What kept him from riding off on his own, however, or at least what he chose to attribute his decision to, was not overcoming his fears, but rather the fact that he was just too wrung out. Emily had dressed his wounds, using Dermabond and butterfly sutures to replace the weakened or broken stitches, and a cup of hot chocolate prepared over a portable camp stove had fortified him, but his energy reserves were still dangerously depleted. So were his supplies of food and ammunition. If he ran, he wouldn't get far. And if it came to another fight, he wouldn't last long.

No, as much as he wanted to believe that he could rise to the occasion, take on whatever the enemy threw at him, there were hard limits to what he could do, and he had reached them.

The ride seemed to pass by quickly, though it was nearly dawn before they reached the fire road where Mikey's truck and the horse trailer waited under eight inches of fresh snow. While Redd and Mikey got the horses loaded, Emily attended to Bekah, reporting that her body temperature, though still low, had come up a few degrees. More importantly, her pulse and breathing were steady. The girl remained unconscious, but Emily showed no inclination to rouse her.

Emily's original plan to call for an emergency helicopter evacuation of her patient had been thwarted by the weather. Although they were able to get a call out to emergency services, with heavy snow falling once more, the rescue helicopters were grounded, so Bekah's fate remained in their hands.

During the drive back to Wellington, in the warm and comfortable interior of Mikey's truck, Redd recounted his odyssey in the mountains. He told his tale with an almost weary formality, as if debriefing after a mission—an after-action review, assessing battle results with clinical detachment and taking full responsibility for his missteps. Each time he mentioned Rubble's heroics, he made sure to pet the loyal dog, who was lying at his feet. Emily and Mikey listened without interruption, though in the dim glow from the dashboard, Redd could see the incredulity on their faces.

The only time Emily gave a visible reaction was when Redd spoke of the blood transfusion he'd received in Strong's camp. He could see the wheels turning in her head, churning out a list of lab tests and prophylactic medications she would order to ensure that he did not contract some blood-borne illness.

They reached the Stillwater County Health Center, where Emily worked as the lead emergency medicine practitioner, just a little after 7:30 a.m. There were no cars in the parking lot, which was covered with a couple feet of snow, making the facility seem almost abandoned, but the ambulance lane had been plowed at some time during the night. Emily had Mikey pull into it. With the help of the clinic staff, she got Bekah loaded onto a gurney and had her wheeled into the emergency department.

Then she turned to Redd. "You. Inside. Now."

He stared back at her. "Em, we don't have time for this. I have to—"

"Make time," she said. "Doctor's orders. My preference would be to have you admitted, but I know I'll never convince you to sit still that long. But I am going to do a CBC, and get you started on broad-spectrum antibiotics." Rather than give him a chance to refuse, she turned to Mikey. "Could you please take the horses back to Chuck's place and let everyone know that we're back? I'm sure they're all worried sick about us. I'll let you know when we're done here so you can come pick us up."

Mikey returned an almost comical salute. "Aye, aye, ma'am." Then he shot Redd a grin. "Probably better just to do what she says."

Redd complied with a sigh. As he got out, Rubble stirred and leaped down from the lifted pickup. He was stretching, first his front legs and then his back hips, as Emily said, "Sorry, boy. No dogs allowed in here."

Redd turned to follow Emily and felt Rubble take up a position just behind him.

"Stay, Rubble," Emily commanded him. But the K9 kept pace with Redd. She stopped and spun around to face the dog. "Stay!"

Rubble raised his head and let out a low growl. Not one that indicated he was being aggressive—Redd had witnessed that plenty in the last day or two—but more as if he was voicing himself, telling her *no*. The rottie rumble, Redd called it. Rubble could speak for himself.

Emily looked from the dog to Redd, then sighed. "Guess after all you two have been through together, there's no splitting you up now."

"Honestly, Em, the poor boy could probably use a little medical attention himself."

"Alright. Let's go."

As Mikey's big truck and trailer disappeared into the swirling snow, Redd let Emily guide him and Rubble into the clinic's warm interior.

FIFTY-TWO

"Matthew?"

As Redd snapped awake at the sound of the voice, his first thought was *I can't believe I fell asleep.*

When Emily had directed him to lie down on the padded table in an examination room while she went to check on Bekah, he had told himself that he wasn't going to succumb to the seductive temptation to sleep. When she then proceeded to cover him with a blanket and dim the lights in the room on her way out, he had vowed to do nothing more than rest his eyes, just for a couple seconds.

His body had other plans.

A quick check of his G-Shock showed that he had been out for only about twenty minutes, but there was no telling how long he might have slept if not for the intrusion. The moment of self-reproach passed quickly. The voice that had roused him was not Emily's. Feeling more than a little vulnerable, he pulled the blanket tight around himself and sat up to face the figure standing in the doorway.

"Sheriff," he said guardedly.

Emily had told him about her visit to Blackwood's office and his refusal to offer any assistance. While he understood the legal bind the man was in, the simple fact of that refusal stung. However, that was not his foremost concern. "If you're here to take me in so you can hand me over to someone claiming to be Homeland Security, then I think we're going to have a problem."

By way of an answer, Blackwood dropped his gaze to his Stetson, which he held in both hands.

Hat in hand, Redd realized.

"I'm here to ask for your forgiveness," Blackwood began. "I messed up, Matthew. I know that now. I never should have doubted you. You're a good man, and after all we've been through together, I should have known that you were on the right side of this thing. I apologize."

The sincerity of the apology left Redd momentarily speechless.

Blackwood, mistaking Redd's lack of response for acrimony, frowned and clenched the brim of the Stetson. "C'mon, Matthew, I'm trying to make this right."

Redd shook his head. "Don't sweat it. Didn't exactly count on your help anyways."

It sounded meaner than he intended.

"Matty!" Emily stepped out from behind the sheriff, fixing him with a death stare. "Will you just listen to what he has to say?"

Redd glowered at her, but his ire was short-lived. As much as he hated to admit it, Emily was usually right about this sort of thing. "Fine. I'm all ears."

Blackwood glanced over at Emily and gave her a nod of gratitude, then returned his attention to Redd. "Yesterday, Special Agent Treadway paid me a visit."

Redd almost answered, *Sammy?* That was the name he associated with Stephanie Treadway because that was the name she had been using when they first met . . . when she threw a great big monkey wrench into his life.

"Suffice it to say," Blackwood went on, "she convinced me that the men purporting to be DHS agents were nothing of the sort and that I ought to be doing everything in my power to protect you. That's why I'm here."

While Blackwood was speaking, Emily came over to Redd's bedside and, with one firm hand, rolled him onto his left side. Because he was giving his full attention to Blackwood, Redd barely even noticed as she tugged down the waistband of his Wranglers, partially exposing one butt cheek, and began swabbing the area with an alcohol prep pad.

"Little pinch," she said, then jammed a large-bore hypodermic needle deep into the flesh of his hip.

"Ow!" he exclaimed, more out of surprise than anything else.

His reaction startled Rubble, who had fallen asleep on the floor next to Redd.

"Hold still," she admonished. "And don't be such a baby."

Redd ignored the dig—and the pain, which wasn't insignificant—and sat up again. "Look, I appreciate what you're saying. The thing is, you can't protect me.

The people that are coming for me won't respect your badge. If you try to get between them and me, you'll just get yourself killed."

"Be that as it may, I'm the law around here. I took an oath to protect the citizens of Stillwater County, and that includes you." He jammed the Stetson onto his head, signaling the transition from apologetic supplicant to lawman. "I'm putting you in protective custody."

Redd shook his head. "I'm not going to let anyone else die because of me."

"It's not up to you—"

"Sheriff," Emily broke in. "Will you give us a minute?"

Blackwood pursed his lips, but then nodded in assent and exited the room.

As soon as he was gone, Redd tried to defend his position, but Emily put a finger to his lips. "Matthew, just listen. I know you think you have to carry these burdens alone, but it's just not true. Let him help."

"He has no idea what he'll be going up against."

"Maybe that's true. Maybe not. But ask yourself, how long can you keep running?"

An image of Josiah Strong appeared in Redd's mind's eye. Strong had successfully dodged federal law enforcement agencies for nearly thirty years—it *could* be done.

But what kind of life was that?

Emily wasn't finished. "Up to now, the people hunting you have managed to hide behind their fake badges, but now that we know better, they might think twice about attacking real law enforcement agents."

Redd was about to point out that the killers had, without any hesitation, already struck "real law enforcement agents" in Oklahoma City, but a knock at the door cut him off.

Redd and Emily answered simultaneously, but his exhortation to "Hold on" was overridden by her "Come in."

The door swung open, but the figure that stepped inside was not Sheriff Blackwood, and this time Redd and Emily spoke in unison.

"Gavin!"

Gavin Kline, looking both relieved and more than a little harried, strode forward, halting almost within arm's reach of Redd. For a moment, Redd thought Kline was going to hug him, and if he had, Redd would almost certainly have hugged him back, but the moment passed and the space between them remained.

"Matt. It's good to see you still among the living."

Redd nodded. "Likewise. I thought you were—" His throat tightened on the word.

"It was a close one. I got my bell rung pretty bad." Kline managed a smile. "Sorry I didn't get here sooner. We can catch up later. Right now we need to get you over to the courthouse."

"Why there?"

"Because I don't think we can make it to the Bozeman field office, and I'm not sure there's anywhere else where you'll be even remotely safe."

Something about Kline's paternalistic manner rubbed Redd the wrong way. "I've done all right so far."

Kline arched an eyebrow. "Really? Could have fooled me."

"You should see the other guys."

Behind him, Emily grasped his biceps, her touch saying more than words could. *Let him help you.*

"I'm not trying to take anything away from you," said Kline. "But the simple truth of it is that you've been lucky. DHS has had a Predator drone tracking your movements the whole time. It's over us right now."

The revelation brought Redd up short. "DHS? The *real* DHS?"

"It's complicated. Long story short, there's a rogue element working inside the Department of Homeland Security, a special operations unit that has carte blanche to pretty much do whatever they please. They're the personal strike force of a very powerful man known as the Praetorian."

"The Praetorian? So this has nothing to do with the Twelve?"

"Oh, it has *everything* to do with the Twelve. He was their inside man in the federal government, bought and paid for. And just to make sure he stayed in line, they threatened to expose his . . . ah, let's say inappropriate behavior. The Praetorian was afraid that Gage would dime him out to save his own skin, so he decided to preemptively remove the threat. And the rest of the Twelve while he was at it. Unfortunately, because you and Gage spent some quality time together, he's afraid that you might know his dirty little secret as well. That's why he's sent his strike force after you."

Redd thought back to the night when he had taken Anton Gage alive in an abandoned nuclear missile launch base. Gage had named a few names, but ever the negotiator, he had hinted at more than he had actually revealed. "He never said anything about this Praetorian."

Kline shrugged. "The Praetorian doesn't know that. And I don't think he'd believe you if you told him. That's the bad news. The good news is, we can stop him. But it's going to take a little time. Keeping you alive until we can pull the plug on his operation is our chief concern."

"And that's why you want to stash me in the courthouse." Redd shook his head. "What makes you think I'll be safe there?"

Kline grimaced. "I can't guarantee your safety anywhere right now. I've requested reinforcements from the Bozeman field office, but I'm not sure we can count on them for help."

He seemed to be on the verge of explaining this statement, but then shook his head and switched gears. "I'm hoping the Praetorian will think twice about attacking a government building in broad daylight, but if I'm wrong and we have to make a stand, I can't think of a better place."

"He's right," Blackwood said from the doorway. "I've recalled all my deputies, and we've got a small arsenal at our disposal. I hope it doesn't come down to a fight, but if it does, we'll give as good as we get."

A frown of concern creased Emily's forehead. "If they've been following our movements with the drone, is it possible they're following Mikey as well?"

"I'd say it's almost a sure thing," Kline admitted gravely.

Emily turned to Redd. "Mikey's on his way to Chuck Boardman's place. Liz and the kids were staying with him. They could all be in danger."

"I'll call Chuck," Blackwood said. "Better yet, I'll send a deputy out there. We'll bring everyone here." He nodded toward Emily. "Your folks too."

Redd looked from Blackwood to Kline and then to Emily, who gave him what he interpreted as an encouraging nod. "It doesn't look as if I've got much choice," sighed Redd. He continued to look at Emily. "How's Bekah doing?"

"Good. She's conscious but still a little out of it. When the roads are clear, I'd like to have her transported to Bozeman for further treatment and observation." She paused a beat, then added, "She's asking to see you."

"Bekah?" inquired Blackwood.

"Bekah Strong," said Redd. "She's the daughter of Josiah Strong."

Both Blackwood and Kline started at the mention of the fugitive's name, but Redd forestalled any questions with a dismissive wave. "Let me talk to her. Then we can go to the courthouse."

FIFTY-THREE

Bekah Strong looked up from her examination bed and smiled when she saw Redd standing in the doorway. She was wrapped in a foil-lined blanket from which sprouted several thick plastic tubes circulating warm water to and from a small heated pump, slowly bringing her body temperature back to normal. Her cheeks were ruddy and slightly abraded, but she looked otherwise alert and healthy.

"Matt!"

"Bekah." He gestured to the bed. "This all feels kind of familiar, only I think we've switched places."

"That lady doctor told me you saved me."

Redd nodded. "I had some help from Rubble."

"Rubble's okay?"

"Somehow he is. He's resting up in another room right now."

Bekah's smile broadened but then just as quickly faded. "What about the others? Kevin and Justin and Devon?"

Redd shook his head. "I'm sorry. We didn't find them. We alerted county search and rescue, but given the conditions . . ." He trailed off, then repeated, "I'm sorry."

She looked away, blinking as if trying not cry. "I didn't want anything to happen to them. I mean, I didn't want to stay, but I didn't want them to . . ."

"I know." He allowed her a moment with her grief, then went on. "Bekah, listen, I'm going to have to leave for a little while. I'm not sure how long—"

"You're leaving?"

"You'll be okay here," he assured her. "I won't be long. And when I come back, we're going to make sure that you have whatever you need."

Her expression became quizzical. "I don't understand."

"You don't need to go back to the Family. We'll help you start a new life. School, a place to live, a job if you want . . . whatever you need."

She stared back at him for a long moment. "I thought we'd stay together. You promised. Remember?"

"I promised to get you someplace safe," Redd reminded her. "You *are* safe here. That doctor who helped you? She's my wife. Her name's Emily. Once I get back, we'll sort things out, and together we'll help you get settled someplace else."

There was a long pause before Bekah spoke again. "She's very pretty."

"She really is," Redd agreed. "Sometimes I feel like she's Beauty and I'm the Beast."

Bekah chuckled; then her face turned serious again. "How do I know you'll come back?"

"I'm not running anymore. I've done that, and I almost got killed. *Twice.*"

"But you *have* to run. Those government agents are still after you. They won't stop until they get you. That's all they do, hunt down people and kill them in cold blood. They don't ask questions. They just start shooting."

"Your dad teach you that?"

"I've seen it with my own eyes."

It hit Redd that he really hadn't a clue what she'd seen in her short life, but he could guess. And it was more than any kid should have witnessed or been exposed to.

Before he could say anything, Bekah continued. "Don't trust them, Matt. The only good federal agent is a dead one."

"You don't mean that, Bekah."

She folded her arms across her chest in a defiant kind of way. "Actually, I do."

Redd saw right through her tough-guy act and knew that deep down she was a scared young girl who didn't know what she believed. He pitied her.

"Trust me," said Redd, "you don't."

"How would you know what I mean?" Bekah asked.

Redd detected a new edge to her voice and decided it was time to come clean.

"Because *I'm* a federal agent, and you helped save my life."

She recoiled, as if he had just taken off a mask to reveal a reptilian creature underneath, and pulled her blanket up to her chin like a shield.

"Not everybody who works for the government is bad, Bekah. I know you were raised to believe that, but it's not true." He turned to open the door and called out, "Gavin, can you join us for a second?"

Kline, who had been waiting right outside, came into the room. As he passed Redd, he murmured, "Matt, we really need to get moving."

"This will just take a second," replied Redd; then turning to Bekah, he said, "This is Gavin Kline. He's an assistant director of the FBI." Redd paused a beat, then added, "He's also *my* father."

This candid statement seemed to surprise Kline as much as it did Bekah, and the corners of his mouth twitched up in a smile.

Bekah, however, looked terrified. "Are you here to arrest me?"

"Arrest you?" asked Kline. "Why would I do that?"

She frowned. "Then you're here to make me help you find my father."

Kline glanced at Redd, then turned back to the girl. "Your father is a wanted fugitive. But the crimes he's wanted for occurred long before you were born. I don't think growing up in his care constitutes a criminal action. Obviously, we'd like to bring him in. Peaceably. And we would appreciate any help you might be able to give us."

Redd quickly added, "Nobody is going to force you to do anything you don't want to do."

Kline shot him a look that said, *Don't make promises you can't keep,* but he did not contradict Redd.

"Gavin, tell Bekah what you told me. About the Praetorian."

Kline gave him another sidelong look but then appeared to grasp Redd's intent. "The men who have been chasing Matt are part of a rogue agency led by a traitor inside the government. Even though they carry badges, they are not above the law. And we—Matt and I—are going to take them down."

"They're the exception, Bekah," said Redd, "not the rule. I don't think your father understands that."

Kline looked over at him again. "We really need to get moving."

Redd nodded, then turned to Bekah. "I have to go, but I'll be back soon, and then we'll help you . . . Emily and me . . . We'll help you with whatever you need. You don't have to run and hide anymore."

"Thank you, Matt. For everything."

Redd smiled. "You saved me first. Now we're even." He turned and followed Kline out of the room.

Emily, Blackwood, and Rubble were waiting just outside the door. As they made their way to the ambulance entrance, where Blackwood's patrol vehicle was idling, Blackwood leaned in and said, "That girl has a major crush on you."

Redd felt his cheeks go hot. "She's just a kid," he said dismissively. "She's lived her entire life in isolation. She doesn't have enough life experience to know what she wants."

A big smile spread across Emily's face. "Men really don't know much about women, do they?" Before either Redd or Blackwood could answer, she wrapped both her arms around Redd's left arm and said, "It's not a crush. She feels safe with you, Matty. That's all. She has good instincts."

"You must have missed the part about 'the only good federal agent is a dead one,'" replied Blackwood.

"She's misguided. Give her time. We don't throw people away."

Emily had a way of always seeing the best in people. Redd loved that about his wife.

Letting go with one of her arms, Emily swung out in front of Redd. "Matty, it's okay. She knows a hero when she sees one. I hope that someday she finds someone just like you." She slid her free arm around his waist and nuzzled her head into his chest. "Every girl should be as lucky as I am."

Don't count your blessings just yet, thought Redd, though he didn't say it out loud. *This isn't over . . . not even close.*

FIFTY-FOUR

The Stillwater County Courthouse was just a couple blocks south of the medical facility. It was a distance that they could easily have covered in five minutes or less, but that would have been five minutes in the open, visible not only to the drone but also to the Praetorian's hit squad, which Redd knew included at least one sniper team.

Rather than utilize the main entrance or the door into the sheriff's department offices, Blackwood pulled around to the rear of the building and into the sally port used by deputies when delivering suspects to the county lockup. Redd felt a mixture of relief and anxiety when he spotted Mikey's truck in the adjacent parking lot, as well as Elijah Lawrence's old Chevy pickup. For better or worse, all his loved ones had been brought together in one place.

Now it was up to him to ensure their safety.

In the nearly two years since his return to Montana, Redd had become intimately familiar with the two-story redbrick structure that was the seat of county government. He vividly recalled his first visit—when he had learned of J. B.'s death in Sheriff Blackwood's office. Not long thereafter, he'd spent a night in the lockup, framed for the murder of a pair of vagrants who had been suspected of killing J. B. and burglarizing Redd's house. Later he argued with the county assessor over unpaid property taxes and had very nearly lost the ranch over it.

Yet not all his experiences there had been negative. He and Emily had visited the county clerk's office to apply for their marriage license. Redd had spent many hours in Blackwood's office hammering out the details of a weapons training program for the deputies.

None of that mattered now. Today the building was a refuge, a last resort for him and his loved ones. There was nowhere else to go. He just prayed that the redbrick walls would preserve them all through the dark hours that lay ahead.

Redd found them gathered in the reception lobby of the sheriff's department: Mikey and Liz with their son Luke, little Matty, and Emily's parents—the Reverend and Mrs. Lawrence. He went to Liz, who was holding Junior, and took his son into his arms, hugging him as tightly as he could without hurting the small child. Redd immediately felt most of his stress melt away, and he cleared his throat in hopes of dislodging the lump he suddenly felt forming there.

"Daddy missed you, buddy," he whispered.

Little Matty, who had been sleeping soundly, started to fuss ever so slightly. Redd kissed his son on the top of his head, then handed him back to Liz, who had an almost superhuman ability to soothe children back to sleep.

"Thank you," Redd said as he handed Junior back over. "For everything."

Liz took Junior in her left arm and then, surprising Redd, wrapped her free arm around him, pulling him into a warm embrace. "That's what family is for, Matt," she said softly.

Redd swallowed hard, the lump in his throat suddenly returning. He was beyond grateful to have such loyal and caring people in his life. Unable to find the words to convey his thoughts, he simply nodded.

Rubble, his forepaws now wrapped in bandages, had been trailing along behind Redd since leaving the clinic but immediately trotted over to the old preacher. Elijah, who had taken an instant shine to the dog when Redd and Emily adopted him, greeted Rubble with a big grin and began scratching behind his ears.

Stephanie Treadway was also there, looking nothing at all like the redheaded surfer girl in his memory. Three sheriff's deputies were present as well— Undersheriff Shane Hall, Garrison Scott, and the department's rookie, David Thornock—along with one other member of the department's staff.

"Maggie?" Blackwood exclaimed. "I told you to go home."

Maggie Albright put her hands on her hips and thrust her chin at him defiantly. "You did no such thing."

"I most certainly did."

"No, you didn't. You gave the order for all nonessential personnel to go home."

She tilted her head forward, glaring at him over the tops of her horn-rimmed glasses. "I hope you aren't suggesting that I am somehow . . . *nonessential.*"

"Now you know that's not what I meant."

Redd, who had come to think of the sheriff's receptionist fondly as the crazy aunt he never had, tried to intercede. "Maggie, of course you're essential. Stuart's just concerned for your safety."

She turned her stare on him and harumphed. "If I'm not mistaken, the reason you and yours are here is for *their* safety. Are you trying to tell me that it's safe for them, but not me?"

Redd felt a pang of sympathy for Blackwood, who had to deal with the stubborn receptionist on a daily basis. He glanced over at Emily, hoping that she would take the initiative to reason with Maggie, woman to woman, but Emily just raised her hands in a *don't look at me* gesture.

Blackwood shook his head in resignation. "Well, if you won't listen to reason, the least you can do is make yourself useful. See if you can't scare us up some hot coffee and maybe something to eat. We could all be here a while."

Kline stepped forward. "On that note, Sheriff, maybe we should be thinking about our defensive situation. If worse comes to worst and we have to fight off an assault, this is probably not where we want to be."

"You make a good point," agreed Blackwood. "Why don't we move this conversation to the break room?"

As the rest of the group followed Maggie deeper into the office, Blackwood turned to the deputies, directing them to secure and cover the exits.

Redd knew there were four primary entrances to the courthouse, not including the roll-up garage door to the sally port, which was always kept locked. The main entrance, which faced Broadway, directly accessed both the county offices and the justice center. There was also the sheriff's department public entrance on the corner of Broadway and Oak Street, the parking lot entrance on the south side of the building, used mostly by employees, and a fire exit on the east side. There were also numerous ground floor windows large enough for an adult male to pass through. Despite being the most secure building in the county, it was a tactical nightmare under the best of circumstances. With just three deputies to keep an eye on the exits, it would be impossible to defend.

As the deputies moved off to carry out Blackwood's orders, Redd closed with the sheriff. Rubble returned to his heels, following his master wherever he went. "Where's the rest of your force?" he asked, keeping his voice down.

There were seven sworn deputies in the Stillwater sheriff's department. With Blackwood, that brought the total to eight. When Blackwood had promised the protection of his entire department, Redd had understood it to mean that all the deputies would be present. But they had only half that number—four officers, along with Kline, Treadway, and Redd himself. Seven bodies to cover four ingress points and protect their family members. Redd's preference would have been to have at least three on each exit and two or three more providing a last line of defense with the families.

"I've got Kurt Oman parked up at the highway intersection," replied Blackwood. "The others will get here when they get here."

Redd felt a knot forming in the pit of his stomach. "That's not enough bodies to cover all the entrances."

Blackwood spread his hands. "We'll have to make do. I can't change what is."

"Is there a problem?" asked Emily. She had come up behind Redd without his taking note.

He gave a nonchalant shrug. "Nothing we can't handle."

Emily fixed him with her stare. "Matty, talk to me. You're not in this alone."

He frowned as he saw others in the group taking an interest in the conversation. But Emily was right. Everyone present had a stake in what was happening. He took a breath, let it out, and then said, "Okay, here's the situation. We don't really know what we're going to be facing, but if the past is any indication, we might have to actively defend ourselves right here. Unfortunately, there's only seven of us and Rubble. It's not enough to cover all the entrances and protect everyone else, so we're going to need to rethink our defensive strategy."

Mikey raised his hand. "You mean *eight* of us."

"Nine," Emily blurted out.

Redd paused a beat before speaking. "I meant seven who are trained to fight."

"Been fighting my whole life, brother," said Mikey. "And thanks to you, I've got my feet wet when it comes to combat. Let me help."

Redd knew Mikey was an excellent marksman and hunter, and the year prior, he'd relied on his friend to cover him while he confronted a group of bikers that ultimately led to Redd being chased and ended with a buffalo stampede. Likewise, Emily knew her way around a gun, and she'd come to Redd's defense on more than one occasion.

"Guys, I don't—"

"We've all got a stake in this," said Emily, cutting him off. "It may not be ideal, but Mikey is right: we can all fight if we have to."

Redd looked past his wife and saw Liz Derhammer. If anyone would object to everyone taking up arms, it would be Liz. But instead of the uneasy expression he expected to see on her face, Redd was surprised to find Mikey's wife nodding in agreement.

"We're all in this together, Matt," said Liz. "I'll admit it, I don't like my family constantly surrounded by danger." Redd felt a pang of guilt, knowing that he was the reason the Derhammers had faced so much danger these last few months. "But if I've learned anything, it's that we're all stronger together."

Redd took note of the fact that Liz included *him* as part of her family. It meant a lot to him and eased some of the guilt he felt. Plus, she was right. They were stronger together, and arming everyone offered their best chance at making it out of this alive.

"Alright," he conceded. "Mikey and Emily can suit up, but I want you guys in a center room with the others. You'll be the last line of defense to protect the kids and everyone else. The rest of us can figure out how best to cover the entrances."

"How many people do you want on the doors?" pressed Mikey.

"Three would be my preference. I'll settle for two at the main entrance, two at the sheriff's door, and two on the south side. We can probably get by with just one person covering the fire door since it only opens out."

"You can put Emily and Mikey on the doors too. Give me a gun. I'll see to the rest of us." Every head turned to look at the man who had made this comment, the last person Redd had expected to hear from.

Emily's father.

Blackwood answered before Redd could. "Reverend Lawrence, I don't want to put you in that position."

"It's not your doing, Sheriff. We didn't pick this fight."

His gaze went to Redd as he said the last part, and his head bobbed in a nod of reassurance, as if to say, *I don't blame you for this.*

But if that was his intent, it had exactly the opposite effect on Redd.

What have I done? he thought.

For the first time in his life, he began to understand why Gavin Kline had run away from the responsibilities of fatherhood and family life. It was one thing to put yourself in danger as a bachelor, laying your life on the line for the greater good, but a family man risked more than just his life—he risked leaving behind a widow and fatherless children.

But Redd's choices had gone far beyond that. The enemies he had made had not merely come after him but had also threatened Emily and Junior. And now his best friends and his in-laws were caught up in it as well. Not to mention Blackwood, Maggie, and the deputies.

No matter what the reverend said or meant, Redd knew he was absolutely to blame. And while he could almost—*almost*—forgive himself for endangering them all, because he was going to do everything in his power to protect them, there was one thing he could not excuse.

"Elijah, I can't ask you to take up arms."

"You didn't." Lawrence gazed back at him, scratching his chin. "I believe I volunteered."

"I think what Matthew means," intoned Kline, "is that we can't ask a man of God to take a life. It wouldn't feel right."

Lawrence regarded Kline, with one craggy eyebrow arched. "Why is that exactly?"

"Well . . . you know. 'Thou shalt not kill' and everything."

A hint of a grin twitched the corner of Lawrence's mouth. "I do enjoy getting preached at by a layman. Perhaps you'd like to hear my thoughts on how law enforcement might be improved."

Kline blushed. "I didn't mean to—"

Lawrence waved him off. "If you attended my sermons—"his gaze slid over to Redd—"or stayed awake for them . . . you'd know that in the original language, the commandment proscribed unlawful killing. *Murder.* The prohibition did not extend to causing death in warfare, and in fact, you don't have to read much further to find God Himself ordering His people to take the Promised Land by violence. Some of God's most faithful servants were warriors—Joshua, Gideon, King David. It's not a sin to take a life if the cause is righteous." He thrust his chin toward the two young boys. "And I'd say protecting them is about as righteous a cause as I'll live to see."

Kline bowed his head. "I stand corrected."

Blackwood continued staring at Lawrence, as if still troubled by the preacher's stance on the subject, but then he shook his head. "Elijah," he said, skipping all formalities, "you sure 'bout this?"

"I am, Stuart."

"All right, then," Blackwood said with a smile that Redd thought was more out of disbelief than his finding anything humorous. "Follow me to the armory and I'll get you set up."

Redd watched as not only Mikey, Emily, and Elijah, but Liz and Mrs. Lawrence—each with a baby in her arms—lined up behind the sheriff. Then Maggie Albright joined the line as well. Redd was both moved and a little discomfited at their willingness to fight to protect him and his family. He prayed that they would not have to put that willingness to the test.

✖   ✖   ✖

The sheriff's department's arsenal consisted of ten Remington 870 12-gauge shotguns, four of which were in patrol vehicles, six Colt AR-15s chambered for 5.56 NATO rounds, and a Remington M700PSS—the law enforcement variant of the rifle Mikey had loaned Redd, which was now either lost somewhere in the mountains or in the possession of Josiah Strong's Family. Additionally, there were several handguns that had been taken out of service but remained on the property books. Blackwood began by setting aside three AR-15s for his deputies and then offered the remaining rifles to Redd, Kline, and Treadway, along with a supply of magazines and several boxes of ammo on stripper clips. He then offered the rest of the group their pick of what was left. Elijah Lawrence took one of the shotguns, as did Emily, while Mikey chose the Remington rifle. Liz, Maggie, and Mrs. Lawrence, looking a little more hesitant, asked for recommendations. Blackwood gave them each a Smith & Wesson Model 10 Police Special .38-caliber revolver, which had been standard issue among most law enforcement agencies until the shift toward semiautomatic pistols. Redd gave them a quick lesson in how to hold and shoot the weapons but did not talk them through reloading procedures. If things got bad enough that they were obliged to fire their weapons, it was unlikely that they would have enough time to reload.

When everyone who was willing to carry a weapon had one, Blackwood re-visited the defensive plan. Undersheriff Shane Hall and Treadway would cover the main courthouse entrance. Scott and Thornock would take the entrance on the south side of the building. Mikey and Emily were assigned to watch the fire door, and Kline, Redd, and Blackwood would act as a quick reaction force, cover-ing the sheriff's department door and moving to contact as needed. Everyone else would remain in the break room, ready to fight or flee as the situation dictated.

Only Emily seemed to take issue with the assignments. As the rest of the group began moving out to cover their respective positions, she took Redd aside. "My place is with you," she said.

"That's not a good idea," replied Redd, striving for a patient tone. "If we were together and, God forbid, something happened to both of us, who would take care of Junior?"

Emily shook her head. "There's no guarantee that any of us will make it through this. If I'm going to die, I'd rather be at your side."

"Emily . . ."

"Stop trying to always protect me, Matty. We're a team. We should be together."

Redd glanced over at Kline, then Blackwood, hoping one or the other would come to his rescue, but both men conspicuously found something else to occupy their attention. Mikey, however, was quick to weigh in. "You know, I can probably handle that fire exit by myself. It's locked from the outside after all, so odds are, nobody's coming in that way, but if they do, I'll just shout for help."

Redd shot him a murderous look, but Emily took the win. "Then it's settled. I'll stay here with you."

Redd tried to think of a better argument, but before he could, Blackwood's radio crackled to life. "Sheriff, this is Kurt Oman, over."

A sudden hush came over the gathering. Blackwood unclipped the radio and keyed the mic. "Go for Blackwood."

"A bunch of big SUVs just turned off the highway, headed into town. I can't be sure, but I think you're about to have company."

Blackwood glanced over at Redd, then nodded. "I copy, Oman. Stand by." He returned the radio to its place on his belt and faced the group. "This is it."

FIFTY-FIVE

They emerged from the veil of falling snow like the Four Horsemen unleashed at the unsealing of the scroll of the Apocalypse, only instead of four horses they rode in seven 2024 Chevrolet Suburbans. The big sport utility vehicles were roomy enough that the entire twenty-six-man force could have been comfortably transported in just four, but for their purposes, mobility and redundancy trumped economy.

They weren't simply visiting the little Montana town. They were invading it.

In the lead vehicle, Cormac Kilmeade paid little attention to what was going on outside. Just as he had been for the last few hours, he was entirely focused on the display of his tablet computer, which showed the feed from the Predator drone presently circling high above Wellington, Montana. Earlier, he had watched Redd and the others depart the clinic in a sheriff's patrol vehicle and had followed them to the nearby courthouse, where, surprisingly, they had stayed. He had expected them to keep moving. Surely Redd would know that it wasn't over—that the next wave was on its way.

Maybe he's tired of running, thought Kilmeade. *But if he thinks he's going to be safe in there, he's got another thing coming.*

Still, he was not about to underestimate Matthew Redd. Colin had made that mistake. Colin had made a lot of mistakes and had paid the ultimate price for them. Cormac would learn from his twin's failures, and he would exact the cost of that lesson in blood. Matthew Redd's blood.

Wellington's main street appeared completely deserted, the businesses all closed, the sidewalks and storefronts buried under deep snowdrifts. Evidently, the weather was keeping everyone at home. That would make things easier. Cormac wasn't too worried about operating in the open. Just as with the destruction of the JPATS transport in Oklahoma City, he was ready with a plausible cover story. He would simply put the blame on Redd, painting him as a madman who took over the county courthouse and killed all his hostages before finally being taken out by Cormac's heroic rescue team. Even so, the fewer eyewitnesses, the better. And nothing brought unwanted attention like accidentally killing a curious bystander.

When the convoy appeared in the video feed, Cormac keyed his radio mic. "All elements, this is Dagger Six. Halt here."

In the driver's seat across from Cormac, Dagger Seven—Darren Richmond—began applying steady pressure to the brake pedal, bringing the SUV to a slow stop. Cormac continued transmitting. "Arrow Six, deploy your teams to their designated overwatch positions. Everyone else, proceed to your assigned sectors of fire and cover the exits."

One by one the subteam leaders called in to acknowledge the orders, and as they did, the vehicles bearing them broke from the line, passing Cormac's Suburban to continue on toward the main objective, peeling off in different directions to begin establishing a security cordon. When theirs was the only vehicle remaining, Cormac waved his hand, giving the *move out* signal.

Richmond eased the SUV forward, advancing toward the courthouse at a pace barely faster than a walk, giving the others time to fully deploy. The big redbrick building seemed to materialize out of a cloud of snow. Richmond continued past the building's front entrance, stopping at the corner, where the glass door marked with the star-shaped badge of the sheriff's department was clearly visible.

"You sure you want to do this?" he asked, giving Cormac a sidelong glance.

Cormac was sure. "I need to look him in the eye."

"Aren't you worried he'll snipe you the second you step into the open?"

Strangely, Cormac wasn't.

When he had learned of Colin's death, one of the first things he had done was review the target package on Redd. A mere glance at the man's military record was enough to convince Cormac that his brother had not even bothered to open the file. If he had, he would have recognized that Redd's training and combat experience were equal to his own, and subsequently would not have lost his own life along with the lives of eleven operators under his command.

It was a pity, really. Redd was the kind of man Cormac would have loved to serve with. Dumb luck that they had ended up on different sides. Bad luck for Colin.

Matthew Redd was a killer, there was no doubt about that, but he was also a professional, and in his own way, a man of honor. Redd wouldn't take the cheap shot. He would find the very thought of a sucker punch abhorrent.

He couldn't explain any of this to Richmond though, so instead he said, "If anything happens to me, burn that place to the ground."

Richmond shrugged. "It's your funeral."

Cormac ignored the comment. He opened his door, feeling the rush of cold on his face as he stepped out onto the packed snow covering the road. After a moment's consideration, he placed his M4 butt down in the footwell and closed it inside the vehicle. Then, with his badge hanging around his neck, he calmly made his way to the sheriff's office entrance.

There was no sign of activity beyond the glass doors. Like the rest of the town, the courthouse seemed abandoned. Cormac tested the door and found it locked.

Well, that's disappointing, he thought.

He rapped his knuckles hard against the glass three times.

Nothing happened.

He waited thirty seconds, then knocked again, not just three times, but several, banging the thick glass so hard that the pane vibrated like a plucked guitar string between each blow. He kept up the insistent pounding until a figure appeared behind the glass—a tall older man with a droopy gray mustache, wearing a brown uniform with a six-point-star badge. Warily, the man—presumably the sheriff—crossed the reception lobby, his right hand resting on the butt of the gun holstered on his hip.

Cormac continued knocking until the old-timer was just a few steps away, then made a show of holding his own badge up to the glass. The sheriff approached the door but stopped just short of opening it, regarding Cormac for a long moment. The man's continued hesitancy told Cormac that his presence was not unexpected.

Cormac decided to push the issue. "Federal officer," he shouted. "Open up."

The old-timer stared back at him, but Cormac could see the indecision in the man's eyes, the war between doing his duty as a sworn officer of the law and protecting a friend from what he knew would be a death sentence. Cormac waggled his badge, emphasizing the former.

The gesture seemed to have the desired effect. The sheriff took another step forward and pushed on the interior panic bar, opening the door just wide enough for his voice to be heard. "What can I do for you?" he asked, trying and utterly failing to sound nonchalant.

"Mind if I come inside?" Cormac gestured to the lobby behind the man.

"I think you're fine where you are."

Cormac returned a thin, humorless smile. "Then I'll just cut to the chase, Sheriff—" he glanced at the sign beside the door—"Blackwood. You know why I'm here. Give me what I want and save yourself and your little town a world of hurt."

Blackwood squared his shoulders. "All right, since we're speaking plainly. Matthew Redd is under my protection. He's not going anywhere with you."

"Matthew Redd is a federal fugitive," sneered Cormac. "If you're protecting him, then you're committing a federal offense."

"Fugitive? My understanding was that he was wanted for questioning."

"Well, that was before he murdered a dozen federal agents."

The sheriff appeared to consider this, but then he shook his head. "Be that as it may, I'm not going to just hand him over to you. There's a procedure to follow."

The sheriff's response was so predictable, he might have been reading from a script. Cormac considered pressing the point but knew it would be a waste of time. He had not really expected this to go any differently than it was.

"If that's how you want to play this . . ." Cormac let the statement hang unfinished, allowing the old-timer to imagine what dire consequences his decision would provoke. He started to turn away, then stopped and faced the sheriff again. "I'd like to have a word with him."

Blackwood shook his head. "I don't see that happening."

"Indulge me. I can tell that you're dead set on sacrificing yourself to protect Matthew Redd, but I think it's only fair that he weighs in. Maybe when he realizes that he's about to throw your lives away in a senseless act of defiance, he'll rethink his position." Then lowering his voice to an almost conspiratorial whisper, Cormac added, "C'mon, Sheriff. All I want to do is talk to the man."

Blackwood shook his head, but before he could voice his objection, someone else called out from the reception lobby, "I'll talk to him."

There was a murmur of conversation from somewhere just out of view, but then the man himself, Matthew Redd, stepped into view and strode across the lobby. He barely resembled the man in the old photograph from the target package, showing a much younger Redd as a freshly buzzed Marine recruit at boot camp, but there was no mistaking the eyes, which, at the moment, looked like they could cut through hardened steel. Cormac did not fail to notice the AR-15 Redd carried at the low ready. He drew in an involuntary breath, recalling Richmond's warning.

Redd spoke first. "I'm not coming with you. Period. And you can tell the Praetorian that I'm coming for him next."

The defiant words did not shock Cormac nearly as much as Redd's casual mention of the Praetorian. *How does he know that? And if he knows, who else does?*

For the first time in a long time . . . maybe for the first time in his life, Cormac felt a sliver of doubt insinuate itself into his resolve.

If the Praetorian's existence had been exposed, then it was only a matter of time before all his secrets were laid bare, not the least of which being the existence of Cormac's special operations teams. Their ersatz credentials would offer zero protection when the *real* Homeland Security investigators began looking into their activities.

I can get out ahead of this, he thought. *Cash in my insurance policy and head to the tropics now, before the net closes.*

Like many veterans of Tier One special operations units, Cormac Kilmeade had planned ahead for rainy days to come, storing up cash and other assets, developing a fake identity, all so that in the event of something exactly like this, he could reinvent himself and start a new life somewhere far, far away.

But that wasn't why he had come here.

He broke eye contact with Redd, looking skyward, drawing in a breath through his nose as if sniffing the air, and then letting it out slowly.

That's not why I'm here, he told himself.

He faced Redd again.

"The name Kilmeade mean anything to you?"

Redd shrugged. "Should it?"

"Do I . . . look familiar to you?"

The question clearly surprised Redd. He narrowed his gaze, studying Cormac's features for several seconds, but then shook his head. "Never seen you before in my life."

"Are you sure? You haven't seen someone who looks like me?"

Redd's shoulders came up in a shrug. "You guys all look the same to me."

Cormac did not lose his cool, but it was a close thing. With an effort, he mastered the volcanic surge of rage that set his blood boiling and then managed another humorless smile. "Well, take a good look. Because this is going to be the last face you see."

Then he spun on his heel and walked away, his fury lending an urgency to his stride. When he reached the idling Suburban, he wrenched the door open, grabbed his M4, and then keyed his radio.

"All units, this is Dagger Six. Execute, execute, execute!"

FIFTY-SIX

As the man vanished into the haze of falling snow, Redd knew that he had missed something important.

"Do I look familiar to you?"

There had been something like real fear in the man's eyes when Redd had dropped the revelation about the Praetorian, and for a fleeting instant, Redd had almost believed that the gambit would work, that self-interest would prevail over allegiance to a traitor, and that the hit team would hastily retreat and disappear into the woodwork to avoid being swept up with their mysterious leader.

It had been a Hail Mary play, half bluff because it was by no means certain that the Praetorian could be brought to justice, but sometimes that was the only way to win the game.

But he'd read the other man all wrong.

"Do I look familiar to you?"

Too late, Redd grasped the significance of the question.

"You haven't seen someone who looks like me?"

Redd hadn't, but it was pretty easy to figure out why the man had asked.

In the dark with their faces covered by night optics and balaclavas, he wouldn't have recognized any of the men who had hunted him in the mountains . . . the men he had killed. Had he taken the time to look, he might have noticed that one of them bore more than a passing resemblance to the man leading the Praetorian's hit team.

A familial resemblance.

A brother. I killed his brother.

Redd's mistake had been in assuming that the man was just here to do a job. Maybe it had started that way, but now it was personal.

He's out for blood.

Redd turned to Blackwood. "Get to cover. It's happening. Right now."

Blackwood stared back at him as if unable to process what Redd was telling him, so Redd grabbed him by the arm and half dragged him back behind the reception desk. As they moved, Redd unclipped the handheld radio from his belt and keyed the mic. "Everyone, stand ready. They're coming."

Almost before the command was out, the hallways of the courthouse building were filled with the din of combat—dull explosions, gun reports, and shattering glass. Redd ducked reflexively, unable to immediately determine where the action was happening. Then his radio crackled to life. Barely audible over the electronically amplified chaos, Treadway could be heard shouting, "Contact, main door. Contact."

Redd glanced over at Blackwood and Kline, who were hunkering down behind the lobby desk. "Watch your sector," he advised. "This could be a diversion."

Almost as he said it, Deputy Scott's voice broke from the radio. "They're blasting the south door. All hell's breaking loose."

Redd muttered a curse. A simultaneous multipronged assault had been his greatest concern. Two people couldn't realistically hold off an attacking element for very long, which was why he had kept himself in reserve, ready to move to wherever he was needed most. But now, with contact in two different places, he was faced with a choice. If he chose wrong, the enemy might overrun the weaker position and gain entrance to the building. And if they made it inside, there was no telling what might happen.

Who needs me the most?

Redd had worked with all of the deputies, putting them through a rigorous, boot-camp-style special weapons and tactics program, and knew well their capabilities and their weaknesses. While they had never trained for a scenario like this, they did have a grasp of the basics. More importantly, they had all learned the tactics the enemy would be using against them. What they lacked was real-world experience. Stephanie Treadway, on the other hand, had that kind of experience.

He keyed his radio. "Treadway, can you hold your position?"

There was the briefest pause before her reply. "Good for now." The words, shouted over the din of near-constant gunfire, were barely intelligible. "Let you know . . ." There might have been more, but it was lost in a haze of white noise. A moment later a concussion like the detonation of a bomb shook the building.

He keyed the radio. "Treadway?"

There was no answer. Then Deputy Scott's voice squawked. "Help! We need help here!"

Redd glanced over at Emily, noting the look of grim determination on her face. "You good?"

She nodded.

"Okay, stay behind me, but be ready for anything."

As Redd headed for the hallway, Rubble stirred from where he'd been napping under the table, shook once, and started to follow, walking gingerly on paws that had been wrapped in gauze and medical tape. The rottie had been so quiet since they'd come over from the clinic that Redd had almost forgotten about him. He felt both sympathy and admiration for Rubble's steadfast loyalty. Despite everything the dog had been through, he was still eager to help his human.

Redd stopped him with a raised hand. "Stay." He pointed to Liz and Maggie, who were holding Lucas and Junior, respectively. "Protect the boys. Keep them safe."

Rubble shifted his forelegs back and forth, then lowered back onto his haunches.

Redd looked over to his father-in-law. "Take care of them."

Lawrence acknowledged him with a nod. "Take care of yourself. And my little girl."

✖ ✖ ✖

The sheriff's department occupied most of the west end of the courthouse's ground floor. Part of that space was used for administrative purposes—Blackwood's office, and smaller offices for the undersheriff and the department's investigators, as well as conference and utility rooms. The rest was reserved for law enforcement uses—the lockup, secure evidence storage, interrogation rooms, and so forth. A narrow hallway separated these two distinct sections and continued toward the justice center, where the courtrooms and county clerk's offices were located.

That hallway was a miasma of smoke and dust. Adding to the sensory overload, the air was filled with the shrill beeping of ceiling-mounted smoke detector units. Without slowing, Redd took a moment to cover his ears with his earmuffs, which only served to reduce the cacophony to a tolerable level. With the ear protection devices in place, he was effectively cut off from radio communication with the rest of the courthouse defenders. When he had trained the deputies, Redd had urged Blackwood to buy tactical headphones that could plug into the radio units, but it hadn't been in the budget. Given the overall din, he probably wouldn't have been able to hear Treadway anyway.

As he neared the end of the hallway, Redd slowed to a walk, crouching low before stepping out into the open. The smoke and dust were even thicker here, greatly reducing visibility, but there was no immediate sign of structural damage or bullet impacts. Cautiously, he edged forward into the much wider hallway that ran the length of the justice center, separating the courtrooms on either side. Off to his right, another narrower hallway led past the elevator and the main stairwell, down to the south exit, where Scott and Thornock were posted, while further down on the left, the broad hallway intersected the main lobby, where the business of the county clerk was conducted, and where, on the north side, a pair of large glass doors served as the main public entrance.

The smoke seemed even thicker here, as if the building were on fire—for all Redd knew, it might be—but there was still a scarcity of debris and other evidence of the dual attacks. Sticking to his original plan, Redd hooked right and headed toward the south exit.

As soon as he rounded the corner, Redd immediately saw what he had been missing. Smoking fragments of masonry and metal littered the hallway. The walls to either side were pocked with bullet holes too numerous to count. Down near the end of the hall, the two deputies were crouched down behind a hasty barricade consisting of a couple heavy wooden desks and a tangle of assorted chairs, unable to move or return fire under the brutal storm of incoming fire. At the end of the hall, the door to the outside was mostly gone, blown away, with just a few twisted pieces of metal hanging from the hinges.

Redd dropped onto his belly and began high-crawling down the hallway, plaster dust and splinters showering down on him as rounds overshot the deputies' position and punched into the walls above him. A glance back showed Emily right behind him, following his example by crawling to avoid presenting a target to the enemy. He had hoped that she would stay back, out of the line of fire, but knew better than to try telling her that.

He reached the deputies a moment later, tapping Thornock on the leg to let him know that help had arrived. The deputy started at the unexpected touch, but then regarded Redd with a relieved expression.

"What's happening?" shouted Redd. "Did they try to come in?"

He had warned them to expect a dynamic entry. The standard military doctrine for raiding a hostile location was to rush the target building and engage targets before they knew what was happening, so Redd had coached the deputies to train their weapons on the doorway. It was a natural choke point, what operators called "the fatal funnel." The goal of the assaulter was to clear the doorway quickly, before the enemy inside could aim and fire, because if the first man inside went down, his buddies would have the added obstacle of a body in their way, increasing their time spent in the fatal funnel.

Deputy Thornock shook his head. "Haven't even seen 'em. They've just been shooting like crazy."

That was a surprise to Redd. Blindly shooting hundreds of rounds at a doorway served no useful purpose, save perhaps to traumatize the defenders inside. The only reason he could think of for keeping up a constant rate of fire at an enemy's defensive position was to provide cover for a flanking assault.

The realization hit him like a slap. That was exactly what the enemy was doing.

Frantic, he brought his radio up and keyed the push-to-talk button. "It's a diversion! Watch your sect—"

He broke off as he saw something sail lazily through the air above the barricade, tumbling end over end as gravity brought it arcing down to the floor about ten feet behind Emily's outstretched legs. Even through the haze, Redd easily recognized the black cylindrical object that looked like a six-inch-long piece of metal pipe, perforated with large holes.

He tried to shout, "Flash-bang!" but before he could get the warning out, the grenade struck the floor and detonated like a supernova.

FIFTY-SEVEN

At first there was only the sound—a high-pitched, constant tone that was eerily familiar, and not at all comforting. Stephanie Treadway knew this sound, even if she couldn't quite put her finger on what it was. After a few seconds other sounds became audible, but they were distorted, like something heard underwater.

And that was exactly how she felt. Underwater. Drowning in a lightless abyss.

She had felt this way before.

Though still effectively deaf and blind, Treadway's awareness returned in a rush, and with it came a terrible thought.

Not again.

Yet she knew intuitively that this time was different. Unlike the explosions in Afghanistan and Oklahoma City, she retained a clear memory of the moments preceding the blast.

The attack had begun suddenly, the big glass doors shattering amid a fusillade of automatic weapons fire. She and Hall had been waiting for their chance to return fire, but none of the assaulters had made themselves visible. Then Redd had called over the radio, asking if she could hold her position. She remembered assuring him that she would try.

She also vividly recalled the flash-bang, which almost seemed to float through space where the large glass doors had stood. She remembered seeing it hit the floor and bounce once, twice, and then . . .

She even remembered telling herself to move right before her world dissolved into light and fury. The grenade's magnesium core deflagrated to produce a six-million-candela flash, accompanied almost simultaneously by a 170-decibel thunderclap. One ear had been covered by an earmuff, but the hearing protection was only rated for 22 decibels, which did not even reduce the noise to the volume of shooting an unsuppressed gun. Her other ear, the one that had been pressed to the radio, had taken the full brunt of the sonic assault. It was the bang, not the flash that created the greatest debilitating effect. The sound was so loud that it disrupted the fluid in the inner ear, creating intense vertigo. Treadway could feel the room spinning all around her.

But those were just symptoms. What truly terrified her was knowing with certainty what the flash-bang presaged.

As near as she could tell, she hadn't lost any time, not like in Afghanistan or OKC, but that realization brought little comfort. Those other times, the explosion had been the climax event. A great big exclamation point at the end of a chapter, with the story picking up again later, after the effects had worn off. This time, however, it was barely a comma. The detonation was merely the initiating event.

Snap out of it!

Stun grenades were typically employed just before an assault team entered a hostile room, rendering anyone inside totally helpless. Defenseless. They would shoot her dead, and she wouldn't even see the muzzle flash of their weapons.

Time to fight back.

Desperate to prevent or at least delay that outcome, she stabbed her AR-15 toward the courthouse entrance—or at least, where she thought it was—and pulled the trigger. The rifle bucked against her shoulder, but the report sounded like a distant thump. She let out the trigger, then pulled again, sweeping the barrel a few degrees left, then right, firing at random. At first she didn't even attempt to identify a target. All she was trying to do was convince anyone thinking of coming in to reconsider their choices.

It must have worked, because she didn't die.

Her vision was clearing with each passing second. The magnesium deflagration was comparable to looking at a camera flash—dazzling, a little painful, but temporary. She couldn't see anything directly in front of her, but her peripheral vision was working just fine, and in the corner of her eye, she saw shapes silhouetted against the entrance. She swung the muzzle of the AR-15 in their general direction and pulled the trigger again. The shapes disappeared like puffs of smoke. Treadway doubted she had hit anyone. At best she'd bought a few seconds of recovery time.

In the momentary lull that followed, she glimpsed the writhing form of Undersheriff Hall, on his back a couple feet away to her right. He was alive, but that was about all she could determine under the circumstances.

"Are you hit?" Although she had shouted the question, she couldn't hear it over the persistent ringing.

Hall didn't respond, but he was moving. His hands were clenched over his chest, and he rocked from side to side. Without lowering her rifle, Treadway knelt beside him, took hold of his arm and shook it. "Are you hit?" she asked again.

If he answered, she didn't hear it, but she didn't see any blood on his hands, or pooling on the ground behind him. She guessed that he might have caught a bullet but that his body armor had stopped it from penetrating. Nevertheless, the impact probably felt like getting kicked by a mule. Between that and the lingering effects of the flash-bang, the deputy was out of the fight, which meant that if the enemy attempted another assault, she would be on her own—one defender trying to repel an unknown number of hostiles.

She didn't like her chances of succeeding, much less surviving.

Stand and fight . . . and probably die? Or fall back and try to join up with the others?

In that moment, what clinched her decision was not fear of dying, but the certain knowledge that, if they got past her, the people she had vowed to protect would almost certainly die.

She fired a couple more shots at the periphery of the empty doorway, just to discourage anyone who might be thinking of making another attempt. Then, keeping her right hand on the pistol grip of the rifle, she grabbed Undersheriff Hall's shirt collar and began dragging him back into the courthouse.

She'd get him to safety, and then she'd stand her ground and give them hell.

FIFTY-EIGHT

Half a mile away at the intersection of Broadway and the highway, Deputy Kurt Oman sat helplessly in his idling patrol vehicle, knuckles white as he gripped the venti iced mocha he'd picked up before starting his shift. An Army veteran who broke both of his legs after falling from a helicopter during his two tours in Iraq before coming back home to Wellington to heal up and join the sheriff's department, he was only too familiar with the sounds that now rolled down the snowed-over streets. There was a gun battle raging nearby. His friends and coworkers were taking fire, facing overwhelming odds. And there wasn't a thing he could do to help them.

Sheriff Blackwood had posted him here, assigned him to keep an eye on who came and went from Wellington. The sheriff had clearly been expecting trouble of some kind, but Oman doubted that Blackwood had anticipated the magnitude of the threat.

Seven vehicles. He hadn't been able to tell how many passengers rode in each of the big SUVs, but he'd seen multiple riders—at least three or four—which could mean upwards of thirty, and possibly as many as forty or even fifty. Oman's gut had told him that the convoy meant bad news, but even so, the eruption of gunfire a few minutes later shocked him to his core.

Unfortunately, the sheriff hadn't given Oman clear directions about what to do next. He had asked, of course, but Blackwood had silenced him with a terse "Stand by." And then, only a few minutes later, the shooting had started.

Oman's first impulse was to turn his car toward the center of town and roll Code 3—lights flashing, siren shrieking—to let both the good guys and the bad guys know that backup was on its way. But the sheriff had definitely told him to stand by, and besides, what could he realistically hope to do against such overwhelming odds, aside from dying a heroic but utterly futile death?

But he couldn't just do nothing.

"C'mon, think," he said aloud as he took another sip of his iced mocha. "You can't take them on alone . . ."

Then it hit. He didn't have to go in alone. He could call for backup of his own. Blackwood had called all the deputies to the courthouse, but three of them were still en route. He could coordinate with them. And he could call the Highway Patrol, have them send in any troopers in the area. It would take time . . . time that the sheriff and the others really didn't have, but it was probably the best chance any of them had to make it out alive.

He grabbed the radio handset, switched to the tri-county dispatch frequency, and was just about to hit the push-to-talk button when another SUV rolled out of the falling snow and turned down Broadway.

It wasn't a big Suburban like the others but a midsized Ford. Oman didn't recognize it—he knew most of the local-owned rigs on sight, especially the newer models, which were not all that common in economically depressed Stillwater County. Through the section of windshield revealed by the sweeping wipers, he could see only one occupant inside, and while he couldn't make out the face, he knew it would not be anyone familiar.

Another stranger, he thought as the Ford cruised past. *Showing up late to the party. Not if I have anything to say about it.*

Impelled by a feeling of grim determination, he returned the radio handset to its cradle, shifted his patrol vehicle's transmission into gear, and started to pull out. At almost the same moment, the Ford's brake lights lit up and the vehicle slowed to a full stop. Oman tapped his own brakes, halting a good fifty yards behind the Ford, feeling both curious and apprehensive about the other vehicle's unexpected stop.

Then the Ford's reverse lights flashed on, and it began rolling slowly backward.

Oman swallowed nervously. He didn't like this one bit.

The Ford's approach was slow, barely a walking pace. If it was the driver's intention to ram the patrol vehicle, he wasn't making any effort to build up momentum. Even so, Oman's instincts told him, *Get out, now!*

He fumbled to unbuckle his seat belt, and then fumbled to work the inside door lever. In the time it took him to do so, the Ford closed to within ten yards of the front end of his vehicle. As Oman finally spilled out onto the snowpack, the Ford's brake lights flared again, and then the reverse lights winked out.

Kurt Oman drew his service weapon—a Glock 22—and brought it up in a two-handed grip, aimed at the driver's side window of the Ford. Now that he was in the open, the sounds of gunfire in the near distance were even more dramatic, but Oman barely heard them over the roar of blood in his ears.

The window began lowering, and the driver's empty hands extended outward.

Sensing a trap, Oman maintained his aim and began moving, swinging out in a wide arc that gave him a better angle on the subject while keeping a good standoff distance. "Keep those hands where I can see them!" he shouted.

The hands remained motionless. After a few more steps, the driver's face was visible in the window opening. A stranger, just as Oman had figured. The man had tousled blond hair and a neatly trimmed beard. He regarded the deputy with steel-blue eyes that radiated quiet intensity.

"Deputy," the man said, his voice quiet but commanding, "we're wasting time here. I'm not the threat." One hand moved, but only a little, the thumb jerking toward the center of town. "The threat is down there, and that's where we need to be."

It was not so much the declaration as the manner of its delivery that left Oman momentarily flummoxed. In most traffic stops, the drivers were either indignant or obsequious.

"Name?" was all Oman could think to say.

The man's mouth tightened into a frown, then his eyes narrowed, focusing on the name tape above the right breast pocket of Oman's uniform blouse. "Deputy Kurt Oman, you do hear that, right?"

Despite himself, Oman took a moment to listen to the battle noise. He swallowed. "Yeah, I hear it."

"And you know what it is?"

Oman nodded.

The man's blue eyes drilled into Oman. "What are you going to do about it?"

The question cut Oman to the quick. Gritting his teeth, he told the truth, his voice almost a wail. "I don't know."

The other man regarded him a moment longer and then slowly lowered his hands. "Let's figure it out together."

FIFTY-NINE

In a rare display of restraint, Cormac Kilmeade stood back and let his men do the fighting. He usually preferred to lead from the front, but this assault had a lot of moving pieces, and he couldn't be everywhere all at once. Besides, the real attack hadn't even begun yet, and when it did, he would be the tip of the spear.

He studied the schematic displayed on his tablet. It was the emergency evacuation floor plan of the Stillwater County Courthouse building, which he had been able to access online through the office of the state fire marshal. With Redd and the others indoors, there was no longer any need for aerial surveillance, though the Predator would remain on station in the unlikely event that Redd somehow slipped through their net. The floor plan couldn't tell him where Redd and the others were hiding inside, but it did show Cormac where to distribute his forces in order to keep the targets bottled up.

He had placed the new recruits at the main door and the south entrance, directing them to lay down heavy suppressive fire but not to attempt a dynamic entry. Although those men had all received the same training in urban assault, they had never worked together as a team. The battlefield was not the place to work through personality and communications issues. Besides, the goal of the operation wasn't to storm the building and kill everyone in sight, but rather to push Redd and the others toward the sheriff's office exit, where Cormac would be waiting to deal with Redd personally.

So far the results had been less than impressive. The newbs had laid down a lot of lead, as he had directed, but when they had ventured inside the main entrance to assess the situation, three of them had been shot, one fatally. Cormac was still waiting to hear from the men assigned to the south exit, but so far, it looked as though Redd's team had drawn first blood.

It was time to ratchet things up.

He keyed his radio. "Arrow One, it's time to open the door."

✖ ✖ ✖

Two hundred and fifty yards away, and one hundred twenty feet above ground, perched on the maintenance catwalk near the top of the town's water tower in the municipal park across the street from the courthouse, Chad Beaudette received the order with an eager grin. He was glad for a chance to do something more than provide overwatch, and not just because it meant he would get to blow something up. He was still stinging from his earlier failure, and even though there had been no further repercussions, he felt he needed to redeem himself by taking a more active role in the mission to terminate Matthew Redd once and for all.

"Roger that, boss," he replied into his radio, then lowered his eye to the AMPR's scope. The magnification extended his visual range, allowing him to seemingly see through the swirling snow, though there wasn't all that much to see. The weapon was aimed at the brick wall of the courthouse building, specifically at a spot about seventy-five feet to the left of the sheriff's office entrance, where Cormac himself had drawn a large X using a piece of chalk.

Behind him, Jack Wagner, who was peering through his spotter scope, gave him a wind call—the adjustment he would need to make to compensate for the wind blowing between their position and the target. It was Wagner's job as spotter to supply this information, but at this range and for their purposes, windage really wouldn't make much difference.

"Open sesame," Chad said and squeezed the trigger.

SIXTY

The detonations radiated shock waves that reverberated through the building like the deep thump of a bass woofer.

Grenades, thought Kline, though whether they were flash-bangs or frags, he couldn't say for certain. He hoped it was the former, since they were less lethal, but either way, it didn't bode well.

Between the radio traffic and the explosions, it wasn't too hard to put together a mental picture of what was happening just a few hundred feet away in another part of the courthouse. The Praetorian's assault team had arrived in force, hitting the courthouse hard in a coordinated two-prong attack. Worse, if Redd's last transmission was correct, the twin assaults were just a diversion to engage the courthouse's defenders while another hostile element attempted a breach somewhere else.

But where?

His every instinct told him to go where the fighting was, to do whatever it took to protect Matthew and Emily and little Matthew Jr. But if those attacks were the diversion, there were just two ingress points where the main assault might come from, and the most likely of the two was the entrance to the sheriff's office—the entrance Kline and Sheriff Blackwood were presently guarding.

Yet it wasn't the impending assault that filled Kline with dread, but rather the possibility that by his actions—or his inaction—he might lose his family.

A little less than two years earlier, when he'd learned that Redd's Marine Raiders unit was heading into a death trap, Kline had done something that even he considered almost unthinkable. After exhausting every other option to derail the doomed mission, he'd sent Stephanie Treadway to make sure that Matthew Redd remained behind. He had rationalized it by telling himself that he was doing it to protect his flesh and blood, as any good father would do.

Treadway had succeeded, and Redd had survived, while his entire team had been annihilated. Her timely intervention had cost Redd his military career, which deepened Redd's animus toward the man who had never really been his father except in the biological sense, but Kline had never regretted what he'd done.

Not until Oklahoma City.

He had a conceptual grasp of survivor's guilt, but it wasn't until the attack on the JPATS transport . . . until nearly every member of his handpicked fly team had been wiped out . . . until *he* was the survivor, that Kline really understood the deeper source of his son's anger. Understood it in a way that Redd himself probably didn't even grasp—the powerlessness that came with surviving an ordeal when everyone else around you didn't.

And now it was happening again; only this time it wasn't his coworkers who were going to die. It was his family.

My family, he thought.

He'd never wanted a family, never wanted to be tied down. He had always believed that emotional attachments were chains that held you back from reaching your best potential, or worse, tore you to pieces when you tried to have the best of both worlds. Having a family made you vulnerable. It gave your enemies leverage that could be used against you.

That was what he had always told himself to justify his refusal to embrace his responsibilities as a father. But despite the fact that all of those things he believed were true, he realized that those emotional connections were what made life worth living. And now, faced with the possibility of losing the family he had never even known he wanted, he felt only regret for all the missed opportunities.

Please, God, if You'll just keep them safe, I promise to be there for them.

After the loud *whump* that had punctuated Redd's last transmission, Kline counted to ten before keying his own radio. "Matt, what's going on in there?"

There was no answer. He decided to try something different.

"Stephanie, do you read me?"

Treadway didn't answer either.

He had heard her garbled last transmission as well and knew that both of them might be too busy to reply.

Or they might be . . .

He didn't even want to finish his thought, but if both Redd's and Treadway's positions had been overrun, then the enemy was already inside the building.

He glanced over at Blackwood, who was crouched down behind the over-turned desk they had dragged out of one of the offices. The sheriff had eschewed use of an assault rifle, choosing instead to meet the attack with his Smith & Wesson .357 Magnum, which he now held in a two-handed grip, pointing at the glass entrance doors.

"Blackwood," Kline hissed.

The sheriff's face did not turn away from the doors, but beneath one steel-gray brow, his eye shifted to look at the FBI director. "What?"

"What if they made it inside already?"

Blackwood's mouth tightened into a frown. "Matthew said to keep watching our sectors. If we pull back now, we're inviting them in."

"I think they're already in. We need to get the women and children some-where safe."

"I'm not sure anywhere's safe," Blackwood replied gravely. "But I hear you. If it comes down to it, we can fall back to the sally port, load everyone in my rig, and make a run for it."

Kline shook his head. "That's exactly what they'll expect us to do. They'll have that exit covered; I guarantee it."

"They're gonna have *all* the exits covered. That's the problem." His voice dropped to a low murmur. "Never figured they'd bring an army."

"If we can't leave, then we have to find somewhere inside the building where we can make a stand. Do you know of such a place?"

Blackwood paused to consider the question. "Well, we could go to the second floor. There's only the two staircases, and of course the elevator—"

A loud detonation, much louder than the previous ones, drowned out the rest of the sentence. Blackwood startled visibly, as did Kline, and the two men exchanged a look.

"What was that?" asked the sheriff.

Kline shook his head. "I don't know, but it was a lot closer than—"

Another blast reverberated through the air, this one even louder than the first.

"I think—" he started to say, but then there was a third blast, and the walls of the lobby shook with a sympathetic vibration that showered the two men with paint flecks and plaster dust.

"They're gonna bring the whole building down," Blackwood gasped.

Kline stared back at him, trying to process what was happening. Then he realized the terrible truth and shook his head. "No. They're blasting through," he shouted, springing to his feet. "We have to fall back!"

SIXTY-ONE

Redd felt like his head had been stuffed with sawdust and set on fire. He had lost his ability to hear anything, aside from a shrill ringing sound—not really a sound at all, but the result of damage to the tiny hairs lining the inner ear that the brain could only interpret as a high-pitched tone.

Still, Redd counted himself lucky.

When he'd seen the grenade coming in, there had been just enough time to cover Emily's head and shoulders with his own body before the flash and bang filled his world.

Redd had trained extensively with stun grenades, which meant occasionally being on the receiving end, and knew what to expect. The dazzling flash was really only a problem if you happened to be looking in the general direction of the deflagration. It was the concussive force and volume that left anyone in close proximity dazed and disoriented, and between his earmuffs and the fact that he had prudently kept his mouth open so the sudden increase in pressure wouldn't blow out his eardrums, Redd had escaped the worst of the effects. It would be hours before his hearing returned to normal, but that was a small price to pay for mostly keeping his wits about him.

He quickly popped up and aimed his AR-15 at the doorway, finger on the trigger. A human silhouette appeared there, one of the assaulters making his move, and Redd fired three shots in rapid succession—two to the chest, one to the head, a shot pattern known as the Mozambique Drill. The would-be intruder pitched backward, exposing a second assaulter trying to move in. Redd dropped him as well. A third shooter, evidently realizing what kind of reception waited for him beyond the doorway, barely managed to pull back before Redd could sight in.

Keeping the rifle trained on the doorway, Redd grasped Emily's shoulder. "Em! Get up. We need to move."

He knew that she probably couldn't hear him but hoped that his body language would convey the appropriate urgency. It must have worked because she lifted her head and looked around. Her mouth moved but he had no idea what she was trying to say. He shook his head and pointed back down the hall.

"That way!" he shouted. "Go! I'm right behind you."

At that moment, a hand holding a compact machine pistol appeared at the edge of the doorway, letting loose a rapid-fire burst. Redd fired back, sparking a round off the metal doorframe, and both hand and weapon disappeared.

Redd figured he had only a second or two before the assaulters tossed in another flash-bang—or something even more lethal, like a fragmentation grenade. It was time to get off the X.

Still holding the AR one-handed, he knelt and shook the nearest deputy—Garrison Scott. The man stirred but was still clearly feeling the debilitating effects of the stun grenade. Redd turned his attention to Deputy Thornock and found him completely unresponsive—unconscious or dead, it was impossible to say. Redd muttered a curse under his breath. He couldn't drag both deputies back and still keep watch on the door. Realistically, saving even one of the men would be a dicey proposition under the circumstances, but he had to try. He wasn't going to leave either man behind, no matter what.

Suddenly Emily was beside him. He was about to order her to retreat, but she wasn't paying attention to him. Instead, she grabbed ahold of Scott's arm and started dragging him down the hallway. The first few steps were a struggle. The deputy outweighed her by a good sixty pounds, but she bent her back, gritted her teeth, and muscled through.

God bless her, thought Redd.

He grabbed the back of Thornock's body armor vest and heaved the man's unmoving body up onto his shoulder. Then after firing a three-round burst through the doorway, just to give the enemy something to think about, he began backing down the hallway, ready to engage if a target presented itself.

He caught up to Emily a few seconds later and was relieved to see that Scott had regained his senses enough to walk—though *stagger* was probably a better way to describe it—with Emily supporting him.

As soon as they reached the main hallway in the justice center, Redd pulled Emily around the corner, out of the line of fire, before easing Deputy Thornock to the floor. As he did, he spotted Treadway hauling Shane Hall away from the main exit. Leaving Emily to assess the other deputies, he hastened over to the FBI agent and relieved her of her burden, freeing her up to move faster.

The significance of Treadway's forced retreat did not escape Redd. They had lost two of the exits, and if they lost any more ground, they would be cut off from the fire exit at the east end of the building—the exit Mikey was watching all by himself.

Redd unclipped his radio and pressed the transmit button. "Mikey, pull back! Now!"

He didn't wait for a reply—he wouldn't have been able to hear it anyway—but hurried back over to rejoin Emily, who was trying to rouse Thornock. Redd took that as a good sign; the deputy was still alive. Deputy Garrison Scott was on his feet, holding his AR-15 as if ready to get back in the fight, but Redd could see that he was still a little shell-shocked. He pointed back toward the hall leading into the sheriff's offices. "Pull back. Get them all to safety."

The message seemed to get through, because the deputy nodded and then bent down to help Emily rouse the others.

Now to take care of Mikey, he thought.

The fire exit was only a couple hundred feet away, but to make it back to them, Mikey would have to run the gauntlet of hostile forces coming in from either side.

Redd tapped Treadway's shoulder to get her attention, then pointed back in the direction they had come. "Cover me!"

She returned a quizzical look, but as there was no way to make her understand, he simply moved out, his AR-15 at the high ready. He pied the corner of the hallway leading down to the south exit and then dashed across. He felt more than heard a couple rounds sizzle through the air behind him, but he was out of the danger zone before the hostiles moving in from that door could sight him in.

He kept going, stopping at the edge of the lobby at the main entrance where he edged around the corner and found himself looking at half a dozen men in full tactical kit, moving cautiously through the maze of shot-up furniture and broken glass. He dropped two of them before they even knew what was happening, but then the others returned fire in a hailstorm of lead that tore into the corner Redd was hiding behind, showering him with debris. The withering assault forced him back. He was pinned down, with nowhere to go but back, and if he didn't do something to change the situation, Mikey would be caught on the wrong side of the firefight.

He waited for a lull in the incoming fire, then dropped to the floor and combat rolled out into the open. Incoming fire chased after him, bullets tearing into the floor all around, showering him with fragments of stone and metal. With the initial momentum of his roll spent, he came to rest in a prone shooting position and immediately began returning fire. He felt something slap his back—a round glancing off his body armor—and then something hot ripped down the back of his left thigh. He ignored both the pain and the mayhem, completely focused on trying to make his own shots count. He saw one of the shooters flinch with an impact, but the man didn't go down. The others stood their ground, spraying the area with bullets. Then, as he knew it eventually would, the AR-15's bolt locked back, and the trigger remained slack. He had shot out the magazine.

Though partially obscured by the haze of smoke and dust, Redd would have sworn he saw the shooters grinning in anticipation.

SIXTY-TWO

Futile though he knew it was, Redd dropped the useless rifle and made a grab for the Ruger in its holster.

Suddenly, a spray of red mist erupted from the head of the shooter farthest to the right. It took a moment for the others to process what had just happened—a moment that not only gave Redd time to break leather, but also saw a second shooter flinch back and go down. Redd got the Ruger up and squeezed off a shot, but the hostiles were already pulling back, diving for cover.

Redd assumed that Treadway had provided the covering fire that had saved him, but then, from the corner of his eye, he saw Mikey kneeling at the opposite side of the lobby, with his borrowed Remington M700PSS braced against his shoulder.

Redd holstered the Ruger, grabbed the AR, and scrambled over to join his friend. He could feel a dull throb in his thigh and the dampness of his blood soaking through the denim of his Wranglers, but the leg held his weight, and that was all that mattered. When he was out of the direct line of fire, he buttoned out the assault rifle's empty magazine and slapped in a fresh one. Then he clapped a hand to Mikey's shoulder, gave him a nod of reassurance, and pointed to the far side of the lobby.

"Go in three!" he shouted, holding up his hand with three fingers displayed. "Got it?"

Mikey returned a thumbs-up.

Redd gave the countdown and on "Three! Go!" rolled into the open again and started firing. The enemy had yet to recover from Mikey's initial intervention, and Redd's hasty shots convinced them to keep their heads down a little longer, giving Mikey plenty of time to dash across the open lobby. Redd followed his friend's progress in his peripheral vision and as soon as Mikey was clear, rolled again, then bounded up and sprinted to join him.

Treadway was laying down suppressive fire toward the south exit, so Redd urged Mikey onward, passing the second free-fire zone to reach Emily and the deputies, all of whom were conscious and, to varying degrees, ambulatory. Redd waved his hand in a chopping gesture, urging the group to keep making their way back into the part of the building occupied by the sheriff's department, before turning to cover their exit.

He made it only a few steps before the Praetorian's shooters began firing from the corner of the main lobby. Redd and Treadway, standing side by side, returned fire, keeping the enemy behind cover and limiting their ability to shoot with precision.

Suddenly, the deep *boom* of a high-explosive detonation filled the air and shook the floor underfoot. Although he couldn't hear the blast, Redd felt it reverberating through his body. The effect wasn't massive like an IED explosion, but still powerful enough to do some damage.

That was no flash-bang, Redd thought. He glanced over at Treadway and saw that she was thinking the same thing.

There was another detonation, more intense than the first. It felt to Redd like the explosion had come from inside the courthouse and from somewhere behind them. He suspected the Praetorian's men were firing small projectile rounds, like the forty-millimeter grenades used in military weapons systems like the M203 grenade launcher or the Mark 19 machine gun—probably the same weapon that had been used to cause the avalanche that had nearly killed him in the mountains. He had no idea what they might be hoping to accomplish by blasting away at the courthouse, but whatever they had planned couldn't be good.

At his back, Emily and Mikey were doing their best to keep the deputies moving while simultaneously ducking and scanning ahead. Redd couldn't spare more than a moment to check on their progress, as enemy shooters kept popping out from the lobby and the south hall, taking potshots at the group.

"Move!" he roared, fearing it was already too late.

Another explosion shuddered through the floor, pummeling them with a shock wave that felt much too close for comfort. Redd couldn't help casting a glance over his shoulder. The air in the long, broad hallway was thick with dust and smoke, but through the haze, Redd could see that the heavy wooden door leading into the courthouse on the north side, only a few steps away from where Emily was standing, had been blasted completely off its hinges and now lay on the floor directly in their path.

That was when it dawned on Redd what the enemy was trying to do. "Stop!" he shouted, almost screaming the warning. "Pull back!"

Emily had already instinctively taken that advice, covering up to avoid flying debris. It was a decision that probably saved her life because just a few seconds later, a fourth explosion flung a spray of high-velocity projectiles out into the wall. Chips of red brick and splinters of wood tore into the opposite wall like a blast from a shotgun. But Redd knew something even worse was coming.

The Praetorian's forces had just blasted a hole in the exterior wall—a hole through which they could send in a fresh wave of shooters.

"Pull back!" he screamed again. "Pull back!"

The cluster of bodies was slow to respond, but when enemy rounds fired from inside the courtroom began creasing the air in front of them, the urgency of the situation finally sank in. Emily and Mikey both turned away, pushing into the still-dazed deputies, trying to redirect them back down the hallway, while Redd and Treadway continued suppressing the enemy at what was now the front of their element.

Everything was happening too fast.

The group hadn't gone more than a few steps when men in snow camo over-whites began pouring out of the courtroom into the hall. They moved with a swiftness and surety that could only come with relentless rehearsal sessions. Two of them took up a high-low shooting position at the doorway and began firing point-blank into the beleaguered defenders, while behind them more shooters swarmed from the courtroom, pushing to the right, moving down the hallway toward the sheriff's offices. Thornock fell, but then Mikey, Emily, and the other two deputies began returning fire.

Out of the corner of his eye, Redd saw Mikey stagger and drop to the ground.

Redd's heart stopped.

"No!" he screamed, his fists clenching on the grips of the AR, muscles flexing like a volcano about to erupt. In that instant, he was ready to charge the Praetorian's men, crush them to death with his bare hands, but the way was blocked by the rest of the group, and the assaulters from both the main lobby and the south hallway were joining the fight in earnest.

The defenders were caught in a crossfire with nowhere to go.

SIXTY-THREE

Kline sprinted through the sheriff's office reception lobby, weaving around the desks and other obstacles they'd placed in preparation for the siege. When the initial assault had begun, he had heard the sound of gunfire as muted pops, muffled by the thick walls and glass, but now he could hear the reports distinctly, as if the gun battle was being fought just down the hall.

It probably was.

Kline was almost certain that the enemy had breached the courthouse walls somewhere nearby. In all likelihood Redd, Emily, and the others were cut off, but that wasn't his foremost concern. If anyone could beat the odds and survive—not only survive, but save everyone with him—it was Matthew Redd. But if he was right, the enemy was now between Redd and the break room where little Matty and the others were sheltering. It was up to him to save them.

But he was already too late.

Kline rounded the last corner just as a man in snow camouflage disappeared through the break room doorway.

No!

Another man was right behind him, still in the hallway but just beginning to turn and follow. When he saw Kline, he pivoted back, bringing the barrel of his M4 toward Kline. Kline fired first, drilling the man center mass with a controlled pair from his rifle. The gunman staggered back but didn't fall, the rounds stopped cold by his body armor. Realizing his mistake, Kline elevated his barrel, going for the head shot, but before he could pull the trigger, a loud report issued from the break room.

Kline winced, knowing with dread certainty that someone in the break room had just died. He had to get in there.

He tried to put his sights between the eyes of the shooter to his front, but the gunman, realizing his peril, scrambled backward, falling and then backpedaling until he reached the opposite end of the hallway, where he dove for cover.

A second *boom* erupted from the break room, along with a spray of red that showered the opposite wall with blood and bits of flesh. Kline recoiled, reflexively, and so narrowly avoided running into the headless figure in winter overwhites—now liberally streaked with crimson—that staggered back through the break room doorway and collapsed in a gruesome heap at his feet.

The reports he had heard hadn't come from the gunman's M4 but from something with a little more *oomph* at close range. Like a shotgun.

Kline almost sagged in relief, then approached the doorway. "Elijah! Friendly, coming in."

He eased around the corner, showing his hands first, just in case the old man hadn't heard him, and then stepped into the open.

A second gunman lay dead just inside. And on the far side of the room, standing erect with the shotgun braced against his shoulder, looking like a pint-sized Eastwood from an old spaghetti western, was the Reverend Elijah Lawrence.

When he saw Kline's face, Lawrence lowered the shotgun and acknowledged his presence with a nod.

"Is everyone okay?" asked Kline. He could hear both Matthew Jr. and Luke crying.

"A little shook up, but otherwise none the worse for wear." Elijah thrust his chin toward the corner of the room, where the rest of the group were hunkered down behind a snack food vending machine. Redd's rottweiler looked up at Kline and gave a little *woof.*

"We can't stay here," said Kline. "Come with me."

Lawrence looked over at the others. "Well, you heard the man. Let's get going."

As Mrs. Lawrence, Liz, and Maggie moved out, Elijah turned back to Kline. "Emily? And Matthew?"

Kline shook his head. "I haven't heard from them, but judging by all the shooting, I'd say they're still in the fight."

The reverend did not seem as relieved by this news as Kline would have expected. "Shouldn't we be helping them out?"

"Right now my only concern is keeping all of you safe. Especially our grandson. Follow me." Kline turned away before the old man could protest and moved back into the hallway, rifle at the ready. The hallway was clear, so he stepped out, guarding the approach while the others filed out of the break room behind him.

Kline knew that at any moment, the gunmen might make another push in their direction, so he urged them on without looking back. "Go! Go!"

Elijah was the last out, but instead of following the others, he stood next to Kline with his shotgun once more at the ready. Kline admired the old guy's guts but knew that the shotgun wouldn't be much good in a prolonged battle.

"We're not staying," said Kline, backing away. "Go with the others. I'll be right behind you."

"This way, Elijah!" shouted Blackwood from the other end of the hallway. "Hurry!"

With Kline covering their rear, the group snaked through the hallways behind the sheriff and soon reached a door marked with an ADA-friendly placard emblazoned with the word *stairs* along with a simple image of rising steps. Blackwood held the door open, urging everyone inside. Rubble bounded up the steps as if this was some new form of playtime. Kline, however, knew that they were only postponing the inevitable.

Eventually, the bad guys would clear the main floor and realize where their quarry had gone and begin moving up. He and Blackwood might be able to hold the top of the stairwell for a while, but once the enemy figured out that there was another flight of stairs, they'd be boxed in.

One disaster at a time, he told himself. He unclipped his radio and keyed the mic. "Matt, if you can hear me, we're moving upstairs. Up. Stairs. Try to reach the main stairwell if you can."

Then without waiting for a reply, he passed through the door and started up the steps.

SIXTY-FOUR

The next five seconds felt like an eternity. Bullets sizzled through the air around Redd. The rifle in his hands bucked with each shot. He heard none of it, his ears still screaming from the flash-bang detonation, but his other senses were dialed up to eleven. The sulfur smell of gun smoke stung his nostrils. He could feel the heat of friction on his skin as the rounds streaked by and the rain of debris from the walls around them. There was a bitterness on his tongue—the taste of defeat. It tasted like dust.

But then from the corner of his eye he saw something that gave him hope.

Behind him, Emily was bent over Mikey's body, assessing his injuries, acting as if she wasn't in the middle of a pitched gun battle, mere moments from having her own life snuffed out.

There was blood on her hands.

Mikey's blood.

But then Redd saw that Mikey was moving.

He's alive.

And not just thrashing in his death throes but moving with a purpose. He had something in his hands . . . A radio. He held it to the side of his head, pushing his earmuffs out of the way to hold the handset closer to his ear. Somebody— Kline, maybe, or Blackwood—was transmitting over the net. Redd wondered how Mikey could hear anything, but then remembered that Mikey hadn't had a flash-bang blow up practically in his face.

Now Mikey was shouting and making urgent gestures. Pointing up.

Up?

Then it made sense to him. *Go upstairs!*

The elevator to the second floor of the courthouse, where most of the county offices were located, was just a few steps down the south hallway, and right across from it was the central stairwell. If they could reach it and make their way to the upper story, they would have the high ground. Stairwells were a nightmare scenario for an assaulting force because the defenders could shoot down at them from anywhere on the upper landing.

The realization that Mikey was alive, coupled with the possibility of an escape route, energized Redd. He tapped Treadway's shoulder and pointed toward the main lobby, hoping that she would get the message to continue suppressing the enemy there. Then he turned and made a mad dash for the south hallway.

He'd only gone a few steps when a gunman popped out, ready to engage the group. His eyes went wide with astonishment as he saw Redd barreling toward him. In the brief fraction of a second it took for him to process and adjust his aim, Redd wiped the surprised look off his face with a three-round burst from the AR. Redd caught up to the dead man before he could fall to the floor, grabbed the front of his tactical rig, and propelled him backward into the south hall.

There were two more shooters positioned just beyond the junction, and they reflexively checked their fire to avoid hitting their comrade, just as Redd had hoped they would, giving him time to close in on them. He didn't attempt shooting them. As close as they were, he might be able to take out one, but in the time it would take him to switch targets, the other would have blasted him. Instead, he let his AR fall on its sling and charged headlong into them, shoving their machine pistols away, even as nine-millimeter rounds hammered into his body armor. Then he reached out with both hands, closed his fingers around their throats, and slammed their heads together.

As he let their limp bodies drop, he spied one more shooter farther down the hall. Rather than fumble for the rifle, Redd whipped out his Ruger and snapped off a quick shot. The gunman went down.

He whirled around and punched the button to summon the elevator, then holstered the Ruger, took up the AR again, and moved back to the corner.

"This way!" he shouted, waving his free hand. When he saw that he had Treadway's attention, he picked up the suppressive fire so the rest of the group could move. Treadway continued firing as well, holding her rifle one-handed, braced against her shoulder, while urging the others forward. Mikey was back on his feet, looking surprisingly ambulatory for someone who Redd had thought was dead. Redd didn't question the miracle.

Emily was right behind Mikey, keeping a steadying hand on his biceps just in case. The deputies were facing the other way, exchanging fire with the invaders who had come in through the courthouse, but once Mikey and Emily started moving, they did too, backing quickly toward the corner, never lowering their weapons. As they passed Treadway, she turned and picked up their sector of fire.

As the group filed past, Redd saw that none of them had escaped injury. Bullet fragments and chips of stone had sliced into exposed flesh, leaving faces and hands streaked with oozing wounds. One of the deputies was limping, blood soaking the leg of his uniform and dripping onto the floor. Another had a large gash above his ear where a bullet had grazed him, and blood was streaming down the side of his head. Redd felt a pang when he saw that Emily's right shoulder was soaked with blood.

But they're alive, thought Redd. *Thank God.*

Mikey moved directly to the stairwell door, opened it, and started up. At almost the same moment, the elevator doors opened. The limping deputy started toward it, but Redd waved him off, pointing to the stairs. Redd knew from experience that the elevator was frustratingly slow. He wouldn't have used it under normal circumstances, and certainly not with armed gunmen just around the corner. His reason for summoning the elevator had nothing to do with transport, but that wasn't something he could explain to the deputy. The man looked confused for a moment but then shrugged and hobbled into the stairwell.

Treadway paused beside Redd, ready to help him cover the retreat, but he pointed up, indicating that she should go with the others. Once she was past the stairwell door, he stepped into the elevator, punched the button for the second floor, then exited quickly as the doors started to close. When the elevator arrived at the second floor, he would go in and hit the emergency stop button, locking the car on the second floor and denying its use to the men below. With that accomplished, he headed through the door into the stairwell.

The stairway consisted of two flights running in opposite directions with a landing at the halfway point. The steps were poured concrete with grooved metal nosing, worn smooth in the middle from many years of foot traffic. A continuous tubular handrail ran the inside length, making a U-turn at the landing. Redd's momentary delay with the elevators had allowed most of the group to make it to the top, though Treadway was practically dragging the deputy with the leg wound up the last few steps. Redd stopped on the landing to let them finish their ascent, keeping his rifle aimed down at the door on the first floor.

Within seconds the door swung open, and one of the gunmen peeked around the doorframe. Redd fired and saw sparks as the round struck the metal jamb. The gunman jerked back out of view.

Satisfied that he had bought a few more seconds, Redd pounded up the remaining stairs to the second-floor landing. The stairwell continued up to the roof, with only a chain barrier and a sign indicating that the roof was off-limits to unauthorized persons. Redd filed this information away as he turned toward the door Treadway was holding open for him.

The hallway outside the stairwell was oddly peaceful. There was hardly any sign of structural damage, and there was only a slight haze of smoke in the air. Redd wondered how long that would last.

SIXTY-FIVE

Kline saw movement at the bottom of the stairwell and popped off a couple rounds. So far the Praetorian's men hadn't made a serious attempt to reach the second floor, but it was only a matter of time before they came in force. When they did, Kline wasn't confident that he and Blackwood would be able to repel the assault.

The sheriff tapped his shoulder to get his attention, and Kline saw that he was holding his radio to his ear. "It's Mike Derhammer. He says they've made it to the second floor at the south stairs. They're shot up, but so far we haven't lost anyone."

Kline let out a sigh of relief. Given the intensity of the firefight, he was amazed that any of them were still alive.

"He wants to know what they should do now," Blackwood went on. "What should I tell him?"

Kline was thinking about his answer when two of the Praetorian's men stepped into the open below. One had his M4 pointed up and immediately began firing bursts up the stairwell. He wasn't aiming, but simply providing covering fire so the second man could lob a stun grenade up onto the midway landing. Kline just managed to drag Blackwood back through the doorway before the entire stairwell was filled with light and noise.

The thick walls contained most of the blast energy, protecting the men at the top from the worst effects, but Kline knew the flash-bang was merely a precursor to something much deadlier.

Here they come, he thought.

He thrust his rifle through the doorway, blind-firing several bursts down the stairwell, then looked over his shoulder. "Elijah! Take the others to the south stairs. Meet up with Matthew. We'll hold them here."

To his credit, the old preacher didn't question or hesitate, but turned away and began briskly urging the small group of women to get moving.

Kline heard the roar of Blackwood's .357 and turned his attention back to the stairwell just as a trio of white-clad gunmen, all firing up at the doorway, reached the middle landing. The volley forced Kline and Blackwood to give ground, but both men kept firing back to keep the enemy from advancing any further. Kline knew the attempt would ultimately fail.

He glanced back over his shoulder again, relieved to see that Elijah and the others had disappeared down the hall, then tapped Blackwood's elbow. "Pull back!"

Blackwood nodded and started backing away, keeping his Magnum up and ready to fire. Kline stayed shoulder to shoulder with the sheriff, firing single shots into the stairwell doorway as they backed toward the hallway junction. When the magazine ran out, he shouted, "Reloading!"

Blackwood took up the slack, the Magnum booming like a little cannon, while Kline hastily dropped the empty mag and slapped in a new one.

His last.

"I'm up!" he shouted, taking aim at the doorway and picking up the suppressive fire again. Blackwood immediately flipped the revolver's cylinder out, shook out the spent brass, and deftly slotted in fresh rounds.

Just then, another flash-bang lofted out of the opening to the stairwell. Kline grabbed Blackwood's shoulder, yanking him the remaining few feet into the adjoining hallway, then closed his eyes tight and turned his head in anticipation of the flash.

It helped, but only a little.

The blast left him reeling. Despite his hearing protection, he was effectively deaf but for the persistent ringing. When he opened his eyes, he saw only a green blob in the center of his visual field. He knew the Praetorian's men were already on their way through the door, so he started firing in what he thought was the direction of the doorway and kept backing down the hallway. As he moved he felt the heat of rounds creasing the air around him. Then something hit his chest with enough force to knock him off his feet. The pain of the impact stole his breath away.

That's it, he thought. *I'm dead.*

Nevertheless, he was determined to go down fighting, so ignoring the pain blossoming across his upper torso, he struggled to raise the AR.

Suddenly he was moving, sliding along the floor without volition. Someone had come up from behind and was dragging him away from the battle. He instinctively tried to fight but the hand gripping his armor vest did not yield. At the edge of the green spot, he saw Blackwood retreating alongside him.

Who's dragging me?

The undignified journey seemed to go on forever, but as his vision continued to clear, Kline realized that he was surrounded by friendly faces. Treadway was standing next to Blackwood, her AR at the ready, and when he tilted his head back, he saw that it was Redd pulling him through the hallways.

"I'm good," he wheezed, finding his breath.

Redd either didn't hear or chose to ignore him. Kline reached up and tapped his son's arm to get his attention, then held up an upraised thumb. Redd met his gaze, nodded, and released him.

Kline still felt a little muzzy, but as the fog cleared, he saw that Redd and Treadway had brought him and Blackwood to the south stairwell where all the others were gathered. Treadway, Redd, Emily, Mike Derhammer, Blackwood and his deputies—they all looked like refugees from a postapocalyptic movie—bloody and battered, but standing defiantly with their guns up, ready to meet whatever the enemy was about to throw at them. Even Elijah and the other women—Mrs. Lawrence, Liz, and Maggie Albright—had their handguns out, looking grim and determined, ready to make their final stand. Rubble, too, had his paws braced on the floor, his shoulders back, his teeth bared defiantly. Only the two children, though still crying from the loud noises and chaos around them, seemed at least somewhat unaffected by what was about to happen.

But when the end came, it would come for them all.

Redd and Blackwood were having an animated discussion, more gestures than actual conversation. Redd was emphatically pointing down, while Blackwood was shaking his head and pointing up.

Matt wants to go down, fight his way out of the building, he thought. *The sheriff wants to go up to the roof.*

Kline's vote would have gone with Redd's plan. They hadn't been able to hold the second floor more than a few minutes, and there was no guarantee they'd have better luck on the roof. And there was only one way down from there.

Well, there's another, he thought, *but that's not really an option.*

But he could also see Blackwood's side of it. Redd was an operator, a shooter. His solution to everything was to go on the attack. But Blackwood was sworn to protect and serve, and that meant *not* leading innocent civilians into a free-fire zone if there was even a chance of preserving their lives a little while longer.

They couldn't have it both ways.

Up or down?

Go out in a blaze of glory, or take our chances with one more retreat?

He looked over at Mrs. Lawrence, who was holding her grandson in her arms.

My grandson.

He reached out to Matthew, put a hand on his shoulder, and then raised his finger and pointed up.

SIXTY-SIX

Cormac Kilmeade stood at the top of the stairs on the second floor of the courthouse and seethed.

He had brought overwhelming force to bear, leading a strike team of more than two dozen seasoned shooters against a single former operator, an FBI suit, and a bunch of local yokel law enforcement officers, and had been beaten. And not just beaten. *Embarrassed.* He had expected losses—raiding a building filled with hostiles was an inherently dangerous proposition—but nothing on this scale.

The twelve prospective recruits he'd posted to hold the front and rear exits had been wiped out to a man. Of the six-man element he'd sent in through the breach in the courthouse wall, three were KIA.

Furious over the fact that they hadn't already finished the job, Cormac himself had led the charge to take the east stairs. It had worked, but at the cost of one more of his shooters—Darren Richmond, Dagger Seven, had gotten the top of his head blown off coming up the stairs.

Sixteen dead.

Leaving him with just five operators—six counting him—to finish the job.

But I am going to finish it.

Quitting wasn't an option. Not while Matthew Redd was still alive.

He keyed his radio. "Arrow Two, Arrow Four, I need you to come to the courthouse. Back up Saber One and Saber Three at the south stairwell. I don't want them getting past us."

Two more bodies might not make that much of a difference, but the spotters weren't really doing anything useful where they were. The snipers, Arrow One and Arrow Three, were less than two hundred yards out, and with his AMPR, Arrow One didn't even need to score a direct hit to be lethal.

The spotters called in to acknowledge the order, and then Arrow Four added, "Boss, we've got movement on the roof."

"Movement?"

"There's a whole bunch of them. I count ten or eleven. All armed."

Ten or eleven? Well, that explained the heavy resistance.

Arrow Four wasn't done. "Holy . . . They've got a couple babies with 'em."

Cormac cringed. He had no compunction about wasting children if it accomplished the mission, but could he count on his men to be so callous?

"Understood, Arrow Four. Continue mission as ordered."

Another voice broke in. "Arrow One here, boss. I can start taking them out right now. I could splash half of them with one shot."

Despite his ire, Cormac grinned. *At least I can count on one of them.*

He almost gave the order, but then remembered his promise to Redd.

The last face you see.

"Stand by, Arrow One. I'll let you know when."

✖   ✖   ✖

As Jack Wagner picked up and moved out, hurrying to follow Dagger Six's orders, Chad Beaudette kept his eye to the high-power scope, peering through the veil of swirling snow as he swiveled the AMPR on its bipod, moving between targets.

Who's going to get it first?

He was curious to see what an HEDP round would do to a human being. The XM109, like its predecessor the Barrett M82, was not intended for use against flesh and blood, but whereas the M82 had quickly become a favorite of snipers because of its extended range and devastating impact, the AMPR was definitely designed for literal hard targets. The high-explosive dual-purpose rounds were meant to penetrate steel. There was a very real possibility that the twenty-five-millimeter charge might pass clean through a human body without detonating. Still lethal, but not very satisfying. But the odds were good that his shots would turn a human body inside out.

He found the cowboy easily enough, towering a full head above everyone else. *Just a little squeeze, and this is over.*

But the boss had been adamant about keeping Matthew Redd alive. *Kill everyone else, but leave him for me.*

It wasn't like Cormac to make it personal, but then Chad supposed these were extraordinary circumstances. The man had lost his twin brother, after all.

Chad moved on, putting the reticle on each target just long enough to differentiate them. He was surprised at the number of women. Some of them were pretty good-looking, all things considered.

What a waste, he thought. *Oh well, that's just the way it is.*

Then he settled the scope on an older woman protectively holding a blanket-wrapped bundle close to her chest—a baby.

A smile curled his lips.

Yeah, I'll start with you.

SIXTY-SEVEN

As he backed slowly up the last flight of stairs leading to the roof, his weapon trained down into the stairwell below, ready to fire at the slightest hint of enemy movement, Redd tried to put aside his misgivings. It wasn't an easy thing to do. His every instinct told him that retreating to the roof was a mistake. It was like climbing a tree to escape from a bear—in the moment it might seem like the only way to survive, but bears were excellent climbers, and being trapped up in a tree by a pissed-off grizzly was not a good place to be.

He favored a bold frontal assault, sweeping down the south stairs and covering the end of the hallway while the least combat-capable members of the group headed for the south exit and the parking lot. It was a risky plan, desperate even, but Redd had always adhered to the wisdom of General Patton—*In case of doubt . . . ATTACK!*

And maybe if it had been only him, he would have done just that. But it wasn't only him. He had Emily to think of. And Mikey and all the others. Some of them were in pretty bad shape. Mikey's body armor had stopped what would have been a center-mass kill shot, but the 5.56-millimeter round had hit with the force of a sledgehammer right below Mikey's heart. The cardiac shock from a hit like that was often fatal, even with a vest. Fortunately, the impact had not stopped his heart, but the skin underneath the Kevlar armor had ruptured, which explained the blood.

Mikey wasn't the only one hurting. Though none of them had sustained a life-threatening injury, almost everyone who had engaged in direct fire with the Praetorian's assault team had been wounded. Redd himself was running on empty. His leg throbbed. He'd been scraped and abraded by debris. A bullet had gouged a stripe across his left biceps. Under his armor, he was a mass of bruises, and he was pretty sure that some of the old knife wounds were bleeding again. None of them were operating at peak performance, and anything less than that would probably be the end of their fight.

Thankfully, Elijah and the small group he had been protecting had escaped harm, but now that they were all together and in the open, they would be as vulnerable as everyone else. So when Kline had given his support to Blackwood's plan, Redd had conceded. Then the sheriff had given him an unexpected escape route.

If Redd understood the sheriff correctly—a big *if* since his hearing was just starting to return—there was a way off the roof that, while not exactly ideal, just might give them all a chance to slip the noose the Praetorian's men were tightening around their collective neck.

The Stillwater County Courthouse had been built in 1936 with straight up-and-down construction—sheer walls with no balconies or gables. In the early 2000s, however, as part of a general renovation, the county had approved construction of the sally port on the south side of the building to allow the sheriff's deputies to safely transfer prisoners between vehicles and the lockup. The sally port was basically a single-story garage jutting out from the main building near the southwest corner. It had been built with conventional 4/12 roof pitch, sloping away from the building about ten feet below the foot-high parapet that ran the full perimeter of the courthouse roof. All of which meant, if they had to get off the roof and couldn't go down by the stairs, it was feasible to drop over the side onto the sally port roof and, from there, drop another ten feet to the ground. From there, they could get to the parking lot, load into their personal vehicles, and make a run for it.

There were some problems with this plan, not the least of which was the likelihood that the Praetorian's men might still be watching the ground floor, just in case. But as Blackwood had correctly pointed out, it was a good bet that most of the hostiles were inside the courthouse on their way up. They would have a better chance dealing with whatever token rear guard was left on the ground than trying to fight their way back out of the building.

There was also the fact that two of their group were elderly, two were young children, and others were injured and not exactly in ideal shape to be jumping off a perfectly good building. The sheriff had argued that the strongest among them would be able to help the others down, and the snow would soften the landings.

It was probably a better plan than going on the attack, and while there were all kinds of ways it could go wrong, Redd was going to do his dead-level best to make it go right, because if it worked, they would all survive—Em and little Matty, Mikey and his family, Elijah and Mrs. Lawrence.

And my father.

Even in his head, it didn't quite sound right. He would always think of J. B. as his real father—the old rancher had more than earned it. But hadn't Gavin Kline redeemed himself? If only a little? Did Redd have the right to ask for more?

He shook his head, trying to bring his focus back to the task at hand. This wasn't the time to work through his daddy issues.

When Blackwood unlocked and opened the roof access door, a snow flurry swept in, swirling around the stairwell. In the chaos of battle, Redd had forgotten about the ongoing snowstorm outside. But as the surrounding air quickly cooled, Redd was reminded of the urgency of getting everyone off the roof and out of the elements.

Blackwood and the deputies hurried out first, providing cover in the unlikely event that the Praetorian's forces had somehow gotten ahead of them. Emily followed with her parents, Liz, and Maggie, along with the children. Mikey came out next, with Kline, Treadway, and Redd—with Rubble at his side—bringing up the rear.

As soon as he was out, Redd slammed the door shut. He would have traded a kidney for something to secure the door—a metal rod or a two-by-four he could jam against the latch plate to hold it shut—but if there was anything like that, it was covered under nearly two feet of snow. Instead, he joined with the FBI agents and Mikey to create a firing line about thirty feet away from the door. If . . . when the enemy tried to come through, they would be met with a wall of lead.

Satisfied that they were ready to meet a frontal attack, Redd looked around, surveying other possible avenues of attack. He didn't like what he saw. The roof of the courthouse was far from an ideal location to establish a defensive position. With the exception of the upraised superstructure that housed the elevator pulley equipment atop of the hoistway along with the south stairwell, the only other object that might provide some degree of cover was the master HVAC unit—a metal cube about ten feet on a side—located about fifty feet east of the superstructure. Aside from that, they had neither cover nor concealment, though anyone shooting from ground level wouldn't have a good line of sight on them as long as they stayed away from the perimeter. But something about the situation nagged at him.

He recalled the big gun that had been used to blow through the courthouse wall and likely to cause the avalanche as well. A weapon like that would be employed by a sniper, someone positioned at a distance and probably from an elevated position.

There were only a few two-story structures in downtown Wellington, most of which lay to the east along Broadway, but the superstructure and the AC unit would provide protection from that quarter. In every other direction, there were just a few two-story houses with peaked roofs, none of which rose as high as the courthouse.

And of course, there was the water tower.

Redd felt his pulse quicken as he turned to look north. Through the swirling snow, he could just barely make out the enormous cylindrical structure two hundred odd yards away. Capable of storing well over a million gallons, used to maintain constant pressure in the city's water supply, the top of the tank rose over a hundred and forty feet into the air, nearly three times the height of the courthouse building, which meant that a sniper perched atop it, or even on the maintenance catwalk twenty feet below, would have an unrestricted view of the roof.

He's up there, Redd realized. *And we're totally exposed.*

"Hey!" he shouted at the top of his lungs. "We need to move. We're too—"

There was a bright flash from one side of the water tower.

"Get down!" he screamed, throwing himself belly down into the snow.

Not everybody heard his cry or was able to grasp the urgency of it, but all of them were moving in some way, just enough so that the first round missed its flesh-and-blood target by scant inches.

Mrs. Lawrence let out a shriek of dismay as the round, tracing curlicues of disturbed snow behind it, slammed through the air a mere eighteen inches from her elbow, but she was already falling forward in response to Redd's warning, cradling Matthew Jr. in her arms as she dropped. The round continued along its slanted trajectory, missed the edge of the roof altogether, and impacted out in the mostly empty parking lot, where it detonated, throwing up a geyser of snow. The boom of the explosion arrived almost simultaneously with the report of the weapon.

Lying prone, Redd didn't see the effects of the blast, but he heard it well enough and knew that the sniper on the water tower was the same one that had tried to kill him with the avalanche. The man had missed with his first shot because his target had been upright, but because of his superior angle, he would not have any difficulty with the next shot, especially since all his targets were now sprawled out in the snow.

"Get to cover," he shouted, pointing at the superstructure. "He's on the water tower."

When taking unexpected fire, one of the first things to do was call out the distance and direction of the enemy force. By identifying the water tower to the north as the sniper's position, Redd was telling everyone to retreat to the south side of the structure. With his anti-materiel weapon, the sniper could conceivably blast the little building to oblivion, probably taking them out long before he completely destroyed it, but doing so would also literally drop a ton of bricks down the stairwell on top of the rest of the Praetorian's force, and Redd didn't think he was going to do that. Not right away at least.

Treadway and Kline immediately grasped what Redd was trying to convey and sprang into motion. Treadway grabbed Liz with one arm and Maggie with the other and pulled them behind her. Kline went for Mrs. Lawrence, half dragging her in his haste to get little Matty to a safer place. Everyone else moved under their own power, running frantically toward the upraised structure.

Suddenly, a section of the roof erupted just a few feet to the right of one of the running deputies. The blast hurled him forward and knocked down everyone else in a ten-foot radius, including Redd, but the detonation felt merely like a hot wind pushing at his back. He was up again in a heartbeat, rushing to assist the deputy, who was already on his feet. Redd expected another shot to follow quickly on the heels of the first. That the first two hadn't killed anyone was a matter of dumb luck. With each miss, the sniper would dial in his targets and figure out where to place the next round to keep them from reaching cover.

But their luck held. The anticipated third shot didn't come, and everyone reached the shelter of the superstructure, lining up against it, huddling together to ensure that no part of their bodies would be visible to the shooter on the water tower.

Too late, Redd realized that while they were out of the sniper's line of sight, they had left the roof access door completely unguarded.

"Watch the corners!" he shouted, edging out on the left side just in time to see movement through the curtain of falling snow. The Praetorian's men were on the roof with them.

Their winter camo made it hard to pinpoint the exact location of the enemy shooters, but Redd didn't need exactitude. He fired several rounds into the white haze, employing a tactic he rarely used—spraying and praying.

His worst fears had come to pass. They were caught, pinned down, unable to reach any avenues of escape. But even as the tentacles of defeatism reached out for him, he struck them aside. He was still alive, and until that changed, he wasn't going to stop fighting. Maybe he wouldn't make it off the roof alive, but he was going to make sure the others did.

"Gavin!" he shouted. "I'm going to draw their fire. When I do, make your move."

"You can't take them on all by yourself," countered the FBI director.

"Watch me."

"Matt—" Kline's protest was cut off by a sudden impact against the brick wall right above his head. He ducked reflexively as a shower of red flakes and bullet fragments rained down on him. There was a palm-sized divot in the wall, about a foot above the place where his head had been a moment before.

Redd bit back a curse.

Another sniper, he thought. *Of course there is.*

SIXTY-EIGHT

The second shooter, positioned somewhere south of the courthouse, wasn't firing explosive rounds, but that was little comfort. With snipers covering both sides of the courthouse and an unknown number of enemy forces on the roof, even his heroic sacrifice would not suffice to ensure the survival of the rest of the group.

Redd did not allow himself the luxury of falling into despair. The sniper to the south didn't have a high-angle perch like his buddy on the water tower—otherwise, he would already have started picking them off. As long as they kept their heads down, they were relatively protected. The immediate threat was from the gunmen already on the roof. Redd edged out again and, failing to see a target, fired blind.

Emily was right beside Redd, her rifle at the ready. On the right corner, Treadway was following Redd's lead, suppressing any attempt by the enemy to circle around the structure and attack from the opposite side. The rest of the group was lining up behind them, preparing to get in the fight as soon as they were needed.

With one exception.

"Matt!" shouted Mikey. "See if you can get him to shoot again!"

Redd glanced back, surprised to find that Mikey had crawled away from the superstructure to the edge of the roof, where he was now peering through the scope of his rifle, looking out over the barely visible townscape.

"Mikey! Get back . . ." Redd let the admonition go unfinished as he realized what Mikey was attempting.

Get him to shoot again.

Mikey was going hunting.

Redd had hunted elk with Mikey and knew that he was an excellent marksman. And he'd been blooded in combat on more than one occasion, which meant he wouldn't hesitate to pull the trigger against a human enemy. If anyone could snipe the sniper, it was Mikey Derhammer. But in these conditions, with the falling snow severely limiting visibility, just finding the shooter's location would require almost supernatural abilities. To pinpoint his target, Mikey would need to watch for the muzzle flash of the sniper's weapon, and to do that, someone—

Me.

—would have to stick his neck out.

Okay, thought Redd. *Let's do this.*

He backed away from the corner, tapped Emily's shoulder, and shouted, "Take over for me."

She nodded, though from her quizzical expression it was clear that she didn't realize what he was about to do. He was having a little trouble believing it himself.

He squirmed back away from the wall, letting Emily take his place. As he prepared to move, the sound of near-constant gunfire behind him blurred into the background.

In some of his earliest military training, he had learned the time-honored infantry technique of moving under fire. To minimize exposure, advances across open terrain were made in three-to-five-second rushes, an interval that could be measured with the spoken cadence, *"I'm up. He sees me. I'm down."*

Redd muttered the words, expecting at any moment to see the flash of the sniper's weapon through the white veil, but nothing happened, and when he threw himself down into the thick bed of snow, he felt a mixture of relief and disappointment. He was still alive, but he had failed to flush out the sniper.

Let's try that again.

He bounded up, shouldering his AR as if ready to engage the enemy all by himself, and began the chant.

"I'm up. He sees me . . . He sees me . . ." Every fiber of instinct screamed at him to get down, but he remained on his feet. Remained in the open. "He sees—"

From a not-too-distant rooftop, a flash of bright yellow light appeared through the falling snow, like a glint of sunlight through lace curtains. Redd threw himself flat just as a high-velocity round broke the sound barrier right above him. The sledgehammer crack of the bullet striking the superstructure preceded the report by an imperceptible fraction of a second.

Redd belly crawled over to Mikey. He took note of the alignment of Mikey's rifle and compared it against his memory of where he'd seen the flash. "A little to the left," he suggested.

"I've got him," replied Mikey. "Just need you to do that one more time."

Redd let out his breath in a sigh. *One more time.*

"All right, but make sure you drop him this time."

"You know it."

Redd took another breath, blew it out, and rose.

Powdery snow clung to his body like a crust, falling away in big chunks as he moved.

I'm up.

He sees me.

He sees me.

He sees me.

He—

Flash.

Redd flopped down into the snow. Beside him, Mikey's rifle boomed, the report drowning out the crack of the sniper's bullet.

Redd waited a moment before asking, "Did you get him?"

"I think so." Mikey did not sound especially confident.

He thinks so. Guess there's only one way to find out.

"Keep an eye out for him. I'm going to draw the rest of them off so you guys can get off this roof."

Mikey nodded, but then Redd's message sank in. "Wait, what?"

But Redd was already gone, fast crawling back to the superstructure. The shooting had stopped, though both Emily and Treadway remained vigilant at their respective corners. Redd made his way over to Kline.

"Mikey thinks he got the sniper," said Redd. "What's the situation here?"

"Nobody's shooting back," replied Kline. "But we're running low on ammo."

Redd nodded. "I'm going to draw their fire. Be ready to make a run for it."

Kline shook his head. "We'll stand a better chance if you stay with us."

"Not with that other sniper on the water tower." When Kline offered no argument, Redd went on. "When I make my move, count to ten and then go."

Kline stared back at him for a long moment, then clapped Redd on the shoulder. "Be careful, Son."

Redd almost said, *You too, Dad*, but the words wouldn't form. Instead, he answered honestly. "Careful won't get the job done."

SIXTY-NINE

"Arrow Three, what's going on over there?" Cormac waited for a reply, but none came. "Arrow Three, give me a sitrep."

Still no answer. Cormac spat a curse. He had cleared Three to start eliminating targets and had heard the report of the sniper's Barrett M82 a couple times, but then it had gone silent. Maybe the man had balked at the idea of killing women and children and simply deserted. Or maybe Redd or one of his group had gotten off a lucky shot.

He keyed his mic again. "Arrow One, what do you see?"

"They're on the other side of that little building," said Chad Beaudette. "I can't tell you anything more than that."

Hunkered down on the opposite side of "that little building," Cormac shook his head. He had lost two more men in the attempt to take the roof and had no idea what had become of Arrow Three. Without effective overwatch from his snipers, the odds were good that he would lose a lot more men before Matthew Redd was finally brought down.

It was time to take the gloves off.

Although dealing with the cowboy up close and personal would have been his preference, he was willing to forego that pleasure if it got the job done.

"Arrow One, we're going to pull back about fifty yards to the east and then attempt to flank them. I expect they'll try to move around to the west side, which should give you a target-rich environment. But if they don't, I want you to knock this brick outhouse down. Take away their cover and force them into the open."

"Righteous plan, boss. Just say the—crap, I've got a rabbit. Moving west . . . It's the cowboy. I have the shot."

Cormac knew that Beaudette was asking for permission to take Redd out and knew that he should give it, but fate had just given him one last chance to avenge Colin. He couldn't say no to that.

He edged from the corner and saw a large dark shape moving through the falling snow toward the northwest corner of the rooftop.

"Stand by, Arrow One," he said. "I'll take care of Redd. Once I'm clear, engage with any targets of opportunity."

He turned to the man nearest him, Dagger Two. "You heard?"

Dagger Two nodded.

"Then move out. I want you to exterminate every one of them." He didn't wait for confirmation but picked up and charged out into the open.

SEVENTY

Something's wrong.

Redd had been out in the open, fully in view of the Praetorian's men on the roof and the snipers to either side, for more than fifteen seconds—an eternity—but nobody was shooting at him.

He knew better than to think that the enemy had retreated. No, they were still out there, watching him, biding their time, waiting . . . but waiting for what?

Had they realized his intention? Were they waiting for the rest of the group to make their move so they could dispatch everyone in one fell swoop?

He slowed, then came to a full stop, just a few steps away from the edge of the roof. He could just make out the shape of the water tower and tried to imagine where the second sniper might be hiding. Without advanced optics, his chances of locating and eliminating the shooter were next to nil, but he could surely give the man something to think about.

Why aren't you shooting at me?

As if in response to his unspoken question, several reports broke the stillness. He whirled around, trying to locate the source of the shots. They seemed to originate from near the superstructure, but he could not tell who was shooting or who was on the receiving end. Either way, it didn't seem to be him.

Sensing that he had made a serious error by separating from those under his protection, Redd started back toward the superstructure, but then froze in place when he spied something moving through the falling snow, right in front of him. He hurriedly shifted the muzzle of his AR toward the vague shape, but before he could pull the trigger, the mass suddenly materialized into a hulking human form right in front of him. Then something lashed out at him like a tentacle. He had barely enough time to recognize the object as the molded plastic buttstock of an M4 before it smashed into his jaw.

It was a glancing blow. An inch further to the left and it would have rammed his teeth down his throat. As it was, the rifle butt tore a long gash along the side of his face, spattering the pristine white around him with a spray of blood droplets.

Yet Redd stayed on his feet, and before the man could draw back for a second attack, Redd caught the weapon in his left hand and wrenched it from the other man's grip. The unexpected counterattack pulled the man forward, close enough for Redd to look him in the eye.

It was the same man he had confronted earlier, the leader of the Praetorian's assault team.

"Do I look familiar to you?"

The man who had come looking for vengeance.

Kilmeade!

Redd felt the resistance abruptly vanish as the man let go of the rifle. Misinterpreting this apparent surrender as a victory, Redd realized too late that Kilmeade was already attacking again, driving his knee like a battering ram into Redd's groin.

Redd went rigid with pain, but he'd been hit below the belt before and knew how to compartmentalize the agony and keep fighting. He twisted away, trying to put some distance between himself and his attacker, but Kilmeade was already pressing his attack. He darted in close and aimed a punch at Redd's face. Redd easily blocked the punch with his forearm, realizing only when he felt his rifle's sling tugging against his shoulder that the real intent of the punch had been to distract him while Kilmeade made a grab for Redd's rifle.

At such close quarters, the AR-15 was more a liability than an asset, and with the sling running over Redd's shoulder and across his back, there was little chance of his foe taking the weapon away from him, but as the muzzle swung toward his face, Redd saw what Kilmeade was trying to do.

He caught the barrel in both hands, howling as he felt the skin of his palms sizzle against the hot metal. Redd held on and tried to shove the business end of the rifle away, though the weapon didn't move. He thought he could feel the hot metal oozing under his scorched skin. The initial pain had passed, replaced by the persistent low-grade throb of a first- or second-degree burn, but he ignored the sensation, leaning into the struggle. Kilmeade had one hand on the heat shield and the other on the pistol grip, which not only gave him a lot more leverage but access to the trigger.

Redd stared down at the face of the man who had vowed to kill him. It was a face contorted with effort, teeth bared, skin reddened with exertion. Kilmeade was a good half a foot shorter than Redd, but with a more advantageous grip on the weapon, he was Redd's equal in strength. The rifle tip seemed to float in the air between them, just a few inches below Redd's chin, trembling a little as each man pushed with all his might. In his peripheral vision, Redd could see the vents on the muzzle brake and the bore opening, less than a quarter inch in diameter. The 5.56-millimeter round made such a small hole, barely larger than a carpentry nail, that many questioned how it could be so lethal. Redd knew the answer. It wasn't the size of the wound that mattered but the hydrostatic shock of a high-velocity penetration, and if his enemy succeeded in moving the barrel of the rifle under his chin and pulled the trigger, one of those bullets would plow through his brain.

His back foot started to slide in the snow, and then, despite his best effort, his front foot did too. His opponent advanced quickly, trying to seize on Redd's instability to move the rifle closer, and while Redd was struggling to hold him off, he was powerless to find his footing. Then his slide stopped abruptly as his back heel struck something hard and unyielding. It was the one-foot-high brick parapet around the edge of the courthouse roof.

I'm losing this fight, Redd realized.

But before that seed of doubt could germinate into defeat, he remembered Patton's advice.

He wasn't going to win in a contest of raw power, but there were other ways to attack. Throwing his head to the side, he stopped pushing and instead pulled the weapon to him. The abruptness of the move caught his foe off guard but only for a moment. He shifted quickly, trying to reinitiate the struggle for control.

Suddenly the weapon discharged, spitting a six-inch-long tongue of flame into the air a hand's breadth from Redd's ear. Either intentionally or by accident, Kilmeade had pulled the trigger. Redd barely noticed the noise of the report, but the spray of hot gases stung his eyes, and the explosive energy vibrated through his scorched palms and up his arms like a lightning strike.

The gun bucked a second time. Then a third.

Yeah, he's definitely doing that on purpose.

Redd felt like he was hanging above a bottomless chasm with only a live high-voltage power cable for a lifeline. He couldn't hold on forever, but if he let go, he was dead.

Another shot. Then another. And then . . . nothing.

The rifle's magazine was empty.

Both men realized the significance of this in the same instant.

Redd let go of the rifle and made a grab for his opponent, but he was half a second too slow. Kilmeade had thrust the weapon away, backpedaling to put some distance between himself and Redd. Then he reached into his tactical rig and drew something out.

Expecting it to be a handgun, Redd moved just as quickly, whipping the Ruger out of his holster, realizing only then that what Kilmeade held was not a pistol but a blade—a black-powder-coated five-inch-long combat knife identical to the one wielded by the man who had nearly killed him up on the mountain.

Redd snapped off a shot, but Kilmeade was already moving. As Redd pulled the trigger, he dodged to the side and then charged. Redd tried to correct his aim, but before he could pull the trigger a second time, Kilmeade slammed into him, one hand gripping the front of Redd's armor vest, the other driving the knife toward Redd's exposed throat. Redd took an involuntary step back, successfully parrying the thrust with the Ruger, but then Kilmeade slammed into him, his momentum carrying them both backward. Redd felt the tops of his boots strike the parapet, then both he and his attacker toppled over the edge.

SEVENTY-ONE

Kline gave Redd his ten count and then some. The long quiet that followed Redd's departure was ominous. Nobody was shooting at him, but what exactly that signified was impossible to say. Had their enemy grown wise to Redd's intended diversion? Were they biding their time, waiting for the rest of the group to step out from behind cover?

The only way to know for sure was to put it to the test.

He called the others into a huddle. "We'll move in groups. I'll lead with Stephanie. Everyone else, cover us. Once we're set, start coming over in groups of two or three. If we start taking fire, suppress it, but keep moving. We're getting off this roof. Everyone got it?"

There were nods, a few grimaces, and a couple of blank stares, but nobody signaled confusion or raised an objection.

"Then let's do this."

Shouldering his AR-15, which he figured still had about ten rounds, he started across the roof, not running but moving fast in a low crouch. Treadway was right beside him, her head on a swivel, sweeping the area to their right with the muzzle of her weapon. Through the falling snow, it was difficult to see more than about twenty feet, but Kline thought he detected movement on the opposite side of the roof.

Matthew?

He considered moving closer to investigate but knew his priority was to get everyone else to safety.

Kline and Treadway quickly reached their objective, knelt, and took up stable firing positions. When he was set, Kline raised a fist and pumped it in the air, signaling for the next group to move across. By some unspoken agreement, Elijah and his wife moved out, the latter huddling close with the blanket-wrapped form of Matthew Jr. The elderly couple moved with surprising speed, but Kline could see that the prolonged exposure was taking its toll. Mrs. Lawrence, who had no body fat to spare, was visibly shivering.

She's flagging, he thought. *They all are. We need to get them somewhere warm, ASAP.*

He leaned out over the parapet and looked down at the sloping roof of the sally port. It seemed a lot farther down than he'd expected. Maybe not much of a drop for someone in reasonably good shape, but a long fall for an old woman. Someone would have to lower her from the roof, with someone else waiting below to guide her down. Not an impossible feat by any means, though the snow might complicate things.

Sudden gunfire jarred Kline out of his musings.

"Here we go," he muttered, trying to orient in on the source. The shots came in quick succession, not a sustained burst of automatic fire, but rapid trigger pulls—*pop, pop, pop*—coming, Kline thought, from the north side of the roof. Then, just as abruptly as it had begun, the shooting stopped.

And then started again.

Someone—one of the deputies—shouted out an abbreviated contact report. "They're behind us!"

Kline snapped his attention around and saw bright muzzle flashes lighting up the snow from the east end of the rooftop. With the group between them and the enemy, there was nothing he or Treadway could do to help.

He waved to the Lawrences, who, alarmed by the gunfire, had paused their crossing and hunkered down in place. "Come on!"

Without waiting for a prompt, Maggie Albright and Liz Derhammer, holding her son in her arms, began their crossing, while Emily and Mikey joined with Blackwood and the deputies in exchanging fire with the Praetorian's men. The two women quickly caught up to the older couple and urged them into motion again.

As soon as they reached their destination, Kline pumped his fist and shouted, "Next up!"

But none of the others even looked back at him. They were so fixated on the enemy to their front that they had forgotten the plan, and Kline's shouts could not reach them over the din of combat.

Kline muttered a curse. "Be right back," he told Treadway, then without further explanation, ran back toward the superstructure.

He was halfway there when the roof exploded.

SEVENTY-TWO

Redd and Cormac Kilmeade grappled as they fell, both men trying to twist around in order to be on top when they hit the ground. It was a struggle that the lighter Kilmeade easily won, and when their freefall journey ended a little more than one second after it began, Redd took the brunt, landing flat on his back. The snow compressed under Redd's body, cushioning his fall a little, but when Kilmeade's bulk slammed down onto him a heartbeat later, he felt like a piece of steel caught between hammer and anvil. The second impact knocked the wind out of him, leaving him gasping and dazed.

They had landed at the base of the courthouse's north wall. From where he lay, Redd could see the familiar glass door with the six-pointed star of the sheriff's department off to his right. To his left there was a six-foot-wide breach in the wall, opening up into a darkened courtroom. The snow in front of the hole was littered with bricks that had been blasted loose under the relentless assault of explosive rounds fired by the sniper on the water tower.

Groaning, Kilmeade rolled off Redd, flopping into the snow. He lay there for a few seconds before struggling up to all fours and then rising to his feet. Blood stained his lips and trickled down his chin. His hands were empty, his knife evidently lost during the fall.

Redd, too, had lost his weapon during the fall. He turned his head, looking around for the Ruger, but saw no sign of it.

Kilmeade swayed unsteadily for a moment, looking around as if searching for his missing blade; then his gaze fell on Redd, and a wicked grin curled his bloody lips. He moved tentatively toward Redd until his boots were just inches from Redd's head and then drew back his right foot.

Redd's brain screamed at him to move. But his body was slow to react. It was as if his limbs had been replaced by bags of lead shot. As Kilmeade's foot began its forward swing, Redd heaved his torso sideways, rolling away from the kick before it could land.

The miss caused Kilmeade to lose his balance. Flailing his arms, he wobbled on one leg for a moment, then fell backward.

Redd willed his limbs into motion, pushing himself up onto hands and knees. His breath had returned, but he still felt like his brain and his muscles weren't communicating very well. A few yards away, Kilmeade was rising again, recovering from his misstep.

Move, Redd told himself. *Get up!*

He felt like a punch-drunk fighter trying to get back on his feet before the referee finished the count. From the corner of his eye, he saw that Kilmeade was up again and headed his way, this time more surefooted in his approach. Redd barely managed to stand up before his foe threw a roundhouse punch that landed on the same jaw that had caught a butt stroke just before the fall.

Redd's head snapped to the side, and an eruption of stars filled his vision, but he stayed on his feet and threw a counterpunch. Kilmeade easily dodged it and attacked again with a rapid series of body blows that drove Redd back several steps. Redd tried retaliating, but his punches were too slow. He felt like he was fighting underwater. Desperate to change the trajectory of the fight, he threw his arms wide and tried to sweep his opponent up in a bear hug, but Kilmeade easily dodged away.

Suddenly, there was a loud boom followed almost simultaneously by an even louder explosion somewhere high overhead.

Redd's heart fell out of his chest.

No!

The big rifle up on the water tower spoke again, and there was another explosion on the rooftop.

Kilmeade looked up for just a moment, then turned back to Redd, his bloody grin even wider than before. "You know what that was?" he said. "That was the sound of everyone you love getting blown straight to hell."

Redd barely heard the taunt. He was overcome with blind rage. Energy surged through his body. Without conscious volition, he hurled himself at Kilmeade.

Unprepared for the ferocity of the attack, Kilmeade drew back for a punch that he never got a chance to throw. Redd was there first, his right fist ramming into Kilmeade's face so hard that he was lifted off his feet. His body flew through the air and slammed into the brick wall.

The impact stunned Kilmeade, and before he could recover, Redd was there. His right hand closed around Kilmeade's neck, lifted him off his feet, and slammed him against the wall, holding him there.

Fear dawned in the killer's eyes, the stark realization that he was about to die. He brought his hands up, tearing at Redd's grip, but the effort availed nothing. Frantic, he began beating at Redd's arm with his fists and kicking out at Redd. He would have had better luck trying to take down a cedar tree. Redd didn't feel a thing.

But then Kilmeade landed a lucky kick to Redd's inflamed left thigh, and the leg folded under him. As Redd fell, a gasping Kilmeade wriggled free and scrambled away, putting some distance between them.

Redd, still in the grip of a murderous rage, rose to his feet and went after Kilmeade, but his injured leg failed him again with the first step, dropping him onto the snow once more. Undaunted, he got to hands and knees and began crawling, dragging himself through the snow toward Kilmeade.

Desperate and just barely clinging to consciousness after nearly being choked out by Redd, Kilmeade began looking around for something he might be able to use to halt Redd's murderous advance. Then he saw it lying in the snow, just a couple feet away from where they had landed after the fall, and his grin returned.

In a move that was half crawl, half dive, he threw himself across the intervening distance, closed his hand around the object, and then brought it up and pointed it at Redd.

The sight of his Ruger in Kilmeade's hands, aimed directly at him, stopped Redd in his tracks, but only for a moment. His rage had lost none of its power, but now it transformed into something cooler, more calculating. He was now less a savage beast and more a machine.

His eyes narrowed, assessing the distance separating them, calculating the surest way to reach Kilmeade and rip his head off. He did not expect to survive. There was no permutation where Kilmeade did not pull the trigger, and at such close range, he would not miss. The only question was whether Redd could stay alive long enough to avenge his loved ones. After that there was no reason to go on living anyway.

Kilmeade must have sensed what was going on behind Redd's eyes, because he took a step back, then another. "Don't even think about it, cowboy."

Redd bared his teeth at the other man and resumed dragging himself forward.

Kilmeade retreated another step. "You've got spirit. I admire that. I really do. But you brought this on yourself when you killed my brother."

Redd kept coming.

Kilmeade shook his head. "Time to end this," he said. He aimed the weapon, lining the sights up on Redd's face, and curled his finger around the trigger. "I told you I would be the last face you see."

Then Cormac Kilmeade blew apart.

SEVENTY-THREE

Two hundred and fifty yards away and one hundred twenty feet above ground, Aaron Decker watched the last remaining member of the Praetorian's assault team disintegrate in an eruption of smoke and gore. He allowed himself a smile of grim satisfaction as he raised his head away from the scope of the XM109 Anti-Materiel Payload Rifle.

"Did you get 'em?" asked Deputy Oman, who knelt beside him, peering down into the haze of swirling snow.

Decker nodded. "Got 'em all."

Kurt Oman let out a relieved sigh, then glanced back at the unmoving form of the sniper Decker had overpowered in order to seize control of the weapon. "What about him?"

Decker shrugged. "Don't ask me. You're the law around here."

SEVENTY-FOUR

Redd was still staring at the scattered bloody remains of Kilmeade two minutes later when the doors to the sheriff's office opened and the survivors began to emerge. His disbelief quickly transformed to surprise and then, when he saw Emily holding Junior, gave way to a relief so profound that he almost wept.

As she ran to him, he struggled to his feet and caught her in an embrace so fierce that Little Matty gave a whimper of protest.

He eased up, but only a little.

"I thought you were . . ." He choked up, unable to finish. It was a thought he never wanted to think again.

"I thought you were too," she admitted, making no effort to hold back her emotions. "I love you, Matty."

"I love you too, Em."

As he became aware of the others streaming from the exit, he let go of her and regarded them one by one, putting check marks on his mental roster, terrified that he would find someone missing. Gavin . . . Treadway . . . Mikey, Liz, and Lucas . . . Emily's parents . . . Blackwood . . . Maggie . . . the deputies.

They were all there. Even Rubble.

Who's a good boy?

Mikey broke from Liz and Lucas and made his way over to Redd. He was limping a bit and covered in dirt, but otherwise seemed okay. Though Redd could tell by the look in his friend's eye that he must have felt worse than he was letting on.

"Remember when I told you a while back that you should call me before you ever take on an army on your own?"

Redd recalled Mikey telling him numerous times to call him before confronting the biker gang months prior. He nodded.

"Well," said Mikey, "lose my number."

For a brief moment, silence hung in the air as the two men stared at each other. Then Mikey smiled and let out a laugh as he put an arm around Redd. As the two men embraced, he said, "It's over now, right?"

"It's over," Redd said with another nod.

At least for now.

Redd hoped it was finally over for good, but at the very least, they had time to recover and regroup. "Thanks for everything, Mikey. Really."

"Hey, what are friends for? Though, and I'm not saying I'm keeping score here, being your best friend should, like, come with a warning or something."

"You're probably not wrong."

"Catch up later?"

"Definitely."

As Mikey turned to head back to Liz and Lucas, Redd looked around, taking in the whole scene yet again. He couldn't believe they made it.

But how?

Looking to Emily, Redd finally found his voice. "What happened?"

"I'm not sure," Emily admitted. "Gavin thought that maybe you took out the sniper on the water tower and used his gun to . . ."

She trailed off when Redd shook his head. "Wasn't me."

"Well, someone was looking out for us." She cleared her throat. "We've got to get to the clinic." She glanced at her own shoulder. "I might need a stitch or two, but a few people are hurt pretty bad." She pulled back, looking at him as if only now seeing him. "My gosh, Matthew. What happened to you?"

Redd wasn't sure what she meant at first, but then realized that he was covered in congealing blood. "It's not mine," he mumbled, though he knew that some of it definitely was. "Well, not all of it."

✖   ✖   ✖

A fire truck rolled up a few minutes later and, shortly thereafter, an ambulance. Volunteer firefighters and EMTs quickly deployed to begin assessing the injuries, loading the most serious onto gurneys and litters for transport to the nearby medical center.

Thankfully, none of the patients required critical care, but Emily and her small staff had their work cut out for them, cleaning and stitching wounds, starting IVs, and writing orders for X-rays, antibiotics, and pain medications.

When he had cleaned up and gotten the worst of his injuries tended to, Redd went looking for Kline. He found him in the lobby of the emergency department, talking to a tall, whippet-lean man with blond hair and intense blue eyes. Redd had never seen the man before but instantly recognized him as a kindred spirit. A dangerous spirit.

Kline spotted Redd and waved him over. "Matthew, there's someone I'd like you to meet." He gestured to the other man. "This is Aaron Decker. Aaron, Matthew Redd."

Decker extended a hand. Redd automatically reached out to take it, but then looked down at the thick wrap of gauze bandages covering the burns on both palms and instead gave an apologetic shrug, which Decker accepted with a nod.

"Aaron is . . . ah . . ." Kline faltered, as if unsure what to say about the man, but Decker quickly filled the silence.

"Gavin and I worked together a long time ago. He calls me now and then when he's got a problem that can't be solved the FBI way."

Redd quickly picked up on the subtext. "You're a freelancer."

"That's as good a word as any."

Realization dawned on Redd. "That was you up on the water tower."

It was Decker's turn to shrug. "I saw an opportunity and took advantage of it."

Redd was not put off by the man's effort to downplay his contribution. "You saved my life. You saved all of us."

Decker just gave a little nod. "I'm just glad I got there in time to help."

Redd shook his head and then held Decker's gaze. "I owe you one, Aaron. If you ever need anything, give me a call."

Decker regarded him for a moment, then nodded again. "I appreciate that."

Redd turned to Kline. "So, what happens now? Is the Praetorian going to keep sending his killers after us?"

Kline returned an odd smile. "I don't think you'll have to worry about the Praetorian anymore."

"Then you're going after him," said Redd. "I want to be a part of that."

Kline shook his head. "That's not how this is going to go."

"Why not? We went after the Twelve, didn't we?"

"This is a . . . slightly different situation. The Twelve used their money and influence to control people in power, but the Praetorian . . . he *is* the power."

"Nobody is untouchable," countered Redd.

"No, but sometimes it's the kind of touch that makes all the difference. Some problems can be fixed with a sledgehammer. Others need—" Kline's eyes flicked to Decker—"a scalpel."

Redd narrowed his gaze at Kline. "He came after me. Me, Gavin. And he put my family in danger. You owe me a shot at him."

Kline stared back at him for a long moment. "Do you remember what you told me when I asked you to come work for me?"

Redd was taken aback by the question, but before he could even begin searching his memory, Kline went on. "You said you weren't like me. That you weren't going to *abandon* your family to go chasing bad guys all around the globe."

"I don't think I said it like that," replied Redd, a little sullen. He *did* remember that conversation, and Kline's recollection wasn't wrong.

"You said, 'There are always going to be bad guys, but you only get one chance at family,'" Kline went on. "And you were absolutely right. Family is the most important thing. And you don't show that by running off after every bad guy who threatens them. You show it by being there for them. Taking care of them. Especially right now. Emily and Junior need you here. You took down Gage. The Twelve are finished. That was our deal. Now it's time to live your life."

Redd looked at him sideways. "Are you firing me?"

"No, of course not," Kline answered, a little too quickly. "There's always going to be a place for you at the Bureau if you want it. But right now I think the place for you is right here in Wellington."

Redd continued to stare at the other man, trying to decide if Kline was kicking him to the curb or actually looking out for him. He wanted to believe it was the latter.

Just then, Emily called out to him from across the room. "Matty? There you are."

When she came over, Redd started to introduce Decker, but in the moment that he'd looked away, Decker had vanished.

Noting Redd's surprise, Kline laughed. "It's just something he does."

Redd nodded, but something told him that wasn't the last time he'd see Aaron Decker.

Emily acknowledged Kline with a nod then returned her attention to her husband. "You should be in bed."

"I'm fine," he said.

"I'll be the judge of that," she countered, then shook her head. "Have you seen Bekah?"

"No. Not recently. Why?"

"Nobody's seen her. When I went to check in on her, she was gone."

"She's got to be around here somewhere," intoned Kline. "I mean, where's she going to go?"

Redd felt a sense of deep foreboding. "What if they took her?"

"Then we'll find her," Kline assured. "Josiah Strong is still a wanted fugitive, and now that we've got a lead on him, we're going to see that he's finally brought to justice. Once that happens, we'll make sure that girl, and everyone else under his sway, gets the help they need."

But Redd wasn't so sure. Not about the FBI's ability to track down Strong or about Bekah's prospects for breaking the mental chains of her father's influence.

"Family," he muttered. "It's everything."

SEVENTY-FIVE

After receiving the expected all clear from the head of his security detail, the director of the Federal Bureau of Investigation thanked the agent and entered his home. The two-story Colonial, half a mile west of the National Cemetery, was probably too much house for him—a divorced workaholic who rarely used it as anything more than a place to sleep—but with housing in and around the nation's capital in such short supply, you took what you could get and held on to it as long as you could.

When he'd bought the house twenty-four years ago, it had been more of a home. He had been married then, already a senior FBI official, and even though he had worked long hours, there had still been enough time in the schedule for social events—weekend barbecues with colleagues, cocktail parties, and such— though if he was honest with himself, there had always been an ulterior motive. The twenty-first-century word for it was *networking,* and he had done it better than anyone else. So much so that he didn't need to do it anymore.

Now everything important happened in his office, and since he no longer had a wife making demands on his time, he was happy to spend twelve to sixteen hours a day there, coming home after dark every night to sleep, shower, and change clothes. He had a housekeeper who dusted, took his laundry to the cleaners, and prepared meals that he might or might not get around to eating, but he rarely saw her, and that was just fine with him.

He stripped off his suit coat and carefully laid it across the arm of a wingback chair in the front room, then loosened his tie as he made his way over to the bar, where he poured a generous helping of Laphroaig into a rocks glass. He downed it in a long gulp, then poured another. The peaty ten-year-old single malt was meant to be savored, but it had been that kind of day.

It had been that kind of week.

He'd spent the last few days fielding calls from elected officials and reporters, all wanting to know what the Bureau was doing about the sudden spate of violent terrorist activity gripping the nation. The attack on the federal prisoner transport in Oklahoma City, followed by a bizarre mass shooting incident that had all but destroyed a rural Montana courthouse, had everyone wondering what would happen next, and his message—"We've got it under control"—did not seem to be getting traction.

Unfortunately, he couldn't tell them the truth, that both actions had been carried out by a rogue faction of Homeland Security agents pursuing a private agenda. Only a handful of people would ever know that part of the story. Trust in the federal government was already at such a historic low that if the truth ever came out, it could conceivably spell the end of the United States of America.

Fortunately, he was well insulated from the blowback. Heads would roll eventually, but not his. He just had to make it through another news cycle or two, and then some new crisis or scandal would come along and give him some breathing room.

He carried his glass into the kitchen and had just opened the refrigerator door in search of a snack when his phone buzzed with a notification. The motion detector on the front porch camera had been triggered. As he was opening the app to look at the video, the doorbell rang.

He hardly ever had visitors anymore and certainly never so late—it was almost 11 p.m. But whoever it was, they would have had to make it past his security detail, so he wasn't too concerned.

His eyebrows came together in a frown when he saw the face staring into the porch camera. He set the scotch down and went to answer the door.

"Gavin?"

Kline gave a nod of acknowledgment. "Director. I know it's late, and I'm sorry for visiting you at home, but this is something that I don't think should be discussed at the office."

The director arched an eyebrow. "That sounds ominous." He stepped back. "Please, come in. Can I get you a drink?"

Kline shook his head. "Nothing for me, sir."

"I've got one already started." He motioned for Kline to follow and then returned to the kitchen. "Let's have it, then. What is so important that my director of intelligence couldn't wait until the morning briefing?"

"It concerns the Praetorian."

The director stared at Kline for a long moment. "Is that supposed to mean something to me?"

"It's the alias of the man responsible for the rogue faction at Homeland Security. Multiple independent sources have confirmed it."

The director gave a slow nod. "I see. Well, have you narrowed the list of suspects?"

"I have."

"It must be someone highly placed at DHS. Investigating them is going to be like negotiating a minefield." He picked up his glass, brought it to his lips, breathed in the smoky aroma.

"I know that you're the Praetorian, sir."

The FBI director stared at Kline over the top of his glass. "I'm sorry, what was that?"

Kline stared back but said nothing.

The director set his glass down. "I suppose paranoia comes with your job, Gavin, but coming here? Coming into my home with these unfounded accusations?" He shook his head. "Not a very savvy career move."

Kline remained statue still.

"Alright," the director finally said, breaking the long silence. "Since you went to the trouble of coming here, I'll let you present your case." He picked up the glass, took a sip, and savored it for a moment. "I'm curious to know what you think you found that's so damning it's worth sacrificing your career and reputation."

"I'm not the one who needs to worry about my reputation," countered Kline. "But I'd be happy to lay it out for you.

"I'll admit, you . . . that is to say, the Praetorian . . . wasn't even on our radar until someone started taking out the Twelve. One of my operators was interviewing Holton Fish just before an assassin took him out. He's the one that told us all about a highly placed government official, someone who knew where all the bodies were buried and who used that information for leverage against . . . well, pretty much everyone. Every elected official, every political appointee. You used your position to investigate them all, discover their darkest secrets, and then blackmail them to grow your own power, seeding your cronies into leadership positions in DOJ, Homeland, the State Department. That shadow government that all the conspiracy kooks are always going on about? You made it a reality. The real power behind the throne, just like the Roman Praetorian Guard.

"Unfortunately, you weren't exactly squeaky-clean yourself, and the Twelve found out about it. They were playing the same game, only what they held over your head wouldn't have just meant the end of your career, but probably jail time. So when we began investigating Anton Gage, they decided to cash in that chip."

The director folded his arms over his chest. "I'm the one who authorized you to conduct that investigation. I gave you a blank check to bring down the Twelve. I even covered for you when your son nearly caused an international incident in Spain so you could stop their crazy plan to poison the food supply."

Kline nodded. "You were in a tight spot. You couldn't openly derail the investigation. That would have been suspicious. So instead, you did the next best thing. You openly supported me and my team, but then undercut us by leaking our progress to Gage and the rest of the Twelve so they could stay one step ahead of us. We always knew we had a highly placed mole—"

"Rachel Culp was the mole," countered the director.

"She was certainly one of them. Your handpicked crony. But when she started talking, you shut her up permanently."

"The Twelve did that."

Kline shrugged. "She was in the federal prison system. It was an inside job. Just like the attack in Oklahoma City. The Twelve might have had motive for those attacks, but they wouldn't have had access to our travel itinerary. That could only have come from someone on the inside. Someone other than Rachel Culp, because she was already dead."

"I'm sorry, Gavin, but if that's the best you've got . . ." The director shook his head. "Don't even bother coming in to clean out your desk tomorrow. You're finished. Leave now, or I'll have you arrested for trespassing." He took out his phone, his finger poised to enter the speed-dial code that would bring his security detail running.

Kline, however, ignored the threat. "Creating your own Praetorian Guard inside HomeSec was a stroke of genius. DHS already has a reputation for playing fast and loose with civil rights, so if you needed any dirty work done, you could send Kilmeade and his hit squad to take care of it, and even if things went sideways, there would be nothing to lead back to you."

The director's finger remained poised over the phone. "You haven't presented a single factual piece of evidence that ties me to this alleged conspiracy."

"I'll admit, you covered your tracks well. When I heard what Fish had to say about the Praetorian, I immediately suspected you."

"Why?"

"Honestly? Because you're the smartest person in Washington. You came up through the ranks; you didn't play politics. You kept your job no matter who was sitting in the White House. That alone is suspicious behavior."

The director laughed. "You suspected me because I'm competent?"

"You don't become the longest-serving director of the FBI since J. Edgar Hoover by merely being competent. But as I said, it was just a suspicion. After what happened in Montana, I took a couple days to do a little digging to see if I couldn't find something more compelling. Chad Beaudette was very helpful in illuminating the inner workings of your secret DHS unit."

The director shook his head. "I don't know who that is."

"He's a disgraced former SEAL team sniper, currently working as a special agent for Homeland Security Investigations. He's also the only survivor of Kilmeade's assault team. He's in custody at a safe house in Denver right now. He admitted to taking part in the assault on the JPATS plane as well as the incident in Wellington. I think he's hoping to get an immunity deal by cooperating.

"But he didn't know the Praetorian's identity. For that I had to go elsewhere, and it turns out there are a few people who were only too happy to share what they knew about you. Including, I might add, some interesting video of you visiting a certain notorious party island."

The director's eyes narrowed. "Which one of them told you?"

Kline cracked a smile. The director wasn't denying it anymore. "Bill Dorfman."

William G. Dorfman was a software entrepreneur, business mogul, and number fourteen on the list of the world's wealthiest individuals. He was also one of the Twelve. Or had been until just a couple days ago.

"Dorfman died in a car accident yesterday," said the director, but then he understood. "Ah, you had something to do with that."

Kline didn't move, didn't say a word. He didn't need to.

"So, based on the testimony of a dead man . . . a man that *you* extrajudicially executed . . . you are accusing me of being this criminal mastermind. How do you think that's going to play in court?"

"I think we both know that you're never going to see the inside of a court-room. You're too well-connected for that."

The director looked at Kline again. "And yet you're here. Why? What are you after?" He nodded slowly. "Do you want in? Is that it? Do you even realize what I've been able to do as the Praetorian? What I've been able to accomplish with that kind of power? You said it yourself. Presidents come and go, but I remain. I'm the glue that holds this republic together. Surely you see that."

Kline said nothing.

"The Twelve . . . they're the real enemy. They treat America and the rest of the world like some kind of video game. Their best solution to social and environ-mental problems is to kill half the population. You know I'm right. Otherwise, you would have taken Dorfman into custody and done this by the book. No, you're just like me, Gavin. You're willing to make the hard decisions, get your hands dirty if that's what it takes.

"We can finish this together. There are only a few of them left, and they're all running scared. Together, you and I can deal with the rest."

"There is no 'you and I,'" replied Kline. "You're finished."

For the first time since Kline's arrival, the FBI director felt a tingle of fear. His finger was still poised over the phone, ready to push the panic button. "So you're going to kill me then?"

"I'm not going to kill you," said Kline. He nodded his head toward a corner of the room behind the director. "He is."

The director caught a fleeting glimpse of the blond man who had been stand-ing behind him unnoticed, before his world faded to black.

Epilogue

MONTANA

FIVE MONTHS LATER

For the first time in his life, Matthew Redd was at peace.

His war with the Twelve was finally, officially over. And he'd won. Much of that had to do with Aaron Decker, of course, but Redd had been the cabal's main target, and he'd held his ground through a blizzard and numerous waves of attacks and come out victorious.

He'd weathered the storm both literally and figuratively.

The Twelve's grip on the world's economy had ended more with a whimper than with a bang as the remaining members of the group, one by one, succumbed to death by natural or accidental causes. Redd guessed that was Aaron Decker's handiwork, but if so, the hits had been executed so professionally that nobody, not even the most conspiracy-minded news outlets, suspected anything other than a run of bad luck for men who, despite their wealth, couldn't buy immortality.

Oddly enough, Redd felt no sense of disappointment at being left out of the final accounting. As Gavin Kline had said all those months ago, he had done his part. It was time to focus on what was most important.

"I'm going to put on a pot of coffee," Emily called from the trailer's makeshift family room. Their house was nearing completion finally, and the contractor had told Redd they could move in within the month.

As far as Redd was concerned, he couldn't get out of the trailer soon enough.

"I'd make breakfast," Emily continued, "but we're out of eggs and bacon. All we have is lunch meat and, well . . ."

"You can't have it." Redd finished lacing up his boots, then stood from his spot by the door. He remembered from last time that lunch meat was off-limits during pregnancy unless it was thoroughly reheated, and Emily wasn't a fan of warm shaved turkey breast.

He rose from the bed-slash-chair and moved toward her, closing the distance in just two steps to put his arms around her. "I still can't believe we're having another baby."

"Junior isn't even going to be two by the time this kid is born. People are going to think we're nuts."

"Good thing we don't hang around many people."

Emily laughed. "Are you happy, Matty?"

Redd eyed her suspiciously. "You know I am. Don't I look it?"

The question had thrown him, because while he wasn't great at expressing his feelings, Redd felt blessed beyond words. He recognized the challenges of having two children who were both so young, but he was ecstatic to be building a family with the woman he loved.

"Actually," said Emily, tilting to meet his eyes, "you do. Been a long, long time since I've seen you so happy, in fact. It's wonderful."

He gave her a playful, flirtatious smile and then kissed her. "I could take my boots back off, you know."

Emily rolled her eyes jokingly, rebuffing her husband's not-so-subtle innuendo. "That's what got us into this predicament," she said, rubbing her stomach.

"It's not like I can get you *more* pregnant, Em."

She slapped him playfully on his shoulder. "You have work to do, cowboy. Get to it."

Redd turned and opened the door. Warm air filled the doorway, the early-morning summer rays just starting to peek above the mountains.

"I'll be back for coffee in a bit," he called over his shoulder as he started toward the barn.

"Hey, Matty!"

He stopped and turned. Emily was leaning out of the trailer, a determined look on her face. He walked back over to her.

"You should call Gavin."

"What for?" asked Redd.

"To tell him the news about the baby. Maybe even invite him to our house-warming party next month."

"He's the new director of the FBI, Em."

She eyed him wearily, a defiant hand suddenly placed on her hip. "He's your *father*, Matty."

"I'll think about it."

✖ ✖ ✖

Redd finished mucking out the last stall in the barn and sat down on J. B.'s old wooden stool. The cattle were grass fed, so the barn itself had an earthy smell to it, but it was far from pleasant. He'd long grown accustomed to the smell of manure, but even he had to admit that the heat made the scent especially ripe this time of the year.

As he worked that morning, his mind drifted from thoughts about friends and comrades he'd lost—most recently Rob Davis and other fallen members of the fly team—to what life would soon be like with two kids, but he kept coming back to Emily's admonition.

"You should call Gavin."

Shortly after the end of what some locals had taken to calling "The Battle of Wellington" and "The Shoot-out at the Stillwater Courthouse," Kline had returned to Washington, DC, to accept an interim appointment as director of the FBI, following the unexpected passing of his predecessor, who had died of a heart attack in his sleep. With his new duties, Kline had little time to communicate with Redd. The last time Redd had seen him in person had been at the funeral for Rob Davis, for which Redd had flown back to Washington, DC, just a week after the final showdown with Kilmeade and the Praetorian's assault team.

Redd had congratulated Kline on his promotion and then, commenting on the timing of his predecessor's demise, had asked the obvious question. "Was he the Praetorian?"

"Whatever gave you that crazy idea?" Kline had said cagily.

Nothing more was said on the subject. There was no need.

Kline had also advised him that a thorough search of the Montana wilderness in Stillwater County and surrounding areas had turned up no trace of Josiah Strong and his Family.

"We'll find them," assured Kline, and Redd thought maybe they would. With modern surveillance technology, it would be a lot harder for the fugitive to stay hidden now that the FBI was aware of his presence. In the weeks and months that followed, Redd kept expecting a phone call to say that Strong had finally been brought to heel, but that call never came. Nor had Kline called to check in or invite him back to the fly team.

Redd wasn't sure how he felt about that.

Theirs had always been a troubled relationship, but things had changed in the last couple of years. Since Kline had revealed to Redd that he wasn't actually a traveling salesman for a chemical company but in truth a high-ranking member of the FBI, the two men had spent more time together than at any point prior. Sure, part of the reason was their mutual interest in bringing down Anton Gage, but Kline had kept Redd involved and had even taken the extraordinary step of making him the de facto leader of the fly team, despite Redd's status as an outside contractor. There was no mistaking it as a sign of Kline's respect for his son's ability. But was it also meant as an olive branch?

The sticking point for Redd, the only truly unforgivable thing Kline had done—far more painful than deserting him when he was a kid—was his involvement in pulling Redd off the mission that resulted in his entire team of Marine Raiders being killed in an ambush in Mexico.

"I'm sorry for what happened, but I'll never apologize for protecting you. It's what a father is supposed to do, no matter what," Kline had said in the aftermath. *"You wait until that kid of yours is born; you'll see."*

At the time, Redd was too angry, too full of guilt to reason. But since then, armed with a fresh new perspective and looking at things through the lens of fatherhood, he was beginning to rethink the exchange. He'd done things since Junior was born that he wasn't proud of, all in the name of protecting his family. But would he ever do what Kline did?

Redd still wasn't sure. But he was willing to admit, albeit not out loud, that it wasn't nearly as black and white as he once thought.

Wiping his forehead with the back of his hand, Redd leaned back and thought over the list of things they'd been through together. Kline had been shot numerous times and risked his own life on several occasions, any of which could have gotten him killed, to protect Redd.

That wasn't lost on him either.

Neither was Kline's constant effort to find any reason to fly out to Montana or call him. He'd always done so under the guise of work-related tasks, but Redd knew deep down that Kline had made a real effort to be involved in his life. More than that, he'd even stepped up financially to help make sure that the debts J. B.

had racked up before his death were paid off. Without Kline, the ranch would have been lost. Redd had never truly thanked him for that. Mostly because he didn't know how.

Redd sighed.

Enough excuses. Just do it.

Leaning forward, he pulled his phone from his pocket. He hesitated a moment, then stabbed the screen with his thumb, finding Kline's contact before hitting Call.

The phone rang for several seconds, and Redd expected it to go to voicemail. He was surprised when Kline's voice suddenly boomed from the speaker.

"Matt, what's up?"

"Just checking in. How are things in DC?"

"Fine here." There was a pause, and then Kline continued, somewhat awkwardly. "If you're calling about work, I don't have anything new to tell you at the moment. We're going to form a new team soon, but there's still a lot of red tape to get through. But when the time comes, I'd welcome your input in selecting the team members."

"Actually, that's not why I'm calling." He took a breath. "Me and Em have some news."

"Everything okay?" Redd detected concern in Kline's voice and regretted the vague opening.

"Oh, yeah. No, nothing bad."

"Whew. So, what is it then? House finally done?"

"Builder says we can move in within the month, so getting close on that front. But no. We, uh, we haven't told anyone else this yet, but we're having another baby. Emily is pregnant." Redd swallowed hard, choosing his next words very carefully. "You're going to be a grandfather again."

As his words hung in the air, it wasn't lost on Redd that this was, in fact, the first time he'd ever referred to Kline as the grandfather of his children. Emily had, but it was a sentiment he'd always resisted. Simply put, to be a grandfather, you had to be a father—and for almost all of his life, he'd never considered Gavin his father.

A man of few words, Redd hoped Kline would pick up on the significance of his message. And a moment later, he did.

"Congratulations," said Kline, his voice thick with emotion. "You're a good father. Jim Bob would have been proud of you, and so am I . . . Matty."

For the first time ever, Redd didn't correct him.

The number of people who were allowed to call him by that name had finally grown to four.

"Thanks, Gavin."

"For your sake, I hope it's a girl—might save you a few bullet holes."

Redd laughed. "That's fair." Then he added, "Look, uh, Em is planning a housewarming party in a couple of months. I know it's probably a long shot given how busy you are and whatnot, but you're more than welcome to—"

"I wouldn't miss it for the world," said Kline, cutting him off, excitement filling his voice. "Just text me the date, and I'll be there."

"Okay, well. Sounds good." Redd suddenly ran out of words. "Well, I gotta get back to work, but I'll shoot you a text later on with the details."

"See you soon," said Kline.

"See you soon, Gavin."

And with that Redd punched off the phone, stood up, and got back to work.

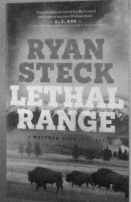

Author's Note

If you've been following along since *Fields of Fire*, then you might have had an idea of where things were heading in this book.

I have long said that the series had to start with *Fields of Fire* in order to introduce Matthew Redd, the Twelve, and set up that specific story arc. That was the natural launch point for this series. It's also true that *Lethal Range*, book two in the series, is the book I always wanted to write—something else I've admitted and talked about in interviews.

I knew when I was sketching out the stories for the first few books that *Lethal Range* was going to be a lot of fun to write because it introduces new characters like Junior, Mikey, Liz, Rubble, and Aaron Decker. If I could have squeezed them all into the first book, I would have. But in order to allow time for Redd and Emily to reconnect, establish Anton Gage, and flesh out the Montana setting, I knew those character introductions needed to wait. And that's okay because, in truth, everything was building and leading to *this* book, which is the hardest thing I have ever written.

At the end of *Lethal Range*, Redd wasn't at peace. He'd won the battle, sure, but the war was far from over. He knew the enemy was out there, planning to come for him eventually. When, he did not know. Nor did he know how great their forces would be.

But he was about to find out. (And so was I!)

When I sat down to write this book, I really challenged myself to deliver an experience that readers would find fulfilling whether they've read the first two books or are just now jumping into the series. But for those readers who've seen

Redd settle down and accept his role as a father and rancher, for those who have seen the family Redd and Emily have built together, I wanted you to really *feel* what he's feeling when someone reaches down and threatens to take that all away from him. I hope I was able to do that.

This book was intimidating to write, but I gave it everything I had. It's longer than my first two books because it needed to be in order to do the story and characters justice. Personally, I liken this book to an *Avengers*-like story. Everyone you've met in the series up until this point returns here, many of them joining forces in hopes of surviving an enemy force that will stop at nothing to get what they want most. And now you know how it all played out. The Twelve have officially been dealt with, closing that story arc for good. But don't worry, this series will continue, as things are far from over for Matthew Redd. I've got plenty more planned for him, Emily, Mikey, and the rest of the gang moving forward, and I'm really excited about the future of this franchise and where things are headed.

The next book, the fourth in the series, will come out next summer, and it introduces new threats for Redd, ones that will probably surprise you.

That's a long way of saying that while the Twelve trilogy is complete, in many ways, I'm just getting started with Matthew Redd. I wish I could tell you the title and details of book four, but unfortunately, it's still too early for that. What I can say, though, is this . . .

Buckle up for the summer of 2025 . . . because Redd will be back, and he's coming in hot.

Ryan Steck
August 31, 2023
Richland, Michigan

Acknowledgments

Once again, I would like to start out by thanking my Lord and Savior, Jesus Christ, who has blessed me far beyond anything I have ever deserved.

To my wife, **Melissa Steck**, who I adore in every way possible, thank you. You are my rock, and I cannot imagine life without you by my side. You inspire me every single day. And when the words don't come as easily, or the story isn't working, and I'm stressed to the max, you're *always* there to help me. It is your patience that has gotten me through the sleepless nights and hard times. I'm so thankful I get to do life with you.

To my children, I love you all so much. **Brynn**, **Jakop**, **Chase**, **Ryan Junior**, **Rylee**, and **Mitchell**, I am so honored and proud to be your dad. Watching you all grow has been the highlight of my life. Brynn was there when I typed *The End* on the first draft of this book, a moment I'll forever cherish. Ryan, Rylee, and Mitchell fueled me with laughter and hugs, and without you, this book would never have been finished. Now, let's have some fun!

To my parents, **James** and **Rhonda Steck**. What a year it's been. Dad, I am so glad you were finally able to retire. The kids and I sure love seeing you every day, and I cannot thank you enough for all that you've done to help me (and our family during some challenging times as I edited this book). And Mom, there were so many nights I was in my office working late, and you stepped in to take Rylee to gymnastics or take the kids out to dinner, or just stopped by to be with them. I am so thankful to be your son, but even more than that, I know how lucky my kids are to have you as their grandmother.

Writing this book was unlike anything else I've ever done. And frankly, the plot idea itself terrified me because I knew it was a lot to try and pull off. At times I wasn't even sure I could do it. As I wrote, I found myself constantly thinking of the authors who came before me, each of them paving the way while also raising the bar, and their works inspired me to finish *Out for Blood*. So, to **Vince Flynn, C. J. Box, Daniel Silva, Brad Thor, Jack Carr, Ted Bell, Brad Taylor, Mark Greaney, Gregg Hurwitz, Don Winslow, T. J. Newman, Connor Sullivan, Chris Hauty, Michael Connelly, Brian Andrews, Jeff Wilson, Joel C. Rosenberg, Marc Cameron, Lee Child, Andrew Grant, Simon Gervais, Don Bentley, Kyle Mills, Brad Meltzer, K.J. Howe, Anthony Horowitz,** and **Nick Petrie**—thank you. I'm sure there are others who I forgot, but the truth is, there are far too many to name.

I mentioned the late **Ted Bell** above, who died in January 2023, but I'd also like to take a moment and single him out here. First, there was nobody quite like Ted. A better writer there was not. One of the most gifted wordsmiths to ever step foot in the thriller world, Ted was larger than life and, in many ways, really was just an older American version of Lord Alexander Hawke. He was also a mentor to me, a close friend, and someone I admired fiercely. Ted conquered the advertising world before retiring and writing *Hawke* (2001), which launched his second career as a *New York Times* best-selling author. Never one to take himself too seriously, Ted opted for fun, over-the-top adventures, often telling me, "People don't want realism. Real life is hard! They want adventure. They want an escape!" I've never forgotten that. And I miss him every single day.

In the grand scheme of things, writing a good book doesn't matter if nobody knows about it. To that end, I owe my biggest thanks to the incredible team at Tyndale for all their hard work and support for me and this series. **Karen Watson, Jan Stob, Stephanie Broene, Andrea Martin, Natalie Wierenga, Wendie Connors,** and **Dean Renninger,** I thank you each for everything that you do for me and for Matty Redd. After I turn a book in, it falls on **Andrea Garcia,** the best marketing manager in the industry, to make sure people know about it. So, Andrea, my sincerest thank-you for all that you do—you're such a huge part of the publishing machine, and I'm incredibly grateful to have you on my side.

Likewise, my brilliant editor, **Sarah Rische, who deserves her own page of acknowledgments, frankly, plays such a critical role in shaping these books into what you, the readers, see when it finally gets into your hands. There's nobody I would rather work with, and yet again, Sarah, I thank you for making me a better writer, and this a better book.**

When *Lethal Range* came out, there were a number of authors who were kind enough to support me at launch, providing incredible endorsements and sharing about the book's launch on social media. It was a dream come true for me to receive a blurb from *the* Nelson DeMille. One of the greatest thriller novelists of our time, it meant so much to me that Nelson not only read and blurbed *Lethal Range*, but then posted about it on his socials. So did Larry Loftis, James Rollins, Steve Berry, Don Winslow, T. J. Newman, Gregg Hurwitz, and Jack Stewart. To all of you, thank you for your support.

To my agent, **John Talbot**, I continue to be so grateful that you took a chance on me all those years ago. Thank you not only for your unwavering support, but also for your friendship, and for being a mentor to me in so many ways. Many times you've gone far above the responsibilities of an agent, and for that I am incredibly thankful. You've listened when I've been stressed, been there to answer every question I've had along the way, and always handled every situation with grace and patience. Thank you so very much for believing in me, John. That alone gives me tremendous confidence.

To **Michael Derhammer**, thank you for always having my back, and Redd's. I appreciate you, my friend, and all that you do for me and my family. To **Emily Derhammer**, who happens to be Mikey's wife but is also one of my closest friends, thank you for everything. And little **Lainey Jo**, who my last book was co-dedicated to, you sure are something, sweet girl. Thank you for making all of our lives fuller just by being here. Thanks also to **Kurt Oman** and his wife, **Kaila**, for treating us like family and hosting a blowout Fourth of July party every year. To **Byrdie Bell**, my new friend and someone I am so glad to know, thank you for your friendship and support.

To **John Robinson**, who is a very talented writer, a world-class doctor, and an even better man, thank you. In many ways, John is the man, husband, and friend I aspire to be. A brilliant physician, John uses his medical knowledge as his ministry, and he was there for me countless times to answer questions as I wrapped up this book. Though we kept it pretty private, my wife had a number of scary and fairly serious health issues pop up while I was in final edits of *Out for Blood*, and on more than a dozen occasions, I sent her reports to John, or texted or called him with questions, concerns, or to translate the medical terms we were hearing. John, your friendship has been a godsend to me, and I thank you from the bottom of my heart for your calming presence and patience.

To that end, I would also like to thank our PCP, Jennifer Squires, as well as the Bronson Urology group and the brilliant minds at the University of Michigan hospitals, not to mention the staff at the Borgess ER, all of whom took exceptional care of my wife these last few weeks.

In addition to their stellar work, I would simply like to thank everyone at

Tyndale for keeping us in their prayers and for treating us like family as I had my attention pulled elsewhere while trying to finish the edits on this book. It was a challenging time, no doubt, but between encouraging emails from Karen and Jan's calm, steady levelheadedness, I never felt the pressure of a looming deadline. I cannot thank you enough for that.

To my **Aunt Marlene**, thank you for continuing to always be there for me. Whether it's letting me vent, offering advice and encouragement, or simply praying for me, I am blessed to have you in my life and appreciate every single thing you do for me.

And finally, to you, the **readers** . . . thank you for diving into my books and following Matthew Redd, Emily, Mikey, Liz, Gavin Kline, and now Rubble around as they deal with each dangerous problem together. It is because of you all that I get to tell stories for a living, and I am beyond thankful that you've spent your hard-earned money on my books, as well as your precious time to read them. I hope you loved *Out for Blood*. I gave this one everything I had, and now that Gage and the Twelve are out of the way for good, I'm excited to show you what the next chapter of Matthew Redd's story looks like next summer!

About the Author

RYAN STECK is an editor, an author, and the founder and editor in chief of The Real Book Spy. Ryan has been named an "Online Influencer" by Amazon and is a regular columnist at CrimeReads. TheRealBookSpy.com has been endorsed by #1 *New York Times* bestselling authors Mark Greaney, C. J. Box, Kyle Mills, Daniel Silva, Brad Thor, and many others. A resident of Michigan, along with his wife and their six kids, Steck cheers on his beloved Detroit Tigers and Lions during the rare moments when he's not reading or talking about books on social media. He can be reached via email at ryan@therealbookspy.com.

KEEP UP-TO-DATE ON NEWS
FROM RYAN STECK AT

therealbookspy.com

RYAN STECK

REDD CHRISTMAS

TURN THE PAGE FOR
BONUS CONTENT!

A MATTHEW REDD NOVELLA

PART I

MONTANA
DECEMBER 24, 2012

"Home is a shelter from storms—all sorts of storms."

—WILLIAM J. BENNETT, former US secretary of education

ONE

Standing by the window, watching thick snowflakes blanket the world around him, it finally sank in for Matthew Redd that this was the last Christmas Eve he would spend at the ranch with his dad before heading off to join the Marines.

Eight years ago, Christmas was just another day. No, actually, it was worse than that, because it was a day when his ten-year-old self was acutely aware of the fact that other kids were celebrating, opening presents, sipping cocoa with their parents, while he . . .

He was not.

Eight years ago, Christmastime was synonymous with disappointment.

Oh, his mother had tried. At first. But as she sank deeper into the grip of addiction, spiraling through a series of increasingly toxic relationships, holiday spirit was one of the first casualties. She had been the last.

Seven years ago, he had found her, dead of an overdose in the filthy bathroom of their trailer in a small and dingy mobile home park in Warren, Michigan. His life up to that point had been hard—and he had been hardened—but nothing could have prepared him for the pain of that loss.

Then, through connections that still weren't completely clear to him, Redd's biological father—a man he did not know but who clearly knew of his existence—showed up and sent little Matthew into the literal wilderness. Specifically, to Western Montana, to live with Jim Bob Thompson, a fourth-generation cattle rancher. It was a far cry from Redd's inner-city upbringing, but once he'd adjusted to the pace of ranch life, he'd fallen in love with it.

He had also rediscovered Christmas.

It hadn't happened all at once. A lifelong bachelor, J. B.—full name James Robert Thompson, and "Jim Bob" to everyone but Redd—knew the value of a simple, uncluttered life. It wasn't that he had any particular dislike for the holidays; he simply didn't have anyone to celebrate them with, so he figured, why bother? When Matthew had come into his life, he had eagerly embraced the idea of celebrating the season, though it had taken a couple years for them to work out exactly what their holiday traditions would look like.

They had a tree, usually one of the young pines growing on the hill behind the house, decorated with colored lights and simple ornaments. Neither of them was much good in the kitchen, so there were no cookies, candies, fudge . . . If they couldn't find it ready-to-eat at the IGA, they did without. They exchanged gifts, but simple, practical things.

Their one reliable tradition was the movies.

J. B., never much of a television watcher, had tried out a few holiday movies and television specials, but Matthew had little affection for the children's classics—Rudolph, Frosty, the Grinch, Charlie Brown—and little patience for mainstays like *Miracle on 34th Street*. He absolutely loathed *It's a Wonderful Life*, which he saw as a movie about a guy who gave up all his hopes and dreams to help a lot of ungrateful and undeserving people and was only appreciated when things got so bad that he actually gave up and decided to take his own life.

How, he often wondered aloud, *is that a positive message?*

Also, it was barely even a Christmas movie.

J. B. offered no defense, though he liked the movie and thought Jimmy Stewart was a fine actor and an even better human being.

They agreed, however, that *A Christmas Story* was an all-around terrific movie, often anticipating some of the film's most memorable lines. It didn't hurt that TBS ran a twenty-four-hour marathon every year, so there were plenty of opportunities for them to watch it together.

When he was just a couple years older, Redd discovered *Die Hard*, which he thought would be a great addition to their Christmas tradition. J. B. had taken some convincing.

"You're tryin' to tell me that *It's a Wonderful Life* isn't a Christmas movie, but *Die Hard* is?"

"Of course it is," Redd argued. "Think about it. It's about a guy who just wants to spend Christmas with his family."

J. B. received this with a skeptical frown but allowed it, though he did give a disapproving cough whenever Bruce Willis's character, John McClane, dropped an f-bomb.

Yes, coming to live with J. B. had restored Redd's faith in the holidays. Which was why this Christmas felt so bittersweet.

"Matty, come sit down by the fire. You need to warm up, Son." J. B.'s voice was permanently hoarse. Redd didn't know why for sure but assumed it was from constantly yelling at cattle, horses, and the government.

"Matty?"

Redd turned. "It's really coming down out there. Maybe we should bring the cattle in for the night."

"Cattle will be fine," said J. B.

He was seated in his favorite dark-brown leather recliner, rocking beside the fire, drink in hand—Wild Turkey, neat. He was wearing his standard everyday attire—green-and-brown flannel button-down, tucked neatly into his Wranglers. His black Stetson rested on the end table next to him, crown down to catch whatever good fortune fell from heaven.

Redd turned back to the window. The snowfall had really picked up over the last twenty minutes, and it was nearing a whiteout now, making it hard to see the barn that stood on the other side of the long driveway, some fifty yards away.

"Matty."

Matty. It was a name Redd hated. In fact, he'd only let three people call him that throughout his life. His mother, of course, had been the first. J. B. was the second, and in truth, it didn't bother Redd when he said it. No, the reason it bothered him today was because it reminded him of the third person who referred to him that way.

"I'm fine, J. B.," said Redd, the flames from the fire casting an orange glow across his face. "Really."

But that was a lie.

Redd turned his head, looking away from the fire. A strong wind gust swirled snow across the picture window next to him as the house creaked against the force of the storm.

Emily loves the snow. Won't be seeing much of that in Texas.

She'd been gone several months, but the hurt her absence had caused had barely receded. It came in waves, he found, with the majority of his pain coming during downtime when he wasn't working around the ranch. For that reason, he silently cursed the storm. Still, he knew it wasn't Mother Nature's fault. Fate had often been cruel to him but that didn't mean he felt sorry for himself. Redd wasn't built that way.

Emily Lawrence had been his high school sweetheart.

The words didn't begin to describe just how important she was to Redd. They were young, yes, but he loved her fiercely. And for a young man who'd only loved two other people in his short life, that was no small admission.

Emily had been the first person to welcome Redd to school a few weeks after he arrived in Wellington. Already an outsider, most of the other kids regarded him as a freak of nature, but not Em. She had been the first person to teach him how to ride a horse. She'd been his first kiss. His first lover. His first love.

He had let her call him Matty, too.

Now she was gone. She'd taken a scholarship to the University of Texas, leaving him behind. But her decision to leave wasn't the real reason for their breakup.

The year prior, J. B. had been thrown from his horse and broken his back. He wasn't the type of man to ask for help, and Redd wasn't the type to make him. No, Matthew Redd just stepped up without being asked, spending every moment he had caring for the herd and working to keep the ranch afloat. He'd saved the ranch but in so doing had pulled away from Emily, along with his best friend, Mikey Derhammer.

Now she was in Texas and well on her way to moving on from him. Redd had never even told her goodbye. Something he regretted deeply.

"Matty." This time, Jim Bob Thompson's gravelly voice was a touch louder.

Redd knew that his dad was worried about him. He, like J. B., wasn't big on talking, so the two never really discussed Emily or her leaving, but J. B. knew how hard he was taking it.

Redd sighed. Then he turned, walked across the room, and plopped down in the chair across from his dad.

"I, uh. Look, Matty . . ." J. B.'s voice trailed off.

"I'm fine." Redd offered a half smile. "Just worried about the herd."

"The herd will be okay, like I said."

"Well, I'm worried about the ranch, then."

J. B. eyed him before taking a sip from his crystal old fashioned glass, a family heirloom that had been passed down along with the house and property. "The ranch is okay too, Son."

Redd nodded. "It's just, you know, a lot of work." He wanted to add *for you to do without me* but didn't.

J. B. laughed. "Being a cowboy ain't easy. You just now figuring that out?"

"I mean it's a lot of work for *one* person."

"Ah." The room was silent for a moment, then J. B. set his glass next to his Stetson and leaned forward in his chair. "Matty, I'll be okay. You did a lot around here while I was hurt, and I can't thank you enough. But, Son, you don't need to worry about me. Or the ranch."

Redd let his gaze fall to the floor.

"Heck, I appreciate the help; you know I do. And if you don't . . . then I'm sorry I didn't express it more clearly. But I don't want you worried about me. I'll be okay. I've ranched my whole life. It's all I know. More than anything, I'll just miss you."

Redd's eyes snapped up. J. B. wasn't one to express emotions openly, or outwardly, for that matter. But then again, their time together was coming to an end. Not forever, of course, but they were nearing the end of an important chapter in Redd's life. And once he shipped out, a new chapter would start.

"I feel bad about leaving."

"Don't you dare carry that, Son. You're not George Bailey."

"George who?"

"Jimmy Stewart in *It's a Wonderful Life*. You always told me how you hated that movie because George . . . Jimmy had to give up on his dreams of traveling the world to take care of folks back home. Well, I won't let you give up on your dreams. Leastwise, I won't be your excuse for giving up on them." J. B. leaned back in his chair, crossing one long leg over the other. "You were born to be a Marine, and there is no greater honor than serving your country. It won't be easy, though, so you best get to stopping your worrying about me and getting your mind ready for what's to come."

It was true. And what he wanted more than anything else was to follow in his dad's footsteps. That was what J. B. had become in every way that mattered: his dad. But it wasn't J. B. the rancher who inspired him. Rather, it was J. B. the hero. Before he'd come back to operate the family ranch, J. B. had been a decorated Marine. Being one of "The Few, The Proud" had been Redd's dream almost as long as he'd lived with J. B.

"I'm ready to serve," Redd finally said. "I always wanted to be a Marine. Crazy how fast time flies."

J. B. nodded. "You know, your father was a Marine. Your real father, I mean."

Redd snorted. "Respectfully, J. B., I don't care what he was or is or wants to become. You're the reason I want to join the Corps."

A chuckle escaped J. B.'s throat. "Been a long time since I was a jarhead. Sure as hell wasn't always easy, but it made me tough. Strong. Got me ready to run this ranch."

"Maybe it'll get me ready to run it after you one day." It was something Redd had been thinking about for years, the chance to run the ranch when J. B. was ready to call it quits. Though, truthfully, Redd couldn't ever see the old man doing anything else. *"Cowboys don't retire,"* J. B. would say. *"They work till they die."*

"I sure hope not," said J. B. It wasn't the reaction Redd was expecting.

He doesn't want me to come back?

"Matty." J. B.'s voice turned serious again. "Nothing would make me prouder than to leave you this ranch. Hell, I ain't got nobody else to leave it to. But you, Son, are destined for far more than just ranching."

"But I love it here." It came out faster and more defensive than Redd intended.

"And I love having you. Still, a couple thousand acres might seem big when you're standing outside looking at it, but that's an awful small place to spend your whole life."

Redd dropped his gaze again.

"This is your home," J. B. went on, "and you are always welcome here. But don't you come rushing back just to help me. It's a big world, and you got a bright future ahead of you."

Redd sighed, the scent of fresh pine filling his nostrils. Earlier that month, he and J. B. had scoured the property for the perfect tree, then cut it down and dragged it inside. Every year, the Christmas tree sat at the same place—in the corner of the living room, next to the picture window. His first year there, they'd only had white lights on the tree. Redd had mentioned liking colored lights, and every year since, that's what they had decorated with.

It would remain there just one more day.

During their time together, Christmas had become J. B.'s favorite holiday, but his favorite day of the year was Christmas Eve. Redd suspected it had to do with the buildup of the holiday season. J. B. liked getting the tree up, then decorating different parts of the ranch throughout the month, but come December 26, he immediately started taking stuff down. Early on, Redd had asked his dad why he did that rather than leave it all up and enjoy it longer, and J. B.'s answer was as simple as the old cowboy himself. *"Christmas is over. No reason to leave it up any longer."*

Redd realized that was what made that brief window of opportunity—from Christmas Eve through Christmas Day—so special. It only happened once a year, and when it was over . . . it was over.

And when this Christmas was over . . .

"Well, I'll always come home for Christmas," he blurted out. "I can tell you that much."

J. B. smiled. "I would love that. However, good luck getting away once you're a Marine. You might get lucky and get leave for the holidays once in a while, but don't count on it."

"Guess I hadn't thought of that," Redd said honestly. He knew it was his last Christmas on the ranch *before* he shipped out, but suddenly he realized it might be years before he was back to spend J. B.'s favorite holiday with him. "How 'bout this . . . Every year, if I can, I'll watch our movies. And then, no matter what, I'll always call you on Christmas Eve. I promise."

"Deal!" said J. B., slapping his knees. "A Christmas Eve phone call so you can tell me what Christmas looks like wherever you're at."

With that, Redd let go of all his heartache, fears, and concerns. If it was the last Christmas Eve he'd spend with his dad for the foreseeable future, then the least he could do was try to have a good time and make a few memories.

And that was exactly what they did.

TWO

That was the last Christmas Eve I ever got to spend on the ranch with J. B., and man, is it a good memory to look back on. I was devastated that Emily had left. Mikey, who before a temporary falling-out was my best friend . . . one of my only friends . . . was with his mom visiting family up in Wyoming at the time, so it really was just me, J. B., and the cattle, but we made the best of it.

Back then, we had some Christmas traditions, but the holiday itself didn't mean quite what it does to me today.

Now, me and Em work hard to get the real message of Christmas across to the kids. Her dad usually leads a Christmas Eve service at church, and then we spend time as a family. It's less about the gifts, though I will admit, the best gift I've ever received once showed up on a Christmas Eve delivered by a man who I had no relationship with when I was eighteen, sealed inside a manila envelope. But more on that some other day.

Back to the presents . . .

J. B. was a simple man, which is one of the many reasons we got along so well. It never did take much to make him happy, and that year—don't laugh—all I got him was a can of Folgers and some double-A batteries.

J. B. had a little transistor radio he liked to carry when he was working the ranch. Sometimes he'd dial up a station to hear a little Johnny Cash or some George Strait.

He also loved Randy Travis. But mostly, he used the radio for weather reports. You get caught out in a winter storm in Montana unprepared, and well, you end up dead real quick. Take it from me, I know all too well about that. Not all that long after I mixed it up with the biker gang that attacked my wife and son on the road, I found myself in an even worse situation. I'll spare you the details, but basically, a bunch of goons who were out for blood followed me up the mountain in the middle of a blizzard, and it was one of the worst experiences of my life.

Who knows, maybe I'll tell that story one day.

But I remember that promise to J. B. like it was yesterday.

To be honest with you, I never imagined then, when I was just an eighteen-year-old kid, how difficult it would be to keep. Maybe you were smart enough to have seen it right away. How can someone give their word that, no matter what, they'll always call a loved one at a certain time once a year? But I'll tell you what, I always fought to keep it.

Anyways, the point here is that I'd give anything to go back and have one more Christmas Eve on the ranch with my dad. I didn't know that would be the last one, but even if I did, I can't think of anything I would have changed. We had a big dinner, got up early and tended to the herd, then came in and exchanged gifts. J. B. got me ammo. What else? That and beef jerky. Two can't-miss items any cowboy would be thrilled with.

So yeah, a memorable if low-key Christmas. And after that, I spoke to J. B. every year like clockwork. Never missed once.

But there was a time when I almost did.

Almost . . .

PART II

NORTHERN IRAQ
DECEMBER 24, 2015

*"No battle plan ever survives the first
encounter with the enemy."*

—COLIN POWELL

THREE

There was a ten-hour time difference between Iraq and Montana, which meant that even though it was 1500 hours—3 p.m.—on Christmas Eve for the men of second platoon, Battle Two-Seven, it was just 5 a.m. back home in Wellington. Way too early for Matthew Redd to make his customary Christmas Eve phone call to his dad.

Not that J. B. would be in bed. He'd already be out doing the morning chores, and since the old guy staunchly refused to own a cell phone—or set up a voice mail box for his landline—the odds of catching him during the early morning, Mountain Standard Time, were pretty slim.

Even that was too early in the day. To Redd's way of thinking, Christmas Eve—the evening before Christmas—didn't start until after sundown. However, in the three years since making his promise to J. B., Redd had learned the importance of flexibility.

"No matter what, I'll always call you on Christmas Eve."

The first year, he'd been on liberty for the holiday period, free to choose when to make the call. The other times had found him completely immersed in his duties, such that finding a working phone had been like a covert mission behind enemy lines.

The next year, he'd been in the middle of a weeks-long training exercise and had been forced to sneak through the California desert under cover of darkness until his phone had enough bars for him to make the call. If he had been caught out, it would have meant a "ninja punch"—non-judicial punishment—which might have resulted in a fine or a reduction in rank, or both. While that would not have been the end of the world, it was definitely not something a squared-away Marine like Redd wanted on his permanent record. Nevertheless, to keep his promise to J. B., he had been willing to take that chance. But this year posed a different sort of challenge.

This was the first time he would spend Christmas deployed overseas.

One of the first things Redd had done upon arriving in country was procure a prepaid cell phone, already connected to the local network, from a fellow Marine who was rotating back stateside. He had done this for the sole purpose of being able to stay in contact with J. B. and especially to make the annual Christmas Eve call. He'd thought about reaching out to Emily Lawrence but never found the right words. The same was true for Mikey Derhammer, who he missed but hadn't spoken to in years now. So, the truth was, Redd didn't have anyone else waiting for him back home.

With the exception of J. B., the Corps was his family and his life.

The coverage was surprisingly good at the forward operating base near Mosul, but out at the remote combat outpost—COP—to which Redd and his platoon had been deployed, the reception was spotty at best. If he stood on top of the perimeter Hesko wall and atmospheric conditions were just right, he could *maybe* get a signal, but standing up there, presenting a nice silhouette to enemy snipers, was not something he wanted to do even for a few minutes. Fortunately, the COP also had satellite internet, which Redd could use to establish a VoIP connection in order to make the call.

He figured he would call at around 2100 hours, just before his next sentry shift, which would not only allow J. B. time to finish up the chores but also give Redd plenty of time to watch both *A Christmas Story* and *Die Hard* on DVD.

He was just heading over to the chow hall to grab a few snacks for his movie marathon when a voice bellowed across the compound. "Redd! Straight to the TOC. Briefing in three minutes."

There was no mistaking the source of the shout—it was Staff Sergeant Gutierrez, Redd's platoon sergeant.

Redd immediately snapped to. "Roger that, Staff Sergeant," he said, turning on his heel and redirecting his momentum along a new trajectory. Neither his tone nor his expression registered even a hint of disappointment at having his afternoon plans thwarted—in truth, getting used to the unexpected had been one of the first lessons he had learned in boot camp—but inwardly, he felt a growing sense of unease.

A briefing meant a mission. A mission meant going outside the wire. And if past experience was any indication, there was no telling when they might come back.

I've still got eighteen hours to make the call, he told himself. *Plenty of time.*

FOUR

The platoon leader, 2LT Stern, waited until all the squad and team leaders were present to begin the briefing, which did not require even half of the allotted three minutes. As a fire team leader, in charge of just three other men, Redd thought it a little unusual that he was being included. Typically information flowed through the chain of command. The LT briefed the squad leaders, giving them the big picture of the mission, and then the squad leaders handed down a much more task-focused version of the same. The only rationale Redd could come up with was expediency.

When the last man filed into the crowded room, SSG Gutierrez called out, "At ease," silencing the low buzz of murmured conversation, and the lieutenant got started.

"An hour ago, an Army Special Forces ODA, working with Kurdish fighters near the border, reported contact with a substantial enemy force approximately fifty klicks to the northwest." He moved over to the large map tacked to the wall and tapped a spot near the Syrian-Iraqi border, only about two inches from the green pin that marked the location of the COP.

"They have sustained numerous casualties and are pinned down. Air support is on its way, but casevac won't fly until there's a secure LZ. That's *our* job. First squad will establish the LZ. Second and third will move to the location of the troops, engage the enemy, and begin transporting the wounded to the LZ." He let his gaze roam about the room. "Any questions?"

Redd had a lot of questions but knew better than to ask them. He was, after all, only a lowly corporal.

His squad leader, Sergeant Austin, had no such reservations. "You said we'll be facing a substantial enemy force. Just *how* substantial we talking here?"

The lieutenant nodded as if this was exactly the sort of question he expected. "Best guess is between seventy-five and one hundred enemy fighters, armed with mortars, RPGs, at least a couple PKs, as well as assorted small arms. Intel indicates that additional enemy forces may be moving to join the fight, so it's imperative that we get in there and get those men out, ASAP."

Another hand shot up. Redd cringed a little when he saw who it was. Corporal Dan Burgess, another fire team leader in third squad—Redd's squad.

Redd had no idea how someone like Burgess could have not only made it through boot but actually earned a second chevron. Redd had once overheard Sergeant Austin call Burgess an "oxygen thief," and the mental image had stuck. It was certainly apropos. The fact that Burgess, a lazy scammer who could be counted on to vanish whenever there was work to be done, had been put in a position of leadership was almost enough to make Redd question his faith in the Corps.

Almost.

Austin hissed a barely audible, "Burgess, stow it," but the lieutenant had already spotted the raised hand.

"Corporal?"

"Uh, shouldn't the QRF be dealing with this?"

It was something everyone in the room, Redd included, was probably wondering. There was always supposed to be a QRF—quick reaction force—standing by, ready to roll out at a moment's notice to assist other troops, no matter their affiliation, in the event of a serious incident. When assigned to QRF, the platoon remained in a state of constant readiness, geared up and in their trucks, just as if they were about to head out on a patrol, and then sat and waited for a call exactly like this. Since they weren't presently the designated QRF, Burgess's question was valid.

It was also something he never should have said out loud. A slacker's question, the equivalent of saying "not my job," something everyone else in the platoon knew better than to do.

Staff Sergeant Gutierrez made a hissing sound through his teeth, both a signal of his displeasure at the corporal's impertinence and a warning that there would be consequences. The lieutenant—a kid, really, about the same age as Redd himself—regarded Burgess with a frown but then answered, "The designated QRF is otherwise occupied. We're the closest element to the action, so we're subbing in."

"Now, if there aren't any more stupid questions," barked Gutierrez, "mount up. We roll in five. Let's go!"

FIVE

Four minutes and forty-odd seconds later, the M-ATV carrying fire team Three Bravo took its place in the line of trucks waiting to roll out.

To their credit, when Redd had relayed the lieutenant's orders to the Marines in his fire team, they had not uttered a single word of complaint, not even a muttered curse or groan. Instead, they had gone to work getting their rig and personal kit in order, which they did in record time.

It was only now, with that initial burst of activity behind them and the gravity of their situation finally sinking in, that they dared give voice to their disappointment.

"Man, this sucks," grumbled Private Chuck Maddox. His voice, transmitted over the internal comms to the noise-cancelling headset worn by each member of the fire team, was barely audible over the rush of air passing over his lip mic. Maddox was the only member of the team not buttoned up inside the armored vehicle. Only his legs were inside the M-ATV. The rest of him was up in the turret, behind a MK19 automatic grenade launcher. "Bad enough that we're spending the holidays over here," he went on. "But going outside the wire on Christmas Eve? That's just all kinds of wrong."

Another voice, that of the driver, PFC Evan Wang, came over the net, sounding much clearer than Maddox's. "I feel you, brother. I was just about to Skype with my mom and dad. Haven't spoken to them in a minute."

Redd pursed his lips, silently sharing Wang's pain. But then Private Jayson Heskett, from his seat in the back, weighed in with a rude noise and ruined the moment. "Skyping with Mom and Dad. Lame." He drew the word out, adding an extra syllable. *Lay-muh.*

Wang answered with an obscene suggestion, and for the next few seconds, the three Marines traded insults. Redd allowed it to continue for a while, knowing that the juvenile banter and ersatz conflict was just a coping mechanism to help the young men think about something . . . anything . . . other than the fact that they were racing toward a showdown with men who were going to do their best to kill them all. But after half a minute with no sign of letup, he barked, "Lock it up, Marines."

The comms instantly fell silent, but then Maddox spoke again, trying to get in the last word. "I'm just saying, it's an awful way to spend Christmas."

"I bet those SF guys out there would agree with you," Redd answered and was gratified by the silence that followed.

Ahead, the platoon had begun moving out. As soon as the truck in front of them started rolling, Wang slipped his foot off the brake, and their M-ATV began moving. A few seconds later, they were through the heavy welded-steel gate and weaving through the chicane.

Then Wang spoke again. "So I guess we're sort of a Christmas miracle for those guys."

"Then that must make me Santa Claus," chirped Maddox. "Ho, ho, ho!"

"More like Rudolph," quipped Heskett.

"Hey, I'll take it. He's the most famous reindeer of all."

Redd just shook his head.

It would take them about two hours to reach the objective, and Redd had a feeling it was going to be a very long two hours. He shot a glance at his G-Shock watch, noting the time.

15:12.

5:12 a.m. back home.

As long as he could make the call to J. B. before midnight Mountain Time—more than eighteen hours from now—he'd keep his promise. Eighteen hours sounded like a long time, but time was funny outside the wire. Minutes could seem like hours, while entire days could pass by, seemingly in the blink of an eye.

I should have called him when I had the chance, he thought.

SIX

Despite Redd's earlier misgivings, the cross-desert sojourn passed quickly and quietly. Once outside the sturdy walls of their compound, the Marines kept the chatter to a minimum and maintained constant vigilance, knowing that the enemy might be anywhere, might attack anytime. Redd kept one eye on the screen of the Blue Force Tracker unit—a computer-GPS device that tracked the location of every friendly element in the area, as well as providing navigational waypoints.

Redd had watched as the distance separating the convoy from the beleaguered Special Forces team shrank steadily. Very soon, maybe in just a matter of minutes, the little dots marking the location of the convoy and the SF team would overlap.

There were two more dots on the display—a pair of AH-64 Apache gunships, providing close air support for the SF guys. With their 30-millimeter chain guns and an arsenal of Hellfire missiles and Hydra-70 rockets, the Apaches could definitely take some of the heat off the ground force, but that was about all they could do. They couldn't take out every enemy fighter, and they definitely couldn't drop in and evacuate the wounded. Nor could they remain on station indefinitely. If the Special Forces soldiers pinned down by ISIS fighters were to have a prayer of surviving, it would be because the Marines of Battle Two-Seven established an LZ so that an Army CH-47 Chinook could swoop in and pick them up.

By the time they were close enough to see distant plumes of dust—kicked up by the rocket strikes and rotor wash of the Apaches—rising into the sky, the sun was almost kissing the horizon to the west. Redd figured they had maybe twenty minutes of full daylight, followed by half an hour of twilight. With any luck, they'd be on and off the objective before full dark.

The voice of the lieutenant came over the platoon frequency, ordering first squad to break off and establish the LZ while the rest of the element continued advancing toward the battlefield, still almost two kilometers away. Redd listened patiently as the team leaders acknowledged the order and when his turn came answered with his call sign. "Three-two, roger. Over."

Directly ahead, four M-ATVs broke off to the right, fanning out to create an overwatch perimeter. Redd switched back to the internal comms and said, "All right, everyone, heads on swivels. We're moving to contact."

Wang answered with an, "Oorah," to which Maddox added, "Get some!"

Redd appreciated the show of bravado. Even with all the armor surrounding them, it wasn't an easy thing to charge *toward* men who were sworn to kill you.

The battlefield was not the chaotic free-fire zone of a Hollywood blockbuster. There were no tracers or rocket trails crisscrossing the air, no buzz of heavy machine guns. But for the helicopter gunships roving overhead and the smoldering, twisted remains of several Toyota Hilux trucks—the Eurasian version of the Tacoma—Redd would have been hard-pressed to tell that there was combat in progress. This was just the reality of a prolonged engagement. Neither side could afford to burn through their ammunition spraying and praying. Instead, it was more of a waiting game—wait for someone to make a move. With the Apaches overhead, the enemy wasn't going to risk giving their position away by popping off a few shots at the men pinned down behind the damaged trucks or at the approaching convoy of armored vehicles.

But Redd knew they were out there, just biding their time.

The M-ATVs belonging to second and third squad quickly circled around the damaged Hilux trucks, spaced out to provide overlapping fields of fire from the crew-served weapons. As soon as Wang brought their vehicle to a full stop, Redd and Heskett exited from the right side—the side facing away from the enemy—and took up covered firing positions at the corners of their truck, while behind them the lieutenant and SSG Gutierrez, along with the platoon's two Navy corpsmen, approached the fighting position where the besieged Special Forces team was holed up.

Redd was only peripherally aware of what was happening behind him. His job—his entire focus—was on the open desert in the opposite direction, where the unseen enemy lurked, but he was still able to piece the scene together from overheard radio traffic.

Two of the Special Forces guys were KIA, and three had sustained critical wounds. Redd felt a lump rise in his throat at this news. Two American warriors would never see another Christmas. Did they leave behind wives? Children?

The situation was much worse for the thirty Kurdish fighters who had been working with the Alpha Team—ten dead, six critical. None of the survivors had escaped injury.

After several minutes of coordinating the situation, Gutierrez's voice came over the comms, designating two vehicles from second squad to begin transporting the most grievously wounded back to the LZ. Redd allowed himself to feel just a bit of cautious optimism. Slowly but surely, they were moving, getting off the X.

Then the Apaches left the sky.

At first Redd took this as a good sign. The gunships wouldn't head back to base if the enemy threat was still extant, right? But of course, there was a much more compelling explanation for their departure—they were running low on fuel and probably needed an ammunition resupply as well.

Still, while losing close air support wasn't ideal, it wasn't the worst thing in the world. Unlike the enemy, the Marines were fresh and ready to fight. The ISIS fighters were probably just waiting for night to fall so they could slink away with their tails between their legs.

Or maybe not.

A deep, thunderous, and all-too-familiar boom echoed across the desert. Somewhere out there, the enemy had just lobbed a mortar into the sky.

SEVEN

Redd screamed, "Incoming!" and then dropped flat and wriggled under the front end of the M-ATV.

It wasn't the first time he'd been on the wrong end of enemy artillery. The COP had been hit numerous times since their arrival, with both mortars and rockets, but those were always hit-and-run attacks, and rarely accurate. This was different. The ISIS fighters had been out there for hours and would have had plenty of time to dial in their target. Only the presence of the Apaches had forestalled their attack, and now that the helicopters were gone, there was no reason for them to hold back.

A few seconds later, the mortar shell detonated without any other warning. There had been no whistling sound to warn of its imminent approach. That was really more of a movie myth than reality because the shell was traveling faster than the sound it created. The only time you heard that cliché shriek was when the shell passed overhead and impacted well away from your position.

The ground shook with the explosion, the shock wave hitting Redd like a gut punch, and then a rain of rock debris and shrapnel rattled against the M-ATV's armor.

Close, thought Redd, *but not too close.* He took a moment to check himself for injuries, then called out, "Bravo, check in!"

Wang, still seated behind the wheel of the armored vehicle, was the first to reply. "I'm up."

"All good!" shouted Maddox from the turret. "But I've got no target!"

"Keep looking," ordered Redd. "Heskett, you still with us?"

There was a long pause, at least a second or two, in which Redd's heart dropped, but then the young private's shaky voice came over the comm. "I'm okay. Dang, that was close."

Before Redd could breathe a sigh of relief, Gutierrez's voice came over the platoon net. "Enemy firing position is approximately two klicks to the northeast—at our eight o'clock. Three-zero, engage and destroy."

Three-zero was Sergeant Austin's call sign, and the meaning of the rest of the order was clear—third squad was going hunting.

"Mount up," shouted Redd, wriggling out from under the truck. As he climbed back inside, he heard another, slightly frantic voice in his ear.

"Sergeant, shouldn't we keep one truck back as a reserve element?"

Redd almost swore out loud. It was Three-three. Corporal Burgess.

This guy.

The thought of going into combat with someone like Burgess . . . of having to count on such a useless Marine to watch his back . . . made Redd want to throw up.

Evidently Sergeant Gutierrez felt the same way because a moment later he said, "Yeah, probably better if you stay in the rear, Three-three."

Redd could hear the note of disgust in the platoon sergeant's tone, as well as the audible relief in Burgess's when he responded, "Roger that."

Redd surprised himself by saying, "Don't worry, Staff Sergeant. We've got this." Then after a glance over his shoulder to confirm that Heskett was aboard, he turned to Wang. "Let's roll."

Wang swallowed nervously but punched the accelerator and pulled away.

As the M-ATV raced across the featureless terrain, Redd felt like he was sitting on a live wire. Adrenaline coursed through his bloodstream. His muscles seemed almost to quiver with anticipation. He peered through the front windshield, scanning ahead for any sign of the enemy fighters he knew had to be lying in wait. A few seconds later, he saw a small plume of smoke rising in the distance. Another mortar had just been fired.

"You've got incoming!" he shouted over the platoon net.

He barely got the warning out before the interior of the armored truck was filled with the deep resonant *thump-thump-thump* of the turret-mounted MK19 throwing 40-millimeter grenades at the enemy position and a simultaneous rain of brass and links falling down inside the vehicle. By Redd's estimation, the mortar team was almost at the limit of the weapon's maximum range, but Maddox knew what he was doing. In the approaching twilight, Redd couldn't make out the line of slow-moving projectiles arcing out across the desert, but he had no trouble spotting the flashes of the 40 mike-mike rounds finishing their journey and detonating. In seconds, the area around the enemy position was curtained behind a wall of smoke and dust.

Redd was so fixated on the action to the front that he didn't even see the RPG round streaking toward them from off to the left, but Heskett did and shouted, "Incoming! RPG!"

By the time the words were out, the rocket-propelled grenade was already whooshing over the front end of the M-ATV. If the RPG gunner had waited a fraction of a second longer, the vehicle would have taken a direct hit on the driver's side. A moment later, Redd heard the sound of bullets impacting the armored exterior.

Maddox reacted quickly, spinning the turret around. The MK19 spoke again, hurling explosive rounds at close range toward the source of the incoming fire. This time, Redd could hear the explosions as the grenades tore up the desert. The enemy barrage ceased immediately.

Sergeant Austin's voice came over the radio. "Three-two, save some for the rest of us, over."

Redd craned his head around and spotted another M-ATV rolling along behind—Team Three's truck, equipped with an M2 Browning .50 caliber machine gun, which presently wasn't doing much of anything.

Redd grinned. "Roger that, Sergeant."

But as former CENTCOM commander General James "Chaos" Mattis— one of J. B.'s oft-quoted personal heroes—was fond of saying, "The enemy gets a vote," and evidently they voted to keep their heads down. The two armored trucks reached their objective without taking any more enemy fire.

Wang slowed the vehicle as he negotiated around several shallow blast craters—the result of Maddox's initial salvo with the MK19. The air was still thick with settling dust and the deepening twilight made it difficult to see anything, but then Maddox called out, "Oh, yeah. They're toast."

"What do you see?" asked Redd.

"Couple of dead bad guys, and something that looks like it used to be a mortar tube."

"Wang, stop here," said Redd. "Heskett, let's go take a look."

The young private was speechless for a moment, but then nodded and, in a small voice, said, "Oorah."

Redd switched to the platoon frequency. "Three-zero, this is Three-two, I'm going extravehicular for a BDA, over."

"Wait one, Three-two. I'm coming with you."

After the briefest delay, when Austin signaled that he was ready, Redd undogged his door and stepped out into the open, immediately bringing his weapon—an M16A4 equipped with an ACOG rifle combat optic and an M203 grenade launcher—to the high ready. Heskett exited right behind him, hefting his M27 Infantry Automatic Rifle and sweeping the open ground to their immediate right. A moment later, Austin joined them, accompanied by Three-one—Corporal Garrett Kovacs—and Lance Corporal Elijah Romero.

At Austin's direction, they formed a picket line and began crossing the impact area. Redd immediately spotted the remains of the ISIS mortar team and felt his gorge rise. One of the enemy fighters lay twisted and bloody but mostly intact—killed, Redd presumed, by shrapnel from one or more grenade detonations.

The other man had literally been torn apart.

"Tell your gunner that was some fine shooting," remarked Austin as he surveyed the damage.

Redd just nodded. He had been in a few engagements since the beginning of this, his first combat deployment, but this was his first time witnessing the aftermath of a battle up close. He reminded himself that these two men had just tried to kill him and his buddies and were directly responsible for at least some of the casualties sustained by the SF team and the Kurdish fighters.

It helped, but only a little.

EIGHT

The image of the dead ISIS fighters lingered in Redd's mind as they completed the hasty search. Only a few hours ago, when he'd been thinking about calling J. B., he'd composed a mental list of things he would talk about. The usual stuff: gripes about eating MREs and the austere living conditions at the COP, stories about the stupid things some of his squad mates did to deal with their boredom. Now he would have something else to talk about.

If he could find the words.

It occurred to him that, in all their long talks about Redd's plans to become a Marine, J. B. had only ever talked about his combat experiences in Panama and Kuwait in the most general terms. One time, Redd had asked his dad if he'd ever killed anyone. J. B. had looked at him for a long moment before replying, "Matty, if someday you decide to serve and, God forbid, find yourself in a situation where you have to take another man's life, you'll know why that's a question best not asked. Or answered."

Young Matty Redd had figured that was J. B.'s way of answering affirmatively without wanting to sound like he was bragging about ending another man's life. Now he wondered if there wasn't a lot more to the story.

The search turned up little of value. The insurgents carried no cell phones, maps, or documents that might have shed light on their affiliations or broader purposes. The mortar tube was cracked and inoperable, as were a pair of AK 47s. The only significant find was an ammunition pack with five Russian-made 82-millimeter mortar rounds, which Austin secured to prevent future use by the enemy.

Once that task was complete, the sergeant gave the order to mount up and they headed back to rejoin the main element. Redd urged his team to be hyper-vigilant as they approached the area where they had earlier taken fire, but if the enemy was still there, they elected to not draw attention to themselves.

As they rejoined the security perimeter, Redd was heartened to learn that the most critically wounded individuals had been loaded into second squad's vehicles and were already heading back to the designated LZ, and even more encouraged by the news that an Army Chinook was on its way, ETA thirty minutes.

Thirty minutes, thought Redd, checking his watch. It was 1721. Even allowing some wiggle room, the helo would arrive at about 1800. With a little luck, they'd be back at the COP by 2000 hours—10 a.m. back home. There would be a hot wash and of course routine maintenance duties, breaking down and cleaning the MK19 and getting the truck ready to roll out again, but that wouldn't take more than a couple hours.

And then he would call J. B. He didn't even care if was only afternoon in Montana—he wasn't going to risk something else coming up and closing the window of opportunity.

Plenty of time.

But time seemed to have ground to a halt. After another check of his watch showed that barely five minutes had passed, he vowed to stop checking.

The helo will get here when it gets here, he told himself.

Kneeling at the corner of the M-ATV, he viewed the desert landscape through his ACOG. It was almost too dark to see anything. Pretty soon, they would have to break out their NODs, finishing the evac under cover of darkness.

Not so long ago, that would have been a comforting thought. During the early years of the Global War on Terror, the US military had owned the night, but there had been recent reports indicating that ISIS had found a source for third-generation night-optical devices. While possessing night vision technology did not exactly level the playing field, it did mean the Marines could no longer trust that the enemy would only attack in the daylight hours.

The more time that passed without incident, the more anxious Redd became.

"Best guess is between seventy-five and one hundred enemy fighters," the LT had told them. *"Additional enemy forces may be moving to join the fight."*

They had only killed two of them. Where were the rest?

They're out there. What are they waiting for?

With the night continuing to deepen, Redd told his men to break out their NODs.

A few minutes later, Redd heard the crunch of footsteps behind him. He quickly turned his head, expecting to see SGT Austin or possibly even SSG Gutierrez, but the man moving toward him in a low combat walk was not someone from the platoon. He wasn't even a Marine.

The man wore desert cammies, with body armor and a chest rig, but there were no name tapes or rank patches. Like Redd, he wore a Kevlar brain bucket and NODs—a different design than Redd's PVS-15, monocular instead of binocular, but bulkier—which covered much of the top half of his face. The bottom half was hidden behind a thick black beard. The latter feature, more than anything else, identified him as one of the Special Forces guys.

That and the pressure bandage wrapped around his left biceps.

And the dark stain soaking the sleeve on the same arm.

"Which one of you is Redd?" the man asked. His voice was raw, his tone heavy. The pupil of his uncovered eye shone weirdly in the display of Redd's NODs.

Redd answered quickly. "I'm Corporal Redd, sir."

"Don't 'sir' me, kid," the man said wearily. "Your PL told me you might have an extra seat in your truck."

"Yes, sir." Redd grimaced and quickly corrected, "I mean, yes, we do."

He'd heard that spec ops guys often eschewed traditional military protocols, though an even more likely explanation was that the man was almost certainly not an officer but a senior NCO. Just like in a line unit, most operators were enlisted men, not officers.

"I've got some walking wounded who need a ride to the LZ. How many can you squeeze in?"

Redd's gaze involuntarily went to the vehicle. The M-ATV was configured to seat four—five if the gunner was included—which meant they had only one empty seat. That hardly seemed sufficient to the needs of the situation.

But then Redd saw a solution to the problem. "How many can you squeeze into three seats?"

"Three?" The SF soldier cocked his head sideways, doing the math. "Where you guys gonna sit?"

"There's just two of us aside from my driver and my gunner. We can ride on the step."

From his crouch at the rear of the truck, Heskett swiveled his head around and fixed his gaze on his team leader. With his NODs on, Redd couldn't see his eyes, but his body language was easy to read.

Ride where? Are these guys crazy?

Standing on the running boards of a moving truck, even one moving at low speed, was a borderline reckless thing to do, a recipe for disaster, and doubly so if they started taking fire, but in his head, it just made sense. They had to get everyone to the LZ as quickly as possible. Multiple shuttle runs with just one or two at a time would only prolong their time on the X, giving the enemy time to organize another attack. Heskett would just have to deal with it.

The soldier regarded him for a long moment, then nodded. "Appreciate it, kid."

He turned and shuffled away, presumably returning to the casualty collection point. When he came back just a few minutes later, he was trailed by five young, dark-haired men wearing old-school woodland-pattern BDUs and a mishmash of old Army surplus gear. None of them wore NODs, and Redd could see the haunted looks in their uncovered eyes. Every single one of them had at least one bandage wrapped around a limb, or covering a head wound, and one of them, though conscious and alert, had his arms draped over the shoulders of two of his comrades, unable to walk on his own.

The SF soldier opened the door of the M-ATV and helped the young men climb inside. All five of them somehow managed to fit into the rear seats. Redd felt a pang of sympathy for the wounded men, packed in like sardines. When the last man was inside, the soldier closed the door and then turned and leaned back against the side of the truck as if dead on his feet. He closed his eyes—or at least the one eye that was visible—but after a few seconds opened them and gazed at Redd. "We should be rolling out pretty soon."

"Roger that."

The man stared back at him for a moment, then managed a tired smile. "I can tell it's killing you not to 'sir' me. The name's Mike."

Without even thinking, Redd said, "That's my best friend's name. Well, we call him Mikey." Even as the words were uttered, Redd felt both silly and a little sad. Silly for thinking that this snake-eater would give a rip about Redd's personal life and sad because what he had just said wasn't really true. He hadn't spoken to Mikey Derhammer in years.

But the other man just chuckled. "Call me 'Mikey' and we're gonna have a problem."

"No, s—I mean, uh . . . You got it, Mike."

Mike nodded and then tilted his head back and closed his eyes again. Redd thought he looked like he was asleep on his feet.

SSG Gutierrez's voice broke over the net. "All elements, saddle up and get ready to roll out."

Even though he'd been expecting it, Redd felt a surge of relief at the order. Finally, they were moving again. There were few things in the world that a Marine hated more than sitting and waiting.

He moved back from the corner of the truck and opened the door, gesturing for Mike to climb in.

But the soldier just shook his head. "Nah, kid. I appreciate the offer, but that's your seat. I'll ride coach."

"You're wounded. I'm not. Get in."

Mike laughed. "I've fallen off better rides than this one. I'll be fine."

Redd saw that he wasn't going to change Mike's mind, but he couldn't imagine choosing the comfort and safety of the interior when others had to take their chances in the open, so he shrugged and then looked past Mike. "Heskett, get up here. You get the shotgun seat."

Heskett's expression went from surprise to relief to guilt, all in the space of a few seconds. "I'm good riding outside," he said, though the slight quaver in his voice suggested otherwise.

"It wasn't a suggestion," barked Redd. "Get in."

Heskett got in.

As Redd closed the door, he saw Mike staring at him with a lopsided grin. "You're all right, kid."

Redd laughed. "Thanks. Just call me Matt or Redd, though. Keep calling me 'kid' and we're definitely gonna have a problem."

NINE

When the squad finally rolled out, Redd and Mike weren't the only ones hanging off the side of their M-ATV. All three of the trucks were packed with noncritically wounded Kurdish fighters and SF guys, and all three had at least two shooters riding on the running boards.

They rolled slow, barely faster than walking speed, which allowed the outside riders to hold onto the truck with one hand while keeping the other on their weapon. At the first sign of enemy activity, they would drop to the ground and engage on foot. The crawling pace also served to keep the dust down, which increased visibility.

Redd scanned the desert to the right, searching for any signs of enemy presence and taking note of large rocks and terrain features that might provide cover and concealment. He saw plenty of the latter, but none of the former. Neither observation was a source of encouragement.

Five minutes passed, then ten. In the far distance, Redd could make out the white glow of IR chemlights marking the location of the LZ, and then, gradually, he was able to distinguish the vehicles and Marines of first squad. Five more minutes brought them inside the secure perimeter, where second squad had established a secondary CCP—casualty collection point—where the most seriously injured had been offloaded and were being monitored by the platoon's

Navy corpsmen. When the M-ATV came to a halt, Redd and Mike both hopped down and began helping the wounded out of the vehicle so that, when the transport arrived, no time would be wasted getting everyone aboard.

After that, it was just a waiting game. Despite his earlier vow, Redd found himself checking his watch again.

Almost 1800. The helo was running behind schedule.

Come on, he thought. *Let's get this done.*

As if in response to his silent summons, the distinctive, rhythmic thump of rotor blades buffeting the air became audible, growing louder with each passing second. Redd scanned the sky to the south, looking in vain for the incoming aircraft. The helo operated without running lights, the pilots relying on night vision devices just like the Marines on the ground.

Despite running under blackout conditions, the CH-47 Chinook was no stealthy attack helicopter. Almost a hundred feet long, with two sixty-foot-diameter rotor assemblies, the enormous aircraft had a lift capacity of more than ten tons—which meant it could transport between thirty and fifty passengers, depending on whether they were fully equipped combat troops. To Redd, the Chinook looked like nothing so much as a big twin-rotor school bus.

He was generally not a fan of helicopters, which always seemed one minor malfunction away from dropping like a stone, but his apprehension was directly proportionate to the size of the aircraft. To his way of thinking, the bigger the bird, the harder the fall. The same went for the Corps' primary transport aircraft, the V-22 Osprey—which largely served the same purpose as the Chinook, but with the added feature of being able to tilt its rotor assembly forward ninety degrees so that it could travel like an airplane after takeoff.

But more than the fear of crashing, the thing that Redd most disliked about flying was giving up control. On the ground, if something bad happened—like contact with the enemy—he could do something about it. Aloft, he was at the mercy of the aircraft crew and, of course, gravity. Fortunately, on this night, he would be keeping his feet firmly on the ground.

Judging by the increasing noise level, he figured the Chinook was still a few miles out, which meant it would be setting down in the LZ in just a couple minutes.

The first indicator of trouble was a sudden burst of light so bright that Redd involuntarily ripped his NODs off. The afterimage of the flash lingered on his retinas, a big green blob, through which he could still see what looked like a burst of fireworks falling from the sky.

He knew exactly what he was seeing. The helicopter had just released a burst of flares, a countermeasure designed to fool a heat-seeking missile. Antimissile countermeasures released automatically when a launch was detected, which meant someone on the ground had just fired at the aircraft.

Suddenly, another bright flash lit up the sky. Though not as brilliant as the flares, which were still falling like white-hot raindrops, it nevertheless revealed, just for an instant, the outline of the big helicopter, juking away in a desperate and ultimately futile bid to evade the missile that had detonated right behind it.

Darkness returned with the finality of a falling guillotine blade, but Redd didn't need eyes to know what had just happened.

An enemy missile had brought down the transport helicopter.

PART III

NORTHERN IRAQ

"Marines don't know how to spell the word 'defeat.'"

—JAMES MATTIS

TEN

Strangely, in the dark nothingness that followed, Redd recalled something J. B. had taught him about thunder and lightning.

"When you see the flash, start counting in your head until you hear the thunder. Light travels faster than sound. If it takes five seconds, you know the storm is a mile away. Less than that, and you could be in for some trouble."

Lightning was a problem in Montana, especially in the summer months, when electrical storms could come out of nowhere, so it was a critical lesson for a young man growing up on a ranch.

It was just as critical in a war zone.

A wave of sound arrived—the boom of a missile launch, the rapid-fire pop and hiss of flares explosively ejected from canisters aboard the Chinook, the much louder detonation of the missile itself, and then a second or two later, the terrible sound of the helicopter impacting on the desert floor.

Redd had not consciously counted the interval between "lightning" and "thunder," but he knew that it hadn't been very long at all. Five seconds? Maybe, but definitely not much longer than that.

The significance of this triggered a cascade of dire revelations.

The Chinook had come down only about a mile from the LZ. The helicopter had come in from the south, along a route that had been considered safe.

The enemy had somehow flanked them, moved around to cut off not only the approach to the LZ but also their escape route.

And they were close.

Yet there was an even more ominous aspect to this development.

The Chinook . . . the helicopter that had been coming to bear away dozens of wounded American soldiers and Kurdish fighters . . . had just been destroyed, likely killing everyone aboard. Its destruction almost ensured that more of the wounded would die. And none of the rest of them would be going anywhere, anytime soon.

For what seemed like a long time—but was probably no more than a second or two—the entire platoon seemed gripped by a collective paralysis.

Then Mike swore aloud and broke the spell. "That was a MANPAD. They've got freaking MANPADS."

MANPAD—man-portable air defense system—was a catchall term for any kind of surface-to-air missile that could be easily transported and fired by an infantry element. ISIS wasn't supposed to have them, but evidently they did.

Mike's identification of the weapon system brought with it a host of second-order problems, but none of those were of immediate concern to Redd and his fellow Marines. What mattered was that the enemy had just attacked again, and it was their job to respond in kind.

Gutierrez barked over the platoon freq, "Three, move out. Find and engage that missile team."

Austin quickly seconded the order. "Mount up, Three. We're rolling."

Redd fumbled for his NODs, switching them off and on again to reset the device, then swiveled them down over his eyes. PVS-15s utilized autogating technology and were designed to shut down if exposed to bright light in order to prevent damage, but either the phosphor tube or Redd's own retinas still carried an afterimage of the dazzling but ultimately ineffective flares. Still, the NODs allowed him to pierce the veil of darkness as he prepared to once more engage the enemy.

But even as he was sliding back into the front seat of the M-ATV, another flash of light in the distance caught his eye—not an explosion, and nothing bright enough to overpower the NODs again, but a distinctive shaft of light connecting earth to sky. An infrared targeting laser.

For a fleeting moment, Redd thought that what he was seeing was part of the enemy's missile system, but then Gutierrez's voice sounded in his ear. "Three-zero, I've got a FRAGO. CAS just took out the missile team, but we need to get to the wreck and check for survivors."

Redd understood now that the laser had not come from an enemy weapon but rather from a friendly aircraft, most likely another Apache gunship flying escort for the ill-fated Chinook.

A lot of good it did them.

"On it," replied Austin.

Redd looked back to make sure that Heskett was aboard and was only a little surprised to see Mike sitting in the other empty seat. He acknowledged the soldier's presence with a nod, then turned to Wang. "Drive."

As the M-ATV peeled off, leading the charge out across the desert, Redd heard Burgess's voice over the comms, asking if he should stay behind as a reserve element. Redd rolled his eyes in disgust but was gratified to hear Gutierrez's sharp reply. "Second squad is the reserve element. Get out there, Three-three."

With his NODs fully functional again, Redd could easily make out a column of smoke rising from the desert floor, marking the crash site. His estimate of the distance to the wreck hadn't been far off—if anything, he'd overestimated. In less than two minutes' time, they closed in on the wreckage. Wang drove around it in a wide circle before finally coming to a stop about thirty yards away.

As he dismounted, Redd could hear the beat of the Apache gunship's rotors as it circled overhead, looking for more enemy fighters to engage. That the aircraft's guns remained silent did not necessarily inspire confidence. The enemy was still out there. Hiding. Waiting.

The Chinook lay on its left side and looked surprisingly intact. But for the fact that the rotor blades had all snapped off and now lay in pieces scattered around the aircraft, and for the enormous hole where the starboard engine nacelle had been and from which black smoke continued to pour, Redd might have believed it possible to simply roll the helicopter over and get it flying again.

As soon as the M-ATV stopped, Redd threw his door open and began a tactical approach to the aircraft. He immediately smelled both the acrid odor of plastic and metal burning and the distinctive kerosene tang of spilled JP8 fuel. The realization that the Chinook was now a firebomb just waiting to ignite caused him to hesitate, but only for a moment. If any of the Chinook's crew still lived, they were inside that firebomb.

He closed the remaining distance in seconds, moving to the front end where he could look through the Herculite windscreen and into the cockpit where the pilots were still strapped into their seats. The man in the right seat hung motionless against his restraints, but the man on the left, crammed down against the interior wall, was stirring.

Still alive.

Redd heaved himself onto the exterior of the fuselage and wriggled up to the open front hatchway. The interior of the aircraft was filled with smoke, so he sucked in a deep breath of fresh air, then lowered himself through the entrance.

He immediately saw the form of a crew member, crumpled against the now-horizontal left wall of the aircraft. There was a safety line attached to his belt, but this had done little to protect him during the crash. Judging by the unnatural angle of his head, Redd guessed that the man's neck was broken, but he took a few seconds to check for a pulse anyway.

Nothing.

Another brave warrior, gone.

Shaking off his despair, Redd crawled through the cockpit and saw the man in the left seat fumbling with his restraints. He still wore his flight helmet and the attached night vision gear was still in place, but he didn't appear to be aware of Redd's presence.

"I'm here to help," Redd said, using a little of the breath he was still holding.

The helmeted head swung toward Redd, bobbing uncertainly. "My NODs switched off," the man said, his voice hoarse from the smoke. "Can't see a thing."

"Just hold still." Redd drew his KA-BAR and carefully inserted it between the pilot's body and the heavy webbing of his five-point safety harness. As he sawed through the belts, Redd began to feel the discomfort of a breath held too long and finally surrendered to the urge to breathe. The acrid smoke burned a little but was tolerable. "Okay, you're free. Are you hurt?"

"Yeah," groaned the man. "I feel all busted up."

"Think you can move?"

The man struggled to reposition himself but immediately let out a wail of pain.

"All right, just sit tight. Let me check on the other guy." He twisted around and looked up at the second pilot, who still hung suspended above him.

The first pilot grunted an affirmative, then added, "What about Peralta? The crew chief?"

"Was he in the back?"

"Yeah."

Redd shook his head but then, realizing that the man couldn't see him, said, "He didn't make it." Then, because he knew he had to keep the man focused on the living, he asked, "Anyone else aboard?"

"Just the three of us."

Redd nodded absently, then reached up to the man in the right seat, squeezing his shoulder and giving it a gentle shake. He felt immeasurable relief when the man jerked suddenly and began flailing his arms as if waking from a dream of falling.

Redd maintained his grip on the man. "It's okay," he said. "You're okay. I'm going to get you out of here."

The assurance had the desired effect, calming the man. He relaxed, then reached up to his helmet and began fumbling with this NODs.

"Don't try to move just yet," advised Redd. "I will get you out of here. I just need to figure out how we're gonna do that."

Realizing that he would never be able to manhandle both men out through the side hatch, Redd reversed his position so that his feet were facing the front windscreen's center pane. Then, with as much power as he could muster, he pistoned his heels into the composite windows, striking with enough force to pop the window out of its frame.

That was when he noticed Mike and several Marines waiting just outside. "Dang," remarked the soldier. "You just like to jump right in with both feet, don't you?"

Redd thought it sounded like a compliment, so he allowed himself a small smile. "That's how things get done."

But his glib reply hid a deeper emotion, one that he wasn't comfortable expressing.

Too many brave men had died this night. Too many families back home would soon receive the worst news ever, and on Christmas, no less.

So yeah, if it meant saving just one life, bringing one father or husband home alive, then Matthew Redd was definitely going to jump in with both feet.

It was the least he could do.

ELEVEN

With help from the Marines outside, the evacuations of the Chinook's flight crew, including the remains of Crew Chief Peralta zipped up in a black body bag, continued apace. While Redd helped from the inside, SGT Austin located a fire extinguisher and sprayed down the smoldering wreckage of the starboard engine to prevent the spilled fuel from igniting.

When the offload was complete, Austin directed Redd to oversee the recovery of the aircraft's weapons—three M240 machine guns—along with a few thousand rounds of linked 7.62-millimeter ammunition. The guns all used the standard pintle mount, and once disconnected from the remote trigger, the two mounted in the nose were easily enough removed. The 240 mounted to the rear deck showed signs of impact and fire damage, so Redd made the decision to leave it in place to be destroyed along with the broken helicopter. Standard operating procedure for any piece of military hardware that could not be recovered from the field was to use incendiary grenades to burn everything to slag.

Once the salvageable weapons were removed, Austin called the entire squad together. Redd heard an uncharacteristic note of apprehension in the sergeant's voice and knew that he wasn't going to like what his squad leader had to say.

"Listen up," said Austin. "Here's our situation. HQ isn't going to send another casevac. Not tonight, anyway. Not until we can guarantee a secure LZ, and that's not going to happen anytime soon. Unfortunately, a lot of our wounded won't last the night if we don't get them to a med unit. So we're gonna load the wounded back onto the trucks and drive them out ourselves."

"There's not enough room!" blurted Burgess.

"That's right," replied Austin, ignoring his subordinate's lapse in discipline. "That's why some of us are staying behind. We'll dig in here and wait for relief to arrive."

Redd took a step forward. "I'll stay."

Austin shook his head. "I'm not asking for volunteers. The roster is already set. All drivers and gunners will stay with their trucks. TLs and automatic riflemen will be in the stay-behind element, which I will be commanding."

Redd did some quick mental math. There were three squads in the platoon, and three fire teams in each squad. That meant eighteen Marines—nineteen if Austin was included—would be giving up their seats so that others, the most critically wounded, would have a chance at surviving the night.

"This isn't a suicide mission," Austin went on. "The enemy doesn't usually fight after dark, but even if they decide to mix it up, the LT believes that we can hold out against a force as great as four to one. So do I."

Not great odds, thought Redd, *but not impossible.*

Not everyone agreed, however. "Four to one?" muttered Burgess. "There's just nineteen of us—"

"Twenty," Mike interjected, breaking his long silence. "I'll stay with you guys."

"Against how many?" pressed Burgess. "Eighty? A hundred?"

"We held out against these idiots for hours waiting for you to show up. They might have shot us up pretty bad, but we gave as good as we got. I doubt there's more than fifty of them left, and a lot of them have probably lost their will to fight."

"Burgess," snapped Austin. "You can snivel on your own time. You're a Marine. Act like it."

Burgess, looking chastened, said nothing more.

Austin knelt and used the blade of his KA-BAR to sketch out a crude diagram of the crash site, assigning his three team leaders to begin setting up fighting positions around the wreckage. The two recovered machine guns would be set up on tripods at the front and rear of the wreck, and once those overwatch positions were established, teams would be sent out to emplace M18A1 claymore antipersonnel mines all around the perimeter.

The plan was solid, and the more Redd heard, the more confident he felt.

They were fresh and ready to fight, while the enemy forces had been out in the open for hours and the few victories they'd achieved had cost them terribly.

We can do this, Redd told himself, and as he moved out with Heskett to his assigned fighting position, for the first time in what seemed like a long time, he checked his watch.

Almost 1900 hours.

The platoon would probably transport the wounded directly to the medical facility in Mosul, a trip that would take about three hours. Figure another hour to refuel and refit, three hours to come back and pick up the stay-behinds, and then two more to get back to base.

Nine hours.

That would put Redd back in the COP at about 0400—6 p.m. in Montana. Even allowing for a visit from the notorious "Mr. Murphy," there would still be plenty of time to keep his promise.

TWELVE

Once the convoy was gone, and with it the Apache gunship, an almost surreal quiet fell over the crash site. Austin had ordered the Marines to observe strict noise and light discipline not only so that they would be able to hear the enemy coming, but also so as not to betray their own position and numbers. But the absence of sound seemed to have extended to the rest of the world as well. No buzz of insect wings, no skittering of rodents or lizards moving about the desert floor. The hush was so absolute that Redd could hear his own heartbeat.

"Not a creature was stirring," he thought mordantly. *Silent night is right. Heckuva way to spend Christmas Eve.*

A long hour passed, and Redd heard the crackle of someone breaking squelch on the comms. Each of the fire team leaders carried an encrypted PRC-148 MBITR radio unit, capable of reaching higher headquarters if connected to a satellite antenna, but presently useful only for local transmissions. The sender was Austin, calling for a radio check. One by one, the team leaders reported in, whispering their team identifier.

Another hour of silence followed, punctuated by another scheduled radio call. Then another.

By prior arrangement, he and Heskett took turns checking in with the other at fifteen-minute intervals to ensure that neither of them fell asleep. Initially,

Redd wouldn't have believed he would have trouble staying awake, not with the threat of enemy in the area still extant, but the enforced inaction sapped his resolve. As a fourth hour passed, Redd's thoughts began to drift, and his eyelids began to droop with increasing frequency. Under any other circumstances, he would have done something physical to wake himself up—just standing up or doing some push-ups—but anything like that would have made too much noise.

A tap on his shoulder startled him back to full wakefulness. He swung his head around to meet Heskett's gaze and gave a thumbs-up. Heskett nodded in return and then returned his attention to their sector of fire. Redd did some isometric stretches, then checked his watch, noting the time.

2330.

"Soon it will be Christmas Day."

Redd grimaced as the song began playing, unbidden, in his head.

Well, maybe that will help me stay awa—

"All elements, this is Two-one. I have movement at eight o'clock. Three hundred meters."

The unexpected radio call sent a surge of adrenaline through Redd's bloodstream, flushing away any lingering drowsiness. In a second, he was wide awake and completely alert. The fighting positions had been oriented with true north as twelve o'clock. Eight o'clock was to the southwest. Redd and Heskett were positioned at five o'clock, facing south-southeast, which meant they didn't have a good line of sight on the visual contact, but Redd craned his head around and scanned the area, hoping to catch a glimpse.

"Looks like four individuals," continued the second squad team leader. "AKs. Black do-rags and woodland cammies."

ISIS fighters didn't have a standard uniform, but black headgear and surplus camouflage was about as close as they got.

"Yeah, they're heading our way."

"Roger, Two-one," replied Austin. Redd thought he heard someone murmuring in the background—probably Mike—and after a brief pause, Austin went on. "Sounds like a scouting party. Probably coming to pick over the helo wreck. When they get within a hundred meters, take them out."

"Should I hit them with the claymores?"

"No. Controlled pairs only. Everyone else, keep watching your sectors. Once the shooting starts, things could get real hot, real quick."

Redd put his eye to the ACOG on his rifle and began scanning from left to right and back again, looking for a target. The 4X power magnification extended his visual reach, but all it showed was an up-close view of nothingness.

All remained still in their assigned sector. Meanwhile, Two-one continued supplying a play-by-play of the enemy scouts' steady approach. Once the fighters reached the 150-meter mark, the updates came in rapid-fire, and the anxiety in Two-one's voice escalated with each.

Two-one—*his name is McCormick,* Redd remembered, *Gage McCormick*—was about to kill someone and he knew it.

"That's it," whispered McCormick. "They're at a hundred meters."

"Do it," urged Austin. "Take the shot."

The loud *pop-pop* of the first controlled pair came almost before Austin finished his transmission, followed quickly by several more staccato reports.

"Targets down," said McCormick, no longer whispering, almost shouting. "Targets down!"

"Stand by," advised Austin. "Keep watching your sectors."

For a long moment, silence returned to the desert, and Redd felt his own anxiety spiking. Then Austin spoke again. "Three-one, Three-two, meet me at the eight o'clock. We're moving out to assess the targets."

Redd keyed his mic. "Three-two, roger."

Then, moving slowly to avoid drawing the attention of any possible enemy gunmen lurking out in the middle distance, he got up and moved stealthily to the southwest corner of the crash site where he found Austin and Corporal Kovacs kneeling beside McCormick and his automatic rifleman. Mike was there as well.

A hundred or so meters farther out lay four shapeless, unmoving forms.

With Redd's arrival, Austin wasted no time. "Let's move out. Wedge formation. I'll take point. Kovacs, you're on the left. Redd go right. Mike . . ." Austin stared at the soldier for a moment, as if uncomfortable giving him an order.

Perhaps sensing this, Mike spoke up. "I'll pick up the right side behind the big guy. That way, if he goes down, I can use him for cover."

He gave Redd's shoulder a punch that was probably meant to be playful but was hard enough to rock Redd sideways.

"All right," said Austin, turning away and stepping out beyond the defensive position. Redd and Kovacs fanned out into their assigned positions, maintaining five meters of separation, and kept their rifles at the high ready.

As they neared their objective, the motionless forms began to look more like what they were—four dead men.

But Redd knew that might not be completely true. One or more of them might still be alive, possibly even unhurt, and just waiting for a bunch of careless Marines to stroll up for a closer look. But Redd resisted the impulse to train his weapon on the bodies. That was Austin's job as the leader. His job was to watch their right flank.

From the corner of his eye, he saw Austin raise a hand, signaling them to halt and take a knee. Redd repeated the signal—an ingrained habit—and then knelt but continued to scan back and forth.

"Mike," whispered the sergeant. "Cover me."

The soldier advanced, keeping his weapon trained on the nearest body as Austin edged closer. He spent nearly a full minute visually checking the corpse, looking for any indication that the man might be wearing a suicide vest, then carefully reached out and checked for a pulse. Satisfied that the man was dead, he moved on, repeating the process with the next body.

As he was moving toward the third man, however, an audible groan broke through the stillness. Austin froze in place, as did everyone else, and this time, Redd couldn't help but look. One of the ISIS fighters was still alive. Wounded, probably dying, but still clinging to the mortal realm.

After a long pause, Austin resumed his slow approach. When he was within reach the man groaned again, his eyes opening as if sensing the Marine's presence in the darkness, and then he began to gibber.

A sudden report, shockingly loud in the stillness, caused Redd to jump. He twisted around, looking for the source of the shot, thinking that they were taking enemy fire, but instead saw Mike, his rifle aimed at the man on the ground, smoke curling from the barrel. Then Redd noticed a spreading dark stain on the ground under the enemy fighter's head.

Mike just shot him in the head, Redd told himself. *Holy*—

Austin had leaped back a step and now gaped at the soldier. "What are you doing?" he cried. "You just . . ." He shook his head, momentarily at a loss for words. Finally he managed an accusing croak. "You shot him. You just murdered that dude!"

"It wasn't murder," replied Mike, as calmly as if disagreeing about a weather forecast. "It was mercy. He was dead the minute he came our way." He cocked his head to the side, still staring at Austin. "Or would you rather have let him lie here suffering until he finally bled out?"

"I would have . . ." Austin faltered. "He was a prisoner. We don't kill prisoners."

"He wasn't a prisoner. He was the enemy. End of story." He gestured to the remaining body. "C'mon. Let's finish this. We've been out here too long as it is."

As shocked as he was by what Mike had just done, Redd understood the cold logic of his decision. It was the same logic J. B. had taught him many years before on the ranch when they'd found one of the herd—a yearling—who had fallen down a short cliff and become entangled in a section of barbed wire fence. The animal had been in terrible pain, lowing frantically, desperate for succor, but J. B. had stopped Redd from running down to free the animal. Through long years of experience, the old cowboy had known that the steer was beyond saving, that its injuries were too severe, and that, even if they somehow managed to free the animal and haul it back to the ranch, call out a veterinarian for treatment, the outcome would be the same. The yearling would be put down, no matter what. The only question was how much it would suffer first.

Redd remembered how J. B.'s eyes had glistened with emotion as he drew his Ruger Vaquero .44. "This is just the way it is, Matty."

It was a hard thing to take a life. Even the life of an animal.

Combat was different. In combat, it was kill or be killed. But what Mike had just done . . . what J. B. had done all those years ago, and what Redd himself had done more than once on subsequent occasions when dealing with sick or injured cattle . . .

The enemy fighter had been mortally wounded. Maybe, with immediate medical attention, his life might have been saved, but the small group of Marines did not have the resources to accomplish that. The man would have died. Maybe in an hour. Maybe in five minutes. The only question was how much pain he would endure before eventually slipping away.

"It was mercy."

Was it, though?

Austin was clearly still struggling with it. He put his hands on his hips, facing the SF soldier. "Don't do anything like that again. Not without talking to me first."

Mike regarded him for a moment. "You think you can make that decision."

"LT put me in charge. So, yeah. I'll do what—"

Something sharp and loud, like the amplified whine of a mosquito, cut him off. The noise ended as abruptly as it had begun, terminating with a wet thud. Redd felt something hot and viscous splatter onto his face and saw dark spots in the display of his NODs, distorting his view of the world. He blinked once, and his eyes came into focus. When they did, he could still see Austin standing there staring at Mike, but now with his left hand clamped tight against the side of his neck, trying and failing to stop the arterial spurt of blood that gushed through his fingers.

"He's hit!' cried Redd. "Man down!"

THIRTEEN

In that moment, Redd's focus narrowed to a pinpoint. He was peripherally aware of what was going on around him, of Kovacs shouting a contact report and Mike shouting, "Sniper!" He heard the sharp report of a single, distant rifle shot, the sound arriving too late to warn of the immediate peril, and heard also the much louder eruptions of the rifles belonging to Mike and Kovacs as they began returning fire. But all of that was just so much background noise for Redd. The only thing that made any kind of impression on him was the dark substance—black in the monochrome display of the NODs—jetting from Austin's neck.

He was at Austin's side in the space of a heartbeat, his own hands clamping over Austin's, pressing down in an attempt to stop the hemorrhage. Even as he did this, he knew it wouldn't be enough, so with one hand, he groped for the pouch affixed to the front of Austin's tactical vest that contained his IFAK—individual first aid kit. He got the little pouch open but fumbled with adrenaline-numb fingers to locate the package containing a pressure dressing, all too aware of the fact that with every passing second, the life of his sergeant—his friend—was pouring out.

"Get down!" shouted Mike.

Redd, still hyperfocused on trying to stop the bleeding, barely heard. He had found the pressure dressing and was trying to tear it open with his teeth. No sooner had he done this than Mike was pulling both men—Redd and Austin—down to the ground, even as bullets snapped through the air around them. The change in position caused Redd's hand to slip away from the wound in Austin's neck, but he moved quickly to replace it, and then, with the pressure dressing finally released from its packaging, moved Austin's hand away, exposing the wound just long enough to clamp the absorbent pad over it.

The fabric covering the dressing darkened in a matter of seconds as the pad became saturated. Redd took a second dressing from the IFAK, tore it open, and pressed it into place over the first.

Through the tumult, he heard someone . . . Kovacs, maybe . . . shouting, "We gotta go. We gotta go!"

Then a hand gripped his shoulder. "Matt!" It was Mike. "We can't stay here. We have to move. *Now!*"

"Can't move him," mumbled Redd. "Have to keep pressure . . ."

"We can't do anything for him out here," insisted Mike. "Tie the dressing off and let's go. Before we're all shot up and left here to die."

Redd shook his head. It wasn't possible to tie an effective pressure dressing on a neck wound because to do so would strangle the victim. But he also knew Mike was right. They had to fall back to the fighting position, get behind cover. Only then would he be able to really help Austin.

He knelt close to Austin, shouting to be heard over the din of ongoing gunfire. "Sergeant. You've got to keep pressure on the dressing." He grabbed the man's hand and placed it over the blood-soaked pads, but it fell away as soon as he let go. Austin had gone limp.

"We have to go!" urged Mike.

He grabbed Redd's biceps, tried to pull him along, but Redd wrenched free of the soldier's grip. With his left hand curled around Austin's neck, squeezing the dressing against the wound, he awkwardly lifted the injured man in his arms. Then, orienting himself toward the crash site, he lurched into motion.

Only now did he realize that he was in the middle of an intense firefight. Bullets creased the air all around. Targeting lasers lanced out from the fighting positions, accompanied by bright muzzle flashes. Tracer rounds streaked out across the desert. Redd knew he should be moving tactically, zigzagging to make himself less of a target, even high crawling, but with Austin in his arms, it was all he could do to simply keep moving.

Something struck him squarely in the middle of his back, the force of it shoving him forward. He stumbled but managed to catch himself without falling.

That was a bullet, he realized. *Someone just shot me.*

The blow hurt, like getting slammed from behind by a football tackle, but didn't feel like what he thought a bullet wound would feel like. Given the location of the hit, he assumed that the SAPI plate in his Interceptor Body Armor had done its job, stopping the 7.62-millimeter AK round from punching a hole clear through him.

If not, he would know soon enough.

He heard more rounds snap through the air nearby, felt the spray of dirt and debris kicked up as bullets impacted the ground behind him, but miraculously, he was not hit again. Thirty-odd seconds after picking up and moving, he was back at the crash site, where he dropped down behind a low barrier of sandbags and eased the unconscious Austin to the ground.

Austin's armor and uniform were completely black, soaked through with blood, as was Redd's left glove and sleeve up to the elbow.

So much blood . . .

But the arterial spurt from the neck wound seemed to have relented. Direct pressure on the wound had done its job, slowing the bleeding, but given the amount of blood he had already lost, the sergeant was probably slipping into shock. Austin needed IV fluids to restore his blood volume, but Redd didn't have enough hands to maintain pressure on the wound and start an IV.

He raised his head, looking for someone to give him a hand, and only then beheld the scope of the firefight. He could see the muzzle flashes of enemy weapons, firing from multiple positions along their southern flank. The Marines were returning fire with reckless abandon, burning through their limited supply of ammunition evidently without a thought for effectiveness.

Shocked at what might well be a fatal lapse in discipline, Redd shouted into his radio mic, "Cease fire!" Then repeated the message again and again—"Cease fire, cease fire!"—waving his hand in front of his face in the signal to stop firing. After a few seconds, he heard the shout echoed, passed along from man to man until the volume of outgoing fire slackened and stopped altogether.

"Remember your fire discipline," Redd barked. "Let them come to us. Wait for a target and then take them out. Single shots only!"

There were a few guilty murmurs of assent over the comms. They all knew that they'd screwed up. Redd didn't belabor the point but returned his attention to Austin. He needed to get some fluids in the sergeant. He realized that Mike was crouched beside him and said, "We need to get an IV started on him."

But Mike just shook his head. "Matt. He's already gone."

Already gone?

That couldn't be right. The bleeding had stopped, hadn't it?

"No," Redd said emphatically. "No, he's gonna make it."

But even as he said it, he saw the truth of Mike's statement revealed in Austin's unseeing eyes.

For a long moment, all Redd could do was stare at his fallen sergeant . . . his friend.

How can you be dead? You were just here a couple of seconds ago.

The voices sounding over the radio now began to filter down into his awareness, pulling him back into the moment. There would be time to grieve later, but first they had to get through the night, and right now, judging by the unstructured babble he was hearing over the comms, nobody had a clue what was going on.

He stared at Austin, then looked at Mike again. "Somebody needs to take charge."

Mike stared back at him. "You're somebody. What are you waiting for? Do it."

FOURTEEN

"Do it."

The words hit Redd like a bucket of ice water in the face. He was a Marine NCO—non-commissioned officer—trained to lead. So what if his rank only put him in charge of a fire team. Leadership was leadership.

He recalled an old quote that his dad had been fond of—Teddy Roosevelt, or so J. B. claimed: *"In any moment of decision, the best thing you can do is the right thing, the next best thing is the wrong thing, and the worst thing you can do is nothing."*

He clicked his mic three times to interrupt the transmissions. "Break, break," he said. "Team leaders, check in. Give me an up."

After a moment of stunned silence, the corporals began calling in with their ACE status—ammunition, casualties, equipment. The quick battlefield report used a color code system—green, amber, red, or black—to indicate combat readiness after contact with the enemy.

The results were not encouraging.

Most of the team leaders were reporting in as amber—meaning they had less than seventy-five percent of their combat load remaining. Some were already red—below fifty percent. The two recovered machine guns were, thankfully, still green, but the gunners were reporting that they would need to make a barrel change.

They were better on casualties, but there were still too few greens. Redd asked for additional clarification on the amber and red reports and learned that most of the injuries were minor scrapes caused by rock and bullet fragments. Three of the Marines, however, had sustained serious injuries. One had taken a round through the right forearm, the bullet shattering both the ulna and radius. Another had been hit in the face by something, a ricochet or a piece of debris, that had lodged in his left eye. The third was the most serious—a chest wound that had somehow angled in through a gap in the Marine's body armor. The wounded had received immediate attention, the men stabilized, but they were out of the fight.

Then an urgent voice sounded over the radio. "Break, break. This is Two-two. I have enemy movement at four o'clock. Three hundred meters out. Looks like . . . four, no, five tangos. Heading our way."

Redd scanned the indicated sector with his rifle scope.

Where are you, you sons of—

He spotted the barely visible figures, creeping across the open ground but clearly heading toward the crash site. He clicked his mic. "Roger, Two-two. They're trying to draw our fire. Make us waste our ammo. Let 'em come closer."

Another sighting came in a moment later—a group of six insurgent fighters advancing from the eight o'clock. Redd repeated his order, adding, "Wait for them to reach one hundred meters. We have to make every shot count."

Then he heard Burgess's whiny voice, not over the comms but from the next firing position over. "Who died and made him the boss?"

Before Redd could even think about how to respond, Mike wheeled around and barked, "Your sergeant died, you pathetic little thumb-sucker, that's who. I suggest you quit your sniveling and do what he says. Who knows? You might just make it out of this alive."

For a moment, there was only stunned silence. Then a lone voice from some-where farther out called back, "Oorah!"

Someone else echoed the sentiment, and then several more joined in.

"All right, all right," said Redd, waving his hand to get their attention. "We'll all hug it out later. Right now, keep it down. And keep calling out those enemy contacts."

As the Marines returned to a state of quiet vigilance, Redd turned to Mike. "I really appreciate what you just said, but maybe you should be the one in charge. I'm sure you've got a lot more experience with this kind of stuff?"

Mike regarded him with a wry grin. "Actually, I have zero experience riding herd on a bunch of jarheads, and I wouldn't take the job if you paid me. You guys are wound a little too tight for my liking." Then he clapped Redd's shoulder. "You got this, Matt. Trust your instincts."

Perversely, Mike's vote of confidence had exactly the opposite effect. Redd was suddenly overcome with self-doubt.

Trust my instincts? What if my instincts end up getting everyone killed?

But then he heard J. B.'s voice in his head. *"The next best thing is the wrong thing."*

Mike's right, he decided. *Don't overthink it. Just do it.*

Then his gaze fell on the unmoving form of Sergeant Austin, a grim reminder of the possible consequences of doing the wrong thing.

FIFTEEN

The three enemy scouting parties—sixteen men in all—continued their slow advance, coming in from different directions, but clearly intent on converging at the crashed helicopter. Some were creeping forward with exaggerated slowness, as if believing that by so doing, they would be hidden from the "night eyes" of the American military, while others moved in quick bounds before dropping to the prone and high-crawling forward—standard infantry movement tactics. Evidently emboldened by the lack of return fire, as they neared the crash site, they actually spent more time walking upright, fully silhouetted. Without NODs of their own, the ISIS fighters were literally groping in the darkness, completely oblivious to the fact that every single one of them was in the sights of a Marine rifleman.

All the while, Redd monitored the radioed reports of their progress.

"Two hundred meters out."

"Wait for it," he advised.

"One fifty."

"Stand ready."

Redd kept the illuminated reticle of his ACOG center mass on the target designated Charlie-three. Each one of the approaching fighters had been assigned a unique identity so that no two Marines would be firing at the same target.

Charlie-three, his head swathed in black cloth, was the third man from the left in the third group from the left, the one approaching from the southwest.

Even at 150 meters, it was an almost-impossible-to-miss shot, but he waited. The Alpha group was lagging behind the others, and he wanted them all within optimal range before any shots were fired.

Come on. Just a little closer.

He waited until all of Alpha was within the kill box and then gave the order. Just one word. "Fire."

Sixteen rifles spoke in almost perfect unison.

Sixteen ISIS fighters died.

Charlie-three didn't stagger or start, but simply folded over and dropped like a rock.

Then all hell broke loose.

The first indication of trouble was a series of flashes from dozens of different points in the far distance—at least four hundred, possibly as much as six hundred meters to the south. Redd barely had time to shout a warning—"Down!"—before the ballistic fury was upon them.

The air around him was suddenly filled with the distinctive crack of supersonic rounds breaking the sound barrier. The volume of fire was incredible. AKs on full auto, but also a heavy machine gun—the LT had said the insurgents might have a PK. Maybe more than one.

Some of the bullets fell short, smacking into the desert floor, only to scatter rock debris and metal fragments across the Marine fighting positions. Some struck the exposed underbelly of the wrecked Chinook, thunking into the metal like hammer blows.

Others found their mark.

Over the din, Redd heard cursing and shouts of "I'm hit!"

In a flash of insight, he realized what the enemy was doing. The scouting parties had been sent out as a pawn sacrifice. Unwitting cannon fodder to get the Marines to reveal their position and numbers.

And it had worked.

"Keep your fire discipline!" Redd barked into the radio. "Target the muzzle flashes!"

Taking his own advice, he sighted the ACOG on one particularly bright flash, finding the correct marking on the reticle to adjust for the distance, and pulled the trigger. Unlike the shot that had dropped Charlie-three, this was by no means a sure thing, and when, after a few seconds, he saw the distant flash again, he knew that his shot had missed.

This is no good, he realized. *We're getting hammered.*

He keyed his mic. "We need more fire on the south side. Leave two lookouts at two and ten o'clock. Everyone else, move to the south."

Even as he gave the order, however, his mind was racing to come up with a better solution. Simply holding their ground and trading fire with the enemy was no way to win this fight. Redd had always favored the wisdom of US Army General George Patton: *"When in doubt, ATTACK!"*

That was the Marine way, after all. Move to contact. Take the fight to the enemy. But there were many different ways to attack, and a full-frontal suicide charge was probably not what Patton had in mind.

A plan quickly took shape, a variation on one of the basic infantry battle drills.

They would need to abandon their present position, fall back with the wounded, putting the crashed helo between themselves and the enemy. Then he would lead anyone still able to walk in a broad flanking maneuver to engage with the enemy in close combat, where they would be able to make the best use of their remaining ammunition.

He keyed his mic. "All elements, cease fire, cease fire."

He paused, waiting until the Marines' rifles quieted. The volume of incoming fire, however, remained undiminished.

"Listen up," he began. "I want a CCP one hundred meters north of the wreck. On my signal, we're going to pick up and move there—"

That was as far as he got.

In the distance, two brilliant points of hot light bloomed into existence and streaked across the desert even faster than a bullet. Not muzzle flashes or tracers but the flame trails of a pair of rocket-propelled grenades.

There was no time to shout a warning, much less try to find cover. All Redd could do was throw himself flat and hope for the best.

SIXTEEN

Designed for anti-armor warfare, the RPG-7 was not ideally suited for use against infantry. So when the warheads slammed into the underside of the fallen Chinook, instead of producing an explosive shock wave, along with a deadly spray of molten shrapnel, the grenade's unique-shaped charge instead created a conical burst of superheated plasma that torched through the metal skin of the aircraft. Because most of the energy of the detonation was focused forward, toward the point of impact, the shock wave it produced, while not insignificant, was not lethal to the Marines huddled in the shadow of the downed aircraft.

Mindful of the possibility of a secondary explosion, Redd waited a few more seconds to raise his head. The first thing he noticed was the flames that were spreading across the exterior of the Chinook's fuselage. The RPG warheads had ignited the spilled jet fuel, transforming the aircraft into a blazing beacon.

The second thing he noticed was that the ranks had broken. Several Marines were already fleeing the area. Many of those still at their fighting positions looked as if they were about to bolt as well.

"Stay at your post!" he shouted. "Hold your ground!"

But Redd's cries were lost in the tumult. The Marines were either unable to hear or too lost in their own panic to remember their training. Then Redd felt a hand on his shoulder. It was Mike.

"You told them to fall back," he shouted. "A hundred meters, you said. It was the right call. We can't do anything here. We need to go."

Redd stared at him, momentarily uncomprehending. It had not been his intention to order a retreat, but rather to regroup in order to initiate offensive action. But there hadn't been time to explain that.

Given the present situation, attempting to mount any kind of attack would be a tall order. Nevertheless, the idea of retreat galled him. The Marine credo—"Never Retreat, Never Surrender"—was something he had believed in even before it was hammered into his brain during boot camp.

He raised up a little higher and looked out across the desert at the enemy position. The intensity of the incoming fire had slacked off a bit. Instead of a steady stream of lead, there were now only short machine gun bursts. Then he saw a large, dark mass moving quickly across the foreground—an enemy assault force, mounting an old-school infantry charge. Led on by the blazing wreckage of the helicopter, they had already crossed half the distance to the crash site in a flat-out run and now were probably less than a minute from reaching their goal.

The ISIS fighters were so tightly clustered together, Redd couldn't get a sense of their numbers—only that there were a lot of them. At least two dozen, but probably closer to twice that. If his Marines had held their ground, they might have been able to turn the tide, but now there weren't enough left to get the job done.

"We have to pull back!" Mike urged again.

Redd nodded dully, but his mind was still turning over the problem. He looked down at the rifle in his hands, knowing that while he might be able to take out several of the onrushing attackers, the rest would be on him as soon as he had to stop to change mags.

Then he remembered that bullets weren't the only thing his rifle could fire.

He shifted to a crouch, facing the oncoming insurgents, and shouldered his rifle. But instead of taking aim and pulling the trigger, he instead elevated the weapon just a few degrees and moved his hand down past the magazine, putting his finger on the second trigger, the one on the M203 grenade launcher attached to the underside of the M16's heat shield.

Like the MK19, the M203 fired a 40-millimeter explosive grenade. Redd's was loaded with the M433 HEDP—high-explosive, dual-purpose. Slower than a bullet, the grenades were most effective when fired in a high parabolic trajectory like an artillery shell, at stationary targets 200 to 400 meters away.

Unfortunately, the vanguard of the enemy advance was already past the

200-meter mark. And unlike the MK19, the M203 was a single-shot weapon that had to be reloaded after every fire.

Redd hoped one shot would do the job.

The weapon discharged with a resonant *thunk*. Then, almost a full second later, there was a flash and a puff of smoke right in front of the horde.

When the smoke cleared, Redd could see that several of the insurgents were down, either cut down by the spray of shrapnel or knocked off their feet by the detonation itself. The rest had probably just hit the deck as a reflex, but the momentum of the charge had been broken. However, more than half of the insurgents were still on their feet, and after only a moment's hesitation, they began advancing again. They moved tactically now, taking turns shooting and moving.

Mike gripped Redd's shoulder again. "We're out of time. Gotta pull back!"

With a grimace, Redd moved his hand back to the M16 trigger and began firing into the attackers until the magazine was empty. Then, with the bitter bile of failure in his mouth, he keyed his mic. "Fall back to the CCP. Fall back! If you're already there, give us covering fire."

As the remaining Marines picked up and began moving, Redd quickly switched out the empty magazine and resumed firing. Beside him, Mike was firing as well, but with just the two of them, the odds favored the attackers. Emboldened by what appeared to be the collapse of the defense, several of the insurgents threw caution to the wind and charged.

"Matt!" shouted Mike. "Time to go!"

Redd nodded but when he bounded up, he did not choose the shortest route around the wreck. Instead, he leapt for the centermost fighting position—the one at six o'clock—and seized hold of the item that had been left there: an olive-drab plastic device that looked a little like a blocky hand grip exerciser with speaker wire sprouting from one end. Eschewing the standard verbal warning, Redd began vigorously pumping the handle.

On the third squeeze, the four claymore mines arrayed across the southern flank of the crash site and daisy-chained together detonated simultaneously.

The force of the explosion shook the ground under Redd, vibrating through his body like the thrum of a deep bass woofer. But he was on the correct side of the claymores, the side upon which the words *BACK M18A1 APERS MINE* had been stamped in the plastic housing. Those on the other side, the side marked *FRONT TOWARD ENEMY*, never knew what hit them.

Each of the four claymores blasted out a spray of approximately seven hundred one-eighth-inch steel ball bearings, traveling at ballistic velocities—lethal to anyone within fifty meters and might ruin someone's day as far as two hundred meters out. Arranged to provide overlapping cones of fire, the claymore blast eviscerated the enemy fighters.

A shroud of smoke and dust hung over the killing field. Redd didn't wait for it to dissipate so he could survey the damage. He had done what he could. It was time to go.

SEVENTEEN

As Redd and Mike went looking for the rest of the element, the fire raging inside the wreckage of the Chinook continued to spread, fully engulfing the aircraft. The flames lit up the surrounding area bright enough to render NODs ineffective. Swinging his up and out of the way, Redd continued across the open desert, chasing his own shadow until he spotted one of the Marines, lying in a prone firing position behind a salvaged M240 machine gun, facing toward the south.

"Friendly coming in," Redd called out.

"Come on in, Corporal," came the answer.

Redd was relieved to see that at least a few of the Marines had remembered their training, establishing security for the casualty collection point. "Any sign of movement out there?" he asked as he passed the gunner.

"Saw a couple of 'em crawling away, but nobody's coming this way."

"That's good. Hopefully we bought ourselves some time."

But any sense of accomplishment he might have felt evaporated when he beheld the toll the battle had taken on the Marines. Redd faltered when he got a look at the CCP. The men looked like refugees of the apocalypse.

About half of them lay flat on the ground, clutching bloody pressure dressings to wounds too numerous for him to catalogue. Some weren't moving at all. A few Marines—he recognized Corporal Kovacs among them—were moving amidst the wounded, assessing and triaging, providing what treatment and comfort they could. Yet as terrible as that tableau was to behold, what stopped Redd in his tracks was the condition of those who appeared to have mostly escaped injury. A group of them sat on the ground, gazing off into nothingness as if completely dissociated from the world—the infamous thousand-yard stare of the shell-shocked. A few were openly weeping.

Overcoming his incredulity, Redd barked, "Suck it up, Marines. This is what we trained for. Break's over. Back to work."

A few heads turned to look at him, including Heskett's—the private's face was streaked with blood and tears—but the rest either didn't hear his exhortation or chose to ignore it. Redd saw Burgess among the latter number and felt his blood begin to boil. He strode forward until he was standing over the corporal, his fists clenched, and shouted directly into the other man's face. "Get up! Lead your men."

Burgess stared past him vacantly for a moment, then shook his head. "Can't. Can't do it."

"*Can't* is not in our vocabulary," Redd fired back. "Now get off your—"

"I don't want to die," sobbed Heskett. "We ain't making it out of this, man. I'm not ready to die."

Redd wheeled on the young man, ready to hurl accusations of cowardice like stones, but the raw emotion in Heskett's eyes stopped him cold.

Before Redd could respond, another Marine said, "I've got a kid on the way. Now I'll prolly never even get to see him. I just wanna go home."

Redd heard the defeat in his voice, and it shook him.

"You think cuz you've got a kid on the way you've got more right to live than the rest of us?" challenged Burgess.

"Enough!" snapped Redd. He took a breath, then slowly let it out, uncurling his fists. "You're right," he said, now speaking slowly, patiently, as if trying to reassure frightened children. "Nobody wants to die. But if we give up now, stop fighting, that's exactly what's going to happen."

He looked around at the little group, trying to make eye contact with each of them. Some, like Burgess, refused to meet his stare.

"You say you don't want to die," he went on. "Well, you better want to live more than you *don't* want to die."

Heskett's lips moved as if trying to form words, but no sound issued. Still, Redd felt like he was finally making progress. He glanced over at Mike and saw the SF soldier watching him with an appraising stare. When they made eye contact, Mike gave him a slow nod.

Go on, he seemed to be saying. *You've got this.*

Redd turned to the triage area. "Kovacs. How bad is it?"

The corporal looked over, revealing a face that was just as haunted and exhausted as any of the others. Redd now saw that Kovacs's right sleeve was stained red and sported a battlefield dressing.

"Well," Kovacs said after a moment's consideration. "Not great. We're pretty shot up, brother. But other'n Aus—" He faltered. Took a breath and then tried again. "Other than the sergeant, we haven't lost anyone. Not yet, anyway."

Despite the caveat, Redd felt immensely relieved by this news. He turned back to the others. "We can get through this, but only if everyone does their part." He checked his watch and was surprised to see that it was almost 0100.

Merry Christmas, everyone . . .

He dismissed the mordant thought. "We just have to hold out a couple more hours," he went on. He let that sink in a moment. "Now, I can't promise that the worst is behind us. We bloodied their nose, but they're gonna know that we're running low on ammo. If they try again, we have to be ready. And we've gotta give them everything we got."

He paused a beat, checking to see if he was finally reaching them. "Burgess, how long do you think we can hold out if they attack again?"

The corporal's eyes flitted back and forth for a moment, as if he was trying to decide whether to engage with the question. Then he shrugged. "Depends on how much ammo we've got left. Maybe half an hour if we're—"

Redd cut him off. "Heskett, what do you think?"

The private jolted in surprise at being singled out. "Umm, I don't know. Half an hour sounds about right."

Redd pointed to another Marine, a private from first squad whose name momentarily escaped him. "You. How long?"

"Uh, well, I guess it depends on how bad they want us."

Redd had already turned away. "Show of hands. Who thinks we can hold out for half an hour?"

Burgess raised his hand. So did a few others. Heskett, however, kept his down, evidently rethinking.

"Who thinks we can hold out longer than that? An hour?"

No hands.

"Who thinks it depends on what the enemy wants?"

This time most of the hands went up.

Redd nodded slowly. "Well, for a bunch of guys who claim they don't want to die, you all seem pretty resigned to it." He let that sink in a moment. "If you think we can only hold out for half an hour, then that's exactly how long you're going to last. If you think it depends on what the enemy wants, then you've already decided that they are going to win."

Burgess ducked his head as if the rebuke was meant for him, but some of the others were nodding in chagrined comprehension.

"The correct answer," Redd continued, "is as long as we have to. And it doesn't matter how bad the enemy wants it. What matters is how bad *you* want it. So . . . how bad do you want it?"

He paused a beat, then turned to the expectant father. "Tell me what you have to live for."

The private swallowed. "I want to see my kid."

Redd nodded. "Good. You will." He pointed at another. "How 'bout you?"

The young private winced. "I don't know."

Redd gave him a fatherly smile—a J. B. smile. "Are you sure you want to go with that?"

"Well, I don't want to die a . . ." He gave a guilty shrug. "I mean, I've never even had a girlfriend."

Redd nodded. "Well, if you are determined to stay alive until you find a girl who will have you, you just might live forever."

The line brought a round of laughter. Redd glanced sidelong at Mike and saw the soldier smiling.

He'd done it. He'd finally broken the spell.

"Keep going. Picture what you have to live for, what you're going to fight to get back to, and don't let it go," Redd went on. "That's how we're *all* going to make it home."

Whether it was to talk to a loved one again or to see the new Star Wars movie, everyone that was conscious and able to speak found a reason to want to stay alive.

"What about you?" Heskett asked. "What you fighting for tonight, Redd?"

Redd had his answer ready. "Few years ago, just before I shipped out, I promised my dad that no matter where I was, no matter where the Corps sent me, I would always call him on Christmas Eve. It was only ever the two of us for Christmas. We didn't have anyone else, so we had to make our own traditions."

Even though he'd known what he was going to say, Redd was surprised at the rush of emotions that recollection triggered. He wondered what J. B. was doing back home.

He's probably done with all the chores . . . Maybe he's sitting in the living room, sipping a bourbon, watching A Christmas Story *or maybe just staring out the window, watching the snow.*

Is it snowing back home? Is J. B. gonna have a white Christmas? I'll have to ask him.

"Anyway," continued Redd, "I didn't get a chance to make that call before we came out here, so that's why I gotta get back. I made a promise to my dad, and I intend to see that through. No way is he going to get a call that I was KIA instead. That can't happen. I'm gonna make it back. *We* will make it back."

"You're too late," said Burgess. "It's after midnight."

Redd frowned at the corporal.

Leave it to the oxygen thief to ruin an inspirational moment.

"It's still Christmas Eve back home in Montana . . . three p.m. I've got nine hours." He smiled. "Plenty of time."

And for once, he was actually starting to believe it might be.

EIGHTEEN

Two hours passed with no indication that the enemy was still in the area.

That was the good news.

The bad news was that two hours passed with no sign of the platoon's return.

At 0230, Redd had put a call out on the radio. Without the sat antenna, he had little hope of reaching HQ, but if the convoy was within range, he wanted to let them know the situation as soon as possible.

That the call went unanswered was no real surprise. His estimate of nine hours had been just that, an estimate. He decided to wait fifteen minutes and then try again.

Despite the casualties they had taken, morale had markedly improved. Even Burgess seemed to be taking his role as team leader seriously, overseeing the inventory and redistribution of ammunition. As much as Redd wanted to take credit for the change in attitude, he knew it probably had more to do with the fact that the long night was almost over. Relief was on the way and the worst appeared to be behind them.

The 0245 call also went unanswered. So did the 0300 call.

Redd tried not to let his disappointment show when letting the team leaders know. "Truth is," he told them, "we don't know how long they're gonna be. No telling what they might be dealing with, but we all know the staff sergeant is going to move heaven and earth to come get us. He won't leave us hanging."

His attempt to reassure them fell flat. He could almost see the wheels turning in their heads, churning out the direst of scenarios. What if the convoy got ambushed somewhere along the way? What if nobody even knew they were out there?

"I'm sure they'll be here soon," Redd went on, not feeling sure at all. "But just in case, let's implement a rest plan. An hour ought to take the edge off. Burgess, can you set up the roster for that?"

"Aye, aye," replied the corporal, sounding a little pleased at being entrusted with the assignment.

Maybe there's hope for him yet, thought Redd. *And hopefully we won't need that rest plan.*

But as 0400 came and went, without so much as a squawk from the radio, cracks began to appear in the half-full glass of Redd's enforced optimism.

What's taking so long?

When he felt a hand on his shoulder, gently shaking him, and heard Mike's voice in his ear saying, "Rise and shine, Matt," he dared to believe that the wait was finally over. He'd barely even closed his eyes, after all.

"Zero-five-hundred," added Mike. "Back to work."

"Zero-five?" groaned Redd, checking his watch, certain that Mike was messing with him. The G-Shock, however, confirmed Mike's statement as factual.

The fire that had consumed the Chinook had long since burned itself out, but the Milky Way overhead was so clear and bright, he could almost see Mike's face by its light.

He sat up, activated his NODs, and swiveled them down. "Any word?"

Mike shook his head. *"Nada."* Then he shrugged. "Higher knows we're out here. They won't leave us in the wind."

"I know. It's just . . ." Redd trailed off. It wasn't something he wanted to talk about.

After a quiet moment, Mike spoke again. "So look, there's something I've got to tell you. I don't want you to get a big head or anything, but . . . you're doing great. I mean, you've really held it together out here. I'm impressed. Even if you're a jarhead."

Redd couldn't help but chuckle. "Thanks. I think."

Mike paused a beat. "Kidding aside. You ever think about a career in special ops?"

The question came from out of left field, but Redd came back with a quick reply. "Yeah, I thought about it, but it sounded too easy, so I joined the Corps instead."

His recruiter had expressed a similar sentiment back when he'd started the enlistment process. *"Forget the Navy SEALs . . . You want to be hard-core? Join the Corps."* The young sergeant had gone on to bemoan the fact that Navy SEALs and Army Special Forces were always in the spotlight, called out for high-profile missions, treated like superheroes by the public, when the Marines were the ones doing most of the real war fighting. It had made his job a lot harder because most of his best prospects were being enticed into signing up for the other services under special operations contracts even though the chances of their making the cut were pretty slim.

For Redd, there had never been any question. He wanted nothing more than to be a Marine. Just like Jim Bob.

Mike grinned. "The Marines have their own operators you know."

"You mean MARSOC. The Raiders. Yeah, I know about them." He shrugged. "I don't know. I'm pretty happy doing what I'm doing."

Mike sobered. "Spec ops ain't like in the movies. Well, I guess some of it is . . . We definitely get better toys. And we don't have to put up with quite as much crap as the line units. But what really matters is being part of the team. You can be the toughest, strongest, bravest whatever, but if you can't work with the team, forget it.

"What you said to those kids tonight? The way you motivated them? That's what I'm talking about right there," said Mike. "You didn't just read them the riot act. You knew exactly what they needed to hear to get back in the fight. You've got the right stuff, believe me. You're being wasted in a line unit."

Redd shrugged again. "I was just doing what needed to be done."

"Yeah. But you were the one who did it." He clapped Redd on the shoulder. "Listen, when you get back, I want you to talk to your CO about putting in for MARSOC assessment. Promise me you'll do that, okay? Raiders could use a dude like you."

"I'll think about it."

Mike shook his head. "Uh-uh. Promise me. That way I know you'll do it because you keep your promises, right?"

Redd suddenly felt sick to his stomach. "Not anymore I don't."

Mike looked at him crosswise. "What are you talking about?"

"My big promise? To call my dad on Christmas Eve? Looks like I blew it."

"You've still got time."

"I've got—" he checked his watch again—"about four and a half hours. It'll take at least two to get back to camp. Maybe even longer."

"There you go," said Mike, extending a hand, palm out. "You've got two extra hours to play with." He clapped Redd's shoulder again. "Keep the faith, brother. We're gonna make it."

Keep the faith, Redd thought miserably.

That was a lot easier said than done.

NINETEEN

Redd stayed awake after that, constantly monitoring the radio and growing more desperate with each silent minute. An anxious hour passed with no change in the situation. Then another. As 0700 drew near, the sky began to noticeably lighten with the approach of dawn, and Redd's uneasiness multiplied. That he might fail to keep his Christmas promise to J. B. no longer concerned him. His fears were now of an existential nature. When the sun rose, their technological edge over the enemy would evaporate.

As it turned out, the insurgents didn't wait for daybreak.

"Movement at five o'clock," came a frantic report over the radio. "About five hundred meters out. I can't tell for sure, but it looks like a pretty big group."

Redd immediately began searching the area using his ACOG for magnification. The twilight sky was already too bright for NODs, but a cloak of shadow still concealed things at ground level. To make matters even worse, the charred wreckage of the Chinook lay in that sector, creating a visual obstacle, which was, no doubt, why the enemy had chosen to approach from that direction. Nevertheless, Redd's eye was drawn to movement. The enemy was out there, and they were coming.

He keyed his mic. "Showtime, Marines. If your buddy is racked out, wake him up now." He paused a beat, then added, "We have to make every shot count. One shot, one kill."

As soon as he ended his transmission, another call came in. "Got something at nine o'clock. Four hundred meters."

Five and nine o'clock, thought Redd. *A textbook flanking attack.*

The ISIS fighters had been busy during the night, moving their forces around while staying well beyond visual range.

"Head on a swivel, everyone," said Redd. "It's the ones we don't see that we really have to worry about."

He resumed scanning to the five o'clock and this time quickly found the enemy fighters, more than a dozen of them, moving tactically in short, seemingly erratic bursts of activity across open ground. He identified one that seemed to be in the vanguard of the element and centered the glowing red chevron reticle of the ACOG directly on the man's chest, tracking him, leading him, waiting for the optimal moment to squeeze the trigger.

"Come on," he muttered. "Hold still for a second."

Another call came over the radio. "This is One-three. I've got the shot."

Redd knew that once the first shot was fired, any semblance of command and control would evaporate. And once the battle started, it probably wouldn't end until one side or the other was completely destroyed.

He wondered if he ought to say something inspirational, urge them all to remember their training and to look out for the guy next to them . . . remind them that they were Marines to the bloody end. Semper Fi! Maybe an inspirational quote from Chesty Puller . . .

"All right, they're on our left, they're on our right, they're in front of us, they're behind us . . . They can't get away this time."

But that just wasn't his style, so instead he simply said, "Take the shot."

The report cracked in the stillness, and just as Redd knew it would, that single shot opened the floodgates.

More reports followed as Marines began taking out targets of opportunity— single shots, just as directed. Through his optics, Redd saw the fighter he had been tracking drop to the prone, bring his AK to his shoulder, and loose a burst. Redd took him out with a head shot and then began looking for another target.

Redd lost all sense of the passage of time. Minutes and seconds ceased to have any meaning. All that mattered was the rhythm of battle. Acquire, aim, fire, repeat. There was no shortage of targets. After each trigger pull, he needed only shift left or right to find the next enemy shooter. His reports overlapped with those of the dozen other Marines who were still able-bodied enough to fight, sounding like a sustained burst from a machine gun. The actual machine guns remained silent. Redd had made the decision to keep the two M240s in reserve.

The din drowned out the bursts from enemy AKs in the distance, but there was no mistaking the supersonic crack of rounds piercing the air overhead or smashing into the sandbag barriers the Marines were using for cover.

And then, just as he was changing out his magazine, he heard a sound that he both expected and dreaded—a cry, more of dismay than pain, but nonetheless dire. "I'm hit!"

Redd didn't recognize the voice, and the wounded Marine was too far away for him to render assistance, so he finished his reload and resumed scanning for targets. All too soon, a different voice called out from somewhere else, but with the same message. More cries of pain followed, but Redd tuned them out. When he felt something pluck at his left sleeve and then a moment later felt a burning sensation along the length of his forearm, he didn't make a sound. He just looked down for a moment, watching as fresh blood mingled with the black crust that already stained his cammies—Austin's blood—and muttered, "Huh."

The wound—just a graze, he decided—began to throb in time with his pulse, but the hand that held his rifle steady seemed to be working just fine, so he resumed his battle rhythm.

Overhead, the sky continued to lighten, revealing enemy positions scattered across the battlefield. There were dozens of them, too many to count, so Redd didn't even bother to try. The main advance to the front seemed to have stalled at about three hundred meters, well within the range of a Marine rifleman, but just far enough out that any movement from the target after the trigger pull might spoil the shot. Despite his best attempts at target acquisition and ammo discipline, Redd's misses outnumbered his hits. He was burning through his ammo—they all were—with no appreciable reduction in the size of the attacking force.

Another desperate shout cut through both the din and Redd's mental filter. "Right flank! Right flank! They're coming!"

This had been Redd's greatest fear. He couldn't be in two places at once. He couldn't fight the enemy to the front *and* still keep an eye on the flanking element. And, just as he'd known they would, the ISIS fighters had worn the defenders down to the point where a mad rush no longer seemed like guaranteed suicide.

Redd knew he had to shift over to the vulnerable area in order to repulse the assault but knew also that in so doing, he would reduce the effectiveness of the forward defense. So, before picking up to move, he took just a moment to send a grenade from his M203 downrange, dropping it amid a cluster of ISIS fighters.

The situation on the right was worse than he could have imagined. Just two Marines—Burgess and his automatic rifleman—remained to take on an advancing force of at least two dozen enemy fighters who were now within a hundred meters. Two more Marines lay writhing on the ground beside them, clutching at bloody wounds, begging for someone to help.

Redd helped the only way he knew how, joining in the fray, moving from target to target with the dispassionate determination of a competition shooter. He wasn't killing men but simply dropping targets.

Targets that would kill his men if he didn't shoot them first.

His intervention gave the two Marines time to reload and get back in the fight, and in a matter of seconds, the advancing force was completely cut to pieces. Nevertheless, Redd could see another group of enemy fighters lurking a couple hundred yards away, biding their time and waiting for another opportunity.

Redd shouted, "Hit 'em with your 203," even as he was ejecting the spent casing from his own weapon to load in another round. Without waiting for Burgess to join in, Redd sighted and fired. The M433 arced high into the air and then came down in the midst of the insurgents, scattering them across the desert floor. Redd deftly loaded in another round, sighted, and fired, but the enemy had already gotten the message and was in full retreat. Redd loaded in another grenade, then turned to Burgess again.

"You got this?"

The corporal stared back at him for a moment then returned a dull nod, but Redd saw real fear in the man's eyes. He was able to see it because out across the desert to the east, the sun was just breaking over the horizon.

He high-crawled back to his original firing position and wasn't surprised to see that, in his absence, the enemy to the front had begun another push. Mike was keeping up a steady rate of fire, as were the three Marines who were still in the fight, but there were just too many.

Redd fired a grenade into the midst of the approaching fighters, reloaded and fired again. The detonations scattered the insurgents, but those that weren't killed or injured outright quickly picked up and kept coming. Mike took advantage of Redd's covering fire to shift over to one of the M240s, whereupon he opened up, swiveling the machine gun back and forth, hosing the enemy and cutting them down in droves.

Yet still they came, driven by some passion or fear beyond comprehension.

Suddenly, the machine gun went silent. Redd glanced over and saw Mike cursing as he opened the feed tray cover and removed the belt of linked ammunition.

A jam, Redd thought, then started crawling toward the gun emplacement.

The M240 was a crew-served weapon, designed to be operated by a two-man team—one man to pull the trigger and another standing ready to clear jams and load in a new belt as needed. Mike was trying to do both jobs. He succeeded in ejecting the unfired round that had caused the malfunction and was in the process of repositioning the ammo belt when Redd reached his side.

"I got it!" Redd shouted, moving into position to Mike's left.

Mike flashed him a grin and raised both hands to show Redd that he was clear. "Go for it!"

The belt was already in the feed tray, so all Redd had to do was slam the cover back down, but he also saw that only about a foot and a half of the ammo belt remained. Another long burst from the machine gun would burn through that. He would need to have the reload ready to go so that there would be no interruption in fire. He flashed Mike a thumbs-up, indicating that he was good to go, then turned and reached for a sealed can of linked 7.62 rounds. From the corner of his eye, he saw Mike nod and grin as he racked the charging handle back . . .

And then he jolted as if touching a live wire.

"Mike?" Redd shouted as he broke the wire seal on the ammo can and undogged the clamp on the hinged lid. "You good?"

He realized on some intuitive level that Mike had caught a round but figured the soldier would just shrug it off and keep fighting. But the machine gun remained silent.

"Mike!" Redd shouted again as he shoved the can toward the gun then turned to the soldier who still lay prone behind the weapon's molded stock, his hand on the trigger, staring down the barrel with sightless eyes as blood streamed from a small hole just above the bridge of his nose.

What the . . .

"No," Redd heard himself say. "No, no, no, no . . . C'mon, Mike!" But it was too late.

Mike was gone.

In a flash, Redd had seen the man engage the enemy, and then nothing. Like someone turned out the light. Unplugged him. His brain struggled to comprehend the gravity of what he'd just witnessed. Redd felt his mouth go dry, and a sudden shiver went up his spine.

Probably not gonna be able to make that call, J. B. I'm so sorry.

Emotion consumed Redd. For numerous reasons.

He wanted to turn back time and try again. Wanted a do-over. Maybe he could save Austin and Mike and others too.

He screamed a curse. His hands balled into fists insentiently.

What now? he asked himself. *What do we do now?*

And then a loud voice, one that sounded a little like Mike, answered Redd in his subconscious. *"Get back in the fight!"* it shouted.

And that's exactly what he did.

TWENTY

Matthew Redd flipped the 240's feed tray open, removed the short ammo belt, and replaced it with the end of the one from the can he'd just opened—a task that took all of ten seconds. Then he eased Mike's unresisting form aside, gently, as if trying to move a sleeping child, snugged the butt of the M240 into his shoulder, looked down the barrel, and started firing.

It was, as the saying went, a target-rich environment.

The enemy was everywhere. Evidently interpreting the cessation of machine gun fire as a signal that the Marines' defense had collapsed, dozens of insurgents were rushing the position in twos and threes.

Redd had to remember to breathe as he shifted the machine gun from one target to the next, letting loose five or ten rounds in a burst with each trigger pull. In a matter of seconds, the leading edge of the wave collapsed. One by one at first, and then en masse, the insurgents lost their nerve, turned tail, and ran.

It did not save them.

Then, between bursts, he heard Burgess screaming, "Right side! Right side! They're overrunning us!"

Without a moment's hesitation, Redd scooped up the 240, still securely attached to its tripod mount and trailing the ammo belt like a long tether, pivoted to the right, and fired over the heads of the two Marines. The combined weight of weapon and tripod was just north of forty pounds, and with the compounding recoil of rapid fire, it was like trying to wrestle a bull, but Redd just bared his teeth and held the trigger down in a long, sustained pull.

A stream of lead cut down half a dozen insurgents like a scythe through wheat stalks. Hot brass and links fell like rain at his feet.

Yet no sooner had he repulsed that attack than he glimpsed movement to his left. He let off the trigger, swung around in that direction, and saw a pair of enemy fighters moving in from the seven o'clock.

He fired short bursts this time, mindful of the need to manage his rate of fire. Continuous fire would overheat the barrel in just a couple minutes. His first trigger pull dropped the insurgent on the right. His second and third missed, but his fourth stitched a bloody line across the man's chest.

Something punched him in the chest, caused him to stagger back. The barrel of the machine gun jerked upward, sending several rounds arcing high out across the desert.

Stay in the fight!

The blow, almost certainly a 7.62-millimeter AK round punching into his front SAPI plate, felt like a mule kick to his diaphragm and left him gasping, but he stayed on his feet and got the heavy machine gun back under control, turning, finding targets, firing.

He was starting to feel the weight of the 240 now. His biceps were burning with the strain of unsupported shooting. A dull but debilitating ache pulsed from the wound in his forearm, and it was all he could do to hold the weapon steady, but he did not relent.

Not until the gun stopped with the abruptness of a head-on collision.

Another jam.

He knew he needed to get the heavy back in the fight, but clearing the jam would take time he didn't think he had, so he dropped the M240 and brought up his M16, sweeping it back and forth, from three o'clock to ten o'clock and back again, and found targets everywhere he looked. The rifle felt feather-light in his hands, its recoil just a gentle tap compared to the heavy.

"I'm out!"

The cry came from someone to Redd's left. He glanced down at the pouches attached to his flak jacket. The covers on all but two of his double mag pouches were open, the magazines stuffed in upside down. Empties.

Grimacing, he tore open one of the remaining pouches, took out both mags, and without looking, tossed them to the Marine who had called.

Two left for me. Thirty rounds plus whatever's left in this mag, Redd noted. *Gotta make it work.*

He burned through his first mag in less than two minutes.

When he felt that unmistakable snap of the bolt locking back, signaling that his last round had been fired, Redd immediately knelt and went to work trying to clear the jammed machine gun. He got the feed tray cover open, letting the ammo belt fall away, then flipped up the feed tray to inspect the firing chamber. The receiver assembly was hot to the touch, burning his fingers as he tried to pry out a stuck cartridge. The unfired round wouldn't budge.

He cursed under his breath, racked the charging handle, shook the gun then beat his fist against the side of the assembly. He guessed that some combination of heat expansion and a defective cartridge had caused the malfunction. The only way to clear it was to let the weapon cool and then run a cleaning rod down the barrel to push the dud back out.

Yeah, I'll have to put that on my to-do list.

He realized then that the world had grown oddly quiet. It was not absolute silence. The pop-pop of AK reports continued without letup, as did the unnerving crack of bullets zipping by too close for comfort. But the louder noise that had been almost constant for . . .

How long had it been since the start of the battle? It felt like forever.

The louder noise that had been almost constant, the thunder of Marine rifles firing back at the enemy . . . That noise was gone now.

Redd felt the sun on his face.

A new day had dawned.

Christmas Day.

He thought about checking his watch but thought better of it. It didn't matter what the numbers said. Time was up. Then he heard something else.

And suddenly, everything changed.

TWENTY-ONE

The Apache was almost right on top of the fighting position before Redd heard the beat of its rotors, a sound that was almost immediately drowned out by the rhythmic *thump-thump-thump* of the gunship's M230 autocannon, delivering a storm of 30-millimeter explosive shells onto the advancing enemy. The chain gun was controlled by an optical targeting system in the pilot's helmet; wherever he looked the gun followed. Redd could tell from the proximity of the detonating rounds that the aircraft was shooting danger close, meaning that Redd and the other surviving Marines were on the cusp of the damage radius of the helo's weapons systems. The enemy had come that close to overrunning their position.

Spent brass fell from the sky like snow, some of it bouncing noisily off his Kevlar helmet, but Redd didn't mind a bit. After a few bursts to clear the area around the fighting position, the Apache began flying in widening circles, but the frequency of fire fell off dramatically following the initial engagement. Redd cautiously looked up, surveying the battlefield, but saw only blast craters and the bodies of dead insurgents.

Without warning, his view was blocked by a line of M-ATVs rolling up in a cloud of dust, passing right in front of where Redd lay. He stared up at the armored vehicles in disbelief, too stunned to move, even when the rear door of the nearest truck was thrown open and Private Maddox emerged.

For a long moment, all Redd could think to do was stare at the other Marine. Then Maddox ran over and knelt down beside him. "Come on!" he shouted. "Load up. We gotta go!"

Redd nodded dumbly, finally beginning to grasp that he wasn't going to die. In the parlance of the Old West, the cavalry had arrived in the nick of time.

Yet, as he looked around the fighting position, saw more of the just-arrived Marines moving amidst the wounded and fallen, carrying those who could not move under their own power to the shelter of the waiting convoy, his initial feeling of relief gave way to sorrow and rage.

"Where were you?" he rasped, shouting into Maddox's face. "What took you so long?"

Maddox, seemingly immune to Redd's wrath, shook his head. "Man, it's been a night. Long story. I'll tell you about it on the way back."

Redd's rage slipped away as quickly as it had come. Maybe there was a good reason for the long delay, maybe not, but there was no call to take it out on the young private.

"You want some help getting him in the truck?" asked Maddox, thrusting his chin toward an unmoving form to Redd's immediate right.

Redd looked and saw Mike, lying right where Redd had left him a few minutes before, staring sightlessly up at the sky.

Redd shook his head. "No. I got it. Go find Heskett. I don't know if he's . . ." The words caught in his throat, but Maddox understood and moved off.

Gently, almost reverently, Redd slid his arms under Mike's shoulders, hooked his elbows up under Mike's arms, and clasped his hands over Mike's chest. Mike was a big guy, almost as big as Redd himself, but Redd lifted him so that only Mike's boots dragged on the ground as Redd shuffled to the open door of the waiting M-ATV. The wound in his forearm began throbbing afresh from the exertion, but he gritted his teeth and toughed it out.

When he got to the vehicle, he had to manhandle Mike over the hump in the middle but managed to get him into the left-side seat, buckling him in and positioning him so that his head was tilted against the window as if taking a nap.

"Almost home," Redd muttered, though he wasn't sure if he was saying it to Mike . . . or to himself.

TWENTY-TWO

The return trip seemed to fly by. Part of this, Redd felt sure, was psychological. On the outbound trip, his senses had been on high alert, increasingly so as they moved toward the objective. Now, as they moved away, the opposite was true. While he knew better than to let his vigilance lapse completely, he could not help but feel that the worst was behind them.

The fact that Wang and all the other drivers were putting the pedal to the metal might also have had something to do with it. In full daylight, following a now familiar trail, the convoy moved at flank speed. Many lives depended on their being able to reach the hospital near Mosul as quickly as possible.

Heskett turned out to be not only alive but relatively unhurt. An enemy bullet had cracked into his helmet with sufficient force to give him a concussion, taking him out of the fight, but the Kevlar had saved his life. While a traumatic brain injury was nothing to laugh at, he would live to fight again. Remarkably, he wasn't the only one.

LT Stern did a hasty debrief over the radio while they rode, and Redd was astonished to learn that, aside from Austin, all of the Marines who had been left behind at the crash site were still alive. A couple were critical but stable. Several more had sustained injuries that would likely end their military career, and nearly all of them, Redd included, would carry the scars of the battle for the rest of their lives, but live they would.

The lieutenant also explained the reason for the platoon's delayed return. There had been several contributing factors. Higher headquarters had initially been reluctant to let the platoon return to the area, for reasons that Stern did not go into but which were clearly still a source of frustration. When they had finally gotten leave to head out again, they had received a report of enemy fighters massing along their route, which had necessitated a long detour. Redd almost felt a little sorry for Wang and Maddox. They might not have gotten shot at, but they had spent the entire night driving around the desert.

Unfortunately, as exhausted as everyone was, there was still a lot of work to do.

Upon arrival at the field hospital near Mosul, Redd immediately went to work helping transport the wounded from the trucks into the triage area. The surgical team, who were still tending to the wounded SF soldiers and Kurdish fighters, was also going to have a busy day.

When a haggard-looking Army medic asked him if he needed to be checked out, Redd just said, "Maybe later."

He had one more thing to take care of.

Rigor mortis had caused Mike's face to contort into a fierce grimace, as if he'd died in the grip of absolute terror. Redd knew that nothing could be further from the truth. Mike had remained calm and professional right to the end, and when death had found him, it had been purely a matter of bad luck.

"I wish I'd gotten to know you a little better," Redd murmured.

He imagined Mike's reply. *"Me too, kid."*

And then, the conjured ghost went on. *"Remember your promise."*

"Promise?" Redd whispered.

"When you get back, I want you to talk to your CO about putting in for MARSOC assessment.

"I want you to promise me. Because you keep your promises."

"You know, I never actually promised that I would."

Then he heard another voice. Not a ghost but a flesh-and-blood Marine. It was Corporal Burgess, walking back to his truck and talking to his driver. As they passed without looking his way, Redd caught some of what Burgess was saying.

"PTSD . . . Just tell them you have nightmares . . . Hundred percent disability . . ."

Redd shook his head in disgust. Burgess, while streaked with dirt and grime, appeared to have come through the night completely uninjured.

Redd sighed as he looked down at the face of a man he would have liked to call a friend and decided he couldn't think of a better way to honor him than to follow up on that unspoken promise.

"Marine Raiders," he mused. "Okay, you talked me into it."

But as he carried Mike's body into the hospital, the memory of that exchange nagged at him.

"Because you keep your promises, right?"

What had he told Mike?

"Not anymore, I don't. My big promise? To call my dad on Christmas Eve? Looks like I blew it."

When he'd said that, he'd figured he would only be a few hours late, but toward the end, he'd begun to doubt that he would ever get to talk to his dad again.

Well, better late than never, he thought. *I just hope the old man is still up.*

He checked his watch and was shocked to see that it was 0952.

9:52 Christmas Day in Iraq was 11:52 Christmas Eve, Mountain Standard Time.

I've still got time.

He hurried Mike inside the hospital, setting him down on the first empty gurney he passed, and then took out his mobile phone.

Full bars. And the clock display next to the signal meter read 9:54.

As he brought up J. B.'s number and hit the dial button, he made his way back outside, looking for some privacy. There was an interminable delay as the signal bounced up into space, moving from one satellite to the next and then back again, but then the ringback tone was cut off midway through and he heard J. B.'s gruff voice over the line.

"Matty!"

"Merry Christmas, Dad."

Even before the words were out, J. B. was speaking again. "Merry Christmas, Son!"

Redd laughed. One of the most frustrating things about long-distance calls was the satellite lag. It took a second or two for the messages to go back and forth, which all too frequently caused some overlap and confusion. "I'm glad you're still—"

"I'm glad you were able to call," J. B. went on. "I was starting to think that maybe . . . Oh, sorry. Yes, I was about to turn in, but thought I'd wait up. Just in case. Good thing, too."

Redd nodded to himself, waiting until he was sure that J. B. was done talking before asking, "How are you doing, Dad? How's the ranch? Everything okay?"

"The ranch is fine, Matty. As for me? Can't complain. Well, I could, but it wouldn't do any good."

Redd smiled at the old joke.

"And how about you, Son?"

Redd's smile sagged. "It was kind of a hard night."

His throat closed up, strangling the last word and preventing him from elaborating. He opened his mouth, but the words wouldn't come. The silence on the line stretched out for several seconds.

"I hear you," J. B. finally said, his tone uncharacteristically quiet. "Had a few of those myself, back in the day. I know how it is."

Redd tried to explain but choked up again. His eyes began to sting, his vision blurring with tears. Redd wasn't a crier. Ever. Not when Emily left. Not when J. B. got injured. Not even when he found his mother dead in their trailer.

He wiped his sleeve across his face, embarrassed at the display of emotions, but instead of absorbing his tears, the fabric, crusted with dried blood, left his skin raw.

"You just take some time to deal with it," J. B. went on. "Sometimes you just gotta sit with your feelings awhile. Trust me, I know."

Redd struggled to find his voice. "I . . . I, uh . . ."

"Well, since you asked about the ranch," J. B. said, "I did have one heckuva time the other day. A hole turned up in the fence to the west pasture, and a few cows got out. Found one of 'em all the way in town, just looking sideways at a McDonald's sign. Poor thing."

Redd knew his dad was talking to cover the silence. He found a spot in the shade against the brick wall of the hospital and leaned his back against it, letting himself slide down into a squatting position. As he did so, he took in the aftermath of the carnage around him. Soldiers were being rushed in for treatment, some of them missing limbs. Others carried on stretchers. Redd wasn't even sure they were still alive. All of them were covered in blood.

As the gravity of it all hit him, he felt his chest heaving. Soon the tears were accompanied by full-on sobs, and embarrassed, Redd muffled the speaker on the phone with one hand while clamping the other over his mouth so that Jim Bob wouldn't hear him. But deep down, on some level, Redd knew that his dad was all too aware. And that's why he kept talking, spending nearly ten minutes covering what he'd been up to and how the ranch was faring during the cold winter they were facing back in Montana.

Some time passed, and eventually, Redd began to collect himself.

"Wish there was something I could do for you, Matty," J. B. finally said.

Redd didn't know how to respond. Not only was he not a crier, but he was also flat terrible at expressing emotions. "You did it, J. B.," was all he managed to get out.

I love you, Dad. He wanted to say it but didn't know how.

There was another two-second delay. Redd imagined his dad nodding to him and felt himself nod back.

"Now that I'm thinking about it, why don't you give me a call tomorrow, say eleven my time. It's getting on, and Christmas or not, I've got to get up early and get the chores done. How does that sound?"

Redd managed to catch his breath. "Yeah. Okay. That's probably a—" He faltered, but then because he didn't want to let his dad go just yet, he blurted out, "Did you get snow?"

There was silence on the line and Redd thought that maybe J. B. had already rung off, but then he heard the old man's voice again. "Sure did. I'm looking out at it right now. It's beautiful. Going to have ourselves a white Christmas here."

The thought nearly brought a smile to Redd's face. As a kid, he had loved winter. Loved watching the snow fall, loved playing in it. As a rancher, working outside for long hours no matter the weather, he'd lost some of his love for the season, but there was something undeniably serene about watching snow fall at night.

He still remembered that last Christmas Eve at the ranch, watching the snow fall and promising J. B. that he would always call.

"I wish I could see it," he murmured.

But J. B. was already speaking again. "And how's Christmas look over there, Son?"

The question, natural enough though it was, caught Redd unprepared. He looked down at his hands, at his uniform and body armor, the camouflage pattern soaked in blood. Some of it was his, but not all. He thought about Sergeant Austin, who had died in his arms. Thought about Mike, and all the others who had died or been maimed.

"Red," he managed to say. "It looks like a red Christmas here, J. B."

And when the tears began to flow back down his cheeks, he let them fall.